# 宋词五百首英译
## 500 Song *Ci* Poems in English

顾正阳　顾怡燕　译

上海大学出版社
·上海·

## 图书在版编目（CIP）数据

宋词五百首英译：汉英对照／顾正阳编译．—上海：上海大学出版社，2023.10
 ISBN 978－7－5671－4826－0

Ⅰ．①宋… Ⅱ．①顾… Ⅲ．①宋词—选集—汉、英 Ⅳ．①I222.844

中国国家版本馆 CIP 数据核字（2023）第 205308 号

责任编辑　严　妙
封面设计　缪炎栩
技术编辑　金　鑫　钱宇坤

### 宋词五百首英译

顾正阳　顾怡燕　译

上海大学出版社出版发行
（上海市上大路 99 号　邮政编码 200444）
（https://www.shupress.cn）　发行热线 021－66135112）
出版人　戴骏豪

＊

南京展望文化发展有限公司排版
上海光扬印务有限公司印刷　各地新华书店经销
开本 890mm×1240mm　1/32　印张 24.25　字数 523 千
2023 年 11 月第 1 版　2023 年 11 月第 1 次印刷
ISBN 978－7－5671－4826－0/I・695　定价　168.00 元

版权所有　侵权必究
如发现本书有印装质量问题请与印刷厂质量科联系
联系电话：0510－86688678

# 序

2018年10月,我在浙江大学出版社出版了《译道与文心——论译品文录》一书,为"中华译学馆·中华翻译研究文库"首辑所收录。书中有不少文章是我为翻译学界同行的优秀探索成果写的序或评。在这本书的自序中,我强调指出:"改革开放后中国的翻译研究,与其他人文学科的发展有相似之处,对于西方的借鉴很多,模仿也很明显,少有创新。对此,我一直有清醒的认识。我知道,人文学科的创新特别不容易,需要继承、积累、探求与交流,也需要质疑,需要思想的交锋。鉴于此,我一直特别关注中国翻译学界的同行在翻译探索之路上所取得的进展,对翻译学界所出现的不同的想法、不同的观点、不同的意见持开放的态度。对于翻译学界的同仁提出的一些具有争议性的观点,我更是持鼓励、肯定、支持的态度,希望能够通过学术争鸣,导向新观点、新发现、新收获。"基于这样的认识,我先后为穆雷的《中国翻译教学研究》、谭载喜的《翻译学:作为独立学科的求索与发展》、沈苏儒的《翻译的境界——"信达雅"漫谈》、奚永吉的《文学翻译比较美学》、胡庚申的《生态翻译学——建构与诠释》、周领顺的《译者行为批评:理论框架》等数十部理论著作写序言,做评论。

每每重读我写下的一篇篇序言或评论,都会不由自主地想到学界老友顾正阳。二十余年来,对顾正阳教授就中国古诗词曲英译展开的系统研究,我一直予以特别的关注。顾正阳教授从2003年到2013年十年间,先后发表中国古诗词曲英译研究著作八部:《古诗词曲英译论稿》《古诗词曲英译理论探索》《古诗词曲英译美学研究》《古诗词曲英译文化探索》《古诗词曲英译文化视角》《古诗词曲英译文化溯源》《古诗词曲英译文化探幽》《古诗词英译文化理论研究》。其中上海大学出版社出版的三部专著都有四十余万字,可谓长篇巨作。他的研究特质鲜明,十分注重文本,从语言、文学、文化、思想等多个维度,深刻探究文本和文本背后的翻译问题,具有启迪性与开拓性。承蒙他信任,我先后为其中的七部著作作序,曾对他的有关探索作了如下评价:"顾正阳的古诗词曲英译研究,不是泛泛而论,而是在跨文化交流的宏大视野下,展开多层面的探索:既有从宏观意义上由技入道、由语言及文化对古诗词曲的传译之道的探讨,也有对古诗词曲英译中所遇到的障碍,有的放矢,具体而微的剖析。无论是对诗歌翻译形而上层面的理论见解,还是古诗词曲英译修辞层面的障碍分析与方法探讨,还是在美学层面上对古诗词曲英译展开的具有开拓意义的研究,都体现了顾正阳教授研究的一贯风格:善于发现,善于思考,善于分析,善于总结。"

前些年,顾正阳先生退休了,我们常有联系。我调入浙江大学后,他曾从上海专程到浙江大学紫金港校区来看望我。交谈中,我得知,近年来他的学术重心有所转移,将全部精力投入古诗词曲的英译与修订中。前日,我接到他的电话,告诉我他精选了他所翻译的宋词,即将出版《宋词五百首英译》。

顾正阳教授这部新作《宋词五百首英译》,我相信在中外译者的宋词英译作品中一定独具特色。我在2006年顾正阳教授所著的《古诗词曲英译文化探索》的序中说过这么几句话:"要真正理解顾正阳教授的这部新作的价值,把握其精神,我认为,不能不了解近二十余年来他在中国古诗词英译领域中执着的研究历程。"顾正阳教授的翻译研究,是以其丰富的翻译实践为基础的。四十多个春秋,他教翻译、做翻译、研究翻译,把翻译实践、翻译的理论探索与翻译人才培养融为一体,互相促进。对他即将出版的这部译著,我有着特别的期待,原因有三:一是我想结合他以前所做的中国古诗词曲的英译研究工作,看看他的翻译实践在何种程度上受其翻译理念与翻译价值观的指引,在翻译方法上有何独到的探索;二是在中国文学史上,宋词有着独特的地位,宋词翻译难度大,我想看到顾正阳教授在宋词翻译的审美层面,尤其是宋词的韵,是如何进行翻译并予以成功再现的;三是对我而言,顾正阳教授的这部巨译有着特殊的意义,他的工作不仅仅是宋词英译历程的一次超越,更是翻译精神的弘扬。杨宪益、许渊冲等老一辈翻译大家的未竟事业需要一代又一代翻译人去传承、去发扬。在这个意义上,已入古稀之年的顾正阳先生的努力便愈发显得珍贵,在此,我要向他致以崇高的敬意。

许 钧

(浙江大学文科资深教授 中国翻译协会常务副会长)

2021年8月16日于南京黄埔花园

# 目录
## Contents

| | | | |
|---|---|---|---|
| 1 | 王禹偁<br>Wang Yucheng | 点绛唇<br>Rouged Lips | 1<br>1 |
| 3 | 寇準<br>Kou Zhun | 江南春<br>Spring in the South of the Yangtze River<br>踏莎行<br>Treading on Grass | 3<br>4<br>4<br>4 |
| 6 | 钱惟演<br>Qian Weiyan | 木兰花<br>Magnolia Flowers | 6<br>6 |
| 8 | 潘阆<br>Pan Lang | 酒泉子<br>Song of Wine Fountain<br>酒泉子<br>Song of Wine Fountain<br>酒泉子<br>Song of Wine Fountain | 8<br>8<br>9<br>9<br>10<br>10 |

| 11 | 林逋 Lin Bu | 长相思 | 11 |
| | | Yearning Forever | 12 |
| | | 点绛唇 | 12 |
| | | Rouged Lips | 12 |
| 14 | 杨亿 Yang Yi | 少年游 | 14 |
| | | Travelling While Young | 14 |
| 16 | 夏竦 Xia Song | 鹧鸪天 | 16 |
| | | Partridge Sky | 16 |
| 18 | 范仲淹 Fan Zhongyan | 苏幕遮 | 18 |
| | | Screened by South Curtain | 19 |
| | | 渔家傲 | 19 |
| | | Pride of Fishermen | 20 |
| | | 御街行 | 20 |
| | | Song of Imperial Thoroughfare | 21 |
| 22 | 柳永 Liu Yong | 蝶恋花 | 23 |
| | | Butterflies in Love with Flowers | 23 |
| | | 甘草子 | 24 |
| | | Song of Licorice Root | 24 |
| | | 雨霖铃 | 25 |
| | | Bell Ringing in the Rain | 25 |

| | |
|---|---|
| 望海潮 | 26 |
| Watching the Tidal Bore | 26 |
| 定风波 | 28 |
| Calming Disturbance | 28 |
| 少年游 | 29 |
| Travelling While Young | 30 |
| 八声甘州 | 30 |
| Eight Beats of Ganzhou | 31 |
| 昼夜乐 | 32 |
| Joy of Day and Night | 32 |
| 采莲令 | 33 |
| Song of Gathering Seedpods of Lotus | 33 |
| 集贤宾 | 34 |
| Gathering of Virtuous Guests | 35 |
| 少年游 | 36 |
| Travelling While Young | 36 |
| 浪淘沙慢 | 37 |
| Slow Song of Waves-Sifting Sand | 37 |
| 卜算子慢 | 39 |
| Slow Song of Divination | 39 |
| 夜半乐 | 41 |
| Midnight Joy | 41 |
| 鹤冲天 | 43 |
| A Crane Flying to the Sky | 44 |

| 木兰花慢 | 45 |
| --- | --- |
| Slow Song of Magnolia Flowers | 45 |
| 迷仙引 | 46 |
| Song Fascinating Immortals | 46 |
| 秋夜月 | 47 |
| The Moon on an Autumn Night | 48 |
| 御街行 | 49 |
| Song of Imperial Thoroughfare | 49 |
| 归朝欢 | 50 |
| Joy of Returning to Royal Court | 50 |
| 婆罗门令 | 51 |
| Song of Brahman | 51 |
| 忆帝京 | 52 |
| Recollecting Imperial Capital | 52 |
| 锦堂春 | 53 |
| Spring in the Brocaded Hall | 54 |
| 引驾行 | 55 |
| Driving a Carriage | 55 |
| 斗百花 | 56 |
| Flowers Blooming Vying in Beauty | 57 |
| 驻马听 | 58 |
| Stopping the Horse and Listening | 58 |
| 曲玉管 | 59 |
| Jade Musical Pipe | 59 |

|   |   | 倾杯 | 61 |
|---|---|---|---|
|   |   | Emptying a Cup of Wine | 61 |
|   |   | 迷神引 | 62 |
|   |   | Song Fascinating Gods | 62 |
|   |   | 安公子 | 64 |
|   |   | Prince An | 64 |
|   |   | 破阵乐 | 65 |
|   |   | The Pleasure of Breaking the Battle Array | 65 |
|   |   | 轮台子 | 67 |
|   |   | Wheels | 67 |
|   |   | 诉衷情近 | 69 |
|   |   | Baring the Heart Face to Face | 69 |
|   |   | 戚氏 | 70 |
|   |   | A Miserable Lady | 70 |
| 73 | 张先 | 更漏子 | 73 |
|   | Zhang Xian | Song of Water Watch | 74 |
|   |   | 醉垂鞭 | 74 |
|   |   | Drunk with a Whip Hanging | 75 |
|   |   | 诉衷情 | 75 |
|   |   | Baring the Heart | 75 |
|   |   | 一丛花令 | 76 |
|   |   | Song of A Cluster of Flowers | 76 |

| | |
|---|---|
| 青门引 | 77 |
| Song of Green Gate | 78 |
| 千秋岁 | 78 |
| A Thousand Autumns | 79 |
| 天仙子 | 80 |
| Song of Immortals | 80 |
| 木兰花 | 81 |
| Magnolia Flowers | 81 |
| 画堂春 | 82 |
| Spring in the Painted Hall | 82 |
| 谢池春慢 | 83 |
| Slow Song of Spring in the Xie Pool | 83 |
| 剪牡丹 | 85 |
| Pruning Twigs of Peonies | 85 |
| 满江红 | 86 |
| The River All Red | 87 |
| 菩萨蛮 | 88 |
| Buddhist Dancers | 88 |
| 相思令 | 89 |
| Song of Lovesickness | 89 |
| 渔家傲 | 89 |
| Pride of Fishermen | 90 |
| 浣溪沙 | 90 |
| Silk-Washing Stream | 91 |

| | | | |
|---|---|---|---|
| | | 惜琼花 | 91 |
| | | Loving Qiong Flower—the Most Beautiful Flower of All | 92 |
| | | 蝶恋花 | 93 |
| | | Butterflies in Love with Flowers | 93 |
| 94 | 晏殊 Yan Shu | 清平乐 | 94 |
| | | Music for a Peaceful Time | 95 |
| | | 玉楼春 | 95 |
| | | Spring in the Jade Boudoir | 95 |
| | | 蝶恋花 | 96 |
| | | Butterflies in Love with Flowers | 96 |
| | | 破阵子 | 97 |
| | | Dance of the Cavalry | 97 |
| | | 诉衷情 | 98 |
| | | Baring the Heart | 98 |
| | | 踏莎行 | 99 |
| | | Treading on Grass | 99 |
| | | 浣溪沙 | 100 |
| | | Silk-Washing Stream | 100 |
| | | 踏莎行 | 101 |
| | | Treading on Grass | 101 |
| | | 少年游 | 102 |
| | | Travelling While Young | 102 |

| 诉衷情 | 103 |
| --- | --- |
| Baring the Heart | 103 |
| 浣溪沙 | 103 |
| Silk-Washing Stream | 104 |
| 清平乐 | 104 |
| Music for a Peaceful Time | 104 |
| 木兰花 | 105 |
| Magnolia Flowers | 105 |
| 诉衷情 | 106 |
| Baring the Heart | 106 |
| 喜迁莺 | 107 |
| Joyous Migrant Orioles | 107 |
| 踏莎行 | 107 |
| Treading on Grass | 108 |
| 撼庭秋 | 108 |
| Autumn in Courtyard | 109 |
| 木兰花 | 109 |
| Magnolia Flowers | 110 |
| 木兰花 | 110 |
| Magnolia Flowers | 110 |
| 踏莎行 | 111 |
| Treading on Grass | 111 |
| 山亭柳 | 112 |
| Willows by Hillside Pavilion | 112 |

| | | 浣溪沙 | 113 |
| | | Silk-Washing Stream | 113 |
| | | 蝶恋花 | 114 |
| | | Butterflies in Love with Flowers | 114 |
| | | 浣溪沙 | 115 |
| | | Silk-Washing Stream | 115 |
| | | 采桑子 | 116 |
| | | Song of Gathering Mulberry Leaves | 116 |
| 117 | 石延年 | 燕归梁 | 117 |
| | Shi Yannian | Swallows Returning to the Beam | 118 |
| 119 | 李冠 | 蝶恋花 | 119 |
| | Li Guan | Butterflies in Love with Flowers | 120 |
| 121 | 宋祁 | 蝶恋花 | 122 |
| | Song Qi | Butterflies in Love with Flowers | 122 |
| | | 木兰花 | 123 |
| | | Magnolia Flowers | 123 |
| | | 锦缠道 | 124 |
| | | Road Covered with Brocade | 124 |
| 125 | 梅尧臣 | 苏幕遮 | 126 |
| | Mei Yaochen | Screened by South Curtain | 126 |

| | | | |
|---|---|---|---|
| 127 | 叶清臣 | 贺圣朝 | 127 |
| | Ye Qingchen | Congratulations to a Sacred Dynasty | 128 |
| 129 | 欧阳修 | 玉楼春 | 130 |
| | Ouyang Xiu | Spring in the Jade Boudoir | 130 |
| | | 生查子 | 130 |
| | | Mountain Hawthorn | 131 |
| | | 采桑子 | 131 |
| | | Song of Gathering Mulberry Leaves | 131 |
| | | 生查子 | 132 |
| | | Mountain Hawthorn | 132 |
| | | 采桑子 | 133 |
| | | Song of Gathering Mulberry Leaves | 133 |
| | | 采桑子 | 134 |
| | | Sone of Gathering Mulberry Leaves | 134 |
| | | 采桑子 | 134 |
| | | Song of Gathering Mulberry Leaves | 135 |
| | | 采桑子 | 135 |
| | | Song of Gathering Mulberry Leaves | 135 |
| | | 采桑子 | 136 |
| | | Song of Gathering Mulberry Leaves | 136 |
| | | 采桑子 | 137 |
| | | Song of Gathering Mulberry Leaves | 137 |
| | | 蝶恋花 | 138 |
| | | Butterflies in Love with Flowers | 138 |

| | |
|---|---|
| 踏莎行 | 139 |
| Treading on Grass | 139 |
| 诉衷情 | 140 |
| Baring the Heart | 140 |
| 南歌子 | 140 |
| Southern Song | 141 |
| 临江仙 | 141 |
| Immortals by the River | 142 |
| 渔家傲 | 142 |
| Pride of Fishermen | 143 |
| 蝶恋花 | 143 |
| Butterflies in Love with Flowers | 144 |
| 玉楼春 | 144 |
| Spring in the Jade Boudoir | 145 |
| 玉楼春 | 145 |
| Spring in the Jade Boudoir | 145 |
| 浪淘沙 | 146 |
| Waves-Shift Sand | 146 |
| 阮郎归 | 147 |
| Return of the Lover | 147 |
| 蝶恋花 | 148 |
| Butterflies in Love with Flowers | 148 |
| 渔家傲 | 149 |
| Pride of Fishermen | 149 |

| | | 浣溪沙 | 150 |
| | | Silk-Washing Stream | 150 |
| | | 望江南 | 150 |
| | | Looking in the Direction of the South of the Yangtze River | 151 |
| | | 少年游 | 151 |
| | | Travelling While Young | 152 |
| | | 朝中措 | 152 |
| | | Way in the Royal Court | 153 |
| | | 采桑子 | 153 |
| | | Song of Gathering Mulberry Leaves | 154 |
| | | 青玉案 | 154 |
| | | Green Jade Cup | 154 |
| | | 玉楼春 | 155 |
| | | Spring in the Jade Boudoir | 155 |
| 157 | 王琪<br>Wang Qi | 望江南 | 157 |
| | | Looking in the Direction of the South of the Yangtze River | 157 |
| 159 | 韩琦<br>Han Qi | 点绛唇 | 159 |
| | | Rouged Lips | 159 |
| 161 | 杜安世<br>Du Anshi | 菩萨蛮 | 161 |
| | | Buddhist Dancers | 161 |

|     |                    |                              |     |
| --- | ------------------ | ---------------------------- | --- |
|     |                    | 卜算子                       | 162 |
|     |                    | Song of Divination           | 162 |
|     |                    | 鹤冲天                       | 163 |
|     |                    | A Crane Flying to the Sky    | 163 |
| 165 | 李师中             | 菩萨蛮                       | 165 |
|     | Li Shizhong        | Buddhist Dancers             | 165 |
| 167 | 司马光             | 阮郎归                       | 167 |
|     | Sima Guang         | Return of the Lover          | 167 |
|     |                    | 西江月                       | 168 |
|     |                    | The Moon over the West River | 168 |
| 169 | 韩缜               | 凤箫吟                       | 169 |
|     | Han Zhen           | Song of Phoenix Flute        | 170 |
| 172 | 阮逸女             | 花心动                       | 172 |
|     | Ruan Yi's daughter | Stirring of Love             | 173 |
| 175 | 王安石             | 桂枝香                       | 175 |
|     | Wang Anshi         | Scent of Laurel Twigs        | 176 |
|     |                    | 千秋岁引                     | 177 |
|     |                    | Song of a Thousand Autumns   | 177 |

|     |              |                                    |     |
| --- | ------------ | ---------------------------------- | --- |
|     |              | 菩萨蛮                             | 178 |
|     |              | Buddhist Dancers                   | 178 |
|     |              | 南乡子                             | 179 |
|     |              | Song of Southern countryside       | 179 |
|     |              | 渔家傲                             | 180 |
|     |              | Pride of Fishermen                 | 180 |
|     |              | 渔家傲                             | 181 |
|     |              | Pride of Fishermen                 | 181 |
| 182 | 章楶         | 水龙吟                             | 182 |
|     | Zhang Jie    | Chanting of Water Dragon           | 183 |
| 185 | 郑獬         | 好事近                             | 185 |
|     | Zheng Xie    | Happiness Approaching              | 185 |
| 187 | 王安国       | 清平乐                             | 187 |
|     | Wang Anguo   | Music for a Peaceful Time          | 188 |
|     |              | 减字木兰花                         | 188 |
|     |              | Shortened Song of Magnolia Flowers | 188 |
|     |              | 点绛唇                             | 189 |
|     |              | Rouged Lips                        | 189 |
| 191 | 晏几道       | 临江仙                             | 192 |
|     | Yan Jidao    | Immortals by the River             | 192 |

| | |
|---|---|
| 临江仙 | 193 |
| Immortals by the River | 193 |
| 蝶恋花 | 194 |
| Butterflies in Love with Flowers | 194 |
| 蝶恋花 | 195 |
| Butterflies in Love with Flowers | 195 |
| 蝶恋花 | 196 |
| Butterflies in Love with Flowers | 196 |
| 蝶恋花 | 197 |
| Butterflies in Love with Flowers | 197 |
| 更漏子 | 198 |
| Song of Water Watch | 198 |
| 鹧鸪天 | 199 |
| Partridge Sky | 199 |
| 鹧鸪天 | 200 |
| Partridge Sky | 200 |
| 鹧鸪天 | 201 |
| Partridge Sky | 201 |
| 鹧鸪天 | 202 |
| Partridge Sky | 202 |
| 鹧鸪天 | 203 |
| Partridge Sky | 203 |
| 鹧鸪天 | 204 |
| Partridge Sky | 204 |

| 阮郎归 | 205 |
|---|---|
| Return of the Lover | 205 |
| 阮郎归 | 205 |
| Return of the Lover | 206 |
| 虞美人 | 206 |
| Great Beauty Yu | 207 |
| 思远人 | 207 |
| Thinking of My Dear Far Away | 207 |
| 六幺令 | 208 |
| Song of the Green Waist | 208 |
| 木兰花 | 210 |
| Magnolia Flowers | 210 |
| 木兰花 | 211 |
| Magnolia Flowers | 211 |
| 玉楼春 | 212 |
| Spring in the Jade Boudoir | 212 |
| 长相思 | 212 |
| Yearning Forever | 213 |
| 清平乐 | 213 |
| Music for a Peaceful Time | 213 |
| 菩萨蛮 | 214 |
| Buddhist Dancers | 214 |
| 采桑子 | 215 |
| Song of Gathering Mulberry Leaves | 215 |

| | |
|---|---|
| 浣溪沙 | 216 |
| Silk-Washing Stream | 216 |
| 御街行 | 216 |
| Song of Imperial Thoroughfare | 217 |
| 归田乐 | 217 |
| Joy of Returning to Field | 218 |
| 生查子 | 219 |
| Mountain Hawthorn | 219 |
| 生查子 | 219 |
| Mountain Hawthorn | 220 |
| 菩萨蛮 | 220 |
| Buddhist Dancers | 220 |
| 少年游 | 221 |
| Travelling While Young | 221 |
| 南乡子 | 222 |
| Song of Southern Countryside | 222 |
| 生查子 | 223 |
| Mountain Hawthorn | 223 |
| 浣溪沙 | 224 |
| Silk-Washing Stream | 224 |
| 浣溪沙 | 224 |
| Silk-Washing Stream | 225 |
| 鹧鸪天 | 225 |
| Partridge Sky | 225 |

| | | | |
|---|---|---|---|
| | | 蝶恋花 | 226 |
| | | Butterflies in Love with Flowers | 226 |
| | | 留春令 | 227 |
| | | Song Inviting Spring to Stay | 227 |
| | | 河满子 | 228 |
| | | Sad Song | 228 |
| 230 | 王观<br>Wang Guan | 卜算子 | 230 |
| | | Song of Divination | 231 |
| | | 庆清朝慢 | 231 |
| | | Slow Song of Celebrating the Good Dynasty | 232 |
| | | 清平乐 | 233 |
| | | Music for a Peaceful Time | 233 |
| 234 | 张舜民<br>Zhang Shunmin | 卖花声 | 234 |
| | | Song of Peddling Flowers | 235 |
| 236 | 魏夫人<br>Madame Wei | 菩萨蛮 | 236 |
| | | Buddhist Dancers | 236 |
| | | 点绛唇 | 237 |
| | | Rouged Lips | 237 |
| | | 好事近 | 238 |
| | | Happiness Approaching | 238 |

| | | 卷珠帘 | 238 |
| | | Rolling up the Pearly Curtain | 239 |

| 240 | 王诜 Wang Shen | 忆故人 | 240 |
| | | Thinking of the Old Friend | 240 |
| | | 人月圆 | 241 |
| | | Reunion under the Full Moon | 241 |
| | | 蝶恋花 | 242 |
| | | Butterflies in Love with Flowers | 242 |

| 244 | 苏轼 Su Shi | 西江月 | 245 |
| | | The Moon over the West River | 245 |
| | | 念奴娇 | 246 |
| | | Charm of a Maiden Singer | 246 |
| | | 浣溪沙 | 247 |
| | | Silk-Washing Stream | 248 |
| | | 浣溪沙 | 248 |
| | | Silk-Washing Stream | 248 |
| | | 浣溪沙 | 249 |
| | | Silk-Washing Stream | 249 |
| | | 浣溪沙 | 250 |
| | | Silk-Washing Stream | 250 |
| | | 浣溪沙 | 251 |
| | | Silk-Washing Stream | 251 |

| | |
|---|---|
| 定风波 | 252 |
| Calming Disturbance | 252 |
| 临江仙 | 253 |
| Immortals by the River | 253 |
| 少年游 | 254 |
| Travelling While Young | 254 |
| 鹧鸪天 | 255 |
| Partridge Sky | 255 |
| 蝶恋花 | 256 |
| Butterflies in Love with Flowers | 256 |
| 蝶恋花 | 257 |
| Butterflies in Love with Flowers | 257 |
| 江城子 | 258 |
| A Riverside Town | 258 |
| 江城子 | 259 |
| A Riverside Town | 259 |
| 江城子 | 260 |
| A Riverside Town | 260 |
| 诉衷情 | 261 |
| Baring the Heart | 262 |
| 定风波 | 262 |
| Calming Disturbance | 263 |
| 定风波 | 263 |
| Calming Disturbance | 264 |

| | |
|---|---|
| 阮郎归 | 264 |
| Return of the Lover | 265 |
| 点绛唇 | 265 |
| Rouged Lips | 266 |
| 洞仙歌 | 266 |
| Song of Immortals in the Cavern | 267 |
| 望江南 | 268 |
| Looking in the Direction of the South of the Yangtze River | 268 |
| 水调歌头 | 269 |
| Prelude to Water Melody | 269 |
| 江城子 | 270 |
| A Riverside Town | 270 |
| 虞美人 | 271 |
| Great Beauty Yu | 272 |
| 永遇乐 | 272 |
| Joy of Eternal Union | 273 |
| 水龙吟 | 274 |
| Chanting of Water Dragon | 274 |
| 江城子 | 275 |
| A Riverside Town | 276 |
| 南歌子 | 277 |
| Southern Song | 277 |
| 菩萨蛮 | 278 |
| Buddhist Dancers | 278 |

| 木兰花令 | 279 |
| --- | --- |
| Song of Magnolia Flowers | 279 |
| 昭君怨 | 280 |
| Grief of Zhaojun | 280 |
| 浣溪沙 | 280 |
| Silk-Washing Stream | 281 |
| 南乡子 | 281 |
| Song of Southern Countryside | 282 |
| 采桑子 | 282 |
| Song of Gathering Mulberry Leaves | 283 |
| 蝶恋花 | 283 |
| Butterflies in Love with Flowers | 283 |
| 江城子 | 284 |
| A Riverside Town | 284 |
| 临江仙 | 285 |
| Immortals by the River | 286 |
| 临江仙 | 286 |
| Immortals by the River | 287 |
| 洞仙歌 | 287 |
| Song of Immortals in the Cavern | 288 |
| 醉落魄 | 289 |
| Drunk in Dire Straits | 289 |
| 行香子 | 290 |
| Burning Incense | 290 |

| | | | |
|---|---|---|---|
| | | 归朝欢 | 291 |
| | | Joy of Returning to Royal Court | 291 |
| | | 沁园春 | 292 |
| | | Spring in the Fragrant Garden | 293 |
| | | 一丛花 | 294 |
| | | A Cluster of Flowers | 294 |
| | | 南乡子 | 295 |
| | | Song of Southern Countryside | 295 |
| | | 南歌子 | 296 |
| | | Southern Song | 296 |
| | | 蝶恋花 | 297 |
| | | Butterflies in Love with Flowers | 297 |
| | | 贺新郎 | 298 |
| | | Congratulations to the Bridegroom | 298 |
| | | 醉落魄 | 300 |
| | | Drunk in Dire Straits | 300 |
| 301 | 苏辙 | 调啸词 | 301 |
| | Su Zhe | An Ancient Song of a Joke | 301 |
| | | 调啸词 | 302 |
| | | An Ancient Song of a Joke | 302 |
| 303 | 李之仪 | 卜算子 | 303 |
| | Li Zhiyi | Song of Divination | 303 |

| | | 临江仙 | 304 |
|---|---|---|---|
| | | Immortals by the River | 304 |
| | | 谢池春 | 305 |
| | | Spring in the Xie Pool | 305 |
| 307 | 舒亶 Shu Dan | 菩萨蛮 | 307 |
| | | Buddhist Dancers | 307 |
| | | 一落索 | 308 |
| | | Chain of Jade Rings | 308 |
| | | 虞美人 | 309 |
| | | Great Beauty Yu | 309 |
| 310 | 孔平仲 Kong Pingzhong | 千秋岁 | 310 |
| | | A Thousand Autumns | 310 |
| 312 | 王雱 Wang Pan | 倦寻芳慢 | 312 |
| | | Slow Song of Seeking Flowers | 312 |
| 314 | 黄庭坚 Huang Tingjian | 清平乐 | 314 |
| | | Music for a Peaceful Time | 315 |
| | | 诉衷情 | 315 |
| | | Baring the Heart | 315 |
| | | 鹧鸪天 | 316 |
| | | Partridge Sky | 316 |

|  |  | 虞美人 | 317 |
|---|---|---|---|
|  |  | Great Beauty Yu | 317 |
|  |  | 水调歌头 | 318 |
|  |  | Prelude to Water Melody | 319 |
|  |  | 望江东 | 320 |
|  |  | Gazing at the East Shore of the River | 320 |
|  |  | 南歌子 | 321 |
|  |  | Southern Song | 321 |
|  |  | 阮郎归 | 321 |
|  |  | Return of the Lover | 322 |
|  |  | 好事近 | 322 |
|  |  | Happiness Approaching | 323 |
|  |  | 南乡子 | 323 |
|  |  | Song of Southern Countryside | 324 |
|  |  | 蓦山溪 | 325 |
|  |  | The Stream by the Mount Mo | 325 |
|  |  | 念奴娇 | 326 |
|  |  | Charm of a Maiden Singer | 326 |
| 328 | 晁端礼 Chao Duanli | 水龙吟 Chanting of Water Dragon | 328 329 |
| 331 | 李元膺 Li Yuanying | 茶瓶儿 Tea Kettle | 331 331 |

| | | | |
|---|---|---|---|
| 333 | 朱服 | 渔家傲 | 333 |
| | Zhu Fu | Pride of Fishermen | 333 |
| 335 | 刘弇 | 清平乐 | 335 |
| | Liu Yan | Music for a Peaceful Time | 335 |
| 337 | 秦观 | 鹊桥仙 | 338 |
| | Qin Guan | Immortals on the Magpie Bridge | 338 |
| | | 画堂春 | 339 |
| | | Spring in the Painted Hall | 339 |
| | | 踏莎行 | 340 |
| | | Treading on Grass | 340 |
| | | 浣溪沙 | 341 |
| | | Silk-Washing Stream | 341 |
| | | 如梦令 | 341 |
| | | Like a Dream | 342 |
| | | 满庭芳 | 342 |
| | | Courtyard Full of Fragrance | 342 |
| | | 满庭芳 | 343 |
| | | Courtyard Full of Fragrance | 344 |
| | | 八六子 | 345 |
| | | Song of Eight and Six | 345 |
| | | 好事近 | 346 |
| | | Happiness Approaching | 347 |

| | |
|---|---|
| 江城子 | 347 |
| A Riverside Town | 347 |
| 减字木兰花 | 348 |
| Shortened Song of Magnolia Flowers | 349 |
| 望海潮 | 349 |
| Watching the Tidal Bore | 350 |
| 水龙吟 | 351 |
| Chanting of Water Dragon | 351 |
| 千秋岁 | 352 |
| A Thousand Autumns | 353 |
| 虞美人 | 354 |
| The Great Beauty Yu | 354 |
| 南乡子 | 355 |
| Song of Southern Countryside | 355 |
| 阮郎归 | 356 |
| Return of the Lover | 356 |
| 调笑令 | 356 |
| Song of a Joke | 357 |
| 南歌子 | 357 |
| Southern Song | 358 |
| 南歌子 | 358 |
| Southern Song | 358 |
| 临江仙 | 359 |
| Immortals by the River | 359 |

| | | 点绛唇 | 360 |
| | | Roughed Lips | 360 |
| | | 桃园忆故人 | 361 |
| | | Thinking of an Old Friend in Peach Orchard | 361 |
| | | 如梦令 | 362 |
| | | Like a Dream | 362 |
| | | 画堂春 | 362 |
| | | Spring in the Painted Hall | 363 |
| | | 满庭芳 | 363 |
| | | Courtyard Full of Fragrance | 364 |
| | | 满庭芳 | 365 |
| | | Courtyard Full of Fragrance | 365 |
| | | 行香子 | 366 |
| | | Burning Incense | 366 |
| 368 | 米芾 | 水调歌头 | 368 |
| | Mi Fu | Prelude to Water Melody | 369 |
| 370 | 赵令畤 | 蝶恋花 | 370 |
| | Zhao Lingzhi | Butterflies in Love with Flowers | 370 |
| | | 菩萨蛮 | 371 |
| | | Buddhist Dancers | 371 |
| | | 蝶恋花 | 372 |
| | | Butterflies in Love with Flowers | 372 |

| | | | |
|---|---|---|---|
| | | 乌夜啼 | 373 |
| | | Crow Cawing at Night | 373 |
| 374 | 贺铸 | 子夜歌 | 375 |
| | He Zhu | Song at Midnight | 375 |
| | | 惜余春 | 376 |
| | | Cherishing the Remaining Spring | 376 |
| | | 半死桐 | 377 |
| | | The Parasol Tree Half Dead | 377 |
| | | 陌上郎 | 378 |
| | | Lover on the Path | 378 |
| | | 减字浣溪沙 | 378 |
| | | Shortened Song of Silk-Washing Stream | 379 |
| | | 减字浣溪沙 | 379 |
| | | Shortened Song of Silk-Washing Stream | 379 |
| | | 芳心苦 | 380 |
| | | A Bitter Heart | 380 |
| | | 捣练子 | 381 |
| | | Song of Pounding Cloth | 381 |
| | | 青玉案 | 382 |
| | | Green Jade Cup | 382 |
| | | 石州引 | 383 |
| | | Song of Shizhou | 383 |

| | | | |
|---|---|---|---|
| | | 小重山 | 384 |
| | | Hills by Hills | 384 |
| | | 芳草渡 | 385 |
| | | Ferry by Fragrant Grass | 385 |
| | | 人南渡 | 386 |
| | | Going to the South across the River | 386 |
| | | 国门东 | 387 |
| | | The East Gate of the Capital | 388 |
| | | 梦相亲 | 388 |
| | | Making Love in the Dream | 389 |
| | | 愁风月 | 389 |
| | | Sorrow for the Wax and Wane of the Moon | 390 |
| | | 西江月 | 390 |
| | | The Moon over the West River | 390 |
| | | 点绛唇 | 391 |
| | | Rouged Lips | 391 |
| | | 台城游 | 392 |
| | | Touring the Palace | 392 |
| | | 望湘人 | 394 |
| | | Yearning for the Dear by the Xiang River | 394 |
| 396 | 仲殊 | 诉衷情 | 396 |
| | Zhong Shu | Baring the Heart | 397 |

| | | | |
|---|---|---|---|
| | | 诉衷情 | 397 |
| | | Baring the Heart | 398 |
| | | 南柯子 | 398 |
| | | Southern Song | 399 |
| | | 柳梢青 | 399 |
| | | Green Tips of Willow Branches | 400 |
| | | 夏云峰 | 400 |
| | | Summer Clouds over the Peak | 401 |
| 403 | 晁补之<br>Zhao Buzhi | 金凤钩 | 404 |
| | | Hook with Gold Phoenix | 404 |
| | | 临江仙 | 405 |
| | | Immortals by the River | 405 |
| | | 摸鱼儿 | 406 |
| | | Groping for Fish | 406 |
| | | 洞仙歌 | 407 |
| | | Song of Immortals in the Cavern | 408 |
| 409 | 张耒<br>Zhang Lei | 秋蕊香 | 409 |
| | | Scent of Autumn Flowers | 410 |
| | | 风流子 | 410 |
| | | Song of Gallantry | 411 |
| 413 | 周邦彦<br>Zhou Bangyan | 满江红 | 414 |
| | | The River All Red | 414 |

| | |
|---|---|
| 兰陵王 | 415 |
| King of Lanling | 416 |
| 拜星月慢 | 417 |
| Slow Song of Worship of the Moon and Stars | 418 |
| 芳草渡 | 419 |
| The Ferry by Scented Grass | 419 |
| 夜飞鹊 | 420 |
| A Magpie Flying at Night | 421 |
| 玉楼春 | 422 |
| Spring in the Jade Boudoir | 422 |
| 长相思慢 | 423 |
| Slow Song of Yearning Forever | 423 |
| 花犯 | 424 |
| Violation of Flowers | 425 |
| 水龙吟 | 426 |
| Chanting of Water Dragon | 426 |
| 苏幕遮 | 428 |
| Screened by Southern Curtain | 428 |
| 大酺 | 429 |
| Drinking while Gathering | 429 |
| 满庭芳 | 431 |
| Courtyard Full of Fragrance | 431 |
| 西河 | 432 |
| The West River | 433 |

| | |
|---|---|
| 解语花 | 434 |
| The Flower Knowing Words | 434 |
| 过秦楼 | 435 |
| Passing the Qin Tower | 436 |
| 浪淘沙慢 | 437 |
| Slow Song of Waves-Sifting Sand | 437 |
| 解连环 | 439 |
| Unchaining Double Rings | 439 |
| 瑞龙吟 | 440 |
| Chanting of the Auspicious Dragon | 441 |
| 六丑 | 442 |
| Six Violations | 443 |
| 关河令 | 445 |
| Song of the Pass and River | 445 |
| 诉衷情 | 446 |
| Baring the Heart | 446 |
| 少年游 | 446 |
| Travelling While Young | 447 |
| 少年游 | 447 |
| Travelling While Young | 448 |
| 尉迟杯 | 448 |
| Wine in the Cup | 449 |
| 渔家傲 | 450 |
| Pride of Fishermen | 450 |

|  |  | 忆旧游 | 451 |
|---|---|---|---|
|  |  | Recollecting the Tours in Old Days | 451 |
|  |  | 一落索 | 452 |
|  |  | Chain of Jade Rings | 452 |
|  |  | 四园竹 | 453 |
|  |  | The Bamboos in the Four Gardens | 453 |
|  |  | 应天长 | 454 |
|  |  | Everlasting Woe | 455 |
|  |  | 还京乐 | 456 |
|  |  | Joy of Returning to the Capital | 456 |
| 458 | 阮阅 | 洞仙歌 | 458 |
|  | Ruan Yue | Song of Immortals in the Cavern | 459 |
|  |  | 眼儿媚 | 459 |
|  |  | Charming Eyes | 460 |
| 461 | 赵企 | 感皇恩 | 461 |
|  | Zhao Qi | Gratitude to Emperor's Favor | 462 |
| 463 | 谢逸 | 蝶恋花 | 463 |
|  | Xie Yi | Butterflies in Love with Flowers | 463 |
|  |  | 江城子 | 464 |
|  |  | A Riverside Town | 464 |
|  |  | 千秋岁 | 465 |
|  |  | A Thousand Autumns | 466 |

| | | | |
|---|---|---|---|
| 467 | 晁冲之 | 临江仙 | 467 |
| | Chao Chongzhi | Immortals by the River | 468 |
| | | 汉宫春 | 468 |
| | | Spring in the Han Palace | 469 |
| | | 感皇恩 | 470 |
| | | Gratitude to Emperor's Favor | 470 |
| 472 | 苏庠 | 鹧鸪天 | 472 |
| | Su Xiang | Partridge Sky | 472 |
| 474 | 毛滂 | 惜分飞 | 474 |
| | Mao Bang | Sorrow for Separation | 475 |
| | | 临江仙 | 475 |
| | | Immortals by the River | 476 |
| | | 烛影摇红 | 476 |
| | | The Candle Shedding a Red Shadow | 477 |
| 478 | 郑少微 | 鹧鸪天 | 478 |
| | Zheng Shaowei | Partridge Sky | 479 |
| 480 | 司马槱 | 黄金缕 | 480 |
| | Sima You | Gold Thread Garment | 481 |
| 482 | 秦湛 | 卜算子 | 482 |
| | Qin Zhan | Song of Divination | 482 |

| | | | |
|---|---|---|---|
| 484 | 徐俯<br>Xu Fu | 卜算子<br>Song of Divination | 484<br>484 |
| 486 | 叶梦得<br>Ye Mengde | 贺新郎<br>Congratulations to the Bridegroom<br>虞美人<br>Great Beauty Yu | 486<br>487<br>488<br>488 |
| 490 | 刘一止<br>Liu Yizhi | 喜迁莺<br>Joyous Migrant Orioles | 490<br>491 |
| 493 | 汪藻<br>Wang Zao | 醉落魄<br>Drunk in Dire Straits | 493<br>493 |
| 495 | 曹组<br>Cao Zu | 忆少年<br>Recollecting Early Youth<br>卜算子<br>Song of Divination<br>青玉案<br>Green Jade Cup | 495<br>495<br>496<br>496<br>497<br>497 |
| 499 | 万俟咏<br>Moqi Yong | 木兰花慢<br>Slow Song of Magnolia Flowers<br>长相思<br>Yearning Forever | 499<br>500<br>501<br>501 |

|     |             | 诉衷情                        | 501 |
|-----|-------------|------------------------------|-----|
|     |             | Baring the Heart             | 502 |
|     |             | 长相思                        | 502 |
|     |             | Yearning Forever             | 503 |
|     |             | 忆秦娥                        | 503 |
|     |             | Recollecting the Beauty in Qin | 503 |
| 505 | 田为          | 南柯子                        | 505 |
|     | Tian Wei    | Southern Song                | 505 |
|     |             | 南柯子                        | 506 |
|     |             | Southern Song                | 506 |
| 508 | 徐伸          | 转调二郎神                    | 508 |
|     | Xu Shen     | Changed Tune of a God        | 508 |
| 510 | 陈克          | 菩萨蛮                        | 510 |
|     | Chen Ke     | Buddhist Dancers             | 510 |
|     |             | 菩萨蛮                        | 511 |
|     |             | Buddhist Dancers             | 511 |
| 512 | 朱敦儒        | 水调歌头                      | 512 |
|     | Zhu Dunru   | Prelude to Water Melody      | 513 |
|     |             | 相见欢                        | 514 |
|     |             | Joy at Meeting               | 514 |

|     |            | 鹧鸪天                              | 515 |
|-----|------------|-------------------------------------|-----|
|     |            | Partridge Sky                       | 515 |
| 516 | 周紫芝     | 醉落魄                              | 516 |
|     | Zhou Zizhi | Drunk in Dire Straits               | 517 |
|     |            | 鹧鸪天                              | 517 |
|     |            | Partridge Sky                       | 518 |
|     |            | 踏莎行                              | 518 |
|     |            | Treading on Grass                   | 519 |
| 520 | 赵佶       | 眼儿媚                              | 521 |
|     | Zhao Ji    | Charming Eyes                       | 521 |
|     |            | 燕山亭                              | 522 |
|     |            | the Pavilion by Hills               | 522 |
| 524 | 廖世美     | 好事近                              | 524 |
|     | Liao Shimei| Happiness Approaching               | 524 |
| 526 | 李清照     | 点绛唇                              | 527 |
|     | Li Qingzhao| Rouged Lips                         | 527 |
|     |            | 减字木兰花                          | 528 |
|     |            | Shortened Song of Magnolia Flowers  | 528 |
|     |            | 醉花阴                              | 528 |
|     |            | Drunk in the Shade of Flowers       | 529 |

| | |
|---|---|
| 如梦令 | 529 |
| Like a Dream | 530 |
| 武陵春 | 530 |
| Spring in the Land of Peach Blossoms | 530 |
| 一剪梅 | 531 |
| A Twig of Plum Blossoms | 531 |
| 凤凰台上忆吹箫 | 532 |
| Playing the Flute on Phoenix Terrace | 532 |
| 菩萨蛮 | 533 |
| Buddhist Dancers | 534 |
| 南歌子 | 534 |
| Southern Song | 534 |
| 永遇乐 | 535 |
| Joy of Eternal Union | 535 |
| 渔家傲 | 537 |
| Pride of Fishermen | 537 |
| 小重山 | 538 |
| Hills by Hills | 538 |
| 怨王孙 | 539 |
| Complaint of Princess | 539 |
| 诉衷情 | 540 |
| Baring the Heart | 540 |
| 渔家傲 | 540 |
| Pride of Fishermen | 541 |

| | |
|---|---|
| 添字采桑子 | 541 |
| Expanded Song of Gathering Mulberry Leaves | 542 |
| 行香子 | 542 |
| Burning Incense | 543 |
| 玉楼春 | 544 |
| Spring in the Jade Boudoir | 544 |
| 满庭芳 | 545 |
| Courtyard Full of Fragrance | 545 |
| 孤雁儿 | 546 |
| A Lonely Wild Goose | 546 |
| 蝶恋花 | 547 |
| Butterflies in Love with Flowers | 548 |
| 声声慢 | 548 |
| Slow, Slow Song | 549 |
| 念奴娇 | 550 |
| Charm of a Maiden Singer | 550 |
| 鹧鸪天 | 551 |
| Partridge Sky | 551 |
| 浣溪沙 | 552 |
| Silk-Washing Stream | 552 |
| 好事近 | 553 |
| Happiness Approaching | 553 |
| 点绛唇 | 554 |
| Rouged Lips | 554 |

|     |     |     |     |
| --- | --- | --- | --- |
|     |     | 庆清朝慢 | 554 |
|     |     | Slow Song of Celebrating the Good Dynasty | 555 |
|     |     | 瑞鹧鸪 | 556 |
|     |     | Auspicious Partridge | 556 |
|     |     | 浣溪沙 | 557 |
|     |     | Silk-Washing Stream | 557 |
|     |     | 殢人娇 | 558 |
|     |     | A Charming and Lingering Beauty | 558 |
|     |     | 如梦令 | 559 |
|     |     | Like a Dream | 559 |
| 560 | 吕本中 | 采桑子 | 560 |
|     | Lü Benzhong | Song of Gathering Mulberry Leaves | 560 |
| 562 | 李持正 | 人月圆 | 562 |
|     | Li Chizheng | Reunion under the Full Moon | 562 |
| 564 | 李邴 | 木兰花 | 564 |
|     | Li Bing | Magnolia Flowers | 564 |
| 566 | 向子䛩 | 秦楼月 | 566 |
|     | Xiang Ziyin | The Moon over the Qin Tower | 566 |
| 568 | 蒋兴祖女 | 减字木兰花 | 568 |
|     | Daughter of Jiang Xingzu | Shortened Song of Magnolia Flowers | 569 |

| | | | |
|---|---|---|---|
| 570 | 李重元<br>Li Zhongyuan | 忆王孙<br>Recollecting Prince | 570<br>570 |
| 572 | 李玉<br>Li Yu | 贺新郎<br>Congratulations to the Bridegroom | 572<br>572 |
| 575 | 吴淑姬<br>Wu Shuji | 小重山<br>Hills by Hills<br>长相思令<br>Song of Yearning Forever | 575<br>575<br>576<br>576 |
| 578 | 乐婉<br>Le Wan | 卜算子<br>Song of Divination | 578<br>578 |
| 580 | 聂胜琼<br>Nie Shengqiong | 鹧鸪天<br>Partridge Sky | 580<br>581 |
| 582 | 陈与义<br>Chen Yuyi | 虞美人<br>Great Beauty Yu | 582<br>582 |
| 584 | 张元干<br>Zhang Yuangan | 兰陵王<br>King of Lanling<br>菩萨蛮<br>Buddhist Dancers | 584<br>585<br>586<br>586 |

| | | | |
|---|---|---|---|
| 588 | 吕渭老<br>Lü Weilao | 薄幸<br>A Fickle Lover<br>选冠子<br>Choosing a Hat | 588<br>588<br>590<br>590 |
| 592 | 朱翌<br>Zhu Yi | 点绛唇<br>Roughed Lips | 592<br>592 |
| 594 | 岳飞<br>Yue Fei | 小重山<br>Hills by Hills<br>满江红<br>The River All Red | 594<br>594<br>595<br>596 |
| 597 | 康与之<br>Kang Yuzhi | 长相思<br>Yearning Forever<br>满庭芳<br>Courtyard Full of Fragrance | 597<br>597<br>599<br>599 |
| 601 | 韩元吉<br>Han Yuanji | 六州歌头<br>Song of Six States | 601<br>602 |
| 605 | 朱淑贞<br>Zhu Shuzhen | 谒金门<br>Pay Homage to the Golden Gate<br>眼儿媚<br>Charming Eyes | 605<br>606<br>606<br>607 |

|  |  | 菩萨蛮 | 607 |
|---|---|---|---|
|  |  | Buddhist Dancers | 607 |
|  |  | 菩萨蛮 | 608 |
|  |  | Buddhist Dancers | 608 |
|  |  | 清平乐 | 609 |
|  |  | Music for a Peaceful Time | 609 |
|  |  | 清平乐 | 610 |
|  |  | Music for a Peaceful Time | 610 |
|  |  | 念奴娇 | 610 |
|  |  | Charm of a Maiden Singer | 611 |
|  |  | 阿那曲 | 612 |
|  |  | A Pleasant Song | 612 |
| 613 | 李吕 | 鹧鸪天 | 613 |
|  | Li Lü | Partridge Sky | 613 |
| 615 | 姚宽 | 生查子 | 615 |
|  | Yao Kuan | Mountain Hawthorn | 615 |
| 617 | 洪迈 | 踏莎行 | 617 |
|  | Hong Mai | Treading on Grass | 617 |
| 619 | 陆游 | 卜算子 | 620 |
|  | Lu You | Song of Divination | 620 |

|     |              |                                      |     |
| --- | ------------ | ------------------------------------ | --- |
|     |              | 钗头凤                               | 621 |
|     |              | Phoenix Hairpins                     | 621 |
|     |              | 秋波媚                               | 622 |
|     |              | Enchanting Autumn Waves              | 622 |
|     |              | 鹊桥仙                               | 623 |
|     |              | Immortals on the Magpie Bridge       | 623 |
|     |              | 诉衷情                               | 624 |
|     |              | Baring the Heart                     | 624 |
|     |              | 恋绣衾                               | 624 |
|     |              | Liking the Embroidered Quilt         | 625 |
| 626 | 唐琬<br>Tang Wan | 钗头凤<br>Phoenix Hairpins        | 626<br>627 |
| 628 | 传陆游妾     | 生查子<br>Mountain Hawthorn          | 628<br>628 |
| 630 | 范成大<br>Fan Chengda | 蝶恋花                      | 631 |
|     |              | Butterflies in Love with Flowers     | 631 |
|     |              | 鹊桥仙                               | 632 |
|     |              | Immortals on the Magpie Bridge       | 632 |
|     |              | 霜天晓角                             | 633 |
|     |              | Morn Horn under the Frosty Sky       | 633 |
|     |              | 鹧鸪天                               | 634 |
|     |              | Partridge Sky                        | 634 |

| | | | |
|---|---|---|---|
| 635 | 杨万里<br>Yang Wanli | 好事近<br>Happiness Approaching | 635<br>635 |
| 637 | 严蕊<br>Yan Rui | 卜算子<br>Song of Divination<br>如梦令<br>Like a Dream | 637<br>638<br>638<br>638 |
| 640 | 张孝祥<br>Zhang Xiaoxiang | 念奴娇<br>Charm of a Maiden Singer | 640<br>641 |
| 642 | 辛弃疾<br>Xin Qiji | 清平乐<br>Music for a Peaceful Time<br>青玉案<br>Green Jade Cup<br>丑奴儿<br>An Ugly Girl<br>定风波<br>Calming Disturbance<br>鹧鸪天<br>Partridge Sky<br>祝英台近<br>Slow Song of Zhu Yingtai<br>汉宫春<br>Spring in the Han Palace | 643<br>643<br>644<br>644<br>645<br>645<br>646<br>646<br>647<br>647<br>648<br>648<br>649<br>649 |

| | |
|---|---|
| 水龙吟 | 651 |
| Chanting of Water Dragon | 651 |
| 念奴娇 | 652 |
| Charm of a Maiden Singer | 653 |
| 贺新郎 | 654 |
| Congratulations to the Bridegroom | 654 |
| 贺新郎 | 656 |
| Congratulations to the Bridegroom | 657 |
| 木兰花慢 | 658 |
| Slow Song of Magnolia Flowers | 659 |
| 永遇乐 | 660 |
| Joy of Eternal Union | 660 |
| 贺新郎 | 661 |
| Congratulations to the Bridegroom | 662 |
| 满江红 | 663 |
| The River All Red | 663 |
| 满江红 | 664 |
| The River All Red | 665 |
| 满江红 | 666 |
| The River All Red | 666 |
| 破阵子 | 668 |
| Dance of the Cavalry | 668 |
| 南乡子 | 669 |
| Song of Southern Countryside | 669 |

| | | | |
|---|---|---|---|
| | 木兰花慢 | 670 |
| | Slow Song of Magnolia Flowers | 670 |
| | 贺新郎 | 671 |
| | Congratulations to the Bridegroom | 672 |
| | 水调歌头 | 673 |
| | Prelude to Water Melody | 673 |
| 675 姜夔<br>Jiang Kui | 点绛唇 | 676 |
| | Rouged Lips | 676 |
| | 鹧鸪天 | 677 |
| | Partridge Sky | 677 |
| | 鹧鸪天 | 678 |
| | Partridge Sky | 678 |
| | 杏花天影 | 679 |
| | Shadows under Apricot Blossom Sky | 679 |
| | 暗香 | 680 |
| | Faint Fragrance | 681 |
| | 疏影 | 682 |
| | Sparse shadows | 682 |
| | 扬州慢 | 684 |
| | Slow Song of Yangzhou City | 685 |
| | 长亭怨慢 | 686 |
| | Slow Song of Farewell Pavilion | 687 |
| | 庆宫春 | 688 |
| | Celebrating Spring in Palace | 688 |

| | |
|---|---|
| 齐天乐 | 689 |
| A Sky of Joy | 690 |
| 念奴娇 | 691 |
| Charm of a Maiden Singer | 692 |
| 侧犯 | 693 |
| Side Invasion | 693 |
| 角招 | 695 |
| Horn Invitation | 695 |
| 解连环 | 696 |
| Unchaining Double Rings | 696 |
| 鬲溪梅令 | 698 |
| The Plum across the Stream | 698 |
| 琵琶仙 | 699 |
| Immortal of Pipa | 699 |
| 凄凉犯 | 701 |
| Violation of a Tune | 701 |
| 霓裳中序第一 | 702 |
| The First One of Rainbow Clothes Tunes | 702 |
| 惜红衣 | 704 |
| Cherishing the Red Dress | 704 |
| 水龙吟 | 705 |
| Chanting of Water Dragon | 706 |

| | | | |
|---|---|---|---|
| 708 | 吴文英<br>Wu Wenying | 莺啼序<br>Prelude to Orioles' Twitter<br>莺啼序<br>Prelude to Orioles' Twitter | 708<br>709<br>711<br>712 |
| 715 | 蒋捷<br>Jiang Jie | 虞美人<br>Great Beauty Yu<br>一剪梅<br>A Twig of Plum Blossoms | 715<br>716<br>716<br>717 |
| 718 | 后记 | | |

# 王禹偁(954—1001)

  宋太宗太平兴国八年(983)进士。做过翰林学士,知制诰(替皇帝草拟诏令的官吏)。在朝廷敢说话,多次受到贬谪。词风含蓄雅丽。本词是当时的名篇之一。他留下的词仅此一首。

**Wang Yucheng(954–1001)**

  He passed the highest imperial examination in 983. He served as a court official and dared to say something in the court. He was demoted many times. The style of his *Ci* poems was restrained and elegant. The following *Ci* poem was one of the well-known *Ci* poems in his time, which is his only *Ci* poem that is extant.

## 点 绛 唇

雨恨云愁,江南依旧称佳丽。水村渔市,一缕孤烟细。 天际征鸿,遥认行如缀。平生事,此时凝睇,谁会凭栏意。

### Tune: Rouged Lips

Though deeply shrouded in the sorrow of the clouds and rains,

The south of the Yangtze still boasts of enchanting landscape.
By the green lake lie a fisherman's fair and a village,
Over the village a lone wisp of cooking smoke rises.

A row of wild geese fly far far away on the horizon southward,
I lean on the railings watching them disappearing in the distance,
My career and big ambition begin to surge in my heart and mind,
How I wish I could leisurely and carefree as them fly far and wide.

# 寇準(961—1023)

宋太宗太平兴国五年(980)进士。一代名相。曾力劝皇上亲征,阻止契丹入侵,稳定了国势。他是朝廷里一位正直的大臣。后来受到贬谪。词风婉转清丽。他的《江南春》是一时脍炙人口之作。

**Kou Zhun(961－1023)**

He passed the highest imperial examination in 980. He was a famous prime minister. He successfully advised the emperor to guard the frontier to stop the invaders stabling the situation of the country. He was a upright court official. Later he was banished from the court. The style of his *Ci* poems was subtle and restrained, simple and elegant. His "Spring in the South of the Yangtze River" won universal praise in his time.

## 江 南 春

波渺渺,柳依依。孤村芳草远,斜日杏花飞。江南春尽离肠断,蘋满汀洲人未归。

## Tune: Spring in the South of the Yangtze River

Without end the clear green waves flow and flow,
With affection sway and sway the tender willows.
By the lonely village the grasses with the scent of our love extend to the horizon,
In the pale sunlight the apricot blossoms fading like my face here and there fly.
I'm heartbroken in the south of the Yangtze River in the spring late,
Clover fern fills the shoal, but my dear has not been back to my bed.

❀❀❀❀❀❀❀❀❀❀❀❀❀

## 踏 莎 行

### 春 暮

春色将阑,莺声渐老,红英落尽青梅小。画堂人静雨蒙蒙,屏山半掩余香袅。　　密约沉沉,离情杳杳,菱花尘满慵将照。倚楼无语欲销魂,长空黯淡连芳草。

## Tune: Treading on Grass

### Late Spring

The enchanting spring is fading little by little,

寇　準

The orioles' voice is growing older bit by bit,
All the red flowers fall and green and small are plum fruits.
Outside the rain drizzling, quiet and still is the painted room,
The screen half open the smoke curls up from the burnt incense.

My dear lover has forgot at all in a sweet tryst our solemn pledge,
But my love to him remains deep forever and ever,
I am tired of making up and dust covers the mirror.
Without a word I lean gazing far on the railings heartbreaking,
Fragrant grass like his robe spreads to the distant sky dimming.

# 钱惟演(977—1034)

曾任保大军节度使。是北宋著名词人,与杨亿唱和。辞藻清新淡雅。

**Qian Weiyan(977 - 1034)**

He served as a court official. He was a well-known poet in the Northern Song Dynasty. He wrote and responded to each other with Yang Yi. His style was fresh and chaste.

## 木 兰 花

城上风光莺语乱,城下烟波春拍岸。绿杨芳草几时休,泪眼愁肠先已断。　情怀渐变成衰晚,鸾镜朱颜惊暗换。昔年多病厌芳尊,今日芳尊惟恐浅。

## June: Magnolia Flowers

On the city gate tower the scenery pretty, the orioles fly to and fro twittering,
At the foot of the city wall the misty waves beat the river shores in the spring.

钱惟演

Year after year with cheer grass and willows put on green clothes,
Tears streaming down my face, I'm filled with unbearable sorrow.

Unlike innocent grass and flowers my heart fades,
I'm shocked to see my face in the mirror changed.
In the past I often in poor health and cups of wine I was tired,
Now I'm afraid in the green jade cups there is too little wine.

# 潘阆(? —1009)

曾任滁州参军。他写了十首回忆杭州的词。交替使用白描、想象、反衬等方法。选景高洁,情调闲雅。

**Pan Lang(? – 1009)**

He served as an official in Chuzhou. He wrote ten well-known *Ci* poems about the beautiful city of Hangzhou. He used simple straightforward skill, imagination and setting off by contrast in turn. The scenes were noble and unsullied. The moods were leisurely and elegant.

## 酒 泉 子

长忆西湖,尽日凭阑楼上望:三三两两钓鱼舟,岛屿正清秋。笛声依约芦花里,白鸟成行忽惊起。别来闲整钓鱼竿,思入水云寒。

## *Tune: Song of Wine Fountain*

So frequently now I think of the beautiful West Lake,
Leaning on railings I watched it with delight all day.

The fishing boats drifted in two or three on the water,
The islets lay leisurely in the clear and cool autumn.

The sweet music of the flute floated out of the reed catkins faintly,
The white birds in a row were started up from the grasses suddenly.
Away from it at leisure I repair my fishing rods with special care,
My missing melts into the white clouds and cold water over there.

※※※※※※※※※※※※※※※※※

## 酒 泉 子

长忆西山,灵隐寺前三竺后,冷泉亭上旧曾游,三伏似清秋。白猿时见攀高树,长啸一声何处去?别来几向画图看,终是欠峰峦!

## Tune: Song of Wine Fountain

Now here I nearly every day recollect the West Hills in Hangzhou City,
It lay leisurely before the Lingyin Temple and after the Hills Heavenly.
How many times by the Cold Spring Pavilion I lingered,
The dog days there were just like in clear cool autumn.

Up the trees so tall the white monkeys climbed,
With long cries they were suddenly out of sight.

Since leaving there so frequently I have watched its pretty paintings,
But I cannot find their peaks with fairy spirit and postures charming.

❀❀❀❀❀❀❀❀❀❀❀❀❀❀❀❀❀

## 酒 泉 子

长忆观潮,满郭人争江上望,来疑沧海尽成空,万面鼓声中。弄潮儿向涛头立,手把红旗旗不湿。别来几向梦中看,梦觉尚心寒。

### Tune: Song of Wine Fountain

I often recollect watching the grand tide in Hangzhou on the scenic spot,
All the people crowded out of the city madly to watch it on the river shore.
The whole sea seemed to be all of a sudden empty,
With sound as a ten thousand drums beating loudly.

The tide players stood on the wave crests,
Holding red flags in their hands not wet.
Since leaving there, many times I dream of the sight,
Awake at midnight, I still shiver and shake with fright.

# 林逋(967—1028)

杭州孤山隐士。种梅养鹤,终身未娶,人称"梅妻鹤子"。词作《长相思》和《点绛唇》写离愁别绪,都是脍炙人口之作。他的《点绛唇》为"咏草之美者"。梅尧臣和欧阳修各填一首题材相同的《苏幕遮》和《少年游》。这三首词被后世称为"咏春草绝调"。

**Lin Bu(967–1028)**

He was a hermit in the Lonely Hill in Hangzhou. He never married, with plum blossoms as his wife and cranes as his son. His *Ci* poems "Yearning Forever" and "Rouged Lips" writing about the sorrow of separation enjoyed great popularity. His "Rouged Lips" was one of the best *Ci* poems writing about grass. Mei Yaochen composed "Screened by South Curtain" and Ouyang Xiu composed "Travelling While Young" about grass. The three *Ci* poems were regarded as "the best *Ci* poems about spring grass" by later people.

## 长 相 思

吴山青,越山青。两岸青山相送迎,谁知离别情? 君泪盈,妾泪盈。罗带同心结未成,江头潮已平。

## Tune: Yearning Forever

Green are the north hills,
Green are the south hills.
They greet boats on the river with delight and with grief see them off,
Who knows completely in our tender hearts our forever parting sore?

From his eyes fall the warm tears,
From my eyes fall the warm tears.
Oh, we fail to make a heart-shaped tie,
The water rising, comes our parting time.

❈❈❈❈❈❈❈❈❈❈❈❈❈❈❈❈❈

## 点 绛 唇

金谷年年,乱生春色谁为主? 余花落处,满地和烟雨。　又是离歌,一阕长亭暮。王孙去。萋萋无数,南北东西路。

## Tune: Rouged Lips

In Golden Vale year after year,
Grow wild grasses so luxuriant.
Where is the devoted songstress of unmatched beauty?

林　逋

The scented pink flowers remaining on the tender twigs,
Shower down on the green ground with the fine drizzle.

The song of farewell with tears I sing,
In the roadside pavilion in the evening.
Farther and farther away he is leaving,
Along roads the green grass like his robe extends,
In south, north, east and west, following his steps.

# 杨亿(974—1020)

被称为神童。与钱惟演唱和。善用典故。

**Yang Yi(974–1020)**

He was called a child prodigy. He wrote and responded to each other with Qian Weiyan. He was good at using allusions.

## 少 年 游

江南节物,水昏云淡,飞雪满前村。千寻翠岭,一枝芳艳,迢递寄归人。　寿阳妆罢,冰姿玉态,的的写天真。等闲风雨又纷纷,更忍向、笛中闻。

## June: Travelling While Young

In the southern land on the coldest days,
The water is turbid and the clouds gray,
The solitary village lies in the snow thick.
Step by step I climb up the green mountain,
I pluck a plum twig with refreshing scent,
And send it far away by post to my friend.

杨　亿

A red blossom fell on the princess's forehead snow-white,

Becoming so popular an ornament in the palace at that time.

In the severe winter she blossoms alone,

She appears in the world pure and cold.

At any time wind and rain will destroy her blossoms fragrant,

I can't bear hearing the flute playing "Falling of Plum Blossoms".

# 夏竦(985—1051)

曾任参知政事、枢密使等职。词《鹧鸪天》没有采用借景抒情的方式,全用女子的口吻直接传达心曲,方法新鲜。最后两行词脍炙人口:"不如饮待奴先醉,图的不知郎去时。"

**Xia Song(985‑1051)**

He once served as a court official. Instead of expressing one's emotion with scene, he used a woman's words to display her mind in "Partridge Sky". It was a way quite new. The last lines won universal praise: "I think I had better get drunk at once as a lord first, /Unconscious when he goes to the end of the world."

## 鹧 鸪 天

镇日无心扫黛眉,临行愁见理征衣。尊前只恐伤郎意,阁泪汪汪不敢垂。 停宝马,捧瑶卮,相斟相劝忍分离?不如饮待奴先醉,图得不知郎去时。

## *Tune: Partridge Sky*

The whole day to draw my brows I have no interest,

夏　竦

I feel sad to see him pack clothes for a long journey.
Reluctant to make my dear heartbreaking,
I try my best to keep my tears from falling.

Stopping his horse for a little time,
I hand him a jade cup of good wine,
And urge him to empty it again and again.
Now and here I am afraid to bid farewell,
I think I had better get drunk at once as a lord first,
Unconscious when he goes to the end of the world.

# 范仲淹(989—1052)

宋真宗大中祥符八年(1015)进士。官至参知政事。他是北宋著名的政治家,也是守卫西北边疆有名的将领。敌人怕他,说他"胸中自有百万兵"。他的边塞词写自己悲凉的情感。

**Fan Zhongyan(989－1052)**

He passed the highest imperial examination in 1015. He was a vice prime minister and a famous politician in the Northern Song Dynasty. He was also a well-known general guarding the northwestern border. The enemy was afraid of him for "he had millions of soldiers in his bosom". His *Ci* poems about the border described his desolate feeling over there.

## 苏 幕 遮

碧云天,黄叶地,秋色连波,波上寒烟翠。山映斜阳天接水,芳草无情,更在斜阳外。　　黯乡魂,追旅思,夜夜除非,好梦留人睡。明月楼高休独倚。酒入愁肠,化作相思泪。

范仲淹

## Tune: Screened by South Curtain

The sky is azure with some white clouds like jade floating,
The land is yellow with all the flowers like beauties fading.
Bleak autumn scene extends to the stream with grief,
Over the waves drifts the tear-like mist cool and green.
The setting sun shines on distant hills, sky and water melting into one,
The grasses without feeling is still luxuriant lying beyond the pink sun.
A soul with intense homesickness,
A traveller with strong loneliness,
Night by night on my bed I keep awake,
Except for sweet dreams of spring days.
Don't lean on the railings of a high building alone in the bright moonlight,
And don't drink, or wine will become lovesick tears falling down the eyes.

## 渔 家 傲

塞下秋来风景异,衡阳雁去无留意。四面边声连角起。千嶂里,长烟落日孤城闭。 浊酒一杯家万里,燕然未勒归无计。羌管悠悠霜满地。人不寐,将军白发征夫泪。

## Tune: Pride of Fishermen

Cold autumn coming to the north-west frontier, bleak is the scene,
The wild geese are flying southward unwilling to stay a night even.
Far and near the horns drearily resound,
Thousands of miserable hills lie around,
The mist drifting and sun setting, the lonely city gate is closed.

Taking a cup of poor wine, I begin to miss my faraway home,
How can we think of going home before defeating the ferocious enemy?
The sad Qiang flute music floats over the ground covered with frost so thick.
No one in the cold tents here can get asleep the whole night,
General's hair turns white, shedding tears the soldiers' eyes.

❀❀❀❀❀❀❀❀❀❀❀❀❀❀❀

## 御 街 行

纷纷坠叶飘香砌。夜寂静,寒声碎。真珠帘卷玉楼空,天淡银河垂地。年年今夜,月华如练,长是人千里。

范仲淹

愁肠已断无由醉,酒未到,先成泪。残灯明灭枕头欹,谙尽孤眠滋味。都来此事,眉间心上,无计相回避。

## Tune: Song of Imperial Thoroughfare

The night seems to be so quite and lonesome.
Yellow leaves shower on the steps so fragrant,
Making the chilly and broken sounds, light though.
The pearly curtain up, the lonely boudoir is shown,
The Milk Way for the separated lovers feels drear.
This night is filled with lovesickness year by year,
The pale moonlight looks like a silk tape,
My pretty dear is thousands of miles away.

My heart is broken and I can drink no longer really,
For the wine turns into tears before it reaches my lips.
In the twinkling candle light on the pillow bleak,
I am gradually awake with the unbearable grief.
Lovesickness grows bit by bit in my mind,
Oh, see on the brows it layer by layer piles.

# 柳永(约 987—约 1053)

　　北宋最杰出的词人之一。他进士七次未能登第。他失望无聊,流连坊曲于繁华的大都市,特别是京城。他过着"浅吟低唱"的生活。宋仁宗景祐元年(1034)进士登第。任地方小官,羁旅于城市和村落之间,夜宿于荒村之中。在乐工和歌伎的鼓舞下,他用俚俗的语言写了两百多首慢词,描写都市的繁华和美丽,以及歌妓浪子的生活,表达了他对这些可怜的女人的同情。他还描写孤独的山水间的旅途生活。他的慢词无论在都市还是在乡村都受到广泛的欢迎,相传当时"凡有井水处,即能闻柳词"。他死于贫穷之中。死后,还是几个知音妓女为其体面落葬。他葬于镇江北固山。他的词对宋词的发展有很大影响。

**Liu Yong( about 987 – about 1053)**

　　He was one of the most outstanding poets in the Northern Song Dynasty. When young, he failed in the highest imperial examination seven times. Disappointed, he lived a dissolute life. He lingered on in the halls for songs and dances in the flourishing cities, especially in the capital. There he lived a life of "drinking wine at leisure and low singing". In 1034, he passed the highest imperial examination. Then, serving as a low-ranking official, he travelled from cities to villages, and often stayed in the lonely villages for nights.

柳　永

Couraged by the musicians and singing girls, in popular spoken language and idioms, he wrote more than two hundred long *Ci* poems, describing the prosperity and beauty of the metropolises, and the life of prostitutes and prodigals, showing his sympathy to the poor women, and his lonely experiences of travelling through mountains and water. His slow tunes were so popular not only in cities but in villages also, as people at that time said:"Where wells are, there waft Liu's poems." He died in poverty. After his death some of his intimates among the prostitutes buried him decently at the foot of the Beigu Mount in Zhenjiang city. His works had a great impact on *Ci* poems.

## 蝶 恋 花

伫倚危楼风细细,望极春愁,黯黯生天际。草色烟光残照里,无言谁会凭阑意。　　拟把疏狂图一醉,对酒当歌,强乐还无味。衣带渐宽终不悔,为伊消得人憔悴。

### *Tune: Butterflies in Love with Flowers*

In a light breeze I lean on the railings high,
To look into the distance, I strain my eyes,
Sorrow seems to be forming on the horizon bit by bit.
The farewell sun shines slanting on the green grasses,
I lean here but who knows really my mental state?

I indulge myself with wine to drive sadness away,
I sing songs in a high voice while drinking,
With grief I get no joy from merrymaking.
I don't regret my belt is looser and looser,
For her I'd rather more and more haggard.

❀❀❀❀❀❀❀❀❀❀❀❀❀❀❀❀❀

## 甘 草 子

秋暮,乱洒衰荷,颗颗真珠雨。雨过月华生,冷彻鸳鸯浦。　池上凭阑愁无侣,奈此个、单栖情绪! 却傍金笼共鹦鹉,念粉郎言语。

### Tune: Song of Licorice Root

At dusk in the cool desolate autumn,
Drops of rain fall on lotuses withered,
As pearls rolling and sparkling.
After a rain the moon is shining,
On the cold pond no pair of mandarin ducks is at play.

She stares sad at the lonely scene leaning on the rails.
The quilt is thin and boudoir is quiet,
And she can't get asleep at midnight.
Turning to the parrot in the golden cage so lovingly,

柳　永

She pours out her feelings to it as to her dear softly.

※※※※※※※※※※※※※※※※※

## 雨　霖　铃

寒蝉凄切。对长亭晚，骤雨初歇。都门帐饮无绪，留恋处、兰舟催发。执手相看泪眼，竟无语凝噎。念去去、千里烟波，暮霭沉沉楚天阔。　　多情自古伤离别，更那堪冷落清秋节！今宵酒醒何处？杨柳岸、晓风残月。此去经年，应是良辰好景虚设。便纵有千种风情，更与何人说？

## *Tune: Bell Ringing in the Rain*

At dusk in the cool autumn the cicadas in the trees sadly cry.
We stand close facing the Farewell Pavilion on the riverside,
Just after shedding tears, a heavy shower.
At the farewell table I feel wine so sour,
Today here we can hardly endure to long part,
The boatman urges me again and again to start.
Holding our hands, we look at each other's teardrops,
Words frozen in our tender hearts, we break into sobs.
With grief I'm leaving her farther and farther away,
The eve haze knits brows over a thousand *li* waves,
The sad gloom shrouds the south shore of the Yangtze River.

Since ancient times to leave one's lover is always heartbroken,
How can I in the clear cold fall stand the sadness?
Where shall I sober up tonight from drunkenness?
On the bank sway the sparse weeping willows,
When the moon sets and morn breeze blows.
I'll be away for years day and night missing my dear,
In the south of the Yangtze on my long journey drear,
I won't bear giving even
A glance at pretty scenes.
Even a thousand thoughts and feelings in my mind I get,
To whom can I with a scented tender heart convey them?

❈❈❈❈❈❈❈❈❈❈❈❈❈❈❈❈❈❈

## 望 海 潮

东南形胜,三吴都会,钱塘自古繁华。烟柳画桥,风帘翠幕,参差十万人家。云树绕堤沙。怒涛卷霜雪,天堑无涯。市列珠玑,户盈罗绮,竞豪奢。 重湖叠巘清嘉。有三秋桂子,十里荷花。羌管弄晴,菱歌泛夜,嬉嬉钓叟莲娃。千骑拥高牙。乘醉听箫鼓,吟赏烟霞。异日图将好景,归去凤池夸。

## *Tune: Watching the Tidal Bore*

In the southeast, with the beauty of the scene, the most famous,

柳　永

And as one of the largest cities in the Kingdom of Wu ancient,
Hangzhou since olden days has been the most flourishing.
The misty willows and painted bridges seem in paintings,
The bamboo curtains hang at the doors and windows,
There are more than hundred thousands of households.
Lining up on the banks of the Qiantang River trees are lost in the sky.
In the broad river the huge waves surge endless eastward snow-white,
The clear river appears to be endlessly long and vast.
In the shops pearls of different sizes and shapes sparkle,
Before the doors shown are pretty colored silk and satin,
The shop owners vie with pride in their riches and luxury.

With inner and outer lakes, hills upon hills, clear and pretty is West Lake.
In autumn here and there floats the intoxicating scent of flowers of bays,
In summer ten miles of lotuses with fragrance are in bloom.
The Qiang pipes play melodious music under the sky blue,
Under the bright moon anywhere the songs of water chestnuts are heard,
Loudly laugh and sing the fishermen and lotus-seedpods-gathering girls.
The guards on horses with colorful flags pass by one by one.

With interest you listen to the drums and pipes when drunk,
Appreciating far and near the green leaves and red flowers.
You recite the poems of the beautiful scene in fine hours.
Before going back, you'd better paint the pictures of them
Which you should to the emperor and high officials present.

❈❈❈❈❈❈❈❈❈❈❈❈❈❈❈❈❈❈

## 定 风 波

自春来、惨绿愁红,芳心是事可可。日上花梢,莺穿柳带,犹压香衾卧。暖酥消,腻云亸,终日厌厌倦梳裹。无那! 恨薄情一去,音书无个。　　早知恁么,悔当初、不把雕鞍锁。向鸡窗,只与蛮笺象管,拘束教吟课。镇相随,莫抛躲,针线闲拈伴伊坐。和我,免使年少光阴虚过。

## *Tune: Calming Disturbance*

Since pretty early spring slowly came to the place,
Sad are willows green and drear feel peaches red,
Nowhere at all my fragrant tender heart can I rest.
The sunshine strokes the flowers' tips,
The orioles play with the willow twigs,
I'm in dreams with him in a sweet quilt.
Thin is my face, enchantingly beautiful and warm,

柳　永

And my dark cloud-like hair is not combed at all,
The whole day without making up I'm out of sorts.
Day and night to forget the days I get no way.
Since my dear fickle lover went so far away,
From him I haven't got any message anyway.

If at that time I had known all these,
I wouldn't have let him so far leave,
I'd have locked saddle of his steed.
I'd have him in the quiet study confined,
And pens and paper I'd readily provide,
I'd let him all the time read and write.
Day and night him I'd be following,
Without even a moment separating,
I'd chat with him gay while sewing.
When we are doing so,
Like body and shadow,
We'd not waste youth.

❈❈❈❈❈❈❈❈❈❈❈❈❈❈❈❈❈

## 少　年　游

参差烟树灞陵桥,风物尽前朝。衰杨古柳,几经攀折,憔悴楚宫腰。　　夕阳闲淡秋光老,离思满蘅皋。一曲阳关,断肠声尽,独自凭兰桡。

## Tune: Travelling While Young

In the misty weeping willows lies the Farewell Bridge,
The scene is just same as that of the previous dynasties.
After a good many years, the willows with knitted brows are old and wither,
Their twigs have been plucked away as gifts for parting friends and lovers,
They are weak and thin as in the Chu palace beauties' waists.

The setting sun is pale and the autumn scenery seems aged,
Parting tears wet the riverside grass.
After a farewell song, the Yang Pass,
In my heart flows the unbearable woe,
I lean alone on an oar in a little boat.

❈❈❈❈❈❈❈❈❈❈❈❈❈❈❈❈

# 八声甘州

对潇潇暮雨洒江天,一番洗清秋。渐霜风凄紧,关河冷落,残照当楼。是处红衰翠减,苒苒物华休。惟有长江水,无语东流。　　不忍登高临远,望故乡渺邈,归思难收。叹年来踪迹,

柳　永

何事苦淹留？想佳人妆楼颙望，误几回、天际识归舟。争知我，倚阑干处，正恁凝愁！

## Tune: Eight Beats of Ganzhou

At dusk a rain falls thick and fast on the Yangtze River,
Washing thoroughly clear the cold withering autumn.
The wind becomes harder and more desolate bit by bit,
The mountains and rivers far and near are so deserted,
The setting sun sheds pale light on the tower's railings.
Oh, the green grasses and the pink flowers are fading,
Gradually leaving is the prime of all the plants.
The Yangtze River remains as before as vast,
In silence flowing fast eastward without a stop.

I can't bear looking far from the railings at all,
For my dear hometown is out of sight,
Homesickness never leaves my mind.
Day by day, year by year alone I wander in alien lands,
Why so far I have not been back to kiss her soft hands?
At home my dear beauty must be upstairs,
Into my direction so often she must stare,
So many times on the horizon among the sails,
She regards one as my returning boat by mistake.
However, she doesn't know, oh, how can she know?

Leaning on the banister I gaze with tears far also.

❋❋❋❋❋❋❋❋❋❋❋❋❋❋❋❋

## 昼 夜 乐

洞房记得初相遇。便只合、长相聚。何期小会幽欢,变作离情别绪。况值阑珊春色暮。对满目、乱花狂絮。直恐好风光,尽随伊归去。　一场寂寞凭谁诉。算前言,总轻负。早知恁地难拚,悔不当时留住。其奈风流端正外,更别有、系人心处。一日不思量,也攒眉千度。

### Tune: Joy of Day and Night

I remember in the boudoir first time we met.
So pure and deep love we together possessed,
We hoped to stay together all our life.
I didn't expect the joy of short trysts,
To turn into the heartbreaking parting grief.
Like my face fading is pretty spring scene,
Oh, here and there, high and low
Fly flowers and catkins with woe.
I think wonderful sight remaining,
Will be following his steps leaving.

柳　永

To whom can I bare my heart lonely and sad?
He made the firm pledge of soon coming back,
But nowadays he has forgotten all about it.
If I had known I'm so painful to leave him,
I would have kept him anyhow here.
So elegant and handsome he appears,
Besides he has a kind of intoxicating charm,
Attracting me into his warm arms and heart.
Even if I put grief away from my brain in a day,
A thousand frowns will show on my fading face.

❈❈❈❈❈❈❈❈❈❈❈❈❈❈❈❈❈❈

## 采 莲 令

月华收,云淡霜天曙。西征客、此时情苦。翠娥执手送临歧,轧轧开朱户。千娇面、盈盈伫立,无言有泪,断肠争忍回顾？　一叶兰舟,便恁急桨凌波去。贪行色、岂知离绪。万般方寸,但饮恨,脉脉同谁语？更回首、重城不见,寒江天外,隐隐两三烟树。

## *Tune: Song of Gathering Seedpods of Lotus*

The round moon filled with tender affection sets,
Clouds pale, frost thick, and day about to break.
As a painful lonely traveller to the remotest west,

Day and night I'm tortured with painful sorrow.
The red door creaks as groaning miserably open,
Holding my hands, she sees me off at a crossroad.
She is so sweet and enchanting,
With grace in silence standing,
Down her face tears streaming,
Heartbroken, how can I bear to turn to increase grief?

Like in a wide river up and down floating a green leaf,
With hurried oars, following the waves, the boat leaves.
The boatman only cares covering the trip,
Knowing nothing at all about my sadness.
With heartbreaking separation melancholy,
I can only keep her deep in my bosom,
To whom can I tell my sweet affection?
Again I turn to look at my pretty lover,
The city and she are out of sight,
Beyond the cold drear water wide,
The misty trees wave me goodbye.

## 集 贤 宾

小楼深巷狂游遍,罗绮成丛。就中堪人属意,最是虫虫。有画难

柳　永

描雅态,无花可比芳容。几回饮散良宵永,鸳衾暖、凤枕香浓。算得人间天上,惟有两心同。　　近来云雨忽西东。消恼损情惊。纵然偷期暗会,长是匆匆。争似和鸣偕老,免教敛翠啼红。眼前时、暂疏欢宴,盟言在、更莫忡忡。待作真个宅院,方信有初终。

## June: Gathering of Virtuous Guests

I have been visiting the little storied buildings and deep lanes in the capital wholly,
There are so many singing girls and dancers heavily powdered in coloured silk.
Of all enchanting young girls,
I like one best, Little Worm.
No portrait can display her elegance,
No flower can match her appearance.
In the long gay nights after drinking,
The scent on our pillow is pleasing,
Our quilt with a pair of painted phoenixes is warm and soft.
We are the only gay pair of intimates in the world and heaven we feel.

Recently I cannot enter her boudoir.
I'm sorrowful we are separated far.
Even we manage to have a tryst,
We can only stay for a short time.

I wish we could be a pair of lovebirds side by side either in rest or play,
There will be neither frown nor tears day and night on her charming face.
At present, I suggest,
We should meet less.
Since we have made a promise so serious,
She shouldn't at all be uneasy and drear.
In the future we will live together all our life in our own house,
No matter how difficult it is, I will keep my promise anyhow.

❈❈❈❈❈❈❈❈❈❈❈❈❈❈❈❈❈❈

## 少 年 游

长安古道马迟迟,高柳乱蝉嘶。夕阳鸟外,秋风原上,目断四天垂。 归云一去无踪迹,何处是前期?狎兴生疏,酒徒萧索,不似少年时。

### June: Travelling While Young

On an ancient road to Chang'an, old capital, goes my horse slow,
The cicadas groan and sigh in a mess in the tall weeping willows.
The sun sets beyond the crows lonely,
On the outskirts blows cold fall wind,

柳　永

Desolation wafts everywhere between the earth and sky.

Far away, my fairy maiden, like a returning cloud flies,
Where is the place of the date we seriously made for today?
My interest to make merry with singers and dancers fades,
Few wine friends again in my house appear,
I'm no longer the young man in those years.

❀❀❀❀❀❀❀❀❀❀❀❀❀❀❀❀❀

## 浪淘沙慢

梦觉、透窗风一线,寒灯吹息。那堪酒醒,又闻空阶,夜雨频滴。嗟因循、久作天涯客。负佳人、几许盟言,便忍把、从前欢会,陡顿翻成忧戚。　　愁极。再三追思,洞房深处,几度饮散歌阑。香暖鸳鸯被,岂暂时疏散,费伊心力。殢云尤雨,有万般千种,相怜相惜。　　恰到如今,天长漏永,无端自家疏隔。知何时、却拥秦云态,愿低帏昵枕,轻轻细说与,江乡夜夜,数寒更思忆。

### Tune: Slow Song of Waves-Sifting Sand

Awake from a beautiful dream at midnight,
A thread of wind through the window I find
Blowing out a faint candle.
Oh, I just sober up and I can

Not bear hearing raindrops without end,
Falling by the window on empty steps.
How should I have been away years from sweet home?
As a lonely guest in a strange area she does not know,
I break my promises serious
With her, my beauty so dear.
I'm unbearably melancholy to change
Happiness of merrymaking in the days
All of a sudden into grief.

With bitterness extreme,
I recollect the hours past.
In the deep warm boudoir,
After I had drunk some wine and listened to her singing love songs,
We shared a quilt embroidered with a pair of mandolin duck so long.
To part from her even a moment, I could not endure,
My heart would be totally broken, I was quite sure.
Our sweet and fragrant love showered
Into our dried hearts hour by hour.

Now the night is so long, so cold and so drear that I can bear hardly,
The water from the water watch falls drop by drop I can hear clearly.
I shouldn't stay alone in the remote area of the world,
When can I again in my warm arms tightly hold her?
The curtains low, on a pillow to her I'll whisper,

How in the sparse willows by the lonely river,
I spent the long cold nights in the small town,
Counting the watchman beating a drum now.

## 卜算子慢

江枫渐老,汀蕙半凋,满目败红衰翠。楚客登临,正是暮秋天气。引疏砧、断续残阳里。对晚景、伤怀念远,新愁旧恨相继。　　脉脉人千里。念两处风情,万重烟水。雨歇天高,望断翠峰十二[*]。尽无言、谁会凭高意?纵写得、离肠万种,奈归云谁寄?

## Tune: Slow Song of Divination

The maples grow old along the bank,
The orchids fade on the nearby land,
The faded red and green fills my eyes.
A traveller alone I climb up the height,
The autumn is quite late.
Under the setting sunray,
Float a few intermittent sounds of cloth pounding.
You, so far away, I can't help so painfully missing,
At dusk I alone look at the dreary scene,

In my heart new sorrow follows old grief.

With tender warm affection,
We look into the directions
Of two places separated by thousands of miles of water and mountains.
Like Cowherd and Girl Weaver looking at each other across the Galaxy.
The sky is higher when rain stops now,
The goddess disapears with rosy clouds,
Leaving in rain the twelve pretty green peaks clear.※
No one knows what is really in my deep heart here,
I keep silence, for even I can write a thousand feelings of sorrow,
No returning clouds will take the lovesick letter to her at home.

※ 翠峰十二即巫山。楚王在梦中与一绝色女子欢会。她临走的时候说:"我乃巫山神女也。旦为朝云,暮为行雨,朝朝暮暮,阳台之下。"

※ King of Chu dreamed of making love with a most beautiful lady. Before leaving, she said:" I'm the goddess in the Mount Wu and I'll come to you in the forms of rosy clouds in the morn and a shower in the eve."

柳　永

## 夜　半　乐

冻云黯淡天气,扁舟一叶,乘兴离江渚。渡万壑千岩,越溪深处。怒涛渐息,樵风乍起,更闻商旅相呼,片帆高举。泛画鹢、翩翩过南浦。　　望中酒旆闪闪,一簇烟村,数行霜树。残日下、渔人鸣榔归去。败荷零落,衰柳掩映,岸边两两三三、浣纱游女。避行客、含羞笑相语※。　　到此因念,绣阁轻抛,浪萍难驻。叹后约、丁宁竟何据! 惨离怀、空恨岁晚归期阻。凝泪眼、杳杳神京路。断鸿声远长天暮。

### Tune: Midnight Joy

Under the sky hang clouds cold,
I take a fast green leaf-like boat,
In high spirits leaving the islet.
We pass many crags and valleys,
Into the deepest stream where Xi Shi washed yarn.※
The great surging waves little by little become calm,
And a favorable wind comes round,
The traders call to each other loud,
All the white sails are lifted so high.
Our boat passes the south bank by.

The streamers of wine shops in the breeze flutter,

The cooking smoke from a village curls upward,
And in it appear lines of the frosted trees.
The slanting sunshine appears to be weak,
To return home, with wood clubs, at boats fishermen knock.
The sweet lotus flowers here and there like faces fade all,
The leaves of the withered weeping willow trees are left only a few.
By water are pretty girls returning from washing in threes and twos,
Who avoid meeting a young man face to face,
Chatting and smiling shy on homeward way.

Her fragrant arms, I regret,
I should not have easily left,
Like a duckweed with water drifting anywhere,
I'm a miserable wanderer going here and there.
Once shedding red tears she urged me to earlier return,
But so far with unbearable woe I fail to go back to her.
Oh, it's already the end of the year,
So grievous I still have to stay here.
With streaming tears, far and wide I look,
To the capital she stays, it is a long route.
I feel heartbreaking under the lonely wide grey sky at dusk,
Seeing a wild goose away from its mate cry for its beloved.

※ 西施列中国四大美人之首。西施少女时在若耶溪边洗纱。不久被选入越国宫廷。越已沦为吴国属国,越王行美人计,将其

柳　永

送与吴王。吴王沉迷酒色,不理朝政,被越王打败,关于井中。西施与相爱之人隐名埋姓,生活在太湖之畔。

※ Xi Shi ranked first on the list of the four most beautiful women in ancient China. In the Spring and Autum Period, a young girl, Xi Shi like a blooming lotus flower, cleaned yarn by the Ruoye Stream with her companions. She was selected to the ruler of the Yue state conquered by the Wu state. The ruler of Yue used a sex-trap sending her to the ruler of Wu. Charmed by her beauty, the ruler of Wu couldn't leave her even a moment. Day and night, with her, he drank wine, enjoying songs and dances, not conducting state affairs. The Yue state defeated the Wu state and the ruler of Wu was put in a well. With her sweetheart, Xi Shi left the court and lived by the Tai lake incognito.

❈❈❈❈❈❈❈❈❈❈❈❈❈❈❈❈❈❈

## 鹤　冲　天

黄金榜上,偶失龙头望。明代暂遗贤,如何向? 未遂风云便,争不恣狂荡? 何须论得丧。才子词人,自是白衣卿相。　烟花巷陌,依约丹青屏障。幸有意中人,堪寻访。且恁偎红倚翠,风流事,平生畅。青春都一饷。忍把浮名,换了浅斟低唱!

## June: A Crane Flying to the Sky

In the highest imperial exam list,
Oh, I lost first place so unlucky.
In the bright flourishing age remains an unselected sage,
What way I wonder painfully in the future should I take?
Since I fail in realizing my ambition,
Shall I pass all my life in dissipation?
I wonder why I give my thoughts to success or failure?
A gifted poet without passing the highest exam imperial,
A minister without scholarly honor I'd be.

On the so famous brothel-gathering street,
I can see dimly the screens with beauties' portraits with charm.
I may be lucky enough to find maiden singers after my heart,
It's worthy to inquire and search.
Holding in arms a charming girl,
I'll make merry to my heart's content all my life.
Oh, beautiful youth is only a little while I realize.
The fame in the world I will stop pursuing,
And I'll drink wine at leisure and low sing.

柳　永

## 木兰花慢

拆桐花烂熳,乍疏雨、洗清明。正艳杏烧林,缃桃绣野,芳景如屏。倾城,尽寻胜去,骤雕鞍绀幰出郊坰。风暖繁弦脆管,万家竞奏新声。　　盈盈,斗草踏青。人艳冶,递逢迎。向路旁往往,遗簪堕珥,珠翠纵横。欢情,对佳丽地,信金罍罄竭玉山倾。拚却明朝永日,画堂一枕春酲。

### Tune: Slow Song of Magnolia Flowers

The paulownias are in bloom purple-white,
A sparse shower probably just at midnight,
Washed the country so clear and refreshing.
The gorgeous apricots seem to be burning,
The pretty peaches appear in the embroidered field,
And the charming scene is just like a colored screen.
The whole city is nearly empty with only willow trees on the roads,
Women take carriages and men ride horses now and then saying hallo,
To the suburb with interest to appreciate the landscape.
Ten thousands of wine shops and halls for songs play,
Musical instruments vying in their music originality.

The ladies graceful with scented skirts in the country
Pick green grasses competing strangeness each other.

Far and near like flowers the singing girls and dancers,
Greet all the persons with a smile full of charm.
By tree-lined roads and on grass-covered paths,
The rich ladies fashionably dressed lose without care
Pearls and jade, gold pins and earrings here and there.
All the tourists happy and joyous
In the sweet places bright and clear
Empty the wine urns and get drunk falling like jade mounts.
Tomorrow they get ready to sleep in painted rooms sound.

❀❀❀❀❀❀❀❀❀❀❀❀❀❀❀

## 迷 仙 引

才过笄年,初绾云鬟,便学歌舞。席上尊前,王孙随分相许。算等闲、酬一笑,便千金慵觑。常只恐、容易蕣华偷换,光阴虚度。　　已受君恩顾,好与花为主。万里丹霄,何妨携手同归去。永弃却、烟花伴侣。免教人见妾,朝云暮雨。

## *Tune: Song Fascinating Immortals*

I clearly remember just over fifteen,
I coiled up my hair with pins green,
And began to learn singing and dancing.
At feasts I attend to officials' offspring,

柳　永

And I am always highly praised.
When I return them a gay face,
They readily give me a thousand ounces of gold at any time,
And to the money I just with sincere thanks turn a blind eye.
I'm day and night worried greatly,
My youth will pass away quickly,
As a rose of Sharon in a day withers.

I am so grateful to your appreciation,
And you'll be my master, as a girl so tender, I warmly hope,
Under the vast blue sky, hand in hand, you'll take me home.
I'll be far, far, away from
The prostitute circle before.
Lest some people around should with interest talk about
My playing fast and loose with love, like a floating cloud.

❈❈❈❈❈❈❈❈❈❈❈❈❈❈❈❈❈❈

## 秋　夜　月

当初聚散,便唤作、无由再逢伊面。近日来,不期而会重欢宴。向尊前,闲暇里,敛着眉儿长叹。惹起旧愁无限。　盈盈泪眼。漫向我耳边,作万般幽怨。奈你自家心下,有事难见。待信真个,怎别无萦绊。不免收心,共伊长远。

## Tune: The Moon on an Autumn Night

Leaving her some time ago at a feast,
Oh, I thought with heartbroken grief,
We can never meet again.
However, oh, just of late,
We meet at the feast again in surprise.
At the same table before cups of wine,
In a chat with me with unbearable sorrow,
Knitting her brows, she sighs and groans,
Raising endless griefs in the past.

Her eyes full of red tears sparkle,
She whispers to me without a stop,
Pouring out her sad complaints all.
On her mind she has something weighing,
I am sorry about it I know at all nothing.
If she determines to stop with others
As before all the romantic relations,
I'll cease love affairs with others in the circle,
And with devoted love live forever with her.

柳　永

## 御 街 行

前时小饮春庭院,悔放笙歌散。归来中夜酒醺醺,惹起旧愁无限。虽看坠楼换马,争奈不是鸳鸯伴。　　朦胧暗想如花面,欲梦还惊断。和衣拥被不成眠,一枕万回千转。惟有画梁,新来双燕,彻曙闻长叹。

### Tune: Song of Imperial Thoroughfare

Days ago I drank a little in a green brothel in spring,
I regretted dismissing the sweet singing and dancing.
At late night, I was very drunk when getting home,
In succession came the old griefs and new sorrows.
Though I met the female singers with versatility and charm,
I knew clearly they were not at all the lovers after my heart.

At midnight I thought of the flower-like face,
When entering a dream, suddenly I awaked.
With clothes on in the quilt alone I could not go to a dream,
On the pillow we shared thousands of thoughts torture me.
Only a pair of swallows on the beam in the nest,
Listened to me sighing so drearily until daybreak.

## 归 朝 欢

别岸扁舟三两只。葭苇萧萧风淅淅。沙汀宿雁破烟飞,溪桥残月和霜白。渐渐分曙色。路遥川远多行役。往来人,只轮双桨,尽是利名客。　　一望乡关烟水隔。转觉归心生羽翼。愁云恨雨两牵萦,新春残腊相催逼。岁华都瞬息。浪萍风梗诚何益。归去来,玉楼深处,有个人相忆。

### Tune: Joy of Returning to Royal Court

On the other shore moor the boats two or three,
The yellow reeds by the water rustle in a breeze.
On the shoal the perching wild geese started fly through thin mist,
In fading moonlight the bridge over water is white with frost thick.
Little by little the dawn becomes clear,
More and more on roads people appear.
The travellers to and fro,
Take carriages or boats,
All of them are busy hankering after fame and game.

My birthplace is beyond rivers and mounts far away.
How I wish I could fly back to her soft arms in my hometown.
My thoughts fly between two places like gloomy floating clouds,
Spring and winter push and press each other.

柳　永

My sweet prime flies away just in a moment.
I'm tired of wandering like a duckweed in water and a leaf in the sky.
Oh, I decide to go back to my native place day and night in my mind.
In the deep jade-decorated scented boudoir,
There's a beauty missing me with a sad heart.

## 婆罗门令

昨宵里恁和衣睡,今宵里又恁和衣睡。小饮归来,初更过,醺醺醉。中夜后、何事还惊起? 霜天冷,风细细,触疏窗、闪闪灯摇曳。　　空床展转重追想,云雨梦、任欹枕难继。寸心万绪,咫尺千里。好景良天,彼此,空有相怜意,未有相怜计。

### *Tune: Song of Brahman*

Last night I slept with clothes,
Tonight, I, with clothes also.
Drinking a bit I come back,
The first watch is just past,
Still as in a sound sleep I'm dead drunk.
After midnight, with a start I sober up.
Cold is the sky of frost,
The breeze blows soft,

Through the curtain,
The candle flickers.

On the lonely bed I toss about missing the beauty after my heart,
On the solitary pillow a dream of love affair only short time lasts.
Ten thousands of thoughts roll in my mind,
In the dream she smiles just before my eyes,
While I'm awake she stays a thousand miles away.
Facing the intoxicating scenery on so sunny a day,
To whom can we in detail tell,
Our amorous feelings intense?

※※※※※※※※※※※※※※※※※※

# 忆 帝 京

薄衾小枕凉天气,乍觉别离滋味。展转数寒更,起了还重睡。毕竟不成眠,一夜长如岁。　　也拟待、却回征辔;又争奈、已成行计。万种思量,多方开解,只恁寂寞厌厌地。系我一生心,负你千行泪。

## Tune: Recollecting Imperial Capital

With a thin quilt and cool pillow in early summer,
All of a sudden I feel sad for our long separation.

柳　永

Counting times with great care just,
The watchman has beaten the drum,
I toss about in the solitary cold bed.
When I get up, I return to bed again.
The whole night I keep awake drear,
Oh, really it seems as long as a year.

Oh, my beautiful charming sweetheart,
I'd better return to your fragrant arms,
But I am on the travel.
How can I come back?
What I should do I do not at all know,
Alone, I'm filled with unbearable woe.
I'll tie you in my tender heart all my life,
And I owe you tears of thousands of lines.

❉❉❉❉❉❉❉❉❉❉❉❉❉❉❉❉❉❉

## 锦　堂　春

坠髻慵梳,愁蛾懒画,心绪是事阑珊。觉新来憔悴,金缕衣宽。认得这疏狂意下,向人消譬如闲。把芳容整顿,恁地轻孤,争忍心安。　　依前过了旧约,甚当初赚我,偷剪云鬟。几时得归来,香阁深关。待伊要、尤云殢雨,缠绣衾、不与同欢。尽更深、款款问伊,今后敢更无端。

## June: Spring in the Brocaded Hall

My hair bun loose, I have no interest to comb hair with care lovely,
My brows knitting, I'm in no mood to draw them like distant hills,
I do not want to do anything at all.
My face looks so sallow and wan,
And my pink clothes and green belt become so loose.
My lovesickness is caused by the young man dissolute,
I still remember clear so lightly he treats me.
I'll dress up more charming than before even.
When thinking of all the time my dear lover's changeable feeling,
How can I feel easy seeing in mirrors my flower-like face fading?

Again he breaks the promise to return to my side.
Since he often did so why at the sad parting time,
He cheated me into cutting a lock of my hair as a pledge.
I'm thinking how to lecture him returning to me some day,
I'll shut him outside the fragrant green boudoir.
If he comes to my bed asking to lie in my arms,
And to make love with me in the quilt embroidered,
Of course I'll refuse him in a very resolute manner.
Until midnight I'll criticize his dissipated affairs one by one,
And ask him to vow never to do such things again even once.

柳　永

## 引　驾　行

红尘紫陌,斜阳暮草长安道,是离人。断魂处,迢迢匹马西征。新晴。韶光明媚,轻烟淡薄和气暖,望花村。路隐映,摇鞭时过长亭。愁生。伤凤城仙子,别来千里重行行。又记得、临歧泪眼,湿莲脸盈盈。　　消凝。花朝月夕,最苦冷落银屏。想媚容、耿耿无眠,屈指已算回程。相萦。空万般思忆,争如归去睹倾城。向绣帏、深处并枕,说如此牵情。

## *Tune: Driving a Carriage*

Over the dust-covered red roads to the old capital, Chang'an,
Hangs the fading sun, shedding pale light on the scented grass.
I feel miserable and lonely,
On long westward journey,
On the old horse so thin and tired.
The sun gets out after a rain fine,
The bright light as water flows in the warm air.
I watch the village with flowers here and there.
Through flowers of different colors the roads are seen unclear,
Lifting the whip suddenly I catch sight of the roadside pavilion.
And at once sadness enters my heart.
I think of the love affairs in the past,
But what touched me the most,

Was the time I was about to go,
Tears wetted her face like a lotus.

She must be nearly heartbroken.
At night with the moon bright and in the morn, flowers in bloom,
Behind the lonely blue screens she is overcome with cold gloom.
Her pink face so enchanting
In sleepless nights is fading,
All the time she is looking forward to my returning date.
Oh, in vain we miss each other so far away night and day,
I'd better go to her arms from a faraway part of the world,
And I'll never anyhow separate even a moment with her.
Behind the curtain and on the fragrant bed,
We will talk about our yearning since then.

❈❈❈❈❈❈❈❈❈❈❈❈❈❈❈

## 斗 百 花

煦色韶光明媚,轻霭低笼芳树。池塘浅蘸烟芜,帘幕闲垂风絮。春困厌厌,抛掷斗草工夫,冷落踏青心绪。终日扃朱户。　　远恨绵绵,淑景迟迟难度。年少傅粉,依前醉眠何处? 深院无人,黄昏乍拆秋千,空锁满庭花雨。

柳　永

## June: Flowers Blooming Dying in Beauty

So brilliant and enchanting is the spring scene,
A thin haze drifts slow over the fragrant trees.
On the pond lie the dimming wild plants,
The curtain hangs and the catkins dance.
All the time the beautiful girl is sleepy and melancholy,
In no mood to join other girls in picking strange grasses,
And going for a spring outing in suburb.
She shuts firmly the quiet red chamber
The whole long lonely day.

Her heart is filled with hate,
The flowers blooming and birds singing, she feels a day as a year.
"Where is my powdered dissolute dear at all?" she thinks so drear,
"On whose bed as before does he get dead drunk?"
Now in the deep courtyard beside her is no one,
She begins to play alone so dreadful on the swing,
Flowers like her face shower down in the evening.

## 驻 马 听

凤枕鸾帷。二三载,如鱼似水相知。良天好景,深怜多爱,无非尽意依随。奈何伊。恣性灵、忒煞些儿。无事孜煎,万回千度,怎忍分离。 而今渐行渐远,渐觉虽悔难追。漫寄消寄息,终久奚为。也拟重论缱绻,争奈翻覆思维。纵再会,只恐恩情,难似当时。

## Tune: Stopping the Horse and Listening

Sharing the pillow and curtain with cheer,

We spent our prime of two or three years,

As fish played with water gurgling.

On fine days in beautiful springs,

We walked arm in arm on paths with flowers,

I'll never forget all my life our happy hours.

In those days all the time,

I stooped to compromise.

Oh, but he

Often to me

Displayed his strong personality.

Since he with me easily parted,

Night and day,

Again and again,

I think of our love in the past

柳　永

With so melancholy the heart.

Now farther and farther away from me he goes,
It's no use regretting leaving him with sorrow.
Even I inform him I love him as before,
I am quite sure it means nothing at all.
Once I think of going on our love,
Considering it long, I give it up.
Even he comes back to my chamber,
Can we keep forever our affection?

❈❈❈❈❈❈❈❈❈❈❈❈❈❈❈❈

## 曲 玉 管

陇首云飞,江边日晚,烟波满目凭阑久。一望关河萧索,千里清秋,忍凝眸?杳杳神京,盈盈仙子,别来锦字终难偶。断雁无凭,冉冉飞下汀洲,思悠悠。　　暗想当初,有多少、幽欢佳会,岂知聚散难期,翻成雨恨云愁?阻追游。每登山临水,惹起平生心事,一场消黯,永日无言,却下层楼。

## June: Jade Musical Pipe

The clouds like her brows fly over peaks high,
On the banks of the river the setting sun shines,

On the railings I gaze long at waves and mist.

The river and passes are so cold and desolate,

For a thousand miles stretches the fall so clear,

I can no longer bear seeing the scene drear.

Now my charming singing girl stays

In the beautiful capital so far away.

I want to send her a long letter telling her my unbearable woe,

But we can't exchange our love and longing on the same pillow.

It is said wild geese can everywhere send letters,

But some fly slow down on the shoal of the river.

Grief breaks my heart.


The short happy past

Now with deep sadness day and night I recollect.

I appreciated her songs and dances now and then.

My heartbroken separation and missing grief

Change into red tears falling from my cheeks,

Stopping me from remembering our merry hours anyhow.

Whenever I see streams leading to the brothel on mounts,

From my heart rise the past feelings

Making me for long heartbreaking.

The whole day I lean alone on the greenish railings without any word,

I get down slow from the high building in the remote part of the world.

柳　永

# 倾　杯

鹜落霜洲,雁横烟渚,分明画出秋色。暮雨乍歇,小楫夜泊,宿苇村山驿。何人月下临风处,起一声羌笛。离愁万绪,闻岸草、切切蛩吟如织。　　为忆芳容别后,水遥山远,何计凭鳞翼。想绣阁深沉,争知憔悴损,天涯行客。楚峡云归,高阳人散,寂寞狂踪迹。望京国。空目断、远峰凝碧。

## Tune: Emptying a Cup of Wine

One by one on the frosty shoal land fall the ducks wild,
And in a line the wild geeze on the distant misty islet lie,
Nature draws the clear scene of fall.
In the evening the fine rain just stops,
By the river, for night, the boatman moors our boat,
I lodge by the mounts in the reed-surrounding post.
Who in a breeze under the moon
Plays the long Hu bamboo flute,
Causing my separation feelings so sad?
On the shore in the thick fragrant grass,
The crickets chirp like miserable wives weaving.

Since I parted with my dear beauty so enchanting,
I have never forgotten her lotus-like face even a moment.

Separated from her by a thousand streams and mountains,
I'm now in a place so lonely and drear,
No carp and wild goose appears, couriers.
She must still be in her boudoir in the deep lone yard,
Unaware at all I'm a withered traveller in a remote part.
Dances and songs die away,
No wine friend at all remains,
I just stay in a lonesome quiet village.
Looking in the direction of the capital.
Oh, before me I can only dimly see
Distant peaks as her hairpins green.

❈❈❈❈❈❈❈❈❈❈❈❈❈❈❈❈

## 迷 神 引

一叶扁舟轻帆卷。暂泊楚江南岸。孤城暮角,引胡笳怨。水茫茫,平沙雁,旋惊散。烟敛寒林簇,画屏展。天际遥山小,黛眉浅。 旧赏轻抛,到此成游宦。觉客程劳,年光晚。异乡风物,忍萧索、当愁眼。帝城赊,秦楼阻,旅魂乱。芳草连空阔,残照满。佳人无消息,断云远。

### Tune: Song Fascinating Gods

The light sails are rolled up and my little boat anchored

柳　永

On the grass-covered south shore of the Yangtze River.
From the wall of a lonely city comes the sound of a horn melancholy,
As the tune from a reed instrument of missing sweetheart distressingly.
The river flows seeming boundlessly long and vast,
At leisure the wild geese gather lying on the bank,
All of a sudden, they fly scattering about.
Mist disappears over cold wood somehow,
The scenery is like a painted screen.
So little the distant green hills seem
Slightly powdered brows of my beauty full of charm.

Oh, so easily I left her sweet and warm green boudoir,
A low-ranking official, I'm tired in travelling boats.
Unconsciously my prime passing away, I grow old.
The scene in an alien region,
Is so lonesome and desolate,
Before my sorrowful eyes.
The capital is out of sight,
Dances and songs seem to be in the end of the world,
In vain my travelling soul everywhere searches her.
To the distant sky stretches grass like her skirt with scent,
The setting sun sheds its pale farewell light from the west.
So far I have got no letter from my dear,
Broken clouds like our love fly far drear.

## 安 公 子

远岸收残雨,雨残稍觉江天暮。拾翠汀洲人寂静,立双双鸥鹭。望几点、渔灯隐映蒹葭浦。停画桡、两两舟人语。道去程今夜,遥指前村烟树。　　游宦成羁旅,短樯吟倚闲凝伫。万水千山迷远近,想乡关何处? 自别后、风亭月榭孤欢聚。刚断肠、惹得离情苦。听杜宇声声,劝人不如归去。

## Tune: Prince An

Over the distant shore a rain stopping, in a boat I see,
The sky and water are shrouded in the dimming eve.
The shoal quiet, away are girls gathering grasses with scent,
In pairs here and there stand leisurely and carefree the egrets.
Some dots of fishing lights far and near glimmer
In dark reed shoots along the mouth of the river.
Stopping their long heavy oars,
Two boatmen in a low voice talk:
"Oh, for the quiet night we'll probably stay…"
Pointing at the village with trees far away.

A low-ranking official I have been travelling for years,
Leaning on the short mast, reciting poems, I gaze drear
Into countless streams and mounts.

柳　永

Oh, where is my dear hometown?
Since that morning with melancholy I said to my beauty goodbye,
I only alone in the farewell pavilion appreciate the moon so bright.
The sad lonely feelings
Make me heartbreaking.
I can't bear the cuckoo crying with woe:
Again and again "You'd better go home."

## 破　阵　乐

露花倒影,烟芜蘸碧,灵沼波暖。金柳摇风树树,系彩舫龙舟遥岸。千步虹桥,参差雁齿,直趋水殿。绕金堤,曼衍鱼龙戏,簇娇春罗绮,喧天丝管。霁色荣光,望中似睹,蓬莱清浅。　　时见。凤辇宸游,鸾舸禊饮,临翠水,开镐宴。两两轻舠飞画楫,竞夺锦标霞烂。馨欢娱,歌鱼藻,徘徊宛转。别有盈盈游女,各委明珠,争收翠羽,相将归远。渐觉云海沈沈,洞天日晚。

### Tune: The Pleasure of Breaking the Battle Array

The dewy flowers are reflected on the Golden Bright Pond clear,
The mist-shrouded grassland spreads to the green bank with cheer,

The green water is warm and pleasant.

Along the bank willows sway gentle,

To the trunks are tied the painted and dragon boats.

Over the pond lies a red stone bridge like a rainbow,

Its rails decorated with wild geese stretching wings graceful

Lead to the big hall seeming floating on the water so tasteful.

On the dyke around the pond,

A hundred players perform,

The beauties in green silk skirts gaily dance and sing

In the quick music of the pipes and flutes resounding.

The spring scene is clear and bright,

The clouds send out five-color light.

With great interest looking round,

I find I enter fairyland somehow.


The emperor comes in an imperial carriage with a purple screen,

Followed closely by lines of high-ranking officials full of glee.

Before the emerald-like water gay and happy,

The emperor lifts a cup of wine and empties it,

All the officials begin drinking fine wine with thanks.

On either boat in pairs in two lines stands a young man,

Rolling two oars like mad trying to win the first place.

All the officials recite the poems of their own to praise

The dynasty just,

Loud one by one.

柳　永

Some of the girls with romantic charm,
Give gifts with smiles to their sweethearts.
Decorate their clothes some shy girls
With glistening green feather of birds.
In pairs they slowly return home with satisfaction,
It's getting dark I feel we are in a celestial cavern.

※※※※※※※※※※※※※※※※※

## 轮　台　子

一枕清宵好梦,可惜被、邻鸡唤觉。匆匆策马登途,满目淡烟衰草。前驱风触鸣珂,过霜林、渐觉惊栖鸟。冒征尘远况,自古凄凉长安道。行行又历孤村,楚天阔、望中未晓。　　念劳生,惜芳年壮岁,离多欢少。叹断梗难停,暮云渐杳。但黯黯魂消,寸肠凭谁表。恁驱驱、何时是了。又争似、却返瑶京,重买千金笑。

## *Tune: Wheels*

Oh, it's really a pity.
On a pillow lonely,
I'm waked up from a fond dream by a near cock's crows.
In a hurry I get on a horse starting my travel with sorrow,
Here and there the thin mist and withered grass fill my eyes.

An autumn breeze blows the decorations ringing on the bridle,

When I quick pass by the frosty wood just,

The heels start the dreaming love-birds up.

With flowing green water in the river and flying dust red,

Since ancient time the roads to the capitals are depressed.

A solitary village I pass by again,

So broad the southern sky remains,

But no first light of dawn appears.


I think my life is hard and drear,

Most of my youth leaves

With the separation grief.

I'm like a peach twig in a brook drifting,

And like dusk clouds in the sky floating.

In broken dreams so melancholy I murmur,

To whom can I confide my woe unbearable?

When can I stop at last

My lonely hard travel?

I'd better go back to the flourishing capital, and to my pretty sweetheart,

Spending a thousand ounces of gold for a sweet smile from her in my arms.

柳 永

## 诉衷情近

雨晴气爽,伫立江楼望处。澄明远水生光,重叠暮山耸翠。遥认断桥幽径,隐隐渔村,向晚孤烟起。 残阳里。脉脉朱阑静倚。黯然情绪,未饮先如醉。愁无际。暮云过了,秋光老尽,故人千里。竟日空凝睇。

### Tune: Baring the Heart Face to Face

After the rain in autumn it is fine and refreshing,
I look far in a high building by a river murmuring.
In the distance the clear gentle water sparkles,
The countless peaks are dyed green with grass.
I can see a path and a broken bridge,
And dimly a distant fishing village.
Under the setting sun rises slow
In the hamlet lone cooking smoke.

Alone leaning on the railings red,
Oh, I feel unbearably depressed.
I get drunk before drinking wine,
My sadness floats to the horizon.
The clouds are on homeward way,
The beautiful autumn scene fades.

In the capital a thousand miles away the charming singing girl thinks of me.
The whole day I gaze so drear in the direction of the merrymaking street.

❈❈❈❈❈❈❈❈❈❈❈❈❈❈❈❈

## 戚　氏

晚秋天,一霎微雨洒庭轩。槛菊萧疏,井梧零乱,惹残烟。凄然,望江关,飞云黯淡夕阳闲。当时宋玉悲感,向此临水与登山。远道迢递,行人凄楚,倦听陇水潺湲。正蝉吟败叶,蛩响衰草,相应喧喧。　　孤馆,度日如年。风露渐变,悄悄至更阑。长天净,绛河清浅,皓月婵娟。思绵绵。夜永对景那堪,屈指暗想从前。未名未禄,绮陌红楼,往往经岁迁延。　　帝里风光好,当年少日,暮宴朝欢。况有狂朋怪侣,遇当歌对酒竞留连。别来迅景如梭,旧游似梦,烟水程何限。念名利憔悴长萦绊。追往事、空惨愁颜。漏箭移,稍觉轻寒。渐呜咽画角数声残。对闲窗畔,停灯向晓,抱影无眠。

### Tune: A Miserable Lady

It is in autumn late already,
On the yard falls a drizzle.
The chrysanthemums fade beside the banister,

柳　永

The leaves of the plane trees by a well wither.
A thin mist rises over the distant wood.
Alone in a secluded village with gloom,
I gaze at the clear stream eastward flowing,
And the clouds floating under the sun setting.
At that time the famous poet Song was unbearably sad
When he climbed mounts facing water in the alien land.
As a traveller with sorrow I am sure,
The way before me is long and cruel,
I am tired of listening to the water gurgle.
The cicadas in withered trees sadly chirp,
The crickets in yellow grass moan and groan,
Their sounds echo to each other high and low.

The inn is lonely and drear,
A day is as long as a year.
The wind calms down and heavier dew becomes,
The quiet and mournful midnight slowly comes.
The blue sky opens her fragrant tender naked arms,
The Galaxy sheds separation tears for sweethearts,
The bright moon, the goddess, solitary seems.
My affectionate heart is filled with deep grief.
I cannot bear looking at the melancholy night views,
I remember the happy affairs years ago, a lad's lure.
With true sweet love but without at all fame and wealth,

I haunted the prostitute-gathering street now and then,
Year by year, day and night I was intoxicated in the joyful hours.

The capital was beautiful and girls looked like blooming flowers.
At that time I was quiet young and unrestrained over there,
Making merry with singing girls and dancers without care.
And sometimes some friends and I gathered very long,
To our heart's content drinking wine and singing songs.
Oh, how fast time especially pretty youth flies,
The happy years becomes dreams of springtime,
The river winds its way to the capital with a tearful fog.
Bogged down by fame and gain I am so sallow and wan.
When I recollect the past joys anyhow,
Unbearable grief appears on my brows.
Seeing the arrow of water watch move quickly,
The night being very late, I feel a little bit chilly.
The lone horn from the city gate gives out sound broken.
I sit lonely behind the window with the rolled-up curtain,
The lights in the small cold inn burn out all,
I'm awake in the moonlight waiting for dawn.

# 张先(990—1078)

宋仁宗天圣八年(1030)进士。官至都官郎中。与柳永齐名。他被称为"张三影",因为他在三首词中写到影子,特别是在《青门引》中写道:"那堪更被明月,隔墙送过秋千影。"使读者从影子想到秋千,从秋千想到姑娘、裙子、香味,经历一段长长的审美之旅。

**Zhang Xian(990‑1078)**

He passed the highest imperial examination in 1030. He was an official in the capital. He and Liu Yong enjoyed equal renown. He was called Three Shadows Zhang, for he wonderfully wrote shadow in three of his *Ci* poems, especially in "Song of Green Gate":"Oh, I can hardly bear to look at the moon so brightly shining and sending/Across the wall the shadow of the swing where with skirt she was playing." The readers from the shadow could imagine the swing, and from the swing to the girl, the skirt, the fragrance and so on. The shadow made the readers experience a long aesthetic journey.

## 更 漏 子

锦筵红,罗幕翠。侍宴美人姝丽。十五六,解怜才。劝人深酒杯。　　黛眉长,檀口小。耳畔向人轻道。柳阴曲,是儿家。门前红杏花。

## Tune: Song of Water Watch

Sparkles the red silk tablecloth of feasts,
And the silken curtains hang low green.
Oh, the singing girl is pretty.
She is fifteen or sixteen only,
She knows to love a scholar brimming with talent,
Urging me to empty cups of wine one after another.

Long are her green brows,
And small, her red mouth.
She says to me in a voice sky, soft and low:
"In the deep shade of green weeping willows,
Before my house in pale blue
The red apricots are in bloom."

❀❀❀❀❀❀❀❀❀❀❀❀❀❀❀❀❀❀

## 醉　垂　鞭

双蝶绣罗裙,东池宴,初相见。朱粉不深匀,闲花淡淡春。细看诸处好,人人道,柳腰身。昨日乱山昏,来时衣上云。

张 先

## June: Drunk with a Whip Hanging

Your skirt is embroidered with a pair of butterflies colorful,
At a happy feast table by the East Pool,
I will never forget I'm so lucky to make your acquaintance.
You are lightly powdered and roughed,
As leisurely flowers display simple and elegant spring scene.

And any part of you is quite delicate and fine,
Your waist is as slender as a branch of a weeping willow tree,
People observing you carefully are surprised.
You're the goddess with showers from the hills last night coming here,
Look, now, still wet your pink silk skirt with sweet love clear appears.

## 诉 衷 情

花前月下暂相逢。苦恨阻从容。何况酒醒梦断,花谢月朦胧。
花不尽,月无穷。两心同。此时愿作,杨柳千丝,绊惹春风。

## June: Baring the Heart

Before flowers under the moon, we had a tryst for the time being,

But our deep sweet love has been being obstructed ring upon ring.
When I sober up, my sweet dream is broken,
And the moon is dim and the flowers wither.

The flowers will be in bloom again,
And the moon will exist without end.
Our two hearts have melted into one.
Oh, you don't know now I really love
To be thousands of the twigs of dancing weeping willows,
To play with the vernal breeze that gentle and warm blows.

## 一丛花令

伤高怀远几时穷？无物似情浓。离愁正引千丝乱,更东陌、飞絮濛濛。嘶骑渐遥,征尘不断,何处认郎踪！　　双鸳池沼水溶溶,南北小桡通。梯横画阁黄昏后,又还是、斜月帘栊。沉恨细思,不如桃杏,犹解嫁东风。

## Tune: Song of A Cluster of Flowers

When will stop the drear feelings in my heart and breast
And no longer I climb heights to look in direction he left?
In the world nothing is as deep and true as love I find.

张　先

The parting woe blows thousands of willow twigs twined,
In the east of the city over paths,
Waft willow catkins near and far.
His horse is going away quick neighing,
Leaving only dust in the distance rising,
Oh, I don't know at all where to find his trails.

In the pool a pair of mandarin ducks is at play,
Men in red and girls in green row boats with cheer.
In the evening the ladder lies still in the loft drear,
The fading moon seeing her thin face through the curtained window.
When thinking of her so miserable situation with unbearable sorrow,
She sighs:"Comparing me with the peach and apricot I'm silly,
Who get married to spring and are held in his arms so tenderly."

❋❋❋❋❋❋❋❋❋❋❋❋❋❋❋❋❋❋

## 青　门　引

乍暖还轻冷,风雨晚来方定。庭轩寂寞近清明,残花中酒,又是去年病。　　楼头画角风吹醒,入夜重门静。那堪更被明月,隔墙送过秋千影。

## Tune: Song of Green Gate

Now a little bit cold, now warm,
In the eve the rain and wind stop.
The courtyard is lonely and drear,
Day of Tomb-worship draws near,
I get drunk before fallen flowers like beauties with red dresses,
Again just as last year, the grief breaks my tender heart nearly.

The sounds of the horn from the city tower and chilly wind sober me up,
At night the courtyard is gloomy and motionless when all the doors are shut.
Oh, I can hardly bear to look at the moon so brightly shining and sending
Across the wall the shadow of the swing where with a skirt she was playing.

❊❊❊❊❊❊❊❊❊❊❊❊❊❊❊❊❊❊

## 千 秋 岁

数声鶗鴂※,又报芳菲歇。惜春更把残红折。雨轻风色暴,梅子青时节。永丰柳,无人尽日花飞雪。　　莫把幺弦拨,怨极弦能

张　先

说。天不老,情难绝。心似双丝网,中有千千结。夜过也,东窗未白凝残月。

## Tune: A Thousand Autumns

Shedding tears a cuckoo utters miserable cries,※
To the passing scented spring saying goodbye.
Loving it I pluck the fading flowers on the branch.
The drizzle falls sparse and the wind blows hard,
The fragrant plum fruits hang on the trees still green and small.
No one else appreciates the willows in Yongfeng Garden at all,
Their catkins shroud the vast sky like a heavy snow all day.

Don't pluck the fourth string for low sad sound it will make,
And it will reveal your sorrow.
The world will never grow old,
Our love will be forever fresh.
And our hearts knit silk nets
With thousands of knots.
Oh, night is nearly gone,
The east window finds still sleeping the innocent daylight,
The fading moon with love accompanies me shining bright.

※ 鶗鴂即杜鹃。据说乃已废蜀主所化。它啼声凄苦,接连不断,直至口中流血:"不如回家,不如回家。"

※ It is said that the cuckoo was transformed from a king of Shu when he had been overthrown. It cries miserably and continually until shedding blood from its mouth: "You'd better go home, you'd better go home."

❀❀❀❀❀❀❀❀❀❀❀❀❀❀❀

## 天 仙 子

《水调》数声持酒听，午醉醒来愁未醒。送春春去几时回？临晚镜，伤流景，往事后期空记省。　　沙上并禽池上暝，云破月来花弄影。重重帘幕密遮灯，风不定，人初静，明日落红应满径。

### Tune: Song of Immortals

Holding a cup of wine I listen to some lines of the melancholy "Water Tune",
I sober up from drunkenness not from sorrow of a dream in the afternoon.
I wonder when it will return, seeing off the spring.
Dressing myself before the mirror in the evening,
I'm so sad to find youth gone with pretty scene on my hair and face,
The past love affairs and solemn promises become memories in vain.

By the water the birds in pairs are in sweet dreams on the sands,

张　先

The moon comes out of clouds and with shadows flowers dance.
To keep the lamp being blown out by wind, I pull down curtains,
But I hear the wind than before blowing harder and harder even,
Oh, at last little by little I begins to feel quiet and calm,
Tomorrow fallen flowers like girls will lie on all paths.

❈❈❈❈❈❈❈❈❈❈❈❈❈❈❈

## 木 兰 花

乙卯吴兴寒食

龙头舴艋吴儿竞,笋柱秋千游女并。芳洲拾翠暮忘归,秀野踏青来不定。　　行云去后遥山暝,已放笙歌池院静。中庭月色正清明,无数杨花过无影。

## Tune: Magnolia Flowers

I wrote the *Ci* poem on Cold Food Day,
in Wuxing in the year Yi-mao(1075).

The young men of Wu in dragon-carved boats take a race madly rowing,
The intoxicating girls in pairs face to face play cheerful on the bamboo swings.
On the green shoal the beautiful girls gather grasses forgetting to go home,

In the beautiful fields the sightseers like an endless stream flow to and fro.

Tourists leaving, distant hills like beauties' brows lie in eve twilight,
Songs floating far away, the countryside becomes empty and quiet.
The yard is bathing in the moonlight of pure brightness,
Without any shadows willow catkins fly away over it.

❈❈❈❈❈❈❈❈❈❈❈❈❈❈❈❈❈❈

## 画 堂 春

外湖莲子长参差,雾山青处鸥飞。水天溶漾画桡迟,人影鉴中移。 桃叶浅声双唱,杏红深色轻衣。小荷障面避斜晖,分得翠阴归。

## June: Spring in the Painted Hall

On the scented lake grow the seed-pods of the lotuses high and low,
The rain-washed green mounts set off white gulls flying to and fro.
The boat floats slow and the water and sky melt into one in the distance,
The reflections of young men and girls move on the water like a

张　先

mirror.

The female singers in apricot silk shirts thin
Sing a sweet love song "Peach Leaves" softly.
To shelter their faces from slanting sunshine, they hold lotus leaves,
When going home, I seem to share their cool pleasant shade of green.

❀❀❀❀❀❀❀❀❀❀❀❀❀❀❀❀❀

## 谢池春慢

### 玉仙观道中逢谢媚卿

缭墙重院,时闻有、啼莺到。绣被掩余寒,画阁明新晓。朱槛连空阔,飞絮知多少? 径莎平,池水渺。日长风静,花影闲相照。　　尘香拂马,逢谢女、城南道。秀艳过施粉,多媚生轻笑。斗色鲜衣薄,碾玉双蝉小。欢难偶,春过了。琵琶流怨,都入相思调。

### *Tune: Slow Song of Spring in the Xie Pool*

#### Meeting a Beauty in a Taoist Temple

Wall by wall, yard by yard,
Now and then, near and far,
I hear the yellow orioles with a bit sorrow sing outside.
The embroidered thin quilt keeps me from cold slight,

The painted boudoir is bright with sunlight in the morning.

The pink banisters connect far and near the high buildings,

The willow catkins like a snow fly here and there.

Days long the green grass grows wild everywhere,

The flowers are reflected on the green pool like a sketch.

The grass and flowers look at each other depressed,

The breeze goes off slow to dream lonesome.

The scent in the air my green horse strokes,

I happen to meet Xie, the beauty,

Just on the road in the south city.

The beauty out of nature is over the one powdered again and again,

Her shy smile displays her matchless beauty and charm of her face.

Her bright-colored shirt shows her graceful figure,

Her jade bracelets are carved into a pair of cicadas.

We look at each other excited without a word even,

Our happy love is far away with the spring breeze.

From pipa her sorrow acute

Flows into the lovesick tunes.

❋❋❋❋❋❋❋❋❋❋❋❋❋❋❋❋

张　先

## 剪 牡 丹

### 舟中闻双琵琶

野绿连空,天青垂水,素色溶漾都净。柳径无人,堕絮飞无影。汀洲日落人归,修巾薄袂,撷香拾翠相竞。如解凌波,泊烟渚春暝。　　彩绦朱索新整。宿绣屏、画船风定。金凤响双槽,弹出今古幽思谁省。玉盘大小乱珠迸。酒上妆面,花艳眉相并。重听。尽汉妃一曲,江空月静。

### Tune: Pruning Twigs of Peonies

#### Listening to Two Beauties Playing Pipa in a Boat

The wild green extends to the horizon distant,
And the blue sky hangs over the clear water,
A broad expanse of white water flows leisurely.
The paths covered with the willows are empty,
The catkins drift in a mess leaving no shadow.
The sun fading, on the shoal travellers go home,
Like fairy maidens with green slender ribbons and pink silk shirts,
Two beauties vie in gathering fragrant grasses and feather of birds.
Smiling, a boat they get on board
And moor it by the shoal very soft.

They change into clothes bright

For the scented and pretty night.

They appreciate the scene of the river and sky near the embroidered screen.

The wind becoming gentle, I invite them very politely to drink wine with me.

The two pipas beautifully-carved begins to play,

Sending out feelings in the hearts through ages,

But at present time the wonderful music who at all can understand?

Sounds rise and fall as pearls of different sizes in a jade plate dance.

The blushes from wine on their pretty faces appear,

Like flowers their charming frowns do not disappear.

Then they play another melancholy tune

Played by the concubine on a horsc who

Was going drear to the bleak north to marry a tribe head far.

The clear, quiet and lonely moon hangs in the open sky vast.

❈❈❈❈❈❈❈❈❈❈❈❈❈❈❈❈❈❈❈

## 满 江 红

飘尽寒梅,笑粉蝶游蜂未觉。渐迤逦、水明山秀,暖生帘幕。过雨小桃红未透,舞烟新柳青犹弱。记画桥深处水边亭,曾偷约。　　多少恨,今犹昨;愁和闷,都忘却。拚从前烂醉,被花迷著。晴鸽试铃风力软,雏莺弄舌春寒薄。但只愁、锦绣闹妆时,东风恶。

张　先

## June: The River All Red

The gentle warm spring breeze had blown all the plum blossoms away here and there,
But the pollen-spreading butterflies and touring bees had not found spring anywhere.
Slowly spring came into view far and near,
The hills became green and the water clear,
The pleasant warmth was felt behind the curtains and screens.
After a fine rain peaches began to blossom, the color not deep,
The new willow leaves were light green and twigs slender and tender.
Oh, I remember near the painted bridge in the pavilion by the water,
We had a sweet tryst.

Oh, it haunts my mind,
And seems to have happened yesterday.
In my deep heart desolation and pain
Have been nearly forgotten in the present.
But fascinated by the flower-like girl then,
I was very often, night and day, drunk as a lord.
Her songs were like a pigeon's bell floating soft,
And as a young oriole in cold spring trying its tongue.
But recently almost all the time I'm afraid very much
Of one day when she would be made up in excitement for wedding,

And the evil east wind would brings unbearable cold in the evening.

## 菩 萨 蛮

忆郎还上层楼曲。楼前芳草年年绿。绿似去时袍。回头风袖飘。
郎袍应已旧。颜色非长久。惜恐镜中春。不如花草新。

### *Tune: Buddhist Dancers*

Missing him, I climb the high building looking far and near,
Before it the fragrant grasses become green year after year.
His robe was as green as the grass in that intoxicating spring,
He turned again and again, in the breeze his sleeves fluttering.

His robe must not be so new as that day,
Its color should at the present time fade.
But I am most afraid his face in the old mirror
Isn't as grass and flowers as fresh and vigorous.

张　先

## 相　思　令

蘋满溪。柳绕堤。相送行人溪水西。回时陇月低。　烟霏霏。风凄凄。重倚朱门听马嘶。寒鸥相对飞。

### Tune: Song of Lovesickness

The clover fern floated here and there on the brook with grief,
The willow trees swayed around the embankment in the breeze.
I saw him off to the west of the water on his long journey with woe,
On my way back I found the moon with knitted brows hanging low.

The fog drifts thick and thick,
Cold and cold blows the wind.
Again I lean on the red door listening to the horse neigh,
I only see a pair of cold gulls fly to and fro without end.

❈❈❈❈❈❈❈❈❈❈❈❈❈❈❈

## 渔　家　傲

### 和程公辟赠别

巴子城头青草暮,巴山重叠相逢处。燕子占巢花脱树,杯且举,瞿塘水阔舟难渡。　天外吴门清霅路。君家正在吴门住。赠我柳枝情几许。春满缕,为君将入江南去。

## Tune: Pride of Fishermen

When I was going a long journey a friend gave me a farewell feast, presenting a *Ci* poem to me. I wrote the *Ci* poem in reply.

On the wall of Ba City the grass sways in the lone eve,
We first time met with delight in the distant hills green.
Swallows return to their nests and flowers everywhere fly,
Let's one after another empty our jade cups of good wine,
I am very afraid in a boat to cross the Jutang Gorge broad and torrent.

Far away stretches a road to Suzhou and Huzhou in the land southern.
My dear friend, you just live in the city of Suzhou,
You give me a weeping willow twig with sorrow.
With homesick feelings and withering spring,
I'll take it to Suzhou so pretty and flourishing.

❀❀❀❀❀❀❀❀❀❀❀❀❀❀❀❀

## 浣 溪 沙

楼倚春江百尺高,烟中还未见归桡,几时期信似江潮? 花片片飞风弄蝶,柳阴阴下水平桥,日长才过又今宵。

张　先

## *Tune: Silk-Washing Stream*

She leans in the high building facing the river and looking far with sorrow,
Through the mist-like valor, she has not so far found his returning boat,
Hardly has he kept his promise of his returning date as the river tides.

The flowers fly far and near and the breeze plays with the butterflies,
In the shade of weeping willows the water is on a level with the bridge,
The long day is gone wholly and the unbearably lonely night just begins.

❈❈❈❈❈❈❈❈❈❈❈❈❈❈❈❈❈

## 惜 琼 花

汀蘋白,苕水碧。每逢花驻乐,随处欢席。别时携手看春色。萤火而今,飞破秋夕。　　汴河流,如带窄。任身轻似叶,何计归得? 断云孤鹜青山极。楼上徘徊,无尽相忆。

## June: Loving Qiong Flower—the Most Beautiful Flower of All

The blooming clover fern was like snow by the water,
The green Tiao Stream water sparkling like emerald.
Often before flowers I wandered, forgetting to leave,
And I was dead drunk here and there at happy feasts.
We appreciated the scenery arm in arm before waving good-bye.
Here I can only see in the air now and then fly glistening fireflies
Breaking the eve drear.

The Bian River is clear,
Like a long lace winding its way to my home.
Even if I become a leaf of a weeping willow,
I cannot go back to see my beauty waiting at the gate at present anyhow.
I find far away over the green mounts a lone wild goose and broken clouds.
I pace about on the red railings of the storied building,
For my dear in my heart flows endlessly the longing.

张　先

## 蝶恋花

移得绿杨栽后院,学舞宫腰,二月青犹短。不比灞陵多送远,残丝乱絮东西岸。　　几叶小眉寒不展,莫唱阳关,真个肠先断。分付与春休细看,条条尽是离人怨。

### Tune: Butterflies in Love with Flowers

The green willow is transplanted in the backyard,
At first she begins to learn so hard the court dance,
In the second month the graceful willow tree is still short.
She feels far better here than near Farewell Bridge at all,
There her twigs were plucked to give travellers as parting gifts.

For severe cold, her leaves are still folded as her brows knitted,
Don't sing the parting song, "Yang Pass", please,
I'm afraid very much it will break her heart indeed.
Fragrant spring, don't watch twigs here,
On them there are parting lovers' tears.

## 晏殊(991—1055)

从神童登科。官至集贤殿大学士、同中书门下平章事兼枢密使。范仲淹、欧阳修、张先皆出自其门下。他在词中常表达他及时行乐的想法。其语言雅致婉丽。《浣溪沙》很有名,其中的"无可奈何花落去,似曾相识燕归来"后世广为传咏,脍炙人口。

**Yan Shu(991–1055)**

Once a child prodigy, and then served as a court official. Fan Zhongyan, Ouyang Xiu and Zhang Xian were his disciples. In his *Ci* poems he often expressed his idea of indulging in pleasure in time. His words were elegant and neat, away from obscenity. The *Ci* poem "Silk-washing Stream" was very famous, in it:"I can't bear to look at the flowers shower down like the charming face,/The pair of the swallows comes back from the south and they seem familiar" were on everybody's lips and won universal praise in later ages.

## 清 平 乐

红笺小字,说尽平生意。鸿雁在云鱼在水,惆怅此情难寄。
斜阳独倚西楼,遥山恰对帘钩。人面不知何处,绿波依旧东流。

晏　殊

## Tune: Music for a Peaceful Time

With small words I fill a sheet of rosy writing paper,
To my heart's content I pour out my true love to her.
Wild geese fly in the sky and fishes swim in the water,
Whom can I ask to send her my letter with affection?

I lean on the rails of the west storied building in the setting sunshine,
The curtain hook gazes at the green distant hills like her brows high.
Oh, where is the enchanting face always in my deep heart and mind?
However the fragrant water still flows with my love east all the time.

❀❀❀❀❀❀❀❀❀❀❀❀❀❀❀❀❀

## 玉　楼　春

绿杨芳草长亭路,年少抛人容易去。楼头残梦五更钟,花底离愁三月雨。　　无情不似多情苦,一寸还成千万缕。天涯地角有穷时,只有相思无尽处。

## Tune: Spring in the Jade Boudoir

By the pavilions the grass gave off scent and willow twigs kissed the face,

My fickle sweetheart with refreshingly green robe so easily went away.
My happy dream is broken by the sound of a drum of a watchman,
The raindrops on the flowers are their tears for our parting miserable.

Those without love don't know the grief of those with tenderness,
An inch of my heart turns into a thousand weeping willow twigs.
However wide and big, the sky and earth have their ends,
But my intoxicating lovesickness without end at all extends.

❋❋❋❋❋❋❋❋❋❋❋❋❋❋❋

## 蝶 恋 花

槛菊愁烟兰泣露,罗幕轻寒,燕子双飞去。明月不谙离恨苦,斜光到晓穿朱户。　　昨夜西风凋碧树,独上高楼,望尽天涯路。欲寄彩笺兼尺素,山长水阔知何处!

## *Tune: Butterflies in Love with Flowers*

In the withering garden here and there in the autumn,
Over the chrysanthemums floats a mist of desolation,
And on orchids roll dewdrops of sorrow.
The pink silk curtain feels a little bit cold,
The pair of swallows flies away from the red beam.

晏　殊

The bright moon is innocent of the separation grief,
Shedding slanting light on the beauty till dawn through the door red.

Last night the green trees and grasses withered in the chilly wind west.
I ascended slowly alone the quiet and drear storied building so high,
Looking into the road leading to the end of the world out of sight.
I want so much to send my intoxicating beauty a letter full of sweet love,
Unaware where she is I just see countless mounts and streams separate us.

## 破　阵　子

燕子来时新社,梨花落后清明。池上碧苔三四点,叶底黄鹂一两声,日长飞絮轻。　巧笑东邻女伴,采桑径里逢迎。疑怪昨宵春梦好,原是今朝斗草赢,笑从双脸生。

### *June: Dance of the Cavalry*

When swallows come back, Shrine Festival of Spring is near,
When peach blossoms fall, Clear and Bright will soon be here.
There appear three or four dots of green moss by the creek,
And there comes one or two warbles of an oriole in leaves,

The weeping willow catkins fly high and low during the long day leisurely.

Two pretty girls meet on the path while gathering the leaves of mulberries,
The west neighbor cracks a joke with the east one in spirits high:
"You look cheerful and you must have had a gay dream last night."
"Really, in the game of picking grasses, I won the first place."
A sweet smile like morn glow appears on the east one's face.

❋❋❋❋❋❋❋❋❋❋❋❋❋❋❋❋❋

## 诉 衷 情

芙蓉金菊斗馨香,天气欲重阳。远村秋色如画,红树间疏黄。流水淡,碧天长,路茫茫。凭高目断,鸿雁来时,无限思量。

## *Tune: Baring the Heart*

The cotton roses and chrysanthemums are in color and scent vying,
The Double Ninth Festival in the cool clear autumn is approaching.
The beautiful picture is the distant village scene,
In the red leaves a few yellow flowers are seen.

The clear water flows calm,

晏　殊

And the blue sky lies vast,
The road in the open country stretches boundless and indistinct.
I ascend the height looking into the drear distance for long still.
When I see the wild geese southward fly,
The countless thoughts come to my mind.

❊❊❊❊❊❊❊❊❊❊❊❊❊❊❊❊❊

## 踏　莎　行

小径红稀,芳郊绿遍。高台树色阴阴见。春风不解禁杨花,濛濛乱扑行人面。　　翠叶藏莺,朱帘隔燕。炉香静逐游丝转。一场愁梦酒醒时,斜阳却照深深院。

## *June: Treading on Grass*

There remain few red petals like girls on the path,
And the fragrant suburb is wild with green grass.
The tower in the deep shade of the trees is seen dimly.
The spring wind knows not to keep the willow catkins
From blowing in showers pretty girls' hair dishevelled.

In the deep green leaves hide some singing warblers,
The red curtains stop a pair of swallows coming their home.
An incense smoke curls up and gossamer flies high and low.

When I'm awake from wine and broken is a miserable dream,
The setting sun spreads its sorrow into the courtyard so deep.

## 浣 溪 沙

一向年光有限身,等闲离别易销魂。酒筵歌席莫辞频。　满目山河空念远,落花风雨更伤春。不如怜取眼前人。

### Tune: Silk-Washing Stream

Life is so short just like a moment,
Any partings make me heartbroken.
Please don't decline feasts accompanied by enchanting singers female.

Gazing at the rivers and mounts I think of my dears in a remote place,
Seeing the wind and rain destroying the flowers I'm sadder uttering sighs.
It would be better for me to love the charming beauties before my eyes.

晏　殊

## 踏 莎 行

祖席离歌,长亭别宴。香尘已隔犹回面。居人匹马映林嘶,行人去棹依波转。　　画阁魂消,高楼目断。斜阳只送平波远。无穷无尽是离愁,天涯地角寻思遍。

## Tune: Treading on Grass

At the banquet in the pavilion by the road,
The beauty sang farewell songs with sorrow.
Through flying scented dust he turned round again and again.
She listened to his horse beyond the wood neighing with pain,
He then took a boat farther and farther away with the rising water.

She is heartbroken when climbing the quiet solitary high chamber.
She stares at the distant wood where with green robe he is out of sight.
The fading sun sees the water off with her tears flowing to the horizon.
Oh, her sorrowful soul goes anywhere to find her dear,
Even travelling to the earth's remotest corner with tears.

## 少 年 游

重阳过后,西风渐紧,庭树叶纷纷。朱阑向晓,芙蓉妖艳,特地斗芳新。　　霜前月下,斜红淡蕊,明媚欲回春。莫将琼萼等闲分,留赠意中人。

### June: Travelling While Young

After Double Ninth Festival in autumn,
The west wind blows harder and harder,
In the yard faded leaves shower down in the morning.
To my great surprise, just out of the long red railings,
The magnolias bloom so pretty and fresh,
As if they specially vie in color and scent.

In the bright moonlight and with the freezing frost,
Red petals and yellow stamens each other set off.
They are so beautiful and brilliant
As if to make spring again appear.
Don't pluck them—emeralds, topazes, rubies,
And leave them so enchanting to my beauty.

❈❈❈❈❈❈❈❈❈❈❈❈❈❈❈❈

晏　殊

## 诉　衷　情

东风杨柳欲青青,烟淡雨初晴。恼他香阁浓睡,撩乱有啼莺。
眉叶细,舞腰轻,宿妆成。一春芳意,三月和风,牵系人情。

### Tune: Baring the Heart

In the vernal breeze the weeping willows sway green,
The rain just stops and a thin mist over them is seen.
Sound sleeping in the small storied building,
She is disturbed by orioles in trees singing.

The willow leaves are her brows slender and beautiful,
And the willow branches, her waist, slim and graceful,
Last night's make-up is faint and thin.
The green willow leaves so affectionate,
And gentle breeze of March,
Link my tender sweet heart.

❀❀❀❀❀❀❀❀❀❀❀❀❀❀❀❀

## 浣　溪　沙

小阁重帘有燕过,晚花红片落庭莎。曲阑干影入凉波。

霎好风生翠幕,几回疏雨滴圆荷。酒醒人散得愁多。

## Tune: Silk-Washing Stream

Through curtain by curtain the swallows fly into the pavilion quickly,
The red petals fall on the green grass in late spring in the yard lonely.
In the cool shimmering waves the twisting railings are clear reflected.

The gentle and warm breeze blows the green screens,
Light showers fall on new round scented lotus leaves.
Awake from wine, a songstress gone, I'm full of grief.

## 清 平 乐

金风细细,叶叶梧桐坠。绿酒初尝人易醉。一枕小窗浓睡。
紫薇朱槿花残。斜阳却照阑干。双燕欲归时节,银屏昨夜微寒。

## Tune: Music for a Peaceful Time

Gentle, gentle, blows the autumn breeze,
One by one, fall the parasol tree leaves.
Drinking the new-made green wine I get drunk so easily,
Behind the little window I sleep sound on a pillow lonely.

The pretty youth of the aster and hibiscus like girls is away,
And the setting sun displays her beautiful face on the rails.
It's the season for pairs of swallows to go to south home,
Last night the silver-decorated screens feel a little cold.

❄❄❄❄❄❄❄❄❄❄❄❄❄❄❄❄

## 木 兰 花

玉楼朱阁横金锁,寒食清明春欲破。窗间斜月两眉愁,帘外落花双泪堕。　朝云聚散真无那,百岁相看能几个? 别来将为不牵情,万转千回思想过。

## Tune: Magnolia Flowers

The emerald pavilion and ruby attic are tightly shut with golden locks,
Cold Food Day and Pure Brightness arriving, spring will soon be gone.
Under the sky the crescent like her brows hangs low sorrowful,
Outside the flowers fall down and I shed tears behind the curtain.

Meetings and partings with deeply loved beauties are beyond control,
How many pairs can accompany each other till a hundred years old?
I have thought that I can get away our parting grief,

But thousands of times I think of our love so deep.

## 诉 衷 情

青梅煮酒斗时新,天气欲残春。东城南陌花下,逢着意中人。回绣袂,展香茵,叙情亲。此情拚作,千尺游丝,惹住朝云。

### June: Baring the Heart

People enjoy wine cooked with green plums, a drink seasonable,
Oh, leaving are just the last days of the charming spring season.
In the east of the city in flowers on the south path,
I meet with the intoxicating beauty after my heart.

I warmly and politely invite the beauty to sit at my side,
And I spread the fragrant embroidered mat with delight,
We pour out our feelings to each other to our heart's content.
Oh, loving the enchanting intimate, I'm so ready at present
To be gossamer measuring ten thousand feet about,
To tie my female celestial, a floating morning cloud.

晏　殊

## 喜迁莺

花不尽,柳无穷,应与我情同。觥船一棹百分空,何处不相逢。
朱弦悄,知音少。天若有情应老。劝君看取利名场,今古梦茫茫。

### Tune: Joyous Migrant Orioles

Oh, the flowers in blossom spread to the ends of the world,
The green willows grow to the remotest corners of the earth,
Their feelings are the same as mine exactly.
I get drunk as a lord to forget my bitterness,
In the future here and there we will meet.

Farewell music flows low with deep grief,
Fewer and fewer will my intimates remain.
The sky will grow old if he is sentimental.
I just advise you, my dear friend, fame and wealth
Are just fond dreams no matter in the past or present.

❈❈❈❈❈❈❈❈❈❈❈❈❈❈❈

## 踏莎行

细草愁烟,幽花怯露,凭阑总是销魂处。日高深院静无人,时时海燕双飞去。　　带缓罗衣,香残蕙炷,天长不禁迢迢路。垂杨只解惹春风,何曾系得行人住!

## Tune: Treading on Grass

In the thin mist the little grass feels sorrowful,
With the cold dew the fragrant flowers shiver,
I am heartbreaking when I lean on railings looking at them each time.
The sun rises high and bright and deep courtyard is lonely and quiet,
The pairs of petrels fly away now and then.

Looser and looser are my silk clothes and belt,
Piece by piece burns out the orchid incense like a heart night and day,
The sky is vast and roads extend far and no obstruction stops her way.
The willows only know to play with spring breeze,
But certainly can not tie my charming lover's feet.

❈❈❈❈❈❈❈❈❈❈❈❈❈❈❈❈❈

# 撼 庭 秋

别来音信千里,恨此情难寄。碧纱秋月,梧桐夜雨,几回无寐。
楼高目断,天遥云黯,只堪憔悴。念兰堂红烛,心长焰短,向人垂泪。

晏　殊

## Tune: Autumn in Courtyard

She is now already thousands of miles away,
How can I send my love to her? Oh, no way.
Behind the green window screen melancholy,
I gaze lonely at the bright autumn moon still,
Or lie in bed listening to rain fall on parasol trees.
So many times I cannot enter state of being asleep.

I climb up the high building to look far,
The clouds hang dark and sky looks vast,
All the time sadness in my heart up and down rolls.
A red candle burns on in the blue hall with sorrow,
Its heart is long but flame short,
It sheds tears for me the night all.

❀❀❀❀❀❀❀❀❀❀❀❀❀❀❀❀

## 木 兰 花

燕鸿过后莺归去,细算浮生千万绪。长于春梦几多时？散似秋云无觅处。　　闻琴解佩神仙侣,挽断罗衣留不住。劝君莫作独醒人,烂醉花间应有数。

### June: Magnolia Flowers

Swan geese, swallows and orioles go sofar,
Thousands of thoughts well up in my heart
Intoxicating youth and love are no longer than spring dreams,
They are like floating fall clouds, once gone no longer seen.

If a talented beauty or a female celestial after your heart wants to go away,
Hard you hold their sleeves even break them, you can't keep them anyway.
I advise you not to be the only one awake from wine,
You should get drunk as a lord in the flowers bright.

### 木 兰 花

池塘水绿风微暖,记得玉真初见面。重头歌韵响铮琮,入破舞腰红乱旋。 玉钩阑下香阶畔,醉后不知斜日晚。当时共我赏花人,点检如今无一半。

### June: Magnolia Flowers

The breeze blows a little warm and gurgles pleasant the green pond

water,
The first time I met the beauty like a fairy maiden I still clearly remember.
She sang with quick overlapped rhythm so exciting,
She danced rapidly and I saw her red skirt circling.

Under the jade hook and railings are scented waterside steps,
Drunk as a lord, I'm unaware now the slanting drear sun sets.
My intimates appreciating flowers with me in those days,
I recollect sadly now only fewer than half here still remain.

❀❀❀❀❀❀❀❀❀❀❀❀❀❀❀

## 踏 莎 行

碧海无波,瑶台有路。思量便合双飞去。当时轻别意中人,山长水远知何处？　绮席凝尘,香闺掩雾。红笺小字凭谁附？高楼目尽欲黄昏,梧桐叶上萧萧雨。

### *Tune: Treading on Grass*

To go to the fairy mounts in the broad east sea, there is no billow,
To dwell in the fairyland along the Peach Stream there is a road.
We wanted to fly there like a pair of phoenixes and find an abode.
But I was easy to leave my beauty after my heart with little sorrow,

Where is she now? The mounts stand high and far the water flows.

A layer of dust lies on her bed scented,
A thin mist drifts over her attic solitary.
Who can send her my love so devoted?
In the eve I gaze far on the high rails so sadly,
At night I listen to rain fall on parasols dreary.

※※※※※※※※※※※※※※※※※

## 山 亭 柳

### 赠 歌 者

家住西秦,赌博艺随身。花柳上,斗尖新。偶学念奴声调,有时高遏行云。蜀锦缠头无数,不负辛勤。　数年来往咸京道,残杯冷炙漫消魂。衷肠事、托何人? 若有知音见采,不辞遍唱阳春。一曲当筵落泪,重掩罗巾。

## Tune: Willows by Hillside Pavilion

### Presenting the *Ci* Poem to the Singer

I lived near the old capital in the west,
I had some important skills very great.
Amid flowers and willows I was the best,
With the tune and music original and fresh.

晏　殊

I learned the songs sang by Nian Nu, a famous palace maid with ease,
Sometimes the flying clouds with great interest stopped to listen to me.
Rolls of the well-known brocade were thrown to stages by my feet,
I contributed success to my unmatched talent and hard work indeed.

Nowadays I travel from the countryside to the old capital to and fro,
Having the remains of dishes and wine in the inns so small and old.
Oh, I am full of heartbreaking sorrow,
And to whom can I pour out my woes?
Oh, if I meet with an old or new intimate,
I will sing all the songs of refined taste.
I can't help shedding tears at feast tables,
With silk handkerchiefs I hide my face.

✳✳✳✳✳✳✳✳✳✳✳✳✳✳✳✳✳

## 浣 溪 沙

玉碗冰寒滴露华,粉融香雪透轻纱。晚来妆面胜荷花。　鬓鬟欲迎眉际月,酒红初上脸边霞。一场春梦日西斜。

### *Tune: Silk-Washing Stream*

In the jade bowl there are pieces of ice dew-like at the pink brim,
Scented sweat wets the silk shirt displaying her snow-white skin.

After being made up in the evening her face is just like the flower of a lotus.

Her hanging hair is ready to greet between the brows moon-like ornament,
A little green wine makes the enchanting eve glow fly to her pretty face.
These happen about sunset time when from a spring dream she is awake.

❋❋❋❋❋❋❋❋❋❋❋❋❋

## 蝶 恋 花

六曲阑干偎碧树,杨柳风轻,展尽黄金缕。谁把细筝移玉柱?穿帘海燕双飞去。 满眼游丝兼落絮,红杏开时,一霎清明雨。浓睡觉来莺乱语,惊残好梦无寻处。

### Tune: Butterflies in Love with Flowers

The twisting railings lean on the green willow trees,
Gently blows the warm and refreshing vernal breeze,
Displaying all their golden slender twigs.
Who plucks the strings of the zither softly?
The pair of swallows flies away through the curtain.

晏　殊

Here and there float willow catkins and gossamer,
Pure Brightness comes, the apricot showing her pink face,
And now and then, thick and fast fall the mourning rains.
I'm waked up from a sound sleep by crying orioles around,
My fond dream is broken and no trace at all can be found.

❋❋❋❋❋❋❋❋❋❋❋❋❋❋❋❋❋

## 浣　溪　沙

一曲新词酒一杯,去年天气旧亭台。夕阳西下几时回？无可奈何花落去,似曾相识燕归来。小园香径独徘徊。

## *June: Silk-Washing Stream*

The singing girl singing one of my new poems, I drink a cup of wine,
Oh, the weather is exactly as last spring, and the pavilion as that time.
When will the setting sun waving farewell with sorrow return again?

I can't bear to look at the flowers shower down like the charming face,
The pair of swallows come back from the south and they seem familiar.
On the scented paths in the garden I pace up and down lonely and drear.

## 采 桑 子

时光只解催人老,不信多情,长恨离亭,泪滴春衫酒易醒。
梧桐昨夜西风急,淡月胧明,好梦频惊,何处高楼雁一声?

## Tune: Song of Gathering Mulberry Leaves

Time only knows how to speed people's aging,
It shows no sympathy at all to our sufferings.
I remember we were heartbreaking at farewell feast in a roadside pavilion,
We quick sobered up and found our spring clothes wet with bloody tears.

Outside a fall wind blows so hard the parasol trees,
In the sky the moon sheds its pale light with grief.
I am awake now and then from sweet dreams at the chilly night,
Where does a wail of a wild goose reach me in the building high?

# 石延年(994—1041)

官至太子中允、秘阁校理。其词以女子口吻写春愁。表明离别愁苦是"为风流",即为男女风流韵事。说上苍将春山的青翠匀在女子眉头的词句"春山总把,深匀翠黛,千叠在眉头",造语别致,时人效者不少。

**Shi Yannian(994–1041)**

He served as a court official. He wrote the spring sorrow in a women's tone which was formed by love affairs between men and women. The lines "With one of the spring hills as a brush,／God carefully paints my brows green." were quite original and were imitated by other poets.

## 燕 归 梁

### 春 愁

芳草年年惹恨幽。想前事悠悠。伤春伤别几时休。算从古、为风流。　　春山总把,深匀翠黛,千叠在眉头。不知供得几多愁。更斜日、凭危楼。

## Tune: Swallows Returning to the Beam

### Spring Grief

The fragrant grass brings deep sorrow year after year.
Day by day I recollect the sweet love in the past drear.
When will spring and parting grief end?
Oh, from the ancient times to the present,
Sorrow of separation comes from love.

With one of the spring hills as a brush,
God carefully paints my brows green.
They hide plenty of unbearable grief.
Alone with tears like a heavy rain when the sun is setting,
I lean in a high building waiting sad for his boat returning.

# 李冠(生卒年不详)

他在词中表达伤春之感,通过琐事,写出了抑扬起伏的感情,为当时词人称颂。苏轼有一首名作受其影响。李冠有五首词存世。

**Li Guan(years of birth and death unknown)**

He expressed his grief for the passing of spring in this *Ci* poem, through the trifles he displayed the feelings rising and falling in this *Ci* poem which was praised by the poets in the time. Su Shi wrote a famous poem influenced by this one. There're five *Ci* poems extant.

## 蝶 恋 花

### 春 暮

遥夜亭皋闲信步,才过清明,渐觉伤春暮。数点雨声风约住,朦胧淡月云来去。 桃杏依稀香暗度。谁在秋千,笑里轻轻语?一寸相思千万绪。人间没个安排处。

## June: Butterflies in Love with Flowers

### Late Spring

By the towers I stroll leisurely at night,
Oh, just away here is Clear and Bright,
I begin to feel sentimental about the spring late.
The spring wind blows away some drops of rain,
Under the drear pale moon the thin clouds float slowly to and fro.

The faint scent of peach and apricot blossoms drifts high and low.
The girls wearing pink skirts play on the swing
With cheer all the time giggling and whispering.
There are thousands of threads of feelings in each inch of my love for her.
Oh, I don't know at all where I should place my lovesickness in the world.

# 宋祁(998—1061)

宋仁宗天圣二年进士(1024)。做过翰林学士、史馆修撰。他的《木兰花》上阕"东城渐觉春光好,縠绉波纹迎客棹。绿杨烟外晓寒轻。红杏枝头春意闹"历代传咏不息,其中"红杏枝头春意闹"一句尤为脍炙人口,因此被时人称为"红杏尚书"。他精于炼字,善于化静为动。

**Song Qi(998 – 1061)**

He passed the highest imperial examination in 1024. He was a senior court official. The upper stanza of his *Ci* poem "Magnolia Flowers" has been on everybody's lips:" In the east suburb of the capital the scene is becoming more and more beautiful,/ The clear water with ripples greets the travelling boats with smiles pleasant,/Beyond the misty green willows the chill of morn is light,/On the twigs of blooming apricots spring is running wide." The last line of the stanza won universal praise. So he was called "Red Apricot Minister". He was good at improving diction and turning stillness into movement.

## 蝶 恋 花

### 情 景

绣幕茫茫罗帐卷。春睡腾腾,困入娇波慢。隐隐枕痕留玉脸,腻云斜溜钗头燕。　　远梦无端欢又散。泪落胭脂,界破蜂黄浅。整了翠鬟匀了面,芳心一寸情何限。

### Tune: Butterflies in Love with Flowers

#### Feelings and Settings

The bed-curtain up, shows the quiet room in the screens.
She is in trance, just awake from a beautiful spring dream,
Her sleepy enchanting eyes slowly roll.
On her face are dim marks of the pillow,
A swallow-shaped pin quivers on the cloud-like hair at the temple.

In the dream with her dear as before she makes love and parts again.
Like a shower of rain fall her warm tears,
The trace of rouge on her face disappears.
She makes up her hair and rouges and powders her face light,
An inch of her little tender sweet heart contains love infinite.

宋　祁

# 木 兰 花

东城渐觉春光好,縠皱波纹迎客棹。绿杨烟外晓寒轻,红杏枝头春意闹。　　浮生长恨欢娱少,肯爱千金轻一笑。为君持酒劝斜阳,且向花间留晚照。

## Tune: Magnolia Flowers

In the east suburb of the capital the scene is becoming more and more beautiful,
The clear water with ripples greets the travelling boats with smiles pleasant.
Beyond the misty green willows the chill of morn is light,
On the twigs of blooming apricots spring is running wide.

Oh, it's a pity in my life as short as a dream I have pleasure so little,
How can I treasure a thousand ounces of gold for a smile of a beauty?
Raising a cup of wine, I beg the slanting sun
To leave shine on the flowers longer at dusk.

## 锦 缠 道

燕子呢喃,景色乍长春昼。睹园林、万花如绣。海棠经雨胭脂透。柳展宫眉,翠拂行人首。　　向郊原踏青,恣歌携手。醉醺醺、尚寻芳酒。问牧童、遥指孤村道:"杏花深处,那里人家有。"

### Tune: Road Covered with Brocade

With cheer the swallows twitter,
The spring days become longer.
Looking far and near at the enchanting spring gardens and parks,
I find flowers seem embroidered on a brocade carpet full of charm.
The crab-apples are rouged beauties with shy smiles after a rain,
The willows unfold the leaves like girls' brows, kissing the face.

We take a stroll so leisurely on the suburban land,
Singing songs to our heart's content hand in hand.
We get a little drunk already,
But I look for fine wine still.
I ask on an old cattle the cowboy,
At the village far away he points:
"In the deep apricots,
There is a wine shop."

# 梅尧臣(1002—1060)

官至都官员外郎。是北宋有名的词人。有一天,作客欧阳修家。有人赞咏林逋的《点绛唇》的词句"金谷年年,乱生春色谁为主?"。他即席赋一同题之作。欧阳修击节赏之,也赋词一首。这三首词被后人称为"咏春草绝调"。

**Mei Yaochen(1002–1060)**

He served as a court official and was a well-known poet in the Northern Song Dynasty. One day as one of the guests he was at Ouyang Xiu's home, and someone admired the lines in Lin Bu's *Ci* poem "Rouged Lips": "In Golden Vale year after year,/Grow wild grasses so luxuriant./Where is the devoted songstress of unmatched beauty?" Mei Yaochen almost at once composed a *Ci* poem of the same theme and rhyme in reply. Ouyang Xiu, beating tune with his fingers, praised the *Ci* poem. He also wrote a *Ci* poem with the same theme and rhyme. The three *Ci* poems were praised as "Acme of the Poems about Spring Grasses".

## 苏 幕 遮

### 草

露堤平,烟墅杳。乱碧萋萋,雨后江天晓。独有庚郎年最少。窣地春袍,嫩色宜相照。　　接长亭,迷远道。堪怨王孙,不记归期早。落尽梨花春又了。满地残阳,翠色和烟老。

## Tune: Screened by South Curtain

### Grass

On the flat dike the white dewdrops gleam,
In the distance lies a lone villa dimly seen.
The spring fragrant grass spreads far and wide,
After a rain the water flows into the bright sky.
Here a young gifted scholar appears.
A deep green official robe he wears
Sets off the fresh light green grass.

He looks at pavilions near and far.
Where is his homeward way?
Himself very much he hates,
He has forgotten his fading dear at home at all.
All the pear blossoms fall and the spring is gone.
The setting sun sheds its last light with sorrow on the ground,
And the green anywhere grows old with a mist floating about.

## 叶清臣(1000—1049)

宋仁宗天圣二年(1024)进士。曾任翰林学士、权三司使等官职。他因词《贺圣朝》而声名卓著。他写情比较曲折,语短情长。与婉约派不同的是,词中既有伤感的情绪,又有豁达乐观的人生态度。他只留下这首词。

**Ye Qingchen( 1000 – 1049)**

He passed the highest imperial examination in 1024. He was a senior official in the court. He was well-known for his *Ci* poem "Congratulations to a Sacred Dynasty". He expressed the feelings tortuously. Different from the subtle school, there were not only painful but also generous and open-minded and optimistic words in his *Ci* poems. Only this *Ci* poem is extant.

## 贺 圣 朝

### 留 别

满斟绿醑留君住,莫匆匆归去。三分春色二分愁,更一分风雨。 花开花谢,都来几许?且高歌休诉。不知来岁牡丹时,再相逢何处?

## June: Congratulations to a Sacred Dynasty

### A farewell Dinner Party

Filling a cup with green wine I invite my friend to stay,
And ask him again and again not to go in a hurry away.
Of three spring scenery,
Two is just bitterness,
And one is wind and showers.

In turn bloom and fall flowers.
How much sorrow at all shall we get in our hearts and minds?
Don't pour out parting grief, sing loudly while drinking wine.
When the pretty peonies in the little garden are in bloom next year,
I wonder where we can meet again and get drunk for our reunion.

# 欧阳修(1007—1072)

宋仁宗天圣八年(1030)进士。知扬州,颍州。官至翰林学士、枢密副使、参知政事。他在扬州建平山堂,壮丽为淮南第一。又在堂前亲手种柳一株,传为千古佳话。退隐后,他住颍州(今安徽阜阳一带)西湖边。他写了十首关于西湖的词,描写了飘扬在西湖上的歌声和音乐以及西湖边的春花秋草,表示了对渐离渐远的青春的眷恋。词风轻松淡然。

**Ouyang Xiu(1007 – 1072)**

He passed the highest imperial examination in 1030. He served as a senior court official and prefects of cities such as Yangzhou where he built the Pingsan Hall, the most magnificent building in the south of the Huai River. Before it he planted a willow, being a forever fantastic story. When he retired, he lived near the West Lake in Yingzhou in today's Anhui Province. He wrote ten *Ci* poems about it, describing the songs and music drifting over the lake and the spring flowers and autumn grass by the lake, to reveal his deep affection for his youth leaving farther and farther away. The style of his *Ci* poems was relaxed and easy, casual and indifferent.

## 玉 楼 春

尊前拟把归期说,欲语春容先惨咽。人生自是有情痴,此恨不关风与月。　离歌且莫翻新阕,一曲能教肠寸结。直须看尽洛城花,始共春风容易别。

## Tune: Spring in the Jade Boudoir

Before wine, I want to tell my beauty my returning time,
But just when I try to open my mouth she bitterly cries.
It is lovers' infatuation that parting melancholy is caused
And nothing to do with the wind and moon on the spot.

An old farewell song already makes us heartbreaking,
Oh, new one, my intoxicating dear, please don't sing.
We should appreciate all the blooming peonies in Luoyang, old capital,
Then we accompany spring mile on mile before saying goodbye drearily.

❀❀❀❀❀❀❀❀❀❀❀❀❀❀❀

## 生 查 子

含羞整翠鬟,得意频相顾。雁柱十三弦,一一春莺语。　娇云容易飞,梦断知何处?深院锁黄昏,阵阵芭蕉雨。

欧阳修

## Tune: Mountain Hawthorn

With shyness she tidies her jet-black hair before the zither she plays,
When she plays the tune to climax she looks at me again and again.
The thirteen strings are like wild geese in the sky flying,
Each gives pretty sound as in spring an oriole twittering.

She so easily leaves like a floating cloud, the fairy maiden,
I'm heartbreaking to realize our sweet dream is here broken.
At dusk in the spring courtyard so lonely and deep,
I listen to the rain shedding tears on plantain trees.

❋❋❋❋❋❋❋❋❋❋❋❋❋❋❋❋

## 采 桑 子

十年前是尊前客，月白风清。忧患凋零，老去光阴速可惊。
鬓华虽改心无改，试把金觥。旧曲重听，犹似当年醉里声。

## Tune: Song of Gathering Mulberry Leaves

Ten years ago at leisure I enjoyed wine,
The breeze was cool and moon bright.
I'm sorrowful to learn many of my friends have passed away,

I'm shocked to know how time flies especially at my old age.

My hair is white but my heart remains unchanged in the present,
I hold a large golden cup filled with green wine to amuse myself.
When I listen to the old songs I enjoyed now and then in those hours,
I seem to be drunk so happy with the beauty like a blooming flower.

❀❀❀❀❀❀❀❀❀❀❀❀❀❀❀

## 生 查 子

去年元夜时,花市灯如昼。月上柳梢头,人约黄昏后。　今年元夜时,月与灯依旧。不见去年人,泪满春衫袖。

### *Tune: Mountain Hawthorn*

I recollect clearly just on the Lantern Festival last year,
The lanterns of various colors as bright as day appeared.
When the moon climbed above the weeping willow trees,
My pretty scented dear lay in my warm arms in high glee.

This year the Lantern Festival comes again,
The moon and lanterns remain just the same.
I wait and wait, but her intoxicating face in the end is not at all shown,

Tears streaming down my cheeks wet the sleeves of my spring clothes.

## 采 桑 子

画船载酒西湖好,急管繁弦,玉盏催传,稳泛平波任醉眠。
行云却在行舟下,空水澄鲜,俯仰留连,疑是湖中别有天。

### Tune: Song of Gathering Mulberry Leaves

In a painted boat on the West Lake drinking is pleasing,
Quick and loud floats the music of the pipes and strings.
We raise jade cups filled with wine again and again with cheer,
Without wind we can lie drunk leaving the boat go far and near.

Below the boat move the clouds in the sky,
The calm broad water is so clear and bright.
At leisure I lift and then hang my head,
I think there is another world in the lake.

## 采桑子

群芳过后西湖好,狼藉残红,飞絮蒙蒙,垂柳阑干尽日风。
笙歌散尽游人去,始觉春空,垂下帘栊,双燕归来细雨中。

### Tune: Song of Gathering Mulberry Leaves

The West Lake is still enchanting when all the flowers wither,
On the ground fall shower by shower like beauties pink petals.
In the air far and near willow catkins fly like a mist,
In the breeze the willows by the railings sigh lonely.

Music and songs fly away, travellers going home,
All of a sudden I find the spring bleak and alone.
I pull down the green silk curtain chilly and quiet,
A pair of swallows has come back from rain fine.

## 采桑子

轻舟短棹西湖好,绿水逶迤,芳草长堤,隐隐笙歌处处随。
无风水面琉璃滑,不觉船移,微动涟漪,惊起沙禽掠岸飞。

欧阳修

## Tune: Song of Gathering Mulberry Leaves

In a little boat with short oars, I especially appreciate
The green water of the West Lake that winds its way.
The long dyke is covered with fragrant fresh grass,
The music of reed pipes floats faintly near and far.

Without wind the water is as smooth as a mirror,
I am unaware of our leisure boat moving forward.
The boat stirs the sparkling ripples slightly,
Started, pairs of birds skim the bank wholly.

## 采 桑 子

天容水色西湖好,云物俱鲜。鸥鹭闲眠,应惯寻常听管弦。
风清月白偏宜夜,一片琼田。谁羡骖鸾,人在舟中便是仙。

## Tune: Song of Gathering Mulberry Leaves

The sky and water setting off each other, the West Lake is charming,
The white clouds and the pink flowers are so brilliant and refreshing.
The gulls and egrets sleep on water leisurely,

Getting used to songs and orchestral music.

With the bright moon and gentle breeze the night boasts prettiest scene,
Oh, the clear scented water seems to be a great expanse of emerald field.
Who desires to take the phoenix-drawn carriage to heaven?
In the little painted boat here no immortal is happier than us.

※※※※※※※※※※※※※※※※

## 采 桑 子

残霞夕照西湖好，花坞苹汀。十顷波平，野岸无人舟自横。
西南月上浮云散，轩槛凉生。莲芰香清，水面风来酒面醒。

### *Tune: Song of Gathering Mulberry Leaves*

The setting sun shining with a red glow, the West Lake is so fine,
The flowers and duckweeds grow luxuriant by water and on isles.
The smooth water flows mile on mile leisurely mirror-like,
By the bank wild with green grass quiet and still boats lie.

In southwest the clouds disperse and the moon rises bit by bit,
The railings and the room feel a little bit cool so gay and happy.

A fresh breeze brings the lotus scent from the water surface,
And it strokes my face and sobers me up from drunkenness.

❊❊❊❊❊❊❊❊❊❊❊❊❊❊❊❊

## 采 桑 子

平生为爱西湖好,来拥朱轮。富贵浮云,俯仰流年二十春。
归来恰似辽东鹤,城郭人民,触目皆新,谁识当年旧主人?

### Tune: Song of Gathering Mulberry Leaves

In my whole life I like the West Lake best.
When young I came here to be the prefect,
Later my career took me here and there, like a cloud floating,
Twenty years has quick passed, like water endlessly flowing.

Now I come back, already old.
The city wall and people, oh,
I'm surprised to find have so greatly changed,
Now who knows me, the master in those days?

❊❊❊❊❊❊❊❊❊❊❊❊❊❊❊❊

## 蝶 恋 花

谁道闲情抛弃久？每到春来,惆怅还依旧。日日花前常病酒,不辞镜里朱颜瘦。　　河畔青芜堤上柳,为问新愁,何事年年有？独立小桥风满袖,平林新月人归后。

### Tune: Butterflies in Love with Flowers

Who says I have thrown leisure sorrow away for a long time?
Oh, I know when one after another charming springs arrive,
Sorrow will come to me again and again.
Before flowers I get drunk day after day,
I can't stop drinking even I see in the mirror my face languished.

By the water grows scented grass and on bank sway willow twigs,
Why does new sorrow appear
In my weak heart year by year?
I stand on the little stone bridge and my sleeves are filled with breeze alone,
The crescent like a beauty's brows rises over the wood, tourists going home.

欧阳修

## 踏 莎 行

候馆梅残,溪桥柳细,草薰风暖摇征辔。离愁渐远渐无穷,迢迢不断如春水。　寸寸柔肠,盈盈粉泪,楼高莫近危阑倚。平芜尽处是春山,行人更在春山外。

### Tune: Treading on Grass

Beside the inn the fragrant and pretty plum blossoms wither,
By the bridge over the brook sway the willow twigs slender,
In the warm and scented breeze I whip my horse on.
The farther I go the more departing grief I have got
As spring water, flowing without end.

Inch by inch her aromatic heart breaks,
Shower by shower her tears fall on her powdered face,
Please don't gaze at the distance leaning on high rails.
The spring hills lie at the end of country wild with green,
Oh, the traveller is beyond the hills like your brows unseen.

❋❋❋❋❋❋❋❋❋❋❋❋❋❋❋❋

## 诉 衷 情

清晨帘幕卷轻霜,呵手试梅妆。都缘自有离恨,故画作远山长。思往事,惜流芳,易成伤。拟歌先敛,欲笑还颦,最断人肠。

### Tune: Baring the Heart

In the early morning the beauty rolls up the curtain with frost thin,
She breathes on her hands to draw a plum blossom on her forehead.
As she has got parting bitterness so strong,
She draws her brows as distant hills as long.

The past happy hours come to her tender heart and mind,
She feels so sad to find so quickly passing her spring time.
And so easily melancholy she becomes.
Before singing on her face grief jumps,
When she is going to smile tears begin falling,
On such occasions, she is nearly heartbreaking.

## 南 歌 子

凤髻金泥带,龙纹玉掌梳。走来窗下笑相扶,爱道画眉深浅入时

欧阳修

无?　　弄笔偎人久,描花试手初。等闲妨了绣功夫,笑问"鸳鸯两字怎生书?"

## Tune: Southern Song

Her phoenix-shaped hair with a sparkling golden ribbon
Is set with a bright dragon-carved comb of precious jade.
Coming to the window, she holds his hand to her bosom,
Asking her bridegroom if her brows in fashion nowadays.

Leaning on him for long she tries to draw flower designs,
But her warm tender heart is so close to his one
That she draws no flower but waste some priceless time,
She asks smiling:"How to spell mandarin duck?"

❋❋❋❋❋❋❋❋❋❋❋❋❋❋❋❋

## 临 江 仙

柳外轻雷池上雨,雨声滴碎荷声。小楼西角断虹明。阑干倚处,待得月华生。　　燕子飞来窥画栋,玉钩垂下帘旌。凉波不动簟纹平。水精双枕,傍有堕钗横。

### June: Immortals by the River

The rain falls on the pool and light thunder sounds beyond the willow trees,
The sound of the rain breaks that of the swaying scented green lotus leaves.
There appears a part of a rainbow in the west corner of the high building.
Yearning for her lover the beauty leans alone quite long on the railings,
The crescent slow climbs knitting brows and shedding tears sympathetic.

The pair of swallows comes back trying to find the red beam painted,
The green curtains hang down from the jade hooks.
The mat with patterns of flowers is even and smooth.
On it a couple of lonely crystal pillows lies,
On her hair is a slanting hairpin on one side.

❊❊❊❊❊❊❊❊❊❊❊❊❊❊❊❊❊

## 渔 家 傲

花底忽闻敲两桨,逡巡女伴来寻访。酒盏旋将荷叶当。莲舟荡,

欧阳修

时时盏里生红浪。　　花气酒香清厮酿,花腮酒面红相向。醉倚绿阴眠一饷,惊起望,船头阁在沙滩上。

## Tune: Pride of Fishermen

Under the lotuses the sound of oars are suddenly heard,
The girl's companions come in a little boat to find her.
They pluck the fragrant lotus leaves as cups to take sweet wine.
The boats drift forward on a large expanse of lotuses carpet-like,
In the green cups the clear ripples appear now and then.

The scent of the flowers and fragrance of wine mix well,
The pink petals set off the blushes on girls' faces.
Drunk, they take a nap in green leaves of lotuses.
They wake up with a start from sweet dreams,
Finding their boats stranded on the sand beach.

## 蝶 恋 花

越女采莲秋水畔。窄袖轻罗,暗露双金钏。照影摘花花似面。芳心只共丝争乱。　　鸂鶒滩头风浪晚。露重烟轻,不见来时伴。隐隐歌声归棹远。离愁引著江南岸。

## Tune: Butterflies in Love with Flowers

In the southern land the girls pluck lotus flowers on the fall water green.
They wear red silk dresses with tight sleeves, singing a song very sweet,
Golden bracelets are seen on their hands that up and down move.
The reflections of their pretty faces are like lotus flowers in bloom.
They are stirred seeing the lotus fibers stay joined even they snap.

At dusk a wind wakes lovebirds in pairs sleeping sound on sands.
The dewdrops on leaves are heavy and mist light in the air,
To her surprise a girl cannot find her companions anywhere.
From a distance faintly come their songs, their boats on way home.
Over the waves of the lotus pool slowly floats their parting sorrow.

❋❋❋❋❋❋❋❋❋❋❋❋❋❋❋❋❋

# 玉 楼 春

洛阳正值芳菲节,秾艳清香相间发。游丝有意苦相萦,垂柳无端争赠别。　　杏花红处青山缺,山畔行人山下歇。今宵谁肯远相随,惟有寂寥孤馆月。

欧阳修

## Tune: Spring in the Jade Boudoir

Luoyang, the old capital, is in the most beautiful spring season,
Everywhere flowers are in bloom and floats delicate fragrance.
The gossamer holds travellers' sleeves asking them to stay a bit time,
The willows without love wave their hands, to them saying goodbye.

The apricots cover a part of a green hill with bright red,
As a traveller I go down the slope and at the foot I rest.
Who would follow me tonight all the way home?
Except for the moon over the inn quiet and lone.

❈❈❈❈❈❈❈❈❈❈❈❈❈❈❈❈

## 玉 楼 春

别后不知君远近,触目凄凉多少闷。渐行渐远渐无书,水阔鱼沉何处问。　　夜深风竹敲秋韵,万叶千声皆是恨。故欹单枕梦中寻,梦又不成灯又烬。

## Tune: Spring in the Jade Boudoir

I know not where you are since you waved goodbye,
Everything is dreary and miserable before my eyes.

The farther you have been away, the fewer letters I have got,
Water wide, fishes deep, nowhere can I get your news at all.

At midnight I hear fall wind blow the bamboos beyond the window,
Ten thousands of green leaves with deep bitterness moan and groan.
I sleep on half of a bed hoping to share with you in a dream pleasant,
I fail to have it finally, furthermore, the pair of candles has burnt away.

❈❈❈❈❈❈❈❈❈❈❈❈❈❈❈❈❈

## 浪 淘 沙

把酒祝东风,且共从容,垂杨紫陌洛城东。总是当时携手处,游遍芳丛。　　聚散苦匆匆,此恨无穷。今年花胜去年红。可惜明年花更好,知与谁同?

## *Tune: Waves-Shift Sand*

Holding a wine cup, I drink to the intoxicating spring breeze,
Let's appreciate the scene leisurely and don't in haste leave.
In the east capital, the roads and paths with green willows
Still remember last year arm in arm with cheer we strolled.
Today we will enjoy ourselves here again to our heart's content.

Our reunion day and night in my tender heart so difficult to get

Is too short leaving endless deep sorrow to us.
This year the flowers are redder than last one.
Than this year next one they will appear more beautiful,
Oh, but who will accompany me here to appreciate them?

## 阮 郎 归

### 踏 青

南园春半踏青时,风和闻马嘶。青梅如豆柳如眉,日长蝴蝶飞。
花露重,草烟低;人家帘幕垂。秋千慵困解罗衣,画堂双燕归。

## June: Return of the Lover

### Taking an Outing in the Country in Spring

Half spring gone, the beauty goes to the south garden for an outing,
In the gentle vernal breeze she hears clear a horse excitedly neighing.
The willow leaves are like girls' brows, and plum fruits, beans,
The days are long and the butterflies fly leisurely and carefree.

The flowers are heavy with dewdrops,
The grass sleeps in a low drifting fog.
Other families have pulled down curtains already,
Down from the swing, she feels tired and sleepy.

Returning to the lone room, she takes off her silk dress to rest,
The pair of swallows has already come back to their old nest.

✿✿✿✿✿✿✿✿✿✿✿✿✿✿✿✿✿

## 蝶 恋 花

庭院深深深几许,杨柳堆烟,帘幕无重数。玉勒雕鞍游冶处,楼高不见章台路。　　雨横风狂三月暮。门掩黄昏,无计留春住。泪眼问花花不语,乱红飞过秋千去。

### Tune: Butterflies in Love with Flowers

Deep, deep, how deep in the courtyard she is,
Over the weeping willows heaps a heavy mist,
Far and near appear curtain upon curtain and screen upon screen.
On the decorated horse, he is going to prostitute-gathering street,
Her searching eyes fail to find his figure in the high building.

The rain sheds tears heavily and wind sighs loud in late spring.
At dusk she shuts tightly the door,
But spring steps she cannot stop.
She asks the miserable fading flowers what she can do drear,
They fly away over the swing on which they play with cheer.

欧阳修

## 渔 家 傲

近日门前溪水涨,郎船几度偷相访。船小难开红斗帐,无计向,合欢影里空惆怅。　愿妾身为红菡萏,年年生在秋江上;重愿郎为花底浪,无隔障,随风逐雨长来往。

## Tune: Pride of Fishermen

These days before the door the water rises in the stream,
My dear lover in a little boat secretly comes to see me.
Putting up a red net to make love I find it too small,
Oh, it's a pity we have no way to do anything at all,
Beside the twin lotus flowers in one stalk we feel drear.

How I wish I could be a charming red lotus flower here,
Year after year blooming on the water in autumn,
And my handsome dear a wave under the lotus.
Oh, there would be no barrier between us anyway,
He could any time come to me with wind or rain.

## 浣 溪 沙

湖上朱桥响画轮,溶溶春水浸春云,碧琉璃滑净无尘。　当路游丝萦醉客,隔花啼鸟唤行人,日斜归去奈何春。

### Tune: Silk-Washing Stream

The painted carts rumble across the bridge with red railings,
The clouds are reflected in a great expanse of water of spring,
The water in the West Lake is clear and smooth like glass without any dust.

On the grass and trees the gossamer holds the arms of tourists being drunk,
The orioles in flowers ask me not quickly to go home,
In the slanting sunshine I go back slowly with sorrow.

❀❀❀❀❀❀❀❀❀❀❀❀❀❀❀❀

## 望 江 南

江南蝶,斜日一双双。身似何郎全傅粉,心如韩寿爱偷香,天赋与轻狂。　微雨后,薄翅腻烟光。才伴游蜂来小院,又随飞絮过东墙,长是为花忙。

欧阳修

## Tune: Looking in the Direction of the South of the Yangtze River

In the southeast of the Yangtze the butterflies
In pairs dance happy in the slanting sunshine.
They steal from the dressing tables powder,
And from beauties' dresses they get aroma,
Heaven offers them character of frivolity.

Towards evening after a short time drizzle,
The afterglow is reflected on their thin sticky wings.
They come to the little courtyard with bees touring,
Then they follow catkins flying away over the wall east.
All the time to be busy for blooming flowers they seem.

❈❈❈❈❈❈❈❈❈❈❈❈❈❈❈❈❈❈❈

## 少 年 游

栏干十二独凭春,晴碧远连云。千里万里,二月三月,行色苦愁人。　　谢家池上,江淹浦畔,吟魄与离魂。那堪疏雨滴黄昏,更特地、忆王孙。

## Tune: Travelling While Young

Alone the beauty leans through the twelve railings in spring,
The scented grass melts into the distant white clouds floating.
The green spreads thousands of miles, oh, so far,
It is pretty and luxuriant in February and March,
The scenery makes the beauty full of sorrow.

She remembers famous poet Xie composed
A line of spring grass: "By the pond grow spring weeds."
And poet Jiang saw here and there the tender grass green,
Writing a parting line: "By the river mouth I saw her off."
And with heartbreaking melancholy she cannot bear at all
A light rain shedding tears without end at dusk,
Her soul flies to him with devoted sweet love.

❀❀❀❀❀❀❀❀❀❀❀❀❀❀❀

## 朝 中 措

### 送刘仲原甫出守维扬

平山阑槛倚晴空,山色有无中。手种堂前垂柳,别来几度春风。
文章太守,挥毫万字,一饮千钟。行乐直须年少,尊前看取衰翁。

欧阳修

## Tune: Way in the Royal Court

### Seeing a Friend off Who Is Going to Assume the Post of Prefect of Yangzhou

On the blue sky the Pingshan Hall seems to lean,
The distant hills are now seen and now unseen.
With my own hands I planted the willow trees,
Since I left they bathe in spring breeze for years already.

I feel happy you become a prefect of wonderful poetry,
In a very short time, you can write hundreds of lines,
Without stop you can empty a thousand cups of wine.
To make merry you must be young,
See how I enjoy myself at feasts just.

❀❀❀❀❀❀❀❀❀❀❀❀❀❀❀❀

## 采 桑 子

清明上巳西湖好,满目繁华。争道谁家？绿柳朱轮走钿车。
游人日暮相将去,醒醉喧哗。路转堤斜。直到城头总是花。

### Tune: Song of Gathering Mulberry Leaves

The West Lake is pretty near Clear and Bright,
The scenery is so flourishing before my eyes.
Oh, the travellers trying to get there earlier fight even,
Under willows run decorated carriages with red wheels.

At dusk tourists group by group return excited,
Those who get drunk talk and laugh like crazy.
The dyke winds its way to the city wall
Filled with the flowers in full bloom all.

---

### 青 玉 案

一年春事都来几？早过了、三之二。绿暗红嫣浑可事。绿杨庭院，暖风帘幕，有个人憔悴。　　买花载酒长安市，又争似、家山见桃李。不枉东风吹客泪。相思难表，梦魂无据。惟有归来是。

### Tune: Green Jade Cup

How much is spring gone so far?
I think at least two thirds is past.

欧阳修

Deep green leaves set off bright red flowers blooming.
In the courtyard sway gentle the green willows weeping,
The spring warm breeze blows the curtain open,
Seeing my face fading like a flower with sorrow.

In the capital I get drunk with female singers and dancers with wine,
But I'd better go back to my wife's warm fragrant arms with delight.
Don't blame the east wind blowing down my tears.
Really I cannot express my yearning for her drear,
Even my soul gets home in dreams, awake, I still fill with grief.
I want to go back to see her standing at the gate waiting for me.

## 玉 楼 春

西湖南北烟波阔,风里丝簧声韵咽。舞余裙带绿双垂,酒入香腮红一抹。　　杯深不觉琉璃滑,贪看六幺花十八。明朝车马各西东,惆怅画桥风与月。

### June: Spring in the Jade Boudoir

The water is wide between the south and north of the West Lake,
The leisure music floats here and there in the spring breeze gentle.
My sweet stops dancing and the green laces of her skirt hang low,

After she drinks a cup of wine, on her pink dimples a flush flows.

My intimates are intoxicated with other girls' dances,
They are not aware of the cups of good wine slippery.
Tomorrow morning in horse-drawn carts we'll say goodbye to each other,
Recalling the breeze and moon over the painted bridge, we'll be miserable.

# 王琪(生卒年不详)

他写了十首《望江南》。每首都以"江南"二字领起,第三字为所咏之题,如"月""柳"等。

**Wang Qi(years of birth and death unknown)**

He composed ten poems beginning with "Looking in the Direction of the south of the Yangtze River". The next words were about topics such as "moon" "willow" and so on.

## 望 江 南

江南月,清夜满西楼。云落开时冰吐鉴,浪花深处玉沉钩。圆缺几时休。　星汉迥,风露入新秋。丹桂不知摇落恨,素娥应信别离愁。天上共悠悠。

## Tune: Looking in the Direction of the South of the Yangtze River

The moon over the south of the Yangtze in clear night
Shines gentle on the lonely west storied building bright.
The moon appears an ice mirror when clouds go away,

Below green waves sinks a hook of the moon like jade.
When will be all time the full moon?

On the Milky Way quick stars move,
The new autumn brings the emerald dew and wind gold.
On the moon the tall laurel doesn't know parting sorrow,
The goddess has suffered separation from her dear
For already ten thousands of lone and quiet years.

## 韩琦(1008—1075)

宋仁宗天圣五年(1027)进士。他曾任枢密副使、宰相等职,反对王安石变法。他写《点绛唇》这首词时,已年老多病,颇为忧郁。他的词风婉约、艳丽。

**Han Qi(1008-1075)**

He passed the highest imperial examination in 1027. He was a senior court official. He opposed Wang Anshi's reforms, he was dismissed. When he wrote this *Ci* poem, he was old, sick and sad. The style of his *Ci* poems was subtle and restrained, and bright-coloured.

## 点 绛 唇

病起恹恹,画堂花谢添憔悴。乱红飘砌,滴尽胭脂泪。　惆怅前春,谁向花前醉?愁无际。武陵回睇,人远波空翠。

## June: Rouged Lips

Recovering from a disease, I'm still weak and weary,
All the flowers fade in the hall so beautifully painted.

The pink petals fall in succession on the courtyard and steps,
Just like the tears with rouge a pretty girl without end sheds.

I'm sorrowful to find the spring gone away in silence,
I haven't appreciated it and got drunk with my lover.
Day and night sorrow fills my tender heart and brain.
I gaze long into the Land of Peach Blossoms she stays,
But in the distance I can only see
On the horizon flowing water green.

# 杜安世（生卒年不详）

北宋前期有名词家。词风与柳永词风相似。他善于描写细节。其词清新、流畅、自然、通俗，像民歌。有八十多首词存世。

**Du Anshi( years of birth and death unknown)**

He was a famous poet in the early age of the Northern Song Dynasty. His style was like Liu Yong's. He was good at describing details. His *Ci* poems were fresh, fluent, natural and popular like folk songs. He left more than eighty *Ci* poems.

## 菩 萨 蛮

游丝欲堕还重上,春残日永人相望。花共燕争飞,青梅细雨枝。离愁终未解,忘了依前在。拟待不寻思,刚眠梦见伊。

## *Tune: Buddhist Dancers*

The gossamer in the air falls and rises at leisure again and again,
The late spring days are long and I look in the direction he stays.
The swallows in pairs flying away, the faded flowers shower down,
After a drizzle the green plum fruits on the slender twigs come out.

The sorrow of separation from my dear is not released at all,
I try to forget him but he is still in my heart as clear as before.
I do my best to think of something else,
But I'll dream of him when I go to bed.

❈❈❈❈❈❈❈❈❈❈❈❈❈❈❈❈

## 卜 算 子

尊前一曲歌,歌里千重意。才欲歌时泪已流,恨应更、多于泪。
试问缘何事?不语如痴醉。我亦情多不忍闻,怕和我、成憔悴。

## Tune: Song of Divination

While I am drinking, the beauty sings a song sweet,
In the air like a cold drizzle is floating her deep grief.
Before she opens her mouth, tears begin to fall,
There should be more sorrow in her heart soft
Than in her dew-like warm tears.

I ask the girl why she is so drear,
In silence, she seems to be drunk totally.
I'm too sentimental to hear her sad story,
Oh, I'm very much afraid
As flowers, we'll both fade.

杜安世

## 鹤 冲 天

清明天气,永日愁如醉。台榭绿阴浓,薰风细。燕子巢方就,盆池小,新荷蔽。恰是逍遥际。单夹衣裳,半笼软玉肌体。　石榴美艳,一撮红绡比。窗外数修篁,寒相倚。有个关心处,难相见,空凝睇。行坐深闺里,懒更妆梳,自知新来憔悴。

### June: A Crane Flying to the Sky

The spring late, Clear and Bright comes,
Days long, with grief she appears drunk.
Thick is the shade of the green trees, pavilion and flower bed,
The warm fragrant spring breeze blows so gentle and pleasant.
The pair of swallows has finished a nest in glee,
The little clear pool is dyed refreshingly green
With the new lotuses enchantingly beautiful.
It's the time to appreciate the scene at leisure.
She wears thick silk dress bright,
Half covering her body jade-like.

Red pomegranate blossoms are charming,
Just like balls of red silk brightly shining.
Some new green bamboos dance outside the windows,
In the eve she leans alone on them feeling a bit cold.

There is someone loving her quite dearly,

Here he's unable to pour out lovesickness,

She gazes in the direction he lives, the faraway land.

She is restless in the deep room, either to sit or stand.

She has no mood to make up her hair and face,

And she knows recently like a flower she fades.

# 李师中(1013—1078)

曾任提点广西刑狱等职。此词为卸任时所作。他精于炼句,工于炼意。其词所描写的景色清丽,感情深挚。写岭南生活的词不多,此词为最好的一首。

**Li Shizhong(1013–1078)**

He was a local official in Guangxi. When he was relieved of his office, he wrote this *Ci* poem. He was good at improving diction and meanings. The scenes in his works were fresh and pretty. The feeling was deep and true. This *Ci* poem was the best one of the few *Ci* poems describing the life in the south of the Five Ridges connecting Guangdong and Guangxi.

## 菩 萨 蛮

子规啼破城楼月,画船晓载笙歌发。两岸荔枝红,万家烟雨中。佳人相对泣,泪下罗衣湿。从此信音稀,岭南无雁飞。

## *Tune: Buddhist Dancers*

The cuckoo cries and fading crescent hangs in the west sky low,

At dawn with music and songs in a painted boat I am going home.
All the banks are covered with the red litchis bright,
The countless houses are in light mist and rain fine.

Face to face the beauty and I sob tears rolling down our cheeks,
Wetting wholly our warm tender hands and fragrant silk sleeves.
Here from now on there will be rare letters really,
No wild goose reaches the south of Five Ridges.

# 司马光(1019—1086)

宋仁宗宝元元年(1038)进士。他是一代名臣和史学家。他小时以机灵出名。

**Sima Guang(1019–1086)**

He passed the highest imperial examination in 1038. He was a well-known court official and historian. When he was a child, he was famous for quick wit.

## 阮 郎 归

渔舟容易入春山,仙家日月闲。绮窗纱幌映朱颜,相逢醉梦间。
松露冷,海霞殷。匆匆整棹还。落花寂寂水潺潺,重寻此路难。

## Tune: Return of the Lover

My fishing boat entered spring mounts, paradise,
The celestial beings there enjoyed a leisure life.
The carved window and gauze curtain reflected a pretty girl's face,
I felt as if I was drunk as a lord and in a dream we together stayed.

At night the dew was cold in pine trees,
At dawn the rosy glow rose in the east.
Wanting to come back, I got the boat ready in a hurry.
Oh, now all the flowers fall shower by shower silently,
The gurgling stream winds its way through mounts to our abode,
But I cannot find it anywhere however hard I search with sorrow.

❈❈❈❈❈❈❈❈❈❈❈❈❈❈❈❈❈

## 西 江 月

宝髻松松挽就,铅华淡淡妆成,青烟翠雾罩轻盈,飞絮游丝无定。
相见争如不见,有情何似无情。笙歌散后酒初醒,深院月斜人静。

### June: The Moon over the West River

Her hair bun is loose greatly,
Her face is powdered lightly.
The green misty silk dress shows off so fine her figure,
While dancing she is like flying catkins and gossamer.

Oh, how I wish I had not seen her pink face so charming,
Affection making me lovesick, I'd better not own feelings.
Music, songs and dances going away, I'm just awake from wine,
The moon hangs slanting over the courtyard so lonely and quiet.

# 韩缜(1019—1097)

宋仁宗庆历二年(1042)进士。曾任淮南转运使、尚书右仆射兼中书侍郎等职。其词特点是巧妙地将草拟人化。句句有草,句句有人,其中融合着古人咏草的名句和含义。下面这首词是咏草的典范之作。他只留下此一首词。

**Han Zhen(1019–1097)**

He passed the highest imperial examination in 1042. He was a court official. He skillfully used personification in his *Ci* poems. In every sentence there was grass and a person with the famous lines or their meanings of the ancient poets about grass. This *Ci* poem was the model of all the poems about grass. Only this *Ci* poem is extant.

## 凤 箫 吟

芳 草

锁离愁、连绵无际,来时陌上初熏。绣帏人念远,暗垂珠露,泣送征轮。长行长在眼,更重重、远水孤云。但望极楼高,尽日目断王孙。　　销魂。池塘别后,曾行处、绿妒轻裙。恁时携素手,乱花飞絮里,缓步香茵。朱颜空自改,向年年、芳意长新。遍绿野,嬉游醉眼,莫负青春。

## June: Song of Phoenix Flute
### Fragrant Grass

Without end spreads the grass green
To lock the unbearable parting grief,
The sun just shines on the winding paths.
My beauty is sad knowing I'm leaving far,
From her eyes fall tears like dew on grass drop by drop
When seeing my carriage for long journey rumbling off.
Farther, farther away with heartbreaking grief I go,
I see nothing but the grass with our love dew grow
Extending to distant water and lone clouds in the sky.
She must be in the high building gazing at the horizon,
In sight is only the green not my figure.

Day and night with sorrow unbearable,
I recollect that day we visited the pool,
With leisure grace her steps she moved,
The green envied her silk skirt like mad.
At that time with delight hand in hand,
Under the showering catkins and flowers,
We walked on carpet-like green for hours.
Youth on my face disappears,

韩　缜

But I see sadly year by year

The grass put on new clothes and sends the scent in the air.

When in the future the grass becomes luxuriant everywhere,

Let's get drunk and visit the pool flowing in our deep hearts again.

Spring, the beauty, waiting for us, she is making up day after day.

# 阮逸女(生卒年不详)

北宋阮逸之女。此词为长词。词人写思妇在一个明媚的春日的春愁春恨。词人把写景、叙事和抒情融为一体,又前呼后应。此词是长调中富有韵味的佳作。

**Ruan Yi's daughter(years of birth and death unknown)**

Daughter of Ruan Yi in the Northern Song Dynasty. This *Ci* poem was a long one. She wrote a young wife's spring sorrow and hatred in a bright and enchanting morning. She blended the scene, thing, and feelings as a whole. This *Ci* poem was an excellent one full of implicit richness in the long tunes.

## 花 心 动

### 春 词

仙苑春浓,小桃开,枝枝已堪攀折。乍雨乍晴,轻暖轻寒,渐近赏花时节。柳摇台榭东风软,帘栊静,幽禽调舌。断魂远,闲寻翠径,顿成愁结。　　此恨无人共说。还立尽黄昏,寸心空切。强整绣衾,独掩朱扉,簟枕为谁铺设。夜长更漏传声远,纱窗映、银缸明灭。梦回处,梅梢半笼淡月。

阮逸女

## June: Stirring of Love

### *Ci* Poem of Spring

The garden is filled with charm of spring,
The peaches in blossom are intoxicating,
Twigs can be plucked away.
Oh, now sunshine, now rain,
Now slight warm, now cold a little bit,
It's time to appreciate flowers beautiful.
In a light breeze willows dance with delight,
Inside the green curtain it is lonely and quiet,
The birds in the trees sing in a voice so sweet and tender.
Her soul goes through mounts and rivers to find her lover,
She strolls along the path where their love sweetened the grass,
Oh, sorrow like water flows into her fragrant and tender heart.

To whom can she tell her grief?
She stands there until the eve,
Oh, she feels inch by inch her heart breaks.
Disappointed, she makes the bed they slept,
And with deep sadness she slowly closes the red door alone.
She sighs:"For whom do I make the bamboo mat and pillows?"
As long as a year the desolate and miserable night appears,
From a distance comes sound of a watchman's drum clear,

Behind a screen a lamp flickers about

Seeming at any moment to burn out.

Awake from a sweet spring dream she sees nothing but

A crescent like her brows shed tears on the tips of plums.

# 王安石(1021—1086)

宋仁宗庆历二年(1042)进士。曾两度为相。他是进步的政治家,推行新法。其词风格高峻豪放。《桂枝香》是他的代表作,为千古绝唱。他写了二十多首词。

**Wang Anshi(1021–1086)**

He passed the highest imperial examination in 1042. He served as a prime minister twice. He was a well-known progressive politician and carried out political reforms. The style of his *Ci* poems was high and powerful. "Scent of Laurel Twigs" was the best one of all his *Ci* poems and acme of perfection through the ages. He wrote more than twenty *Ci* poems.

## 桂 枝 香

### 金 陵 怀 古

登临送目,正故国晚秋,天气初肃。千里澄江似练,翠峰如簇。征帆去棹残阳里,背西风酒旗斜矗。彩舟云淡,星河鹭起,画图难足。　　念往昔,繁华竞逐,叹门外楼头,悲恨相续。千古凭高对此,谩嗟荣辱。六朝旧事随流水,但寒烟衰草凝绿。至今商女,时时犹唱,《后庭》遗曲。

## Tune: Scent of Laurel Twigs

### Ascending the Height in Jinling, the old capital, I think of the past.

Ascending the height I look far and near,
The old capital in the late autumn appears,
The weather begins to be a little bit chilly.
A clear river of a thousand *li*, a lace of silk,
Peaks over water are pins on a beauty's hair high and low.
In the setting sun all the sails are on the journey to and fro,
Against west wind the wine shop streamers wave slanting.
The painted touring boats drift in the pale clouds flying,
The egrets start up out of the vast Milky Way.
Compared with the scene, paintings are pale.

I remember clear with all sorts of feelings in the past
In luxuriousness and extravagance the rich vied hard.
The tower of the gate saw the emperors enjoying songs and dances inside,
While enemy troops with sparkling weapons were already arriving outside.
People like climbing heights in the past and present,
Sighing with deep emotion for the failure and success.
The Six Dynasties floated away with the water unseen,

王安石

Leaving nothing but cold mist and old grass dark green.
Singers still sing the sweet song at all hours
By the king in captivity, "Backyard's Flowers".

❈❈❈❈❈❈❈❈❈❈❈❈❈❈❈❈❈

## 千 秋 岁 引

别馆寒砧,孤城画角,一派秋声入寥廓。东归燕从海上去,南来雁向沙头落。楚台风,庾楼月,宛如昨。　无奈被些名利缚,无奈被他情担阁,可惜风流总闲却。当初谩留华表语,而今误我秦楼约。梦阑时,酒醒后,思量着。

### Tune: Song of a Thousand Autumns

In the hotel I hear the sounds of pounding cloth to make clothes
And of the painted horn from the high wall of the old city lone,
The autumn wind sends them to the open country.
Returning swallows fly out to the sea in a hurry,
The wild geese going south slow rest on the beach.
The gentle wind making the king of Chu pleased,
The bright moon the poet Yu praised,
Oh, they were the same as yesterday.

Restrained by ranks and wealth,

Excited by failure and success,
For a long time I have been away from the loose affairs.
I regret having been again involved in officialdom there,
And failing to have a tryst with my love so charming.
When I am awake from the pleasant dream of spring
And sober up completely from wine,
Her pretty face comes to my mind.

❄❄❄❄❄❄❄❄❄❄❄❄❄❄❄❄❄

## 菩 萨 蛮

数家茅屋闲临水,轻衫短帽垂杨里。花是去年红,吹开一夜风。
梢梢新月偃,午醉醒来晚。何物最关情? 黄鹂一两声。

## Tune: Buddhist Dancers

Several thatched huts lie quiet by the green water,
In casual clothes I stroll under willows at leisure.
A vernal breeze blows all the night without end,
All the flowers are blooming as last year as red.

I get drunk as a lord alone in the whole afternoon,
Awake in the eve I see on treetops a crescent moon.
Now I'm interested most

王安石

In the singing of an oriole.

※※※※※※※※※※※※※※※※※※

## 南 乡 子

自古帝王州,郁郁葱葱佳气浮。四百年来成一梦,堪愁。晋代衣冠成古丘。　绕水恣行游,上尽层楼更上楼。往事悠悠君莫问,回头。槛外长江空自流。

### *Tune: Song of Southern countryside*

For long Nanjing City had been a capital,
All year round it is luxuriant and fragrant.
Four hundred years becomes a dream,
Thinking of it people are full of grief,
High-ranking officials in the Jin Dynasty lie in the desolate hills.

Along the bank I enjoy to my heart's content the beautiful scenery,
I ascend the terraces one after another and the gate tower again.
Don't ask me to comment on success or failure of historic events,
Turning round, beyond the railings I find
In vain the Yangtze flows to the distant sky.

※※※※※※※※※※※※※※※※※※

## 渔 家 傲

灯火已收正月半,山南山北花撩乱。闻说洊亭新水漫,骑款段,穿云入坞寻游伴。　却拂僧床褰素幔,千岩万壑春风暖。一弄松声悲急管,吹梦断,西看窗日犹嫌短。

## Tune: Pride of Fishermen

The Lantern Festival is away and all the lamps have been taken in,
The flowers are dazzling in the south and north of the mountains.
I hear after a rain the suburb is refreshing everywhere,
With a great interest I ride a donkey slow going there,
Through clouds and across valleys I seek fellow tourists at leisure.

Tired, going to the temple, I clear up the bed and raise the curtain,
From the crags and water blows a breeze pleasant and warm.
Suddenly, a gust of wind blows hard pines as the flute sobs,
Waking me up still sleepy from a sound dream,
The sun setting I hope to return to it so sweet.

王安石

## 渔 家 傲

平岸小桥千嶂抱,柔蓝一水萦花草。茅屋数间窗窈窕。尘不到,时时自有春风扫。　午枕觉来闻语鸟,欹眠似听朝鸡早。忽忆故人今总老。贪梦好,茫然忘了邯郸道。

## Tune: Pride of Fishermen

The small bridge over the flat bank lies still in the peaks' arms,
The clear water day and night accompanies flowers and grass.
In the hills hide the thatched huts quiet and deep,
The red dust outside cannot find them with ease,
But spring breeze gets here gently stroking them.

Awake from an afternoon nap, I hear birds twitter,
Going to court in the morn I heard cocks crow,
It occurs to me all of my friends become old.
I enjoy the leisure and carefree dreams in afternoon naps here,
Forgetting Lu's dream of passing the imperial exam with cheer.

## 章楶(1027—1102)

宋英宗治平二年(1065)进士。朝廷高官。词风婉约。苏轼欣赏其所作描写柳絮的《水龙吟》,也写了一首《水龙吟》。其词只留两首。

**Zhang Jie(1027–1102)**

He passed the highest imperial examination in 1065. He was a senior official. The style of his *Ci* poems was subtle and restrained. Appreciating this poem, Su Shi also wrote a *Ci* poem about willow catkins, "Chanting of Water Dragoon". Only two of his *Ci* poems are extant.

## 水 龙 吟

燕忙莺懒芳残,正堤上、柳花飘坠。轻飞乱舞,点画青林,全无才思。闲趁游丝,静临深院,日长门闭。傍珠帘散漫,垂垂欲下,依前被、风扶起。　　兰帐玉人睡觉,怪春衣、雪沾琼缀。绣床旋满,香球无数,才圆却碎。时见蜂儿,仰粘轻粉,鱼吞池水。望章台路杳,金鞍游荡,有盈盈泪。

章 粢

## June: Chanting of Water Dragon

The swallows fly happy far and near,
The orioles are too lazy to sing here.
The flowers fade.
In a casual way,
The catkins from the willows
Over the dyke fly high and low.
Without creativeness, but in glee,
They embellish all the green trees.
Following gossamer leisurely,
They enter the courtyard still,
So long seems to be the day and firmly shut is the red door.
On the pearly curtain into the boudoir they are trying to fall,
Anyway, again and again, but
By a breeze they are sent up.

In the blue curtain a young wife is sleeping,
Awake, she finds her thick clothes of spring
Are stuck with catkins snow-white.
And the embroidered bed is piled
With the catkin balls transparent,
And into pieces they are broken.
The bees with interest here and there

Smell the fragrant powder in the air,

The fish swallow the floating catkins on the water clear and calm.

The beauty sighs:"Away from me brothel-gathering street is far,

You are getting down from a horse at the gate of a brothel so glad,

Please see the falling catkins—they are my bloody tears so sad."

# 郑獬(1022—1072)

宋皇祐五年(1053)进士。他是朝廷官吏,因得罪丞相王安石被贬为知县。此词为当知县时所作。作者当时虽处境不佳,仍保持高洁品格。

**Zheng Xie(1022–1072)**

He passed the highest imperial examination in 1053. He served as an official in the court. Offending Wang Anshi, the prime minister, he was demoted to a county magistrate. During that time, he composed this *Ci* poem. Though in a sad plight, he kept his noble and unsullied character.

## 好 事 近

把酒对江梅,花小未禁风力。何计不教零落,为青春留得。　　故人莫问在天涯,尊前苦相忆。好把素香收取,寄江南消息。

## June: Happiness Approaching

I hold a cup of wine to the riverside plum tree,
The blossoms are too little to bear the breeze.

I can neither help them not to wither
Nor keep their beauty a little longer.

Don't ask my situation in the place remote,
While drinking I miss you with deep sorrow.
I will pluck twigs of blossoms in southeast with faint scent,
And send them to you with my missing, my dearest friend.

# 王安国(1030—1076)

王安石的弟弟。官至大理寺丞、集贤校理。与兄政见不合。其兄罢相后,他被免职归田。他很清高,就像杨花,虽到处飘扬,却不愿进入画堂朱门。其词内容多写离情别绪,善于刻画人物的内心世界。

**Wang Anguo(1030‑1076)**

He was a younger brother of Wang Anshi. He was a senior official. In many respects they had different political opinions. When his elder brother was dismissed, he was removed from office. He was lofty, like willow catkins though drifting everywhere unwilling to enter the painted room and red houses of bigwigs. Most of his *Ci* poems described the sorrow of parting, and he was good at depicting the inner world of characters.

## 清 平 乐

### 春 晚

留春不住,费尽莺儿语。满地残红宫锦污,昨夜南园风雨。 小怜初上琵琶,晓来思绕天涯。不肯画堂朱户,春风自在杨花。

## Tune: Music for a Peaceful Time

### Late Spring

Spring does not slow her step going away,
Though orioles continually beg her to stay.
The dirty palace brocades on the ground are the fallen flowers,
Last night the south garden felt cold in the wind and showers.

From pipa by the new singing girl, "Little Love", comes the music drear,
In the whole morn her thoughts travel everywhere to look for her dear.
The snow-white catkins fly here and there carefree and leisurely,
Unwilling to enter the painted rooms and red houses of bigwigs.

※※※※※※※※※※※※※※※※※※

## 减字木兰花

画桥流水,雨湿落红飞不起。月破黄昏,帘里余香马上闻。
徘徊不语,今夜梦魂何处去。不似垂杨,犹解飞花入洞房。

### Tune: Shortened Song of Magnolia Flowers

The painted bridge lies over the singing stream,
In a drizzle red petals shower down in the fields.

At dusk the moon displays her pretty face through the thin haze,
From the curtain of a carriage drifts to me a young lady's scent.

The carriage gone, dismounting I pace up and down in silence,
Where does my soul in a long dream wander tonight? I wonder.
I feel envy when I see the catkins fly
Into the boudoir of the beauty I admire.

## 点 绛 唇

秋气微凉,梦回明月穿帘幕。井梧萧索,正绕南枝鹊。　宝瑟尘生,金雁空零落。情无托。鬓云慵掠,不似君恩薄。

## *Tune: Rouged Lips*

The summer gone, it is a bit chilly in the early autumn,
Awake from a dream, I see moonlight enter the curtains.
The withering parasol trees groan and moan beside an old deep well,
Starting a pair of magpies flying round the branches again and again.

The zither lies idle with wild geese on the pegs with dust.

I write a long letter to the emperor full of my tender love,

No one would send it to him.

Now I have no at all interest

To comb my fluffy fragrant pitch-black hair.

Though thin it's thicker than his love and care.

# 晏几道(1038—1110)

晏殊第七子。曾任乾宁军通判、开封府判官等。词与其父齐名。词风近其父。多写四时之景,男女之情。较之其父,更工于情感。他在两位朋友家作词,让莲、鸿、蘋、云四位歌女演唱。后两友家道中落,诸伎云散。他的词描写他与歌伎们心心相印,爱情永驻。《临江仙》是他的代表作,也是婉约词的绝唱。

**Yan Jidao(1038–1110)**

He was Yan Shu's seventh son and he once served as a low-ranking official. He was equally famous with his father. The style of his *Ci* poems was like his father's. They often wrote the scenes and love between men and women. But he paid more attention to the feeling than his father. In his two friends' home, he composed *Ci* poems for the four songstresses to sing. Later the two friends suffered a decline in family financial situation. The songstresses scattered. His *Ci* poems depicted their mutual deep love. "Immortals by the River" was the represetive work of all his *Ci* poems, also the acme of perfection in subtle and restrained poems.

## 临 江 仙

梦后楼台高锁,酒醒帘幕低垂。去年春恨却来时。落花人独立,微雨燕双飞。 记得小蘋初见,两重心字罗衣。琵琶弦上说相思。当时明月在,曾照彩云归。

### Tune: Immortals by the River

Awake from a spring dream, I see the hall for songs closed,
And sobering up slow, I see her curtain hanging with sorrow.
Oh, since last spring left here, all the time I am full of woe.
Like tears flowers falling shower by shower, I stood alone,
Through the drizzle a pair of swallows flew high and low.

I remember clear I met beautiful Little Apple the first time
She wore silk clothes embroidered with double hearts bright,
She displayed her love from pipa, plucking strings delightful.
Now just as the last year flows the clear and gentle moonlight
When she as goddess full of love with clouds flew out of sight.

晏几道

## 临 江 仙

斗草阶前初见,穿针楼上曾逢。罗裙香露玉钗风。靓妆眉沁绿,羞脸粉生红。　流水便随春远,行云终与谁同? 酒醒长恨锦屏空。相寻梦里路,飞雨落花中。

### Tune: Immortals by the River

On the seventh of the seventh month,
I saw her first time on the steps vying with the girls in strangeness of green grasses.
Again, on the fifth of the fifth month,
I met her again, learning needle skills from the Girl Weaver in her room scented.
She wore a silk skirt with dew from flowers and hairpins shaking in a breeze,
And her brows so carefully drawn like the distant hills were pleasantly green,
She feeling shy, blush appeared on her face lightly powdered.

With the aromatic spring time, far, far away, floats the water.
With whom at all does the intoxicating beauty like the goddess go?
Sobering up and seeing the lone brocade screens, I'm full of sorrow.
In dreams through mounts and water, I seek her trace,

In the showering fragrant pink flowers and light rains.

❈❈❈❈❈❈❈❈❈❈❈❈❈❈❈❈

## 蝶 恋 花

醉别西楼醒不记,春梦秋云,聚散真容易。斜月半窗还少睡,画屏闲展吴山翠。 衣上酒痕诗里字,点点行行,总是凄凉意。红烛自怜无好计,夜寒空替人垂泪。

## Tune: Butterflies in Love with Flowers

She singing sad, I got drunk in the west tower, awake, forgetting the scene.
Oh, just like the flying autumn clouds and so short a sweet spring dream,
Our reunion is gone so easily leaving nothing but sorrow.
The crescent sheds drear light on me sleepless with woe,
The screens leisurely display the green mounts in the land southern.

The wine stains are on my clothes and my poems on pieces of paper,
All dots and lines full of love change
Into deep grief flowing into my brain.
The red candle has no way to help me out of sadness,
Only sheds tears drop by drop to show me sympathy.

晏几道

## 蝶 恋 花

初撚霜纨生怅望。隔叶莺声,似学秦娥唱。午睡醒来慵一饷,双纹翠簟铺寒浪。　　雨罢蘋风吹碧涨。脉脉荷花,泪脸红相向。斜贴绿云新月上,弯环正是愁眉样。

### *Tune: Butterflies in Love with Flowers*

Twisting the fan in her snow-white hand, she is in thought deep.
The oriole twitters with cheer in the refreshing green thick leaves,
As a young girl sings sweetly and merrily.
Awake from a nap for long she feels lonely,
The double-veined bamboo mat displays cool waves surging.

The rain stops and gentle breeze blows the green water rising.
The affectionate lotus flowers in full bloom red
Look at one another with tear-like drops of rain.
The new crescent slow climbs up again the green clouds,
Just like under black hair my dear beauty's knitted brows.

## 蝶 恋 花

梦入江南烟水路,行尽江南,不与离人遇。睡里消魂无说处,觉来惆怅消魂误。　　欲尽此情书尺素,浮雁沉鱼,终了无凭据。却倚缓弦歌别绪,断肠移破秦筝柱。

### Tune: Butterflies in Love with Flowers

I dream of travelling in the southeast through misty water.
Oh, although everywhere with deep sorrow I have covered,
Nowhere at all can I find my gentle charming love.
In the dream I can't confide my sadness to any one,
Awake, even harder it tortures me.

I want to write her telling my grief,
No errand sends my lovesickness, fishes in water, wild geese, sky,
Even if I get it sent to the remotest place, I can hardly get her reply.
Oh, no way at all, here I can play only
A low tune to convey my parting misery.
Many times when with bitterness I adjust the strings,
The zither always gives forth the sound heartbreaking.

晏几道

## 蝶 恋 花

千叶早梅夸百媚,笑面凌寒,内样妆先试。月脸冰肌香细腻,风流新称东君意。 一稔年光春有味,江北江南,更有谁相比。横玉声中吹满地,好枝长恨无人寄。

### Tune: Butterflies in Love with Flowers

The plum displays her petals so charming,
Greeting with gay smiles the chilly spring,
Like plum-adorned beautiful maids in the imperial palace.
Her face is the moon, her skin ice, and her scent delicate,
Her grace and gentleness most please the spring deity.

Once a year, the cold plum with her charm and beauty,
In the north and south of the Yangtze River anywhere,
No way can other flowers or blossoms be compared.
The music from a jade flute blows blossoms showering down,
Oh, why are the charming twigs of the blossoms not sent out?

❈❈❈❈❈❈❈❈❈❈❈❈❈❈❈❈

## 更 漏 子

柳丝长,桃叶小。深院断无人到。红日淡,绿烟晴。流莺三两声。 雪香浓,檀晕少。枕上卧枝花好。春思重,晓妆迟。寻思残梦时。

## Tune: Song of Water Watch

The willow twigs are long and slender,
And the peach leaves short and tender.
The deep courtyard never sees a guest.
Into it the pale light the morn sun sheds,
A green mist hangs low over the trees.
Once or twice the oriole twitters sweet.

Her snow-white skin sends forth scent rich,
Her blush on the pretty face remains a little.
How beautiful are the flowers on a twig on the pillow.
Her tender sweet heart is filled with the spring sorrow,
Still sleepy, she dresses up very late when the sun already rises high,
Thinking of the happy tryst with her dear love in the dream last night.

晏几道

## 鹧 鸪 天

小令尊前见玉箫,银灯一曲太妖娆。歌中醉倒谁能恨?唱罢归来酒未消。　　春悄悄,夜迢迢。碧云天共楚宫遥。梦魂惯得无拘检,又踏杨花过谢桥。

### Tune: Partridge Sky

At the feast accompanied by songs I saw the beauty,
Under bright lamps singing sweet, she was so pretty.
I didn't regret getting drunk with wine and her songs,
Coming back, my drunkenness remained quite long.

The spring is quiet and alone,
Oh, the night is long and cold.
Like a goddess in the paradise,
She is far away from my side.
My soul in the fond dreams is so easy and carefree,
In snow-white catkins I walk to her chamber green.

## 鹧 鸪 天

醉拍春衫惜旧香,天将离恨恼疏狂。年年陌上生秋草,日日楼中到夕阳。 云渺渺,水茫茫。征人归路许多长。相思本是无凭语,莫向花笺费泪行。

### Tune: Partridge Sky

Drunk, I hold in my arms her spring clothes,
And smell the remaining scent with sorrow.
Though born with indulgence, I can't dispel my sadness.
Year after year the paths in autumn are wild with grasses,
Day by day enters my room drear setting sunlight.

Boundless is the blue sky with flying clouds white,
And vast looks the misty water.
On a long way back is my lover.
Lovesickness can hardly be expressed clear,
So on the rosy paper, don't waste warm tears.

## 鹧 鸪 天

斗鸭池南夜不归,酒阑纨扇有新诗。云随碧玉歌声转,雪绕红琼舞袖回。　今感旧,欲沾衣。可怜人似水东西。回头满眼凄凉事,秋月春风岂得知!

### Tune: Partridge Sky

By the pool we watched duck-fighting games the whole night,
Drunk, at leisure on her green silk fan I wrote the lovesick lines.
The clouds float around my beauty's songs sweet,
The snow flies round her dancing-dress's sleeves.

When I think of our deep love before,
Tears fall on my robe drop by drop.
We are water ways, one flowing to the east, the other the west.
Day and night I recollect our intoxicating affairs in those days,
Everything before my eyes is heartbreakingly miserable,
The fall moon and spring breeze know nothing of them.

## 鹧 鸪 天

彩袖殷勤捧玉锺,当年拚却醉颜红。舞低杨柳楼心月,歌尽桃花扇影风。　　从别后,忆相逢,几回魂梦与君同? 今宵剩把银釭照,犹恐相逢是梦中。

### June: Partridge Sky

With snow-white hands in colored sleeves and with deep affection,
You urged me to empty jade cups of good wine one after another,
And again and again I drank fragrant fine wine to my heart's content.
You danced till the moon was drunk leaning on the willow in the west,
You sang with a fan blowing peach blossoms into morn glow high.

Since you with tears streaming down your pink cheeks waved bye,
Never for a moment have you left my heart soft and sweet,
So many times you lay in my arms smiling to me in dreams.
Tonight I hold the bright lamp so near to your face,
Afraid still in a dream we together so happily stay.

晏几道

## 鹧鸪天

一醉醒来春又残,野棠梨雨泪阑干。玉笙声里鸾空怨,罗幕香中燕未还。　　终易散,且长闲。莫教离恨损朱颜。谁堪共展鸳鸯锦,同过西楼此夜寒!

## Tune: Partridge Sky

When I sober up I find spring gone so quickly again,
From pink pear blossoms fall tear-like drops of rain.
I play the reed pipe conveying in my deep heart the sorrow,
Behind the scented curtains is the empty nest of the swallows.

Happy reunion lasts a very short time,
I'd better live a leisure and carefree life
To keep my face from fading
As in a rain a flower falling.
Who would spread with me the silk quilt with lovebirds embroidered
To spend the cold lonely night bosom to bosom in the west chamber?

## 鹧 鸪 天

守得莲开结伴游,约开萍叶上兰舟。来时浦口云随棹,采罢江边月满楼。　花不语,水空流,年年拚得为花愁。明朝万一西风动,争奈朱颜不耐秋。

### Tune: Partridge Sky

She waits and waits until the lotuses bloom so beautiful,
Then she takes a boat to pick seedpods with her company,
They push duckweeds apart before moving slowly the boat.
In the river mouth over their oars the morning clouds floats,
Returning to the bank she sees pavilions full of moonlight.

The fragrant lotus flowers seem sleeping sound and quiet,
The clear water flows alone to the east in vain,
Year after year she feels sad for flowers to fade.
When the cold west wind brings here autumn,
All the charming flowers will wither in water.

晏几道

## 阮 郎 归

旧香残粉似当初,人情恨不如。一春犹有数行书,秋来书更疏。衾凤冷,枕鸳孤。愁肠待酒舒。梦魂纵有也成虚,那堪和梦无。

### Tune: Return of the Lover

The powder she used in the past is as fragrant as today's,
But her dear's love for her is not as deep as in those days.
In the spring he still writes her a few lines of letters,
His letters become fewer and fewer since the autumn.

In the quilt embroidered with a pair of phoenixes she feels cold,
On the pillow with a couple of mandarin ducks she feels alone.
To get drunk she wish
To dispel her sadness.
Though it's quite meaningless to see him in the sweet dreams,
But without a moment of happiness, she can't bear deep grief.

❈❈❈❈❈❈❈❈❈❈❈❈❈❈❈❈❈❈

## 阮 郎 归

天边金掌露成霜,云随雁字长。绿杯红袖趁重阳,人情似故乡。

兰佩紫,菊簪黄,殷勤理旧狂。欲将沉醉换悲凉,清歌莫断肠!

## Tune: Return of the Lover

Dew becomes frost in the plate of Bronze Man under the sky,
Pulling rosy clouds in a line, the wild geese far, far away fly.
Oh, on the Double Ninth Festival,
In red sleeves with white fingers,
The beauty takes a green cup urging me to drink again and again,
Here human feelings are just as thick as in my dear native place.

Purple orchids on the waist and yellow chrysanthemums in the hair,
Feeling I become young and handsome again, I put on a cheerful air,
And I try to be in the old way of unruliness.
I want to exchange drunkenness with misery,
Asking the songstresses to sing songs pleasing
Instead of the ones sorrowful and heartbreaking.

❀❀❀❀❀❀❀❀❀❀❀❀❀❀❀

## 虞 美 人

曲阑干外天如水,昨夜还曾倚。初将明月比佳期,长向月圆时候望人归。 罗衣著破前香在,旧意谁教改?一春离恨懒调弦,犹有两行闲泪宝筝前。

晏几道

## Tune: Great Beauty Yu

Beyond the winding rails the sky is as water as clear,
Last night for a long time I also leaned on them drear.
People think when the moon turn round lovers will meet,
So night by night I watch it and expect him to come to me.

The silk dress worn, its fragrance remains as in those days,
Who could make our true love in hearts of the past change?
Separation grief breaking my heart, I'm too sad to play the zither,
There are still two lines of dried scented tears on the instrument.

## 思 远 人

红叶黄花秋意晚,千里念行客。飞云过尽,归鸿无信,何处寄书得? 泪弹不尽临窗滴。就砚旋研墨。渐写到别来,此情深处,红笺为无色。

## Tune: Thinking of My Dear Far Away

Red are maple leaves and yellow, chrysanthemums—autumn late,
Day and night I yearn for my lover though a thousand miles away.

The rosy clouds leisurely fly across the blue sky in a breeze,
The returning swan geese bring no message from him to me,
Where can I send him my unbearable sorrow?

Tears fall into the ink stone before the window,
I rub it with ink stick to write him a letter with love in my heart.
When I come to the heartbreaking sight we were about to far part,
From my heart drop by drop the true and sweet affection
Falls on the pink pieces of paper and they lose the color.

❉❉❉❉❉❉❉❉❉❉❉❉❉❉❉❉❉

## 六 幺 令

绿阴春尽,飞絮绕香阁。晚来翠眉宫样,巧把远山学。一寸狂心未说,已向横波觉。画帘遮币。新翻曲妙,暗许闲人带偷掐。 前度书多隐语,意浅愁难答。昨夜诗有回文,韵险还慵押。都待笙歌散了,记取留时霎。不消红蜡。闲云归后,月在庭花旧阑角。

## *June: Song of the Green Waist*

Pink spring leaves, green shade being deep and thick,
The catkins like snow fly round the pavilion scented.
In the eve like green distant hills my brows are drawn

晏几道

According to latest fashion of the maids in the court.
My burning affection for the sweetheart untold to anyone,
But affectionate waves in my eyes are noticed by my love.
Behind painted curtains one after another at the feast,
Oh, I do my best to play well the tunes new and sweet,
Not caring about them stolen out and sung anywhere.

Days ago he sent me a letter with argots somewhere,
And just last night very late,
He handed me a verse again
With narrow rhymes.
Neither have I replied.
I hate wasting time to work my brain.
Wait until the music and songs end,
Then we stay for only a short period,
We needn't bring a red candle here.
When the white clouds in the blue sky at ease and leisurely fly away far,
The moon hangs over the blooming flowers and old railings in the yard.

## 木 兰 花

秋千院落重帘暮,彩笔闲来题绣户。墙头丹杏雨余花,门外绿杨风后絮。 朝云信断知何处?应作襄王春梦去。紫骝认得旧游踪,嘶过画桥东畔路。

### Tune: Magnolia Flowers

Screen upon screen,
Curtain upon curtain,
The swing sways, the scent left from her floating in the yard lone,
With a colored brush she writes leisurely poems in the red windows.
Over the wall after a rain the red apricots fade shedding tears,
Out of the door, the willow catkins fly in a breeze far and near.

Where does my sweetheart like a morn cloud fly?
Probably with another lover, she is having a tryst.
My purple steed is familiar with the house beautifully decorated,
And it neighs passing the road near the east of the painted bridge.

## 木 兰 花

小莲未解论心素,狂似钿筝弦底柱。脸边霞散酒初醒,眉上月残人欲去。　旧时家近章台住,尽日东风吹柳絮。生憎繁杏绿阴时,正碍粉墙偷眼觑。

### Tune: Magnolia Flowers

Little Lotus knows nothing of passing her affection to her lover,
Her unruliness is just like the warm music from her green zither.
When she sobers up, her blush like morning glow goes away,
The dark green moon-like pigment between her brows fades,
The moon setting, she is about to leave.

She lived near brothels-gathering street,
The whole day catkins flew high and low.
But in the late spring what she hated most
Was the apricot trees heavy with green leaves and red fruits,
For they kept her from stealing at her dear lad an eager look.

## 玉 楼 春

东风又作无情计,艳粉娇红吹满地。碧楼帘影不遮愁,还似去年今日意。　　谁知错管春残事,到处登临曾费泪。此时金盏直须深,看尽落花能几醉!

## *Tune: Spring in the Jade Boudoir*

The evil east wind has done the ruthless thing again this year,
Blowing down the bright powder and tender red far and near.
The green tower and painted curtain can't keep me from seeing the scene,
Just like in the last late spring arc the withering scenery and growing grief.

I shouldn't be too miserable when seeing spring fade,
Tears streaming down my cheeks on heights in vain.
I should drink wine as much as possible to spend painful hours,
How many times can I get drunk as a lord before falling flowers?

❈❈❈❈❈❈❈❈❈❈❈❈❈❈❈

## 长 相 思

长相思,长相思。若问相思甚了期,除非相见时。　　长相思,长相思。欲把相思说似谁,浅情人不知。

## Tune: Yearning Forever

I miss you all the time,
I miss you far and wide.
When will the missing cease?
Except when we happily meet.

I miss you all the time,
I miss you far and wide.
Even if I can tell my friends what is my missing,
No one can understand it without deep feelings.

❋❋❋❋❋❋❋❋❋❋❋❋❋❋❋❋

## 清 平 乐

留人不住,醉解兰舟去。一棹碧涛春水路,过尽晓莺啼处。　渡头杨柳青青,枝枝叶叶离情。此后锦书休寄,画楼云雨无凭。

## Tune: Music for a Peaceful Time

I ask him to stay again and again but fail,
Drunk, he unties the boat and goes away.

The boat floats on the green spring waves,
The yellow orioles sing sweet on his way.

By the ferry the weeping willows are green and green,
Their tender twigs and leaves fill with grief and grief.
From now on you shouldn't send any letter to me,
Our prostitutes' love can't be trusted and believed.

❀❀❀❀❀❀❀❀❀❀❀❀❀❀❀❀❀❀

## 菩 萨 蛮

哀筝一弄湘江曲,声声写尽湘波绿。纤指十三弦,细将幽恨传。
当筵秋水慢,玉柱斜飞雁。弹到断肠时,春山眉黛低。

### *Tune: Buddhist Dancers*

On the zither a sad tune, the Xiang River, she plays,
Every syllable describes the sad raging green waves.
Her tender fingers pluck thirteen strings slow,
In detail giving forth her deep lovesick sorrow.

At the feast clear fall water is her enchanting eyes,
The jade strings are like wild geese flying in a line.
When she enters slowly the heartbreaking situation,

She knits her brows, like green hills in the distance.

## 采 桑 子

西楼月下当时见，泪粉偷匀。歌罢还颦。恨隔炉烟看未真。
别来楼外垂杨缕，几换青春。倦客红尘，长记楼中粉泪人。

### Tune: Song of Gathering Mulberry Leaves

Oh, I met you under the bright moon in the west chamber,
Secretly you rubbed powder with tears on the face even.
After singing a song you still knitted your brows,
I can't see you clear through stove smoke around.

Since our parting, still wave the green twigs of the willows,
But how many times have they already put on new clothes?
Though of this human world I'm so tired,
Your powdered face never leaves my mind.

## 浣 溪 沙

二月和风到碧城,万条千缕绿相迎,舞烟眠雨过清明。　　妆镜巧眉偷叶样,歌楼妍曲借枝名。晚秋霜霰莫无情。

### *Tune: Silk-Washing Stream*

In the second month the gentle breeze comes to the green city,
Ten thousands of willow twigs open their arms to welcome it,
They dance in mists and sleep in rains through Qingming Festival.

Young beauties draw their brows like willow leaves before mirrors,
Halls for dances and songs use "Willow Twigs" as a drear farewell song,
But in late autumn, they will be destroyed cruelly by the freezing frost.

❀❀❀❀❀❀❀❀❀❀❀❀❀❀❀

## 御 街 行

街南绿树春饶絮,雪满游春路。树头花艳杂娇云,树底人家朱户。北楼闲上,疏帘高卷,直见街南树。　　阑干倚尽犹慵去,几度黄昏雨。晚春盘马踏青苔,曾傍绿阴深驻。落花犹在,香屏空掩,人面知何处?

## Tune: Song of Imperial Thoroughfare

In the south street round trees the catkins fly like snow,
Covering here and there the green spring paths and roads.
On the trees the gaudy flowers are displayed,
Under them stands the house with a red gate.
The north storied building at leisure I climb,
There the green curtains are rolled up high,
The tall trees are so clearly seen in the street now.

I lean through the rails but reluctant to get down,
How many showers have fallen in the evening?
I rode a horse on the green moss in late spring,
In the deep shade by her chamber I waited for her in air sweet.
The fallen flowers like my beauty lie here and there with grief,
The fragrant screens feel lonely,
Where is the pretty face scented?

❋❋❋❋❋❋❋❋❋❋❋❋❋❋❋❋❋❋

## 归 田 乐

试把花期数。便早有、感春情绪。看即梅花吐。愿花更不谢,春且长住。只恐花飞又春去。　　花开还不语。问此意、年年春还会否。绛唇青鬓,渐少花前语。对花又记得、旧曾游处。门外垂杨未飘絮。

## June: Joy of Returning to Field

I count days before flowers blooming time.
Before the scented spring full of life arrives,
Oh, I have already got sorrow.
Seeing plums about to open,
I wish they would never fade.
Oh, spring, please long stay.
I fear flowers will soon leave with spring season.

Finally here and there plums blossom in silence.
I wonder if every spring
Knows their deep feelings.
The beauties with red lips and black hair in the tower
Are my sweet companions before the opening flowers.
Fewer and fewer of them I meet of late.
Facing the gorgeous flowers I recollect
Once my enchanting dear and I had a tour hand in hand so happy here,
We didn't see the willows before her door wafting catkins far and near.

❀❀❀❀❀❀❀❀❀❀❀❀❀❀❀

## 生 查 子

关山魂梦长,塞雁音书少。两鬓可怜青,只为相思老。　　归傍碧纱窗,说与人人道:"真个别离难,不似相逢好。"

### Tune: Mountain Hawthorn

I often dream of going home through passes and mountains,
But I have not got any of her letters from the remote region.
Looking in the mirror at my frosted hair at the temples,
Oh, only for deep love I become much older, I complain.

In a dream I return to our chamber with green screens at last,
I tell my intoxicating sweetheart in a very low voice so sad:
"Oh, my dear, there I'm terribly lone and drear,
Separation can't be compared with reunion here."

❈❈❈❈❈❈❈❈❈❈❈❈❈❈❈❈

## 生 查 子

长恨涉江遥,移近溪头住。闲荡木兰舟,误入双鸳浦。　　无端轻薄云,暗作帘纤雨。翠袖不胜寒,欲向荷花语。

## Tune: Mountain Hawthorn

All the time I think I am too far away from a long river,
So I move near to the stream to see my dissolute lover.
To gather lotus seedpods I leisurely row my boat winding its way,
I enter a river mouth by mistake seeing pairs of lovebirds at play.

Unexpectedly the fickle clouds floating
Change into a drizzle thickly sprinkling.
My thin silk dress cannot keep out the cold,
I confide to the lotus flowers my deep sorrow.

❈❈❈❈❈❈❈❈❈❈❈❈❈❈❈

## 菩 萨 蛮

相逢欲话相思苦,浅情肯信相思否。还恐漫相思,浅情人不知。
忆曾携手处,月满窗前路。长到月来时,不眠犹待伊。

## Tune: Buddhist Dancers

Meeting her I want to tell her of my long separation grief,
I'm afraid without deep love for me she won't believe me.
If I confide to her my unbearable lovesickness,

Oh, how will she with fickle feelings know it?

I remember with cheer arm in arm we strolled
On the path with flowers before her window.
When the crescent like her brows shines bright,
I toss about on the bed waiting for her all night.

❋❋❋❋❋❋❋❋❋❋❋❋❋❋❋❋

## 少　年　游

离多最是，东西流水，终解两相逢。浅情终似，行云无定，犹到梦魂中。　　可怜人意，薄于云水，佳会更难重。细想从来，断肠多处，不与者番同。

### Tune: Travelling While Young

From her I suffer greatly the long separation.
Even two streams flow in different directions,
Somewhere they'll meet.
Without true love to me
She is like coloured clouds floating,
But she haunts my dreams of spring.

Oh, what a pity!

With love thin,
She won't basically as before sleep in my arms.
When I think of our romantic affairs in the past,
Unbearable grief fills my heart and mind,
I still hope one day she'll come to my side.

❈❈❈❈❈❈❈❈❈❈❈❈❈❈❈

## 南 乡 子

新月又如眉。长笛谁教月下吹？楼倚暮云初见雁,南飞。漫道行人雁后归。　　意欲梦佳期。梦里关山路不知。却待短书来破恨,应迟。还是凉生玉枕时。

### Tune: Song of Southern Countryside

Like brows, the crescent appears.
Who plays the long flute so drear?
Leaning in the storied building, I see wild geese with dusk clouds
Flying at leisure and carefreely to their remote home in the south.
I hope after them my dear will return to me.

I can only look for my beauty in the dreams,
But I lose my way in passes and mountains.
All the time I wait for her sweet love letter,

Oh, so far away she has forgot me at all I'm afraid.
Fall coming I'll lie alone on the cool pillow of jade.

❋❋❋❋❋❋❋❋❋❋❋❋❋❋❋❋❋❋

## 生 查 子

金鞭美少年,去跃青骢马。牵系玉楼人,绣被春寒夜。消息未归来,寒食梨花谢。无处说相思,背面秋千下。

### Tune: Mountain Hawthorn

With a golden whip the handsome lad
Rode his green and white horse so fast.
The young man is in her heart and mind all the time,
With silk quilt on a lonely bed she feels cold at night.

She hasn't got any letter from him anyway,
Cold Food Day gone, pear blossoms fade.
To whom can she confide her love for her sweetheart so deep?
She stands by the swing where she played with a skirt in glee.

❋❋❋❋❋❋❋❋❋❋❋❋❋❋❋❋❋❋

## 浣 溪 沙

日日双眉斗画长。行云飞絮共轻狂。不将心嫁冶游郎。 溅酒滴残歌扇字,弄花熏得舞衣香。一春弹泪说凄凉。

### *Tune: Silk-Washing Stream*

Day after day with great care I draw my brows.
I'm like flying fickle catkins and floating clouds,
But anyhow I will never get married to a fickle prodigal.

At the feast wine splashes on my fan blurring lines on it,
The flowers on my head send the scent to my dancing dress.
In the whole spring telling my feelings, desolate tunes I play.

## 浣 溪 沙

唱得红梅字字香,柳枝桃叶尽深藏。遏云声里送离觞。 才听便拚衣袖湿,欲歌先倚黛眉长。曲终敲损燕钗梁。

晏几道

## Tune: Silk-Washing Stream

She sings the song "Red Plum", making every word full of refreshing scent,
Others' songs like "Willow Twigs" and "Peach Leaves" are cast into the shade.
The songs rise to stop clouds to see the traveller off at the feast.

Hearing her first sound, he sheds tears wetting his green sleeves,
Before singing, she drew her brows like long distant hills,
He beats time with her hairpin and at song's end breaks it.

❀❀❀❀❀❀❀❀❀❀❀❀❀❀❀

## 鹧 鸪 天

十里楼台倚翠微。百花深处杜鹃啼。殷勤自与行人语,不似流莺取次飞。　　惊梦觉,弄晴时。声声只道不如归。天涯岂是无归意,争奈归期未可期。

## Tune: Partridge Sky

Against green hills lean storied buildings of ten miles,
In the depth of the flowers in bloom the cuckoo cries.

It again and again talks to travellers with affection deep,
Unlike the orioles flying freely indifferent to the people.

When fine I'm awakened by the cuckoo alone:
"You'd better go home. You'd better go home."
I know, I hate staying in this remote place,
But I have not decided the returning date.

❀❀❀❀❀❀❀❀❀❀❀❀❀❀❀❀❀

## 蝶 恋 花

欲减罗衣寒未去,不卷珠帘,人在深深处。残杏枝头花几许。啼红正恨清明雨。　　尽日沉烟香一缕。宿酒醒迟,恼破春情绪。远信还因归燕误。小屏风上西江路。

### June: Butterflies in Love with Flowers

Cold remaining, I give up the idea of wearing less clothes of silk,
As sleeping in the spring breeze the pearly curtain hangs low still,
In the green brothel I stay deep in the boudoir alone.
Few apricot blossoms remain on twigs with sorrow,
Fading red shedding tears is afraid of coming Clear and Bright rains.

The eaglewood incense burns on quiet and lonely the whole lone day,
I awake very late from wine last night,
Spring sadness fills my heart and mind.
The swallows hurry home forgetting a letter from my dear sweet,
I watch the road along the west river he will appear on the screen.

❋❋❋❋❋❋❋❋❋❋❋❋❋❋❋❋

## 留 春 令

画屏天畔,梦回依约,十洲云水。手撚红笺寄人书,写无限伤春事。　　别浦高楼曾漫倚。对江南千里。楼下分流水声中,有当日凭高泪。

### Tune: Song Inviting Spring to Stay

The scenery on the painted screen seems in the remotest place,
From a short intoxicating spring dream, I am gradually awake,
I dimly remember the flying clouds and flowing water in fairyland.
The pieces of pink paper filled with words of love are in my hand,
The letter to be sent to the celestial being
Is full of the unbearable sorrow of spring.

By the river mouth in the building high

With heartbroken grief we said good-bye.
Now I lean through the railings of the building alone,
Looking into a thousand miles of the south with woe.
Before it in the gurgling water drear,
Remain that morn my bloody tears.

❀❀❀❀❀❀❀❀❀❀❀❀❀❀

## 河 满 子

绿绮琴中心事,齐纨扇上时光。五陵年少浑薄倖,轻如曲水飘香。夜夜魂消梦峡,年年泪尽啼湘。 归雁行边远字,惊莺舞处离肠。蕙楼多少铅华在,从来错倚红妆。可羡邻姬十五,金钗早嫁王昌。

### *Tune: Sad Song*

With the green figured zither and silk fan,
She expresses in detail her feelings so sad.
Most of rich dandies are frivolous
Like the flowers on flowing water.
Night after night she wakes up from tragic dreams,
Year by year she exhausts her bloody tears of grief.

The wild geese forming a character return with no letter from her dear,

In the heart-shaped mirror, seeing her fading face, she feels quite drear.

Many beauties in brothels heavily rouged and powdered with green clothing

Regret greatly day and night wasting charming scented time of early spring.

She admires her neighbor, a fifteen years old intoxicating girl,

Marrying a rich man and enjoying so happy a life in the world.

# 王观(1035—1100)

宋仁宗嘉祐二年(1057)进士。做过翰林学士。皇上宴请后妃,令其作词,以写欢乐之情。他奉诏当场作《清平乐》词,描写皇上的愚蠢和放纵。太后一眼看出词中对皇上的亵渎之意,叫儿子次日将其赶出宫门。其后他自称为"逐客"。

**Wang Guan(1035 - 1100)**

He passed the highest imperial examination in 1057. He was a court official. Once the emperor gave a banquet to his concubines, asking him to write a *Ci* poem about pleasant atmosphere, he composed the *Ci* poem "Music for the Peaceful Time" on the spot. He described a fatuous and self-indulgent ruler. Knowing he was insulting the emperor, the mother of the emperor drove him out of the court. Later he called himself "a driven guest".

## 卜 算 子

### 送鲍浩然之浙东

水是眼波横,山是眉峰聚。欲问行人去那边?眉眼盈盈处。
才始送春归,又送君归去。若到江南赶上春,千万和春住。

王 观

## June: Song of Divination

Seeing a friend off who is going back in the east Zhejiang, I apply the words of a wife missing her husband far away.

The sparkling clear spring water is her eyes,
Her knitted brows are hills green and high.
My dear friend, really I want to ask where you are going now?
The place the beauty stays in with clear eyes and knitted brows.

I just see off with sorrow the charming spring,
Again I'll watch you leaving with tears falling.
If you catch up with spring in the south of the Yangtze River,
You must live with it, the beauty, in your tender heart forever.

❈❈❈❈❈❈❈❈❈❈❈❈❈❈❈

## 庆清朝慢

### 踏　青

调雨为酥,催冰做水,东君分付春还。何人便将轻暖,点破残寒。结伴踏青去好,平头鞋子小双鸾。烟郊外,望中秀色,如有无间。　　晴则个,阴则个,饾饤得天气有许多般。须教镂花拨柳,争要先看。不道吴绫绣袜,香泥斜沁几行斑。东风巧,尽收翠绿,吹在眉山。

## Tune: Slow Song of Celebrating the Good Dynasty

### Taking an Outing in the Country in Spring

Into sweet dew the rain is made,
Clean water the ice is changed.
Spring god asks it to return anywhere.
First of all who presents the warm air
To drive away the remaining severe cold?
Girls in company for a spring outing go,
They wear shoes embroidered with pairs of lovebirds.
The silk-like mist hangs over the green distant suburb,
They try to appreciate the scene but can't see it clear,
For a moment it appears and for another it disappears.

Now it is sunny,
Now it is cloudy,
The weather changes all the time.
The girls of early spring all try
Their best to first smell red flowers and kiss green willow leaves.
Their tender legs all of a sudden stick to the earth soft and sweet,
Lines of mud appear on their socks colored.
The vigorous soft spring breeze is so clever,

王　观

It gathers all the green around,
Blowing it on the girls' brows.

❀❀❀❀❀❀❀❀❀❀❀❀❀❀❀

## 清　平　乐

黄金殿里,烛影双龙戏。劝得官家真个醉,进酒犹呼万岁。　　折旋舞彻《伊州》。君恩与整搔头。一夜御前宣住,六宫多少人愁。

### Tune: Music for a Peaceful Time

In the deep court golden and fragrant,
In the light of two candles, as dragons,
The emperor and a concubine dance cheerfully.
She urges him to drink until he gets drunk a bit,
Each time she presents wine, saying "Long Live".

She begins dancing "Yizhou" in rhythm quick and light.
He strokes so gently her sweet jade hairpins with delight,
And asks her in a soft voice to accompany him tonight.
Six palaces fill with woe of jealousy of the concubines.

## 张舜民(生卒年不详)

宋英宗治平二年(1065)进士。曾为朝廷高官。后被放逐。此词写于贬谪路上,表达其痛愤之情。其工诗文,亦能词,但存词甚少。

**Zhang Shunmin(years of birth and death unknown)**

He passed the highest imperial examination in 1065. He once served as a senior court official in the capital. The poem was written on the way when he was banished from the court to a remote area expressing his pain and hatred. He was good at composing poetry and prose as well as Ci poems, but only a few Ci poems are extant.

### 卖 花 声

#### 题 岳 阳 楼

木叶下君山。空水漫漫。十分斟酒敛芳颜。不是渭城西去客,休唱《阳关》。　醉袖抚危阑。天淡云闲。何人此路得生还。回首夕阳红尽处,应是长安。

张舜民

## Tune: Song of Peddling Flowers

Ascending the gate tower of Yueyang City,
I wrote the *Ci* poem.

The leaves of trees shower down on the Jun Mountains,
To the distant sky flows the vast Dongting Lake water.
The pretty songstress fills a cup of wine for me drear.
As a demoted official, I won't go to the west frontier,
Please don't sing the Yang Pass, the sad song parting.

Drunk, I lean through the railings of the high building,
In the wide sky leisurely white clouds fly.
From this road who can come back alive?
Turning, I look at the end of the setting sun again and again,
It should be our flourishing capital I think of night and day.

# 魏夫人(生卒年不详)

北宋丞相曾布之妻。人们喜欢她的词就像喜欢李清照、秦观和黄庭坚的词一样。他们的词风相近。

**Madame Wei (years of birth and death unknown)**

She was the wife of Zeng Bu, a prime minister in the Northern Song Dynasty. In popularity, she could compare with Li Qingzhao, Qin Guan and Huang Tingjian. Her style was akin to theirs.

## 菩 萨 蛮

溪山掩映斜阳里,楼台影动鸳鸯起。隔岸两三家,出墙红杏花。
绿杨堤下路,早晚溪边去。三见柳绵飞,离人犹未归。

## *Tune: Buddhist Dancers*

The stream and hills far and near are bathing in the setting sun,
The shadows of the towers moving, pairs of phoenixes start up.
Along the banks lie two or three lone cots,
Out of the high wall climbs a pink apricot.

魏夫人

A path winds its way under weeping willow trees,
Along it I walk to the stream in the morn and eve.
I have seen the willow catkins fly away three times,
But my dear lover has not yet returned to my side.

❈❈❈❈❈❈❈❈❈❈❈❈❈❈❈

## 点 绛 唇

波上清风,画船明月人归后。渐消残酒,独自凭栏久。聚散匆匆,此恨年年有。重回首,淡烟疏柳,隐隐芜城漏。

### *Tune: Rouged Lips*

The cool and refreshing breeze blows over the flowing water,
Under the bright moon, he takes a painted boat to the distance.
Awake gradually from strong wine,
I alone lean on the rails a long time.

Oh, always so short are our happy meetings,
Year by year I have heartbreaking partings.
I turn and gaze at the lone and sad ferry with grief,
Over the two lines of sparse weeping willow trees,
Hangs a thin mist with a frown, and from Yangzhou City
Comes the moans of the drum of a watchman very faintly.

## 好 事 近

雨后晓寒轻,花外早莺啼歇。愁听隔溪残漏,正一声凄咽。　　不堪西望去程赊,离肠万回结。不似海棠阴下,按《凉州》时节。

### Tune: Happiness Approaching

After a rain it is a little bit cold in the early morning,
Beyond the flowers the young orioles stop twittering.
Across the creek comes the sound of a drum
Announcing dawn like a miserable sob just.

I can't bear to look at the road along which he went to the west,
Oh, for it would make my tender heart and mind filled with pain.
I remember we sat under crab-apples so happy,
Playing "Liangzhou", the desolate frontier music.

❁❁❁❁❁❁❁❁❁❁❁❁❁❁❁❁❁

## 卷 珠 帘

记得来时春未暮,执手攀花,袖染花梢露。暗卜春心共花语,争寻双朵争先去。　　多情因甚相辜负,轻拆轻离,欲向谁分诉。泪湿海棠花枝处,东君空把奴分付。

魏夫人

## June: Rolling up the Pearly Curtain

The spring was not late when we came here,
Together we plucked the flowers with cheer,
And our sleeves were wet with the dewdrops from the twigs.
Whispering to the flowers, I divined my destiny of marriage,
We vied in finding the twin flowers in one stalk.

Why has he forgotten my sweet true love at all?
Without sorrow he so easily left me,
To whom can I confide all my grief?
My tears wet the branches of the crab-apples,
Why does the god of spring make me so sad?

# 王诜(1048—1104)

娶宋英宗女魏国大长公主,为驸马都尉。善诗词、书法,其词清丽,情致缠绵。

**Wang Shen(1048 – 1104)**

He married a daughter of the emperor and served as a court official. He was good at poems and calligraphy. The words of his *Ci* poems were clear and sweet, expressing abiding affection.

## 忆 故 人

烛影摇红,向夜阑,乍酒醒、心情懒。尊前谁为唱《阳关》,离恨天涯远。　　无奈云沉雨散。凭阑干、东风泪眼。海棠开后,燕子来时,黄昏庭院。

## Tune: Thinking of the Old Friend

A candle shakes its red flame,
The night is already very late.
Just awake from good wine,
I'm still drowsy and tired.

Why did I sing the farewell song sadly for you at the dinner?
My parting grief followed you all the way to a remote corner.

I sigh sadly:"You had to leave me in this brothel with grief."
I lean on railings gazing at distant grass like your robe green,
And in the breeze shedding tears drop by drop.
The petals of crab-apples shower by shower fall,
The pair of swallows has come back here,
The courtyard lies at dusk quiet and drear.

❀❀❀❀❀❀❀❀❀❀❀❀❀❀❀❀❀❀

## 人 月 圆

### 元 夕

小桃枝上春来早,初试薄罗衣。年年此夜,华灯盛照,人月圆时。禁街箫鼓,寒轻夜永,纤手同携。更阑人静,千门笑语,声在帘帏。

## June: Reunion under the Full Moon

### On the Night of the Lantern Festival

Oh, the spring is still early,
Peaches blossom on twigs,
To wear silk clothes I try.

Oh, year after year, tonight,

Lanterns of different colors and shapes brighten any place,

The moon is full and people have reunions happy and gay.

Pipes and drums sound anywhere in capital streets,

Slight is the cold and endless the night seems to be.

Here and there the lovers stroll arm in arm.

When it is late the streets lie quiet and calm,

All the families still talk and laugh at home loud,

Of green curtains the pleasant sounds come out.

## 蝶 恋 花

小雨初晴回晚照。金翠楼台,倒影芙蓉沼。杨柳垂垂风袅袅。嫩荷无数青钿小。 似此园林无限好。流落归来,到了心情少。坐到黄昏人悄悄。更应添得朱颜老。

## Tune: Butterflies in Love with Flowers

After a drizzle it's fine and appears glow of evening.

All the golden resplendent and magnificent buildings

Are reflected in the clear water of the lotus pool.

The willows in the gentle breeze dance graceful,

On the water float countless lotus leaves like coins green.

In my beautiful garden lies leisurely the brocade-like scene.
I return after a wandering career,
And I have no happy mood here.
Until dusk I sit alone,
And I find I grow old.

## 苏轼(1037—1101)

宋仁宗嘉祐二年(1057)进士,欧阳修为考官。时称老师。曾为京官。因反对王安石的政治改革,多次被贬而任杭州、扬州等地的地方官。在扬州,他很幸运,就住在欧阳修建的平山堂。他们两人都在那儿写过不朽的词作。他是宋代首屈一指的词人,词风豪放、清雅。其中两首词最负盛名。一首是《念奴娇》,前两行为:"大江东去,浪淘尽,千古风流人物。"另一首是《水调歌头》,前两行是:"明月几时有?把酒问青天。"

**Su Shi(1037 – 1101)**

He passed the highest imperial examination with Ouyang Xiu as his examiner in 1057, called teacher in ancient times. Opposing Wang Anshi's political reforms, many times he was demoted from the court to some areas as an official such as Hangzhou, Yangzhou and so on. In Yangzhou, he was lucky enough to live in Ouyang xiu's Pingshan Hall, where they composed many immortal *Ci* poems. He was the best poet in the Song Dynasty. His style was mainly powerful and free, and elegant. Two of his *Ci* poems were the most famous. One was "Charm of a Maiden Singer", beginning with the lines "The Yangtze flows east into the sea great, /Its huge clear surging waves taking away/Oh, the great heroes in all the times." The other was "Prelude to Water Melody", beginning with the lines "When did the moon begin to shine in the sky?/I ask the blue sky holding a cup of good wine?"

## 西 江 月

春夜行蕲水中,过酒家饮,酒醉,乘月至一溪桥上,解鞍曲肱少休。及觉,已晓。乱山葱茏,疑非尘世也。书此词桥柱。

照野弥弥浅浪,横空隐隐层霄。障泥未解玉骢骄,我欲醉眠芳草。　　可惜一溪风月,莫教踏碎琼瑶。解鞍欹枕绿杨桥,杜宇一声春晓。

### Tune: The Moon over the West River

At night getting drunk at home, I rode a horse to a bridge across the Xi stream where I dismounted to have a rest. Awake, I saw green on the mountains all over. I suspect I entered a fairyland. I wrote the *Ci* poem on the posts of the bridge.

On the gurgling creek in the fields the moon shines,
The pale clouds appear indistinct in the bright sky.
The horse stands raising its head with its saddle,
But I want to sleep drunk in the fragrant grass.

How beautiful is the creek with the bright moon and cool breeze,

How can I let the horse tread the grass and water like jade green?
The saddle as a pillow, under green willows I lie on the bridge,
When I am waked up by a cuckoo, it is spring daybreak already.

❈❈❈❈❈❈❈❈❈❈❈❈❈❈❈❈

## 念 奴 娇

### 赤 壁 怀 古

大江东去,浪淘尽,千古风流人物。故垒西边,人道是、三国周郎赤壁。乱石穿空,惊涛拍岸,卷起千堆雪。江山如画,一时多少豪杰。　遥想公瑾当年,小乔初嫁了,雄姿英发。羽扇纶巾,谈笑间、樯橹灰飞烟灭。故国神游,多情应笑我,早生华发。人生如梦,一樽还酹江月。

## Tune: Charm of a Maiden Singer

### At the Red Cliff, Thinking of the Past

The Yangtze flows east into the sea great,
Its huge clear surging waves taking away
Oh, the great heroes in all the times.
At the west the old battle field lies,
Point near with great respect some white-haired natives:
"It is the Red Cliff General Zhou defeated strong enemy."
Into the flying white clouds penetrate the crags,

苏　轼

The big raging waves threaten to break the banks,
Thousands of heaps of the snow up and down rolling.
The green mountains and river seem to be in a painting,
Here is a stage where performed so many heroes.

So clearly I remember, the famous general Zhou
Just married the most beautiful lady, Qiao junior.
So young at that time he was heroic and valiant.
Taking a feather fan and wearing a green silk scarf,
With many subordinates he loud talked and laughed,
He defeated the enemy by burning their boats down.
Here with great interest visiting the old battle ground,
I laugh at my sentiment about failure and success
Oh, making my black hair too early turn grey.
Life is so short just as a dream.
Lifting a cup of wine with grief,
I drink to the shining moon and the turbulent Yangtze River,
I envy them seeing the heroes and beauty in Three Kingdoms.

✿✿✿✿✿✿✿✿✿✿✿✿✿✿✿✿✿✿

## 浣 溪 沙

簌簌衣巾落枣花,村南村北响缫车,牛衣古柳卖黄瓜。酒困路长惟欲睡,日高人渴漫思茶,敲门试问野人家。

## Tune: Silk-Washing Stream

Rustling, rustling, the jujube flowers shower on my scarf and clothes,
Over the south and north of the village, spinning wheels' sounds float,
A peasant is selling cucumbers, on an old willow half leaning.

On the long and long trip, sleepier and sleepier I am becoming,
I'm also getting thirsty with the hot sun rising so high,
I knock at the door asking a villager for tea of any kind.

❀❀❀❀❀❀❀❀❀❀❀❀❀❀❀

## 浣 溪 沙

游蕲水清泉寺，寺临兰溪，溪水西流

山下兰芽短浸溪，松间沙路净无泥。萧萧暮雨子规啼。 谁道人生无再少？门前流水尚能西。休将白发唱黄鸡。

## Tune: Silk-Washing Stream
### Visiting a Temple Facing a West-Flowing Stream

At the foot of the hill the young orchid buds spread to the green

creek,
So clean without mud is the sandy path winding through the pine trees.
The cuckoos sing with delight in the pattering evening rain.

Who says old people can't return to blooming youth again?
The water before Clear Spring Temple can flow westward.
Don't moan and sigh for your white hair and face withered.

❈❈❈❈❈❈❈❈❈❈❈❈❈❈❈❈❈❈

## 浣 溪 沙

### 咏 橘

菊暗荷枯一夜霜,新苞绿叶照林光,竹篱茅舍出青黄。 香雾噀人惊半破,清泉流齿怯初尝,吴姬三日手犹香。

## June: Silk-Washing Stream

### Ode to the Tangerine

After a night frost the chrysanthemums and lotuses wither,
The yellow oranges and their green leaves set off each other,
In the yellow and green, the bamboo fences and thatched cots are seen dimly.

A girl in the south of the Yangtze peals an orange and sprays scented mist,
The cold sour juice begins to flows through her teeth,
After three days her hands still have fragrance sweet.

❋❋❋❋❋❋❋❋❋❋❋❋❋❋❋❋❋

## 浣 溪 沙

元丰七年十二月二十四日,从泗州刘倩叔游南山。

细雨斜风作晓寒,淡烟疏柳媚晴滩。入淮清洛渐漫漫。　雪沫乳花浮午盏,蓼茸蒿笋试春盘。人间有味是清欢。

### Tune: Silk-Washing Stream

On the way to the place of my office, with a friend I toured the South Mountain on the 24th day of the 12th month in the seventh year of Yuanfeng (1084).

With a fine rain and slanting wind in the early morn, it's a bit cold.
A thin mist floats when the sun rises over the bankside sparse willows,
The spring scene here is so beautiful and fragrant.
The clear Luo Stream joins the muddy Huai River,
The vast turbid water flows to the high sky.

苏 轼

With the scented afternoon tea milk-white
And different dishes sweet
of spring vegetables green,
I enjoy the life so simple.
It's a life delicious really.

❀❀❀❀❀❀❀❀❀❀❀❀❀❀❀

## 浣 溪 沙
### 春 情

道字娇讹苦未成。未应春阁梦多情。朝来何事绿鬟倾。 彩索身轻长趁燕,红窗睡重不闻莺。困人天气近清明。

## Tune: Silk-Washing Stream
### Stirring of Love

Just like a spoiled pretty little girl, she speaks not clear,
In her chamber she is too young to dream of her dear.
Why is her pitch-black hair in the morning so fluffy?

Like a swallow she plays on the colored swing lively,
Sleeping sound behind the window, she doesn't hear orioles sing with delight,
It is drowsy in the scented spring, near warm comfortable Clear

and Bright.

�֍֍֍֍֍֍֍֍֍֍֍֍֍֍֍֍֍֍

## 定 风 波

三月七日,沙湖道中遇雨。雨具先去,同行皆狼狈,余独不觉。已而遂晴,故作此词。

莫听穿林打叶声,何妨吟啸且徐行。竹杖芒鞋轻胜马,谁怕?一蓑烟雨任平生。　料峭春风吹酒醒,微冷,山头斜照却相迎。回首向来萧瑟处,归去,也无风雨也无晴。

### *Tune: Calming Disturbance*

On the 7th day of the 3rd month, on the way back from the Sha Lake, we were caught in a rain. Without rain gear, others' clothes were wet through. I paid no attention to it. Soon rain stopped and the sun came out. I wrote the *Ci* poem.

Don't listen to a rain beating the branches and leaves of the trees,
Why not recite poems while I'm going on leisurely and carefree?
With a bamboo stick and straw shoes I feel better than on a horse,
And with an old raincoat of straw on earth I have no fear at all,
Through mist and rain I can live a whole life.

苏　轼

Early spring wind blows me awake from wine,
I feel a bit chilly, but I am greeted
By the slanting sun over the hills.
Turning to gaze at the near place
Where I met the wind and rain.
Oh, to my thatched cottage with satisfaction I return,
Caring neither rain nor wind, nor shine in the world.

❊❊❊❊❊❊❊❊❊❊❊❊❊❊❊❊❊❊

## 临 江 仙

### 夜 归 临 皋

夜饮东坡醒复醉，归来仿佛三更。家童鼻息已雷鸣。敲门都不应，倚杖听江声。　　长恨此身非我有，何时忘却营营？夜阑风静縠纹平。小舟从此逝，江海寄馀生。

## Tune: Immortals by the River

### Drunk, with a stick I am coming back home.

On the eastern slope I get drunk, awake I again drink wine,
When slowly coming back home I feel it is nearly midnight.
Sleeping sound, the houseboy loudly snores.
I knock at the door but I get no answer at all,
I lean on a bamboo stick by the river, listening to surging waves.

In all my life I hate so much I cannot at all control my own fate,
When can I get away wealth and fame from my heart completely?
The wind calming down and ripples lying even, the night is still.
Today taking a little boat, the dusty world I'll forever leave
To spend the last days easy and leisurely by rivers and sea.

❀❀❀❀❀❀❀❀❀❀❀❀❀❀❀❀

## 少 年 游

润州作,代人寄远

去年相送,余杭门外,飞雪似杨花。今年春尽,杨花似雪,犹不见还家。 对酒卷帘邀明月,风露透窗纱。恰似姮娥怜双燕,分明照、画梁斜。

## Tune: Travelling While Young

In Runzhou (Zhenjiang), I wrote the *Ci* poem with the words of a wife missing her husband far away.

I still remember clearly I saw him off drear
Out of the gate of Hangzhou city last year,
The snow was like catkins flying.
Gone is this intoxicating spring,
The flying willow catkins are like snow,

苏　轼

But so far still he hasn't come back home.

Rolling up the red curtain and holding a cup of wine,
I invite the cool and sweet moon to come to my side.
However, the window gauze, the wind and dew get through,
And showing love to the pair of swallows, the tender moon
Sheds slanting light at ease
On the painted green beam.

## 鹧 鸪 天

林断山明竹隐墙,乱蝉衰草小池塘。翻空白鸟时时见,照水红蕖细细香。　村舍外,古城旁,杖藜徐步转斜阳。殷勤昨夜三更雨,又得浮生一日凉。

## June: Partridge Sky

At the wood end the mountain leans on the sky clearly,
The thick fresh bamboos hide the old red walls dimly,
The cicadas chirp in withered grass by the pond green,
The pairs of white birds fly high and low at their ease,
On the water, faint scent the red lotuses give off.

Under the fading sun beyond the lone village cots,
By the city small and old,
with a wood stick I stroll.
Oh, the kind heaven fell a shower at midnight,
Giving a cool and sweet day to my drifting life.

## 蝶 恋 花

花褪残红青杏小。燕子飞时,绿水人家绕。枝上柳绵吹又少。天涯何处无芳草。　　墙里秋千墙外道。墙外行人,墙里佳人笑。笑渐不闻声渐悄,多情却被无情恼。

## Tune: Butterflies in Love with Flowers

The red flowers fall and green apricot fruits hide in leaves.
The pairs of swallows far and near fly so easy and carefree,
Around the lonely village the clear green water in high glee flows.
The breeze blows catkins away, fewer and fewer left on willows,
Everywhere fragrant grass grows under the vast sky.

Inside the wall sways a swing and a path lies outside.
Leisurely a traveller strolls on the path,
While on the swing a pretty girl laughs.

苏　轼

Oh, though the intoxicating sweet laughter slowly goes away,
The unintentional laugh makes love surge in his heart in vain.

❋❋❋❋❋❋❋❋❋❋❋❋❋❋❋❋❋

## 蝶　恋　花

记得画屏初会遇。好梦惊回，望断高唐路。燕子双飞来又去。纱窗几度春光暮。　　那日绣帘相见处。低眼佯行，笑整香云缕。敛尽春山羞不语。人前深意难轻诉。

### Tune: Butterflies in Love with Flowers

I still remember we met between the painted screens.
All of a sudden our love stopped like a broken dream,
Though missing her day and night since then I haven't even once seen her.
The pair of swallows on the beam comes in spring and leaves in fall by turns,
Several times the screens see the charming spring passing away.

I'll never forget I saw her between the beautiful screens that day.
Though pretending to be leaving,
She tidied her hair while smiling.
She knitted her brows like distant spring hills, out of shyness.

How could she confide her love to a man as a young beauty?

## 江 城 子

墨云拖雨过西楼,水东流,晚烟收,柳外残阳,回照动帘钩。今夜巫山真个好,花未落,酒新篘。　　美人微笑转星眸,月花羞。捧金瓯。歌扇萦风,吹散一春愁。试问江南诸伴侣,谁似我,醉扬州。

### Tune: A Riverside Town

The dark clouds pull the rain past the west chamber.
The clear and green water murmurs happy eastward,
The thin mist disappears in the eve.
The setting sun beyond willow trees
Sheds light on the silver hook on the scented curtains shining.
Tonight my beauty like a fairy maiden looks so intoxicating,
The flowers are in full bloom,
The newly made wine is good.

While smiling, she turns her right and left enchanting eyes,
Before her feel ashamed the pretty flowers and moon bright.
She raises the cup filled with wine to me with cheer again and again,
Singing, she waves her scented fan blowing my spring sorrow away.

苏　轼

My friends in the southern land,
From my deep heart now I ask:
"Who is as happy as I getting drunk in
Beautiful and flourishing Yangzhou City?"

❋❋❋❋❋❋❋❋❋❋❋❋❋❋❋❋❋

## 江 城 子

### 乙卯正月二十日夜记梦

十年生死两茫茫。不思量,自难忘。千里孤坟,无处话凄凉。纵使相逢应不识,尘满面,鬓如霜。　夜来幽梦忽还乡,小轩窗,正梳妆。相顾无言,惟有泪千行。料得年年肠断处:明月夜,短松冈。

## June: A Riverside Town

### On the 20th Day of the 1st Month in the Year Yi-mao(1075): A Dream at Night

For ten years there is no message between the living and dead.
Although my wife I deeply love I do not very often recollect,
I cannot at all forget her flower-like face.
Her lone tomb lies a thousand miles away,
To whom can I confide my desolation and grief?
We won't know each other even one day we meet,

Dust covers my face wrinkled wholly,
My hair at the temples becomes frosty.

In a dream before the mirror, she is smartly dressing,
We look at each other, into our hearts words flowing,
From our faces fall a thousand lines of tears.
Oh, I'm sure she is heartbroken year by year,
On the moonlit night she left sadly my side,
On the mound growing the sparse short pines.

## 江 城 子

### 别 徐 州

天涯流落思无穷！既相逢,却匆匆。携手佳人,和泪折残红。为问东风余几许？春纵在,与谁同！　　隋堤三月水溶溶。背归鸿,去吴中。回首彭城,清泗与淮通。欲寄相思千点泪,流不到,楚江东。

## *Tune: A Riverside Town*

### Saying Good-bye to Xuzhou

I wander far away from home, countless, my thoughts.
It is lucky here we have a happy meeting very short,

苏　轼

Then in a hurry I am ready to far leave.
Holding a hand of the beauty so sweet,
With tears on a tree I pluck a remaining flower red.
I ask myself how much warm spring breeze is left,
Oh, even the intoxicating spring still stays here,
With whom can I appreciate the scene this year?

Beside the Sui Dyke is green water rising.
Against the swan geese homeward flying,
To the south of the Yangtze I'm on a journey.
Turning round again and again so melancholy,
I see dimly, so far to the long Huai River the clear Si River flows.
I ask the Si River to take her my thousands of teardrops of sorrow,
But it can never arrive at my sweetheart' side,
It flows east, the opposite direction I realize.

❋❋❋❋❋❋❋❋❋❋❋❋❋❋❋❋❋❋❋

## 诉 衷 情

### 琵 琶 女

小莲初上琵琶弦,弹破碧云天。分明绣阁幽恨,都向曲中传。
肤莹玉,鬓梳蝉,绮窗前。素娥今夜,故故随人,似斗婵娟。

## Tune: Baring the Heart

### A Beauty Playing Pipa

Little Lotus plucked pipa's strings with fingers snow-white,
Then the clear and melodious music flying to the high sky.
Clearly she reveals her deep sorrow
Through her tune newly composed.

Her tender skin looks like jade sparkling,
Her hair is combed like a cicada's wings.
Before the window so beautiful,
The moon tonight with jealousy
All the time everywhere closely follows her
To compare with her in beauty in the world.

❈❈❈❈❈❈❈❈❈❈❈❈❈❈❈❈❈

## 定 风 波

常羡人间琢玉郎,天教分付点酥娘。自作清歌传皓齿,风起,雪飞炎海变清凉。 万里归来年愈少,微笑,笑时犹带岭梅香。试问岭南应不好,却道,此心安处是吾乡。

苏　轼

## Tune: Calming Disturbance

I admire you, a handsome man with lovesickness,
Or, heaven offers you the clever and deft beauty.
Through her teeth flows out fresh songs of her own,
All of a sudden the cold wind begins to hard blow,
Flying snow makes the hot south of Dayu Mountains a cool place.

She comes back home looking much younger thousands of *li* away,
While smiling to us with intoxicating sweet charm,
Her mouth gives forth scent of the mountain grass.
"Do you think it's a lonesome region?"
To my surprise, she at once answers:
"There I feel
Quite at ease."

❈❈❈❈❈❈❈❈❈❈❈❈❈❈❈❈

## 定 风 波

### 红　梅

好睡慵开莫厌迟。自怜冰脸不时宜。偶作小红桃杏色,闲雅,尚余孤瘦雪霜姿。　　休把闲心随物态,何事,酒生微晕沁瑶肌。诗老不知梅格在,吟咏,更看绿叶与青枝。

## June: Calming Disturbance

### The Red Plum

Don't blame the red plum for opening late, she is sleeping soundly.
Realizing her icy face is not at all compatible with the times totally,
Occasionally like the peach and apricot, she displays red appearance.
However, all the time she remains her bearing so leisurely and elegant,
Of quality of aloofness and arrogance of ice, she still boasts.

She never with worldly way changes her heart lone and noble,
Maybe it's wine that makes her jade-like face flush.
A famous poet does not know the quality of the plum,
Oh, it is a pity in some of his well-known poems by mistake he believes
Different from the peach and apricot she has no green twigs and leaves.

## 阮 郎 归

### 初 夏

绿槐高柳咽新蝉,薰风初入弦。碧纱窗下水沉烟,棋声惊昼眠。
微雨过,小荷翻。榴花开欲燃。玉盆纤手弄清泉,琼珠碎却圆。

苏　轼

## June: Return of the Lover

### Early Summer

The young cicadas stop singing in the high willows and green locust trees,
In the distance floats the melodious and gentle music of the South Breeze.
Inside the green window screen the smoke of eaglewood incense slow rises,
In the afternoon a young beauty in sweet dream is waked by chess pieces.

Now, a light drizzle stops just,
The little lotus leaves turn up,
The pomegranates in blossom seem to be burning.
She stretches her snow-white scented hand, playing
With the clear water in the little sparkling basin of jade,
On the lotus leaves waterdrops are pearls, easy to break.

❈❈❈❈❈❈❈❈❈❈❈❈❈❈❈❈❈❈❈

## 点　绛　唇

红杏飘香，柳含烟翠拖轻缕。水边朱户。尽卷黄昏雨。　　烛影摇风,一枕伤春绪。归不去。凤楼何处。芳草迷归路。

## Tune: Rouged Lips

The pink apricot blossoms give off pleasant faint scent,
The green willows contain thin mist and pull silk threads.
The red gate stands near
The water gurgling drear.
The beauty rolls up the curtains with grief
Seeing a shower shedding tears in the eve.

The candlelight shaking, on the pillow I fill with sorrow of spring,
We seem separated by vast green grasses and long streams flowing.
Where is at present her warm fragrant boudoir?
In the sweet grasses I lose my way to her arms.

## 洞 仙 歌

冰肌玉骨,自清凉无汗。水殿风来暗香满。绣帘开,一点明月窥人,人未寝,欹枕钗横鬓乱。　起来携素手,庭户无声,时见疏星渡河汉。试问夜如何？夜已三更,金波淡,玉绳低转。但屈指西风几时来,又不道流年暗中偷换。

苏 轼

## Tune: Song of Immortals in the Cavern

With skin like ice and jade
She is cool without sweat.
A breeze fills the hall by the water with fragrance.
Up rolled is the beautifully-embroidered curtain,
The tender bright moonlight seems coming in,
Bathing the beauty in scented dew awake still,
Disheveled is her hair with a slanting pin on the pillow.

Getting up, hand in hand the beauty and I leisurely stroll,
Quite and still is the courtyard full of charm,
Now and then stars cross the Milk Way fast.
Watching the sky long I wonder what is the time now,
Thrice a watchman has beaten a drum, midnight about.
Fading seems to be the moonlight,
Sleepy feels Plough in the east sky.
Counting days, we ask ourselves:"When will west wind come here?"
But with flowing water unnoticed our precious youth will disappear.

## 望 江 南

### 超 然 台 作

春未老,风细柳斜斜。试上超然台上看,半壕春水一城花。烟雨暗千家。　寒食后,酒醒却咨嗟。休对故人思故国,且将新火试新茶。诗酒趁年华。

## Tune: Looking in the Direction of the South of the Yangtze River

### Climbing up the Aloof Platform

The beautiful and fragrant spring is not at all old,
In gentle breeze sway slanting the twigs of willows.
I climb up the Aloof Platform to appreciate the scenery wonderful,
The city fills with flowers and in half the moat flows spring water,
Thousands of roofs are in a misty rain.

Gone so far away is Cold Food Day,
Awake from wine, now and then I groan and sigh.
Don't talk hometown for I can't bear grief I realize,
I just use new fire to make the fresh tea in high glee.
Drink and compose poems to enjoy gay time, please.

苏　轼

## 水调歌头

丙辰中秋,欢饮达旦,大醉,作此篇。兼怀子由

明月几时有?把酒问青天。不知天上宫阙,今夕是何年。我欲乘风归去,又恐琼楼玉宇,高处不胜寒。起舞弄清影,何似在人间!　转朱阁,低绮户,照无眠。不应有恨,何事长向别时圆?人有悲欢离合,月有阴晴圆缺,此事古难全。但愿人长久,千里共婵娟。

### Tune: Prelude to Water Melody

At the Mid-Autumn Festival in the year of Bing-chen (1076), drinking till dawn, I got dead drunk and thought of my brother.

When did the moon begin to shine in the sky?
I ask the blue sky, holding a cup of good wine.
In heaven I know at all nothing
About what day is this evening.
I think of returning to the jade towers and pavilions,
But over there I cannot bear the severe cold I fear.
In the gentle moonlight with my shadow so cheerfully I dance,
Life in heaven can't be as happy and free as in the world of man.

The moon moves slowly around the pavilions red,

Through the gorgeous window her love she sheds
On me on a lonely pillow sleepless.
To men she should have no hatred,
Oh, I wonder why she is full and bright when we leave.
Men have grief when they part and joy when they meet,
The moon waxes and wanes, bright and dim in turn,
Oh, of all ages nothing can be perfect in the world.
Let's hope we will live quite long and healthy remain,
Sharing the beauty of the moon a thousand miles away.

❄❄❄❄❄❄❄❄❄❄❄❄❄❄❄❄

## 江 城 子

### 密 州 出 猎

老夫聊发少年狂,左牵黄,右擎苍,锦帽貂裘,千骑卷平冈。为报倾城随太守,亲射虎,看孙郎。 酒酣胸胆尚开张,鬓微霜,又何妨。持节云中,何日遣冯唐？会挽雕弓如满月,西北望,射天狼。

## Tune: A Riverside Town

### Hunting in Mizhou

Really crazy, I behave like a young man,
Taking a yellow hound with my left hand,

苏　轼

And with right one, a grey falcon.
Wearing a silk hat and fur garment,
I lead a thousand soldiers on horses surging past the mound.
Tell all the people of the city to follow me, the prefect, out,
You'll see clearly how I kill a tiger with one or two arrows,
As Sun, the ruler of Wu in the Three Kingdoms did alone.

Getting drunk, I'm more heroic,
Now my hair dyes a bit frosty,
But with ambition in my heart I do not care at all.
I hope the emperor will return me the position lost
To guard the far northwest frontier of thousands of *li*.
I'll bend a hundred pound bow like a full moon at ease,
In the direction of the northwest, I
Will shoot down dog star in the sky.

# 虞　美　人

## 有美堂赠述古

湖山信是东南美,一望弥千里。使君能得几回来? 便使尊前醉倒更徘徊。　　沙河塘里灯初上,水调谁家唱? 夜阑风静欲归时,惟有一江明月碧琉璃。

## Tune: Great Beauty Yu

At a banquet in the Beautiful Hall the prefect leaving his post gave to his subordinates. He asked me to write the *Ci* poem.

Mounts and lakes are the prettiest in southeast,
One can clearly see the land of thousands of *li*.
Oh, I wonder when you will come back to me,
Today we'll get drunk and stagger at the feast.

Hangzhou is brightened by the coloured lights,
Who sings Water Melody, the sad song nearby?
Night late, wind calm, and we are to say bye,
The clear water baths in the bright moonlight.

❀❀❀❀❀❀❀❀❀❀❀❀❀❀❀

## 永 遇 乐

彭城夜宿燕子楼,梦盼盼,因作此词

明月如霜,好风如水,清景无限。曲港跳鱼,圆荷泻露,寂寞无人见。紞如三鼓,铿然一叶,黯黯梦云惊断。夜茫茫、重寻无处,觉来小园行遍。　　天涯倦客,山中归路,望断故园心眼。燕子楼空,佳人何在,空锁楼中燕。古今如梦,何曾梦觉,但有旧欢新

苏　轼

怨。异时对、黄楼夜景，为余浩叹。

## June: Joy of Eternal Union

In the Swallow Pavilion, I dreamed of Panpan,
a charming and devoted singer and dancer.

The full moon is bright like frost,
A breeze, the water cool and soft,
Without end spreads the scene intoxicating.
Fishes leap on the Mirror Lake meandering,
Pearl-like dewdrops roll on the lotus leaves,
Oh, no one else sees the quiet solitary scene.
At midnight I am awakened from a dream of love
By three clear sound of a distant watchman's drum
And of a tree leaf falling on the ground.
I seek the traces of the dream just now,
But darkness extends wide and far,
I stroll all over the pretty little garden.

I can't find a path home in mounts, a traveller at the world's end,
Oh, I strain my eyes to get a glimpse of my native place, but fail.
The Swallow Pavilion sleeps drear and lonely,
Where is the devoted and charming songstress?
In the pavilion a pair of swallows' nest remains.
Oh, life is nothing but dreams through ages,

But so far who wakes up from them?
For anybody has grief and merriment.
In the future people for me will also now and then sigh,
Watching the scene of Yellow Pavilion I built at night.

## 水 龙 吟

### 次韵章质夫杨花词

似花还似非花,也无人惜从教坠。抛家傍路,思量却是,无情有思。萦损柔肠,困酣妖眼,欲开还闭。梦随风万里,寻郎去处,又还被、莺呼起。　　不恨此花飞尽,恨西园、落红难缀。晓来雨过,遗踪何在,一池萍碎。春色三分,二分尘土,一分流水。细看来,不是杨花,点点是离人泪。

## Tune: Chanting of Water Dragon

### Following the Tune of Zhang Zhifu's *Ci* Poems of Weeping Willow Catkins

The catkins are like flowers, but not flowers anyhow,
No one takes pity on them, leaving them fall down.
They leave fragrant homes,
Falling by paths and roads.
Cold to anyone they appear,

苏 轼

But they have feelings drear.
Like married pretty young ladies,
They miss their dears melancholy,
Their eyes are unable to open wide with spring grief.
In a dream with the wind they travel ten thousand *li*,
Looking for their talented sweethearts,
Orioles wake them up on the way half.

I don't hate all the catkins flying away here and there,
I hate in the west garden the flowers falling anywhere.
I can't see any trace of catkins after a shower in the morning,
In the pool there are catkins like broken duckweeds drifting.
The spring scene is made up
With green earth, scented dust
And flowing water.
Looking at them,
I am surprised they are not catkins at all,
They are parting loves' tears drop by drop.

❄❄❄❄❄❄❄❄❄❄❄❄❄❄❄❄

# 江 城 子

### 湖上与张先同赋，时闻弹筝

凤凰山下雨初晴，水风清，晚霞明。一朵芙蕖，开过尚盈盈。何处飞来双白鹭,如有意,慕娉婷。 忽闻江上弄哀筝,苦含情,遣谁听!
烟敛云收,依约是湘灵。欲待曲终寻问取,人不见,数峰青。

## Tune: A Riverside Town

In a boat on the West Lake with poet Zhang Xian,
I heard the zither playing.

At the foot of the Phoenix Mountain, rain just stops,
Over the green water the breeze blows clear and soft,
So bright is the glow of the evening.
Though a pink lotus flower is fading,
It looks still so pretty and plump.
Where does a pair of egrets come?
Wanting to appreciate its beauty clear,
They stand with admiration quite near.

All of a sudden from somewhere floats
Out the music of the zither with sorrow,
Making all the listeners miserable unbearably.
The rosy clouds lose color and mist disperses,
Their bleak stories the goddesses of the Xiang River tell.
I look for the players here and there when the music ends,
But nowhere the players can be seen,
In sight, green hills lying with grief.

苏　轼

# 南　歌　子

## 游　赏

山与歌眉敛,波同醉眼流。游人都上十三楼。不羡竹西歌吹古扬州。　　菰黍连昌歜,琼彝倒玉舟。谁家水调唱歌头。声绕碧山飞去晚云留。

## Tune: Southern Song

### Going Sightseeing

The brows of the singing girl is just like the distant green hills,
When she gets drunk, her eyes are clear waves flowing.
All the tourists ascend the Thirteen-storied Buildings,
Admiring no longer West Bamboo Pavilions in Yangzhou City.

At the table, good wine falls into the jade cups from the pot,
And simple but very delicious are the foods.
Who begins singing with grief Water Tune?
The song flies round green hills, and the rosy eve clouds stop.

## 菩 萨 蛮

### 西 湖

秋风湖上萧萧雨,使君欲去还留住。今日漫留君,明朝愁杀人。
尊前千点泪,洒向长河水。不用敛双蛾,路人啼更多。

### Tune: Buddhist Dancers

### The West Lake

On the lake the autumn wind rustles and rain thick and fast falls,
You want to go back now but by them for a while you are stopped.
Oh, if I keep you today your heart will break
Tomorrow when with tears we bid farewell.

You shed a thousand teardrops in the cup at the dinner,
Like showers falling on the water of the Qiantang River.
Though with deep sorrow you needn't knit your brows,
On the road many people see travellers off crying loud.

苏　轼

## 木兰花令
### 次欧公西湖韵

霜余已失长淮阔,空听潺潺清颖咽。佳人犹唱醉翁词,四十三年如电抹。　　草头秋露流珠滑,三五盈盈还二八。与余同是识翁人,惟有西湖波底月!

### Tune: Song of Magnolia Flowers
#### Following the Tune of My Honourable Master Ouyang Xiu's *Ci* Poems on the West Lake in Yingzhou

In late fall the Huai River seems not broad,
I hear the water murmur as if it sadly sob.
Now everywhere beauties sing Ou's poems sweet still,
Forty three years has passed as flash of light as quick.

On grasses roll dewdrops like pearls sparkling,
The bright charming full moon begins waning.
The followers of well-known poet Ou in those days,
Remain I and the moon on the waves of West Lake.

## 昭 君 怨

### 金山送柳子玉

谁作桓伊三弄,惊破绿窗幽梦。新月与愁烟,满江天。　欲去又还不去,明日落花飞絮。飞絮送行舟,水东流。

### Tune: Grief of Zhaojun

#### Seeing a Friend off at Jinshan Temple

Who is playing the music on the bamboo flute nearby so sweet,
Awakening me in the green window at night from a fond dream?
The new crescent hangs low with brows knitted,
The sky and the river are shrouded in drear mist.

You have already said a thousand byes but still linger here,
It is the season with flowers and catkins flying far and near.
Tomorrow catkins will see off your travelling boat,
And the water flows eastward with our tears of woe.

## 浣 溪 沙

麻叶层层檾叶光,谁家煮茧一村香?隔篱娇语络丝娘。　垂

苏　轼

白杖藜抬醉眼,捋青捣麨软饥肠,问言豆叶几时黄?

## Tune: Silk-Washing Stream

The leaves of the hemp pile up layer by layer glistening,
Who cooks cocoons giving forth fragrance so refreshing?
Beyond the fences floats weavers' talking sweet.

In a hurry with a new stick of a branch of a tree,
A white-haired man lifts his eyes drunken,
Getting in the green wheat to be powdered.
I ask him in a voice anxious and low:
"When will soya leaves grow yellow?"

❋❋❋❋❋❋❋❋❋❋❋❋❋❋❋❋❋

# 南 乡 子

### 重九涵辉楼呈徐君猷

霜降水痕收,浅碧鳞鳞露远洲。酒力渐消风力软,飕飕。破帽多情却恋头。　佳节若为酬,但把清尊断送秋。万事到头都是梦,休休。明日黄花蝶也愁。

## Tune: Song of Southern Countryside

At the Double Ninth Festival at a banquet,
I presented the *Ci* poem to a friend, a prefect.

In time of Frost's Descent the traces of the water on the bank disappear,

The green rippling water is shallow and in the distance a shoal appears.

A breeze mild, wine effect abates,

And still a little bit chill remains.

The worn-out hat leans on my head with affection.

How to spend the coming Double Ninth festival?

To send away the autumn, just drink wine,

Everything will become a dream in time.

Oh, since nothing else but drinking wine I can do, let them alone.

Tomorrow butterflies on chrysanthemums will also feel sorrowful.

❈❈❈❈❈❈❈❈❈❈❈❈❈❈❈

## 采 桑 子

多情多感仍多病,多景楼中。尊酒相逢,乐事回头一笑空。 停杯且听琵琶语,细撚轻拢。醉脸春融,斜照江天一抹红。

苏　轼

## Tune: Song of Gathering Mulberry Leaves

I'm so affectionate and sentimental but often ill.
In the riverside Beautiful Views Building Storied,
We lift our cups of wine to celebrate our gathering,
It wins me a smile but in a moment is left nothing.

Putting down my green wine cup I listen to the music from pipa,
A prostitute plucks strings lightly giving forth love from her heart.
Her fragrant drunken face with flush
Sets off the shine of the setting sun.

## 蝶　恋　花

蝶懒莺慵春过半。花落狂风,小院残红满。午醉未醒红日晚,黄昏帘幕无人卷。　　云鬓鬆松眉黛浅。总是愁媒,欲诉谁消遣。未信此情难系绊,杨花犹有东风管。

## Tune: Butterflies in Love with Flowers

Butterflies are lazy, orioles languid and half of spring gone.
In the hard wind, the charming pink flowers in showers fall,

In the little garden here and there sigh and groan the broken red petals.
In the afternoon she gets drunk and she is not awake when the sun sets,
At twilight down the window curtain remains.

Her hair buns are loose and drawn brows fade.
Everywhere grief slow rises,
To no one can she confide it.
Anyhow her sad feelings cannot be floating forever here and there,
Even flying willow catkins are controlled by a east wind with care.

## 江 城 子

### 孤山竹阁送述古

翠蛾羞黛怯人看。掩霜纨,泪偷弹。且尽一尊,收泪唱《阳关》。漫道帝城天样远,天易见,见君难。　画堂新构近孤山。曲栏干,为谁安? 飞絮落花,春色属明年。欲棹小舟寻旧事,无处问,水连天。

## June: A Riverside Town

### Seeing a Friend off for a Prostitute in a Bamboo Pavilion on Lonely Hills in Hangzhou

The green brows show a look shy,

苏　轼

With a round silk fan snow-white,
The pretty girl hides her eyes shedding tears.
She urges him to empty a cup of wine drear,
And then she begins to sing a miserable farewell song, the "Yang Pass".
"Don't say the capital is as far as heaven," she says with a heavy heart,
"Oh, heaven is easy to see,
But you are hard to meet."

Near the Lonely Hills by the water is built the high hall so beautiful,
She can't accompany him to lean on the twisting railings with interest,
Appreciating the wonderful scene of the West Lake.
The white willow catkins fly and pink flowers fade,
Now the charming spring scenery can be found nowhere.
She wants to seek in a boat the traces of the happy affairs,
But about them, no one at all knows,
Before her to the sky the water flows.

❀❀❀❀❀❀❀❀❀❀❀❀❀❀❀❀❀❀

## 临 江 仙

### 送 钱 穆 父

一别都门三改火,天涯踏尽红尘。依然一笑作春温。无波真古井,有节是秋筠。 惆怅孤帆连夜发,送行淡月微云。尊前不用翠眉颦。人生如逆旅,我亦是行人。

## Tune: Immortals by the River
### Seeing a Friend off in Hangzhou

We have been away from the capital for three years,
You have been treading red dust in the world drear.
We give chilly spring warmth with a gay smile.
Outside the door in an old well no waves rise,
Integrity is autumn charm.

Your sad boat at night starts,
I see you off with the pale moon and thin clouds.
Before the wine, beauties, don't knit your brows.
Life is a short journey,
We are travellers only.

❀❀❀❀❀❀❀❀❀❀❀❀❀❀

## 临 江 仙
### 送 王 缄

忘却成都来十载,因君未免思量。凭将清泪洒江阳。故山知好在,孤客自悲凉。 坐上别愁君未见,归来欲断无肠。殷勤且

苏　轼

更尽离觞。此身如传舍,何处是吾乡。

## June: Immortals by the River

### In Hangzhou Seeing off My Deceased Wife's Brother

I have been away from Chengdu for ten years,
You remind me of your dead sister, my dear.
Please take my bloody tears to the river near her old grave.
The mounts and waters in my hometown remain the same,
I'm so miserable in an alien place far away from you alone.

At the farewell dinner you were unaware of my deep sorrow,
Back to my home, thinking of our charming hours I am heartbreaking.
Again and again I empty the wine cup to drown grief for your parting.
Oh, life is as short as in a hotel in the world,
Where is my eternal home beyond the earth?

❋❋❋❋❋❋❋❋❋❋❋❋❋❋❋❋❋❋

## 洞　仙　歌

江南腊尽,早梅花开后,分付新春与垂柳。细腰肢、自有入格风流。仍更是、骨体清英雅秀。　　永丰坊那畔,尽日无人,谁见金丝弄晴昼?断肠是飞絮时,绿叶成阴,无个事、一成消瘦。又莫是东风逐君来,便吹散眉间一点春皱。

## Tune: Song of Immortals in the Cavern

The winter is gone in the south of the Yangtze River,
When the early vigorous charming plum is in blossom,
Spring god assigns the willow to make up new scene.
With her waist soft and slender as a young girl indeed,
Her charm best she shows.
More than that she is also
Graceful and elegant and gives off faint scent here and there.

In Yongfeng Garden famous for weeping willows anywhere,
Oh, it's a pity no other appreciator is seen the whole day.
On fine days the golden silk-like leaves at leisure sway,
She is sad seeing catkins fly far and near.
Her groaning leaves give the shade drear,
The days are long and she is bored to death,
She becomes thinner and thinner in the end.
Oh, lucky enough,
East breeze comes,
Blowing away her brows' wrinkles
And also her elegance and beauty.

苏 轼

## 醉落魄

### 离京口作

轻云微月,二更酒醒船初发。孤城回望苍烟合。记得歌时,不记归时节。　巾偏扇坠藤床滑,觉来幽梦无人说。此生飘荡何时歇?家在西南,常作东南别。

## Tune: Drunk in Dire Straits

### Leaving Jingkou (Zhenjiang)

The thin clouds at leisure float and the pale moon hangs low,
When I'm awake, the boatman tells me he just starts the boat.
Turning, I see the lonely city is wholly shrouded in a mist.
I remember I was intoxicated by the girl's songs beautiful,
But I do not know how I came back to the boat at all.

My cane bed is slippery, scarf slants, and red fan falls,
To no one I can tell my dream, I find.
When can I finish my wandering life?
I have been travelling in the southeast for official affairs,
But I often dream of my hometown in the southwest there.

## 行 香 子

携手江村,梅雪飘裙。情何限、处处消魂。故人不见,旧曲重闻。向望湖楼,孤山寺,涌金门。 寻常行处,题诗千首,绣罗衫、与拂红尘。别来相忆,知是何人。有湖中月,江边柳,陇头云。

### Tune: Burning Incense

We strolled in the village in the suburb of Hangzhou by the river,
Like snow shower by shower fell on our clothes plum blossoms.
We enjoyed ourselves here and there,
And we were intoxicated everywhere.
Today though you are not here,
The old songs float far and near.
I think of the high beautiful Building of Watching the West Lake,
Lone Hills Temple and Gold Emerging Gate we often visited gay.

I also remember the other spots scenic
We together with interest appreciated
Were inscribed with a thousand poems still dimly seen.
The enchanting beauties with embroidered silk sleeves
Wiped away the thick dust.
Since I left Hangzhou just,
Who has been thinking of me? Oh, who?

苏　轼

Over the lake hangs the round bright moon,
By the water sway the graceful willows with charming eyes,
And over the green hills fly easy and carefree clouds white.

❈❈❈❈❈❈❈❈❈❈❈❈❈❈❈❈❈❈

## 归 朝 欢

### 和苏坚伯固

我梦扁舟浮震泽,雪浪摇空千顷白。觉来满眼是庐山,倚天无数开青壁。此生长接淅,与君同是江南客。梦中游、觉来清赏,同作飞梭掷。　　明日西风还挂席,唱我新词泪沾臆。灵均去后楚山空,澧阳兰芷无颜色。君才如梦得,武陵更在西南极。《竹枝词》、莫谣新唱,谁谓古今隔。

## Tune: Joy of Returning to Royal Court

### Leaving a friend, I presented him the Ci poem with tears.

At midnight I dream of taking a boat on the vast Taihu Lake,
To the sky surge a thousand hectares of snow-white waves.
When I'm awake the Lu Mountains fill my eyes,
The countless crags seem to lean against the sky.
Oh, in my life here and there I have to travel,
We are both the guests in the southern land.
Thinking of the difficult days far and near,

I always feel unbearably desolate and drear,
Our happy time is as a shuttle through the air as short.

Tomorrow in a west wind in a small boat you'll set off,
I'll sing new poems of my own,
Shedding red tears on my clothes.
In the southwest great poet Qu wandered bleakly,
In the region all the mountains seem to be empty,
In Liyang thoroughworts lose luxuriant green.
Your talent is as well-known poet Liu Yuxi's.
In Wuling in the faraway southwest over there,
Liu's ancient folk songs are heard everywhere.
Your new poems will also be popular in the world's remote part,
Oh, who can say there is separation of the present from the past?

## 沁园春

情若连环,恨如流水,甚时是休。也不须惊怪,沈郎易瘦;也不须惊怪,潘鬓先愁。总是难禁,许多魔难,奈好事教人不自由。空追想,念前欢杳杳,后会悠悠。　　凝眸。悔上层楼。谩惹起新愁压旧愁。向彩笺写遍,相思字了,重重封卷,密寄书邮。料到伊行,时时开看,一看一回和泪收。须知道,□这般病染,两处心头。

苏　轼

## June: Spring in the Fragrant Garden

Love is a chain of rings,
Hatred, water flowing,
When will they stop?
Neither am I shocked
To see my waist so thin,
Nor am I surprised a bit
To find my hair grizzled at the temples.
In my life I have no way at all to prevent
So painful hardships from happening to me.
She never leaves my heart a moment even.
I recollect with sorrow
Happy affairs long ago,
Our reunion seems in the world's other side.
.
I stare for a very long time at the horizon.
The high building I regret climbing up,
Causing the old sorrow and new one.
I write her a long love letter
Filling pieces of rosy paper.
I seal it with special care,
And in secret post it there.
When the letter reaches her place,

She will read it again and again.
Each time she reads it quite drear,
Her eyes will be filled with tears.
Yearning between us has
Broken two hearts so sad.

## 一丛花

### 初春病起

今年春浅腊侵年,冰雪破春妍。东风有信无人见,露微意、柳际花边。寒夜纵长,孤衾易暖,钟鼓渐清圆。　　朝来初日半衔山,楼阁淡疏烟。游人便作寻芳计,小桃杏、应已争先。衰病少惊,疏慵自放,惟爱日高眠。

### Tune: A Cluster of Flowers

#### Recovering from an Illness in Early Spring

In the early spring it is severely chilly,
The ice and snow break spring's beauty.
Who feels spring here?
But it does clear appear
On the tips of flowers and willows.
Though the night is long and cold,

苏　轼

With the lonely quilt I feel warm enough,
Clear and serene sound the bell and drum.

The red sun lies in the mount's mouth in the early morning,
The thin mist floats over the pavilions and storied buildings.
Tourists here and there appreciate pretty scene,
Like young beauties the pink apricot and peach
First show their faces pleasant.
From a disease I just recover,
Languid, I'm quite unbridled,
Sleeping till the sun rises high.

❈❈❈❈❈❈❈❈❈❈❈❈❈❈❈❈❈

## 南 乡 子

### 送 述 古

回首乱山横,不见居人只见城。谁似临平山上塔,亭亭,迎客西来送客行。　　归路晚风清,一枕初寒梦不成。今夜残灯斜照处,荧荧,秋雨晴时泪不晴。

## *Tune: Song of Southern Countryside*

### Seeing a Friend off

Turning round I see the mountains lying in disorder,

In the city I can no longer find my intimate's figure.
Unlike the pagoda on the Linping Mountains
Without feelings at all, standing high and still,
I greet him with cheer and see him off with grief.

A clear and cool breeze begins to blow in the eve,
I cannot have a dream on a chilly pillow.
Tonight there are only a few lights cold
Shedding their dim light far and near,
Autumn rain stopping, I still shed tears.

❈❈❈❈❈❈❈❈❈❈❈❈❈❈❈❈❈

# 南 歌 子

雨暗初疑夜,风回忽报晴。淡云斜照著山明。细草软沙溪路马蹄轻。　　卯酒醒还困,仙材梦不成。蓝桥何处觅云英? 只有多情流水伴人行。

## *Tune: Southern Song*

The rain stops and I think it is still at night,
The breeze blows clouds away and it's fine.
In the early morn over the mounts the pale moon hangs low,
My horse runs on the fresh grass on the riverside sandy road.

苏　轼

Though awake from wine I am still sleepy,
Oh, where can I find the fairy Blue Bridge?
Nowhere the female celestial I can seek,
Only the sweet stream accompanies me.

❋❋❋❋❋❋❋❋❋❋❋❋❋❋❋❋❋❋

## 蝶 恋 花

### 密 州 上 元

灯火钱塘三五夜,明月如霜,照见人如画。帐底吹笙香吐麝,更无一点尘随马。　　寂寞山城人老也！击鼓吹箫,却入农桑社。火冷灯稀霜露下,昏昏雪意云垂野。

## Tune: Butterflies in Love with Flowers

### At the Lantern Festival in Mizhou

Hangzhou filled with colored lights on Lantern Festival night,
The gentle bright moon shed its frost-like light in the blue sky.
The people appreciating the lanterns were like in paintings everywhere,
Behind curtains beauties played the reed pipes giving forth scent in the air,
No dust far and near could be seen after the horses.

Now I'm old in the lonely and quiet mountain city.

Somewhere come the music of flutes and sound of drums with cheer,
People, young and old give the Shrine Festival a warm welcome here.
Night is late, frost and dew falling, lights sparse and fires cold,
The dark clouds hang low over fields and it is going to snow.

❈❈❈❈❈❈❈❈❈❈❈❈❈❈❈❈❈

## 贺 新 郎

乳燕飞华屋,悄无人、桐阴转午,晚凉新浴。手弄生绡白团扇,扇手一时似玉。渐困倚、孤眠清熟。帘外谁来推绣户? 枉教人梦断瑶台曲。又却是、风敲竹。 石榴半吐红巾蹙,待浮花浪蕊都尽,伴君幽独。秾艳一枝细看取,芳心千重似束。又恐被、秋风惊绿。若待得君来向此,花前对酒不忍触。共粉泪、两簌簌。

### *Tune: Congratulations to the Bridegroom*

A young swallow flies into the room beautiful,
In the eve with scent drifting it is lone and still.
The shade of the paulownia trees turns to the west,
The enchanting beauty feels a bit cool being bathed.
She plays with a white round silk fan,
Like jade are the fan and her little hands.

苏　轼

Just as a fairy maiden so sleepy she feels,
Then alone with sorrow she goes to sleep.
Who is rolling the curtain and pushing window and door?
Oh, but no one stands outside the fragrant boudoir at all.
Awake from a dream in paradise,
To her surprise she finally finds
A gust of wind in the dark
Blows the bamboos hard.


Feeling shy the pomegranate shows half of her face red and tender.
When the charming blossoms of peaches and pears fall on the water,
Winding its way gurgling to the distance drear,
The pomegranate alone accompanies her here.
She looks at a twig of red intoxicating blossoms with great care,
Thousands of threads of deep love from the heart drift in the air.
She is afraid that the cold west wind coming
Will blow green leaves far and near floating.
When her lover comes,
And they lift wine cups,
Their tears and petals will sough
Melancholy falling to the ground.

❀❀❀❀❀❀❀❀❀❀❀❀❀❀❀❀❀

## 醉落魄

### 苏州阊门留别

苍颜华发,故山归计何时决!旧交新贵音书绝,惟有佳人,犹作殷勤别。 离亭欲去歌声咽,潇潇细雨凉生颊。泪珠不用罗巾裛,弹在罗衫,图得见时说。

### Tune: Drunk in Dire Straits

At a farewell banquet I gave the *Ci* poem as a present to a singing girl near Chang Door of Suzhou.

Unnoticed my hair becomes grey and my face fades,
When can I decide the date to go to my native place?
No friend sends me any letter,
Only the pretty girl, my lover
Like a fading pink flower comes to see me off here.

Before she sings she chokes in the farewell pavilion,
The parting grief like a cold drizzle falls on our cheeks.
Don't wipe away our bloody tears with the silk kerchiefs,
And let them wet the sleeves of our silk clothing,
One day when we meet we'll recollect our crying.

# 苏辙(1039—1112)

苏轼之弟。与苏轼同年同登进士科。同为京官。也反对王安石变法,一再遭贬。

**Su Zhe(1039‑1112)**

He was Su Shi's younger brother. He passed the highest imperial examination together with his elder brother in the same year. Also as a court official, as his elder brother he opposed Wang Anshi's political reforms and was demoted again and again.

## 调 啸 词

归雁,归雁,饮啄江南南岸。将飞却下盘桓,塞北春来苦寒。苦寒,苦寒,寒苦,藻荇欲生且住。

## Tune: An Ancient Song of a Joke

A returning wild goose here,
A returning wild goose here.
It drinks and pecks in the south shore of the Yangtze,
It is about to fly far away to the north but lingers still.

In the north it's cold.

In the north it's cold,

Oh, there the cold is really severe in the early spring,

It's better to stay in aquatic plants for the time being.

❄❄❄❄❄❄❄❄❄❄❄❄❄❄❄❄❄

## 调 啸 词

渔父,渔父,水上微风细雨。青蓑黄箬裳衣,红酒白鱼暮归。暮归,暮归,归暮,长笛一声何处。

## *Tune: An Ancient Song of a Joke*

I'm a fisherman now,

I'm a fisherman now.

Over the water a drizzle falls and light breeze blows,

I wear a green bamboo coat and yellow cattail clothes.

At dusk on my way back with white fish and red wine,

Satisfaction and happiness flow into my heart and mind.

When I return home it is in the eve,

I play a long bamboo flute carefree.

# 李之仪(1038—1117)

宋英宗治平四年(1067)进士。历官提举河东常平。从苏轼于定州幕府。词风近秦观。《卜算子》人人可吟咏。

**Li Zhiyi(1048 - 1117)**

He passed the highest imperial examination in 1067. He served as an official and once worked under Su Shi. The style of his *Ci* poems was like that of Qin Guan. The *Ci* poem "Song of Divination" has been recited by many people.

## 卜 算 子

我住长江头,君住长江尾。日日思君不见君,共饮长江水。
此水几时休,此恨何时已。只愿君心似我心,定不负相思意。

## *June: Song of Divination*

I live at the Yangtze River's head,
And you live far away at its tail.
Day and night I think of you but I cannot meet you,
It's lucky I drink the water of the river, and you too.

When will the water stops flowing?
When will my grief cease growing?
I wish your tender heart would be like mine,
And you would live up to my love and mind.

❋❋❋❋❋❋❋❋❋❋❋❋❋❋❋❋

## 临 江 仙

### 登凌歊台感怀

偶向凌歊台上望,春光已过三分。江山重叠倍销魂。风花飞有态,烟絮坠无痕。 已是年来伤感甚,那堪旧恨仍存! 清愁满眼共谁论? 却应台下草,不解忆王孙?

## Tune: Immortals by the River

### Ascending Lingxiao Platform with Thoughts

By chance I ascend the Lingxiao Platform looking at the scenery,
About one third of the beautiful fragrant spring is gone clearly.
Seeing mounts and water melting into the sky I feel depressed.
The pink flowers float here and there with affection and grace,
Without trace catkins shower down drear.

I have been so miserable for some years,
How can I bear the old sorrow remaining from the past?

李之仪

New grief filling my eyes, to whom can I bare my heart?
Does the scented green grass near the platform know
To show sympathy to the traveller far away from home?

## 谢 池 春

残寒销尽,疏雨过,清明后。花径敛余红,风沼萦新皱。乳燕穿庭户,飞絮沾襟袖。正佳时,仍晚昼。著人滋味,真个浓如酒。　频移带眼,空只恁、厌厌瘦。不见又相思,见了还依旧。为问频相见,何似长相守? 天不老,人未偶。且将此恨,分付庭前柳。

## Tune: Spring in the Xie Pool

The remaining cold melts away,
And has stopped the light rain.
Clear and Bright, the day of Tomb-worship is away here.
The paths are covered with red fallen flowers far and near,
A breeze blows making new wrinkles on the water of the pool.
The naughty young swallows fly to and fro in the painted room,
Catkins stick to the sleeves.
Still so pretty is the scene,
The dusk comes already.

In my life I feel really
What I experience in the places is stronger than wine.

Oh, I have been tightening my belt in the present time,
In vain I'm unbearably grievous
To find myself thinner and thinner.
In separation I yearn for you with a heavy heart,
After a reunion I still think of you after you part.
Oh, really I don't want to meet and separate so often,
I hope we'll stay forever as two flowers in one stalk.
Heaven is still so young,
I remain single here but.
For the time being I'd better leave my sorrow
Before the gate to the green weeping willows

# 舒亶(1041—1103)

宋英宗治平二年(1065)进士。任朝廷高官。其词多写恋人分别、朋友分手。词风婉约曲折。

**Shu Dan(1041‑1103)**

He passed the highest imperial examination in 1065. He served as a high official in the court. In his *Ci* poems, he often wrote partings between men and women or farewells between friends. The style was subtle and tortuous.

## 菩 萨 蛮

画船捶鼓催君去,高楼把酒留君住。去住若为情,西江潮欲平。江潮容易得,只是人南北。今日此樽空,知君何日同!

### *June: Buddhist Dancers*

I ask my dear to drink wine again and again, begging him to stay,
But the drum on the painted boat sounds, urging him to go away.
To leave or to stay, you must decide at once,
Look here, the rising tide is about to come.

Oh, the flood tide you can get so easily,
But in south and north we'll be separated.
Today we empty cups of wine here,
But when can we have our reunion?

❋❋❋❋❋❋❋❋❋❋❋❋❋❋❋❋❋

## 一 落 索

### 蒋园和李朝奉

正是看花天气,为春一醉。醉来却不带花归,消不解看花意。试问此花明媚。将花谁比?只应花好似年年,花不似人憔悴。

## *Tune: Chain of Jade Rings*

### In a Garden with a Friend

It is the season to appreciate flowers just,
For the beautiful spring I get dead drunk.
But I come home without bringing any,
I seem too silly to appreciate them really.

So bright and charming flowers are,
Who can compare with them? I ask.
Year after year flowers remains the same,
But beautiful girls without exception fade.

舒亶

## 虞美人
### 寄公度

芙蓉落尽天涵水，日暮沧波起。背飞双燕贴云寒，独向小楼东畔倚阑看。　浮生只合尊前老，雪满长安道。故人早晚上高台，赠我江南春色一枝梅。

## Tune: Great Beauty Yu
### Posting the *Ci* Poem to a Friend

All the lotuses fall and in the water bathes the sky,
At dusk the bright waves in the river begin to rise.
In different directions under the cold clouds a pair of swallows flies drear,
On the rails of the east of little building I lean alone looking far and near.

In my life I just enjoy drinking while growing old,
The road to the capital is covered with thick snow.
My intimate will climb up a balcony every day, gazing far and missing me,
He'll send me a twig of plum blossoms with spring scene in the southeast.

# 孔平仲(1044—1111)

宋英宗治平二年(1065)进士。曾任秘书丞、集贤校理等职。多写男女恋情。词《千秋岁》写闺中对游子的思念以及闺中想象游子对她的想念。词风婉约曲折。

**Kong Pingzhong(1044‒1111)**

He passed the highest imperial examination in 1065. He served as a court official. In his *Ci* poem "A Thousand Autumns", the young wife yearned for her wandering man and thought he missed her. The style was subtle and tortuous.

## 千 秋 岁

春风湖外,红杏花初退。孤馆静,愁肠碎。泪余痕在枕,别久香销带。新睡起,小园戏蝶飞成对。　　惆怅人谁会,随处聊倾盖。情暂遣,心何在。锦书消息断,玉漏花阴改,迟日暮,仙山杳杳空云海。

## *Tune: A Thousand Autumns*

A spring breeze comes here beyond the lake,

孔平仲

The red apricot blossoms begin to fly away.
In the inn quiet and lonely,
She feels sad unbearably.
Her tears stop but the stains on the pillow are still clearly seen,
He is away long and gone is the scent on her belt and sleeves.
Oh, in the afternoon awake from a melancholy dream broken,
She sees pairs of butterflies play in the garden with pleasure.


No one knows day and night he is filled with deep sorrow.
He stops his cart talking with familiar people on the roads.
Oh, he just wants to dispel grief a short time.
But where at all is his heart all the time tied?
He hasn't received her letter written by her snow-white hands at all,
The shade of flowers moves and from the watch water falls drop by drop.
Evening comes to the long spring day at last,
His dear seems beyond the clouds in fairyland.

# 王雱(1044—1076)

王安石之子。他喜欢写长调。这是一首短词。当时很流行,至今读者能背咏。

**Wang Pan(1044 - 1076)**

He was Wang Anshi's son. He liked to compose long tunes, and this was the only short *Ci* poem. It was so popular at that time. Even now people can recite it.

## 倦寻芳慢

露晞向晚,帘幕风轻,小院闲昼。翠径莺来,惊下乱红铺绣。倚危墙,登高榭,海棠经雨胭脂透。算韶华,又因循过了,清明时候。 倦游燕,风光满目,好景良辰,谁共携手?恨被榆钱,买断两眉长斗。忆高阳,人散后,落花流水仍依旧。这情怀,对东风,尽成消瘦。

## *Tune: Slow Song of Seeking Flowers*

Towards evening the scented dew dries,
A gentle breeze blows the curtain light.

王 雱

After a drizzle the little garden is quite and drear,
The orioles fly over the green paths far and near,
Ticking the red down on the green grass.
I lean in the high hall with a heavy heart,
The pink crab-apples blooming
With raindrops are so charming.
The beautiful springtime fades,
And Clear and Bright flies away.


I am just like a worn-out swallow,
After a long journey coming home.
Seeing the wonderful scene,
I fill with unbearable grief.
With whom can I hand in hand appreciate it with great interest?
A thousand of ounces of gold cannot unfold my brows knitted.
To me my intoxicating beauty shedding tears with blood said farewell,
Awake from wine I find flowers falling and water flowing as that day.
With grief in a breeze vernal,
I become a great deal thinner.

## 黄庭坚(1045—1105)

宋英宗治平四年(1067)进士。做过校书郎,并参加修订《神宗实录》。后遭贬谪。为"苏门四学士"之一。他是江西派的开山大师。与秦观齐名。早年词近柳永,多写艳情,风格婉约。晚年近苏轼,深于感慨,风格豪放。

**Huang Tingjian(1045–1105)**

He passed the highest imperial examination in 1067. He once served as a senior court official. He was one of the four disciples of Su Shi, and the founder of Jiangxi school of poetry. He enjoyed equal renown with Qin Guan. In his early years, like Liu Yong, he mostly described love affairs in subtle style. In his later years, like Su Shi, he sighed with deep emotion in powerful and free style.

## 清 平 乐

春归何处?寂寞无行路。若有人知春去处,唤取归来同住。　春无踪迹谁知?除非问取黄鹂。百啭无人能解,因风飞过蔷薇。

黄庭坚

### *Tune: Music for a Peaceful Time*

Where does spring return?
I feel so lonely without her.
I hope someone knows where now she is,
And I'll invite her to live with me certainly.

Her trace no one at all knows,
I can only ask the oriole yellow.
It nods repeatedly singing sweet songs but no one knows what it means,
And then it flies away over the weeping red roses with the gentle breeze.

❋❋❋❋❋❋❋❋❋❋❋❋❋❋❋❋❋❋

## 诉 衷 情

小桃灼灼柳鬖鬖,春色满江南。雨晴风暖烟淡,天气正醺酣。
山泼黛,水挼蓝,翠相搀。歌楼酒斾,故故招人,权典青衫。

### *Tune: Baring the Heart*

The peaches are in blossom and the willow twigs sway in the breeze,
The south of the Yangtze River is filled with enchanting spring scenes.
Showers stop, the breeze blows warm and mist drifts thin,

The spring sights and scent make appreciators intoxicated.

The hills are splashed with black pigment,
Dyed blue is the fragrant murmuring water,
And the green sleeps quite sound near and far on the paths and bank.
In the breeze the streamers of halls for songs and of wineshops flap,
To the tourists they seem to be waving a friendly greeting,
It's worthy to pawn good wine with my clothes of spring.

❀❀❀❀❀❀❀❀❀❀❀❀❀❀❀❀❀

## 鹧 鸪 天

座中有眉山隐客史应之和前韵，即席答之

黄菊枝头破晓寒。人生莫放酒杯干。风前横笛斜吹雨,醉里簪花倒著冠。　　身健在,且加餐。舞裙歌板尽清欢。黄花白发相牵挽,付与时人冷眼看。

### *Tune: Partridge Sky*

For a Guest, a Hermit

Over the yellow chrysanthemums drifts the morn chill.
In life time people shouldn't let the cups of wine empty.
I play the bamboo flute in a drizzle and cold air,
When drunk, I wear chrysanthemums in my hair,

黄庭坚

And a hat upside down.

Oh, being healthy now,
Eat and drink more.
In the songs so soft,
By the scented dance skirts,
I enjoy myself in the world.
My white hair with yellow flowers stay together,
Oh, let the vulgar people give me a cold shoulder.

❋❋❋❋❋❋❋❋❋❋❋❋❋❋❋❋❋

## 虞 美 人

### 宜州见梅作

天涯也有江南信,梅破知春近。夜阑风细得香迟,不道晓来开遍向南枝。　玉台弄粉花应妒,飘到眉心住。平生个里愿杯深,去国十年老尽少年心。

## Tune: Great Beauty Yu

### Seeing the Plum Blossom in Yizhou

To the remotest corner of the earth comes information of the southeast of spring,
The red plum buds are ready to burst, the intoxicating spring

approaching.
In the light breeze, I smell their faint scent at midnight,
This morn blossoms appear on sunny branches, I find.

Jealous of powder and rouge a beauty used to make up before dressing table,
A red plum blossom flew between the brows of the pretty princess to stay.
When young, I enjoyed wine to my satisfaction before charming scenery,
Far away from the palace for ten years, now old, I have lost such interest.

※※※※※※※※※※※※※※※※※※※

## 水 调 歌 头

瑶草一何碧,春入武陵溪。溪上桃花无数,花上有黄鹂。我欲穿花寻路,直入白云深处,浩气展虹霓。只恐花深里,红露湿人衣。 坐玉石,倚玉枕,拂金徽。谪仙何处,无人伴我白螺杯。我为灵芝仙草,不为朱唇丹脸,长啸亦何为?醉舞下山去,明月逐人归。

黄庭坚

## Tune: Prelude to Water Melody

The celestial grass is charmingly green,
Spring arrives at Peach Blossom Stream.
Along it, many peach trees in blossom gently sway,
The orioles sing sweet songs in them happy and gay.
I go through the blossoms to find a path
To enter the white clouds, fairy and vast,
My heroic spirit rises to the rosy glow.
I'm afraid red dew will wet my clothes
In the thicket of peaches in bloom.

Sitting on a stone cool and smooth,
Leaning on another one as a pillow at leisure,
I begin to play softly upon the golden zither.
Where is the famous poet Li Bai drinking wine all the time?
But now here no one accompanies me to enjoy the fine wine.
Than an official I'd rather be grass readily,
Useless is to groan and moan melancholy.
Drunk, downward the hills I dance,
The bright moon follows me back.

## 望 江 东

江水西头隔烟树,望不见江东路。思量只有梦来去,更不怕、江拦住。　灯前写了书无数,算没个、人传与。直饶寻得雁分付,又还是秋将暮。

### Tune: Gazing at the East Shore of the River

On the west shore of the river stand trees in mist,
Keeping me from seeing the east shore he lives.
I could only be a soul in dreams, I think again and again,
Flying to his warm and fragrant bed without being afraid
Of the surging waves low and high.

I write many letters in candle light,
Who can send to my dear my true love?
Even at last when a wild goose comes
To me, the letter carrier, already late will be the autumn,
And it will fly south, the opposite direction of my lover.

❀❀❀❀❀❀❀❀❀❀❀❀❀❀❀❀❀

黄庭坚

## 南 歌 子

槐绿低窗暗,榴红照眼明。玉人邀我少留行。无奈一帆烟雨画船轻。　　柳叶随歌皱,梨花与泪倾。别时不似见时情。今夜月明江上酒初醒。

### Tune: Southern Song

The green locust tree shade by the window dims the boudoir bright,
And the red pomegranate blossoms all of a sudden brighten my eyes.
My dear beauty invites me to stay for a little time,
But I have to take in misty rain a painted boat light.

She sings with knitted brows like a willow leave,
Down her face like a pear blossom tears stream.
I cannot bear comparing gathering joy with parting grief.
Awake from wine I see the full moon over the river green.

❋❋❋❋❋❋❋❋❋❋❋❋❋❋❋❋❋

## 阮 郎 归

### 效福唐独木桥体作茶词

烹茶留客驻金鞍。月斜窗外山。别郎容易见郎难。有人思远山。　　归去后,忆前欢。画屏金博山。一杯春露莫留残。与郎扶玉山。

## June: Return of the Lover

### Ode to Tea

I brewed tea to invite him eagerly on a horse to stay for the night.
The moon climbed hills shedding on us on the pillow jealous light.
It's easy to bid farewell to him, but too difficult to meet him again,
The distant hills keep me shedding tears from seeing him far away.

Since that day with tears I saw him leave here,
I often recollect our merrymaking hours drear.
Oh, just here in the warm fragrant beautifully-decorated chamber,
Hung screens with paintings, burning incense in a bronze burner.
I urged him to empty a tea cup,
Helping him to the bed so drunk.

❄❄❄❄❄❄❄❄❄❄❄❄❄❄❄❄❄❄

## 好　事　近

### 太平州小妓杨姝弹琴送酒

一弄醒心弦,情在两山斜叠。弹到古人愁处,有真珠承睫。　　使君来去本无心,休泪界红颊。自恨老来憎酒,负十分金叶。

黄庭坚

## Tune: Happiness Approaching

A young prostitute played the
stringed instrument and toasted me.

As soon as my dear beauty plays the tune touching my feeling,
Romantic charm comes to her brows, two hills lying slanting.
When she plays to the grief in ancient beauties' hearts,
With pearl-like tears her lashes begin to brightly sparkle.

As an official I transfer here and there now and then without grief,
Beauty, don't cry and leave your tears fall down your pink cheeks.
I'm very sorry I'm too old to drink too much good wine,
Disappointing your hope I reject your wine many times.

❈❈❈❈❈❈❈❈❈❈❈❈❈❈❈❈❈❈

## 南 乡 子

重阳日,宜州城楼宴集,即席作

诸将说封侯,短笛长歌独倚楼。万事尽随风雨去,休休,戏马台南金络头。 催酒莫迟留,酒味今秋似去秋。花向老人头上笑,羞羞,白发簪花不解愁。

## Tune: Song of Southern Countryside

### An Extempore Verse at an Feast on Gate Tower in Yizhou on the Double Ninth Festival

The generals talk about winning of the title of marquis with great interest,
I alone lean on the railings singing accompanied on the flute by a beauty.
Failure and success are gone with wind and rain,
Since we can do nothing, let them pass anyway.
Where are the traces of Horse Displaying Platform the emperor built so high?

Urged by the charming female singers, let's readily empty the cups of fine wine,
As the last one the flavor of the wine is same this autumn.
The pretty flowers on my head laugh at me with sarcasm:
"Oh, you should know you are shameless indeed,
How can we on the white head melt your grief?"

❀❀❀❀❀❀❀❀❀❀❀❀❀❀❀❀❀❀❀❀

黄庭坚

## 蓦山溪

### 赠衡阳妓陈湘

鸳鸯翡翠,小小思珍偶。眉黛敛秋波,尽湖南、山明水秀。娉娉嬝嬝,恰似十三余,春未透,花枝瘦,正是愁时候。　寻花载酒,肯落谁人后。只恐远归来,绿成阴,青梅如豆。心期得处,每自不由人,长亭柳,君知否,千里犹回首?

### Tune: The Stream by the Mount Mo

#### Giving the *Ci* Poem as a Present to a Prostitute in Hengyang

The halcyon and mandarin ducks,
Though small they treasure love.
Autumn waves are her eyes,
My dear's brows are just like
In the south the scene picturesque.
She is not fourteen years old yet,
In the early spring of youth she is
Matchlessly graceful and beautiful.
She is like the branches slender,
And she is in the time grievous.

To appreciate flowers with wine I am the first

On the scented spring day to warmly invite her.
I am afraid when I come here again,
The green trees will form thick shade,
The plum fruits will be like soya beans small.
Oh, we all know Heaven always makes fun of
Lovers' sincere hopes.
But don't you know?
A thousand *li* away, I turn with bloody tears on my sleeves
To gaze into the willows by the pavilion we parted with grief.

※※※※※※※※※※※※※※※※

## 念 奴 娇

八月十七日,同诸生步自永安城楼,过张宽夫园待月。偶有名酒,因以金荷酌众客。客有孙彦立,善吹笛。援笔作乐府长短句,文不加点。

断虹霁雨,净秋空,山染修眉新绿。桂影扶疏,谁便道,今夕清辉不足? 万里青天,姮娥何处,驾此一轮玉。寒光零乱,为谁偏照醽醁? 　　年少从我追游,晚凉幽径,绕张园森木。共倒金荷,家万里,难得尊前相属。老子平生,江南江北,最爱临风笛。孙郎微笑,坐来声喷霜竹。

### Tune: Charm of a Maiden Singer

On the 17th day of the 8th month, while my nephews as guests

黄庭坚

and I were drinking famous wine and appreciating the moon, my friend Sun played the bamboo flute intoxicating.

The rain stops and a rainbow appears,
The autumn sky seems washed clear,
Like a girl's brows, the hills are dyed new green.
The shadow of the laurel in the moon can be seen,
Oh, all the people in the world will say
Brightest light the moon tonight displays.
The sky of ten thousands of miles is blue,
Where is Chang'e, goddess of the moon,
In the broad sky driving the great round jasper?
Why does the moon shed cool light on purpose
On the green fine wine in our gold cups?

With me tours anywhere the man young,
Strolling on the cold paths,
In thick trees in the garden.
Let's pour the wine into the cups of gold,
Thousands of miles away are our homes,
It is a rare chance we can together enjoy wine.
I recollect clear with great interest in all my life,
In the south and north of the Yangtze River so excitedly,
I enjoy myself listening to the music of the flute in wind.
With a sweet smile the well-known player of it, my bosom friend
Sits before the frosty bamboos playing music to his heart's content.

## 晁端礼(1046—1113)

宋神宗熙宁六年(1073)进士做京官。不少词是宫廷因制而作。另有词描写男欢女爱以及个人宦游生活。词风含蓄清婉。

**Chao Duanli(1046–1113)**

He passed the highest imperial examination in 1073. Once serving as a court official, he wrote many *Ci* poems about the banquets in the court ordered by the emperor on the spot. He also composed some *Ci* poems about love affairs and travelling experiences as an official in a reserved and mild and gentle style.

## 水 龙 吟

倦游京洛风尘,夜来病酒无人问。九衢雪小,千门月淡,元宵灯近。香散梅梢,冻消池面,一番春信。记南楼醉里,西城宴阕,都不管、人春困。　屈指流年未几,早人惊、潘郎双鬓。当时体态,如今情绪,多应瘦损。马上墙头,纵教瞥见,也难相认。凭阑干,但有盈盈泪眼,把罗襟揾。

晁端礼

## Tune: Chanting of Water Dragon

I'm tired of visiting the halls for songs and dances in the capital,
When I drank myself blotto, no one gave me tenderness pleasant.
Now the remaining snow covers some of the streets,
On thousands of doors the moon sheds pale sheen,
The Lantern Festival is about to come.
The scent drifts from the tips of plums,
The ice on the ground disappears,
The beautiful spring scene appears.
At the time in the south building when I was drunk as a lord,
And in the west city, when the guests at feasts were all gone,
No one came with warmth to my side.
In the springs I was languid and tired.

Though I'm young still,
I'm shocked to notice
At the temples my hair becomes gray.
She is so melancholy in these days,
Her waist so graceful in the past
In the present time is thinner far.
So beautiful and handsome in those hours,
Even we are lucky to meet on a road now,
We will certainly regard each other as a stranger I know.

She leans on the railings in a high building with sorrow,
And sheds tears without end,
Unconscious of her skirt wet.

## 李元膺(生卒年不详)

他当过地方官。他是丞相蔡京的朋友。一天,蔡京在西池旁宴请几个官吏,不小心掉落池中。李元膺知道这个事情后,笑着对蔡京说:"你把心中的文章都弄湿掉了。"这使蔡京心中大怒,再不提拔他。

**Li Yuanying(years of birth and death unknown)**

He served as a local official, a friend of Cai Jing, the prime minister. One day Cai Jing gave a banquet to some officials by the West Pool. He carelessly fell into the pool. Knowing the accident he laughed at Cai: "You wet your writings in your mind." Cai was furious, never promoting him.

## 茶 瓶 儿

去年相逢深院宇,海棠下、曾歌《金缕》。歌罢花如雨。翠罗衫上,点点红无数。　今岁重寻携手处,空物是人非春暮。回首青门路。乱红飞絮,相逐东风去。

### Tune: Tea Kettle

Last year we sat quiet face to face,

In the yard in crab-apples' shade,

She sang the song "Dress of Gold Thread".

When the moving song came to an end,

Flowers like tears dropped.

Countless pretty pink dots

Covered all over her charming green silk clothes.

This year I seek the place arm in arm we strolled,

She is not here though so enchanting is the spring scene still.

Turning to look at the roads to the Green Gate of the capital,

I find the flying red flowers and catkins green

All going away with the gentle spring breeze.

# 朱服(1048—?)

宋神宗熙宁六年(1073)进士。做过朝官。后放逐一县,卒于该地。词仅存一首,他为此词甚为得意。

**Zhu Fu( 1048 –?)**

Zhu Fu passed the highest imperial examination in 1073. He served as an official in the court. Finally he was banished to a county and died there。He left only one *Ci* poem which he was proud of.

## 渔 家 傲

小雨纤纤风细细,万家杨柳青烟里。恋树湿花飞不起。愁无比,和春付与东流水。　　九十光阴能有几?金龟解尽留无计。寄语东城沽酒市。拚一醉,而今乐事他年泪。

## Tune: Pride of Fishermen

In the light breeze a cool drizzle on the city is falling,
Ten thousands of houses are in misty willows weeping.
The wet flowers stay here for loving the trees.

Oh, go away in my heart the unbearable grief
With water flowing east with spring night and day.

Oh, it's a pity, how many days of the spring are left?
Even I change my gold turtle for wine I can't keep it a bit time.
In the east city, please tell all the owners of the shops of wine,
There it is certain with merriment as a lord I'll get drunk,
Today's pleasure will cause tomorrow's tears with blood.

# 刘弇(1048—1102)

宋神宗元丰二年(1079)进士。曾为朝官。宋词中悼念正室的以苏轼的《江城子》和贺铸的《半死桐》最为感人。至于悼念爱妾,则应推苏轼的《西江月》和这首了。

**Liu Yan( 1048 – 1102)**

He passed the highest imperial examination in 1079. He once served as a court official in the Song Dynasty. The most moving *Ci* poems written in memory for one's deceased wife were Su Shi's "A Riverside Town" and He Zhu's "The Parasol Tree Half Dead". And the most famous *Ci* poems in memory for one's deceased concubine were Shu Shi's "The Moon over the West River" and this one.

## 清 平 乐

东风依旧,著意隋堤柳。搓得鹅儿黄欲就,天气清明时候。　去年紫陌青门,今宵雨魄云魂。断送一生憔悴,能消几个黄昏!

## Tune: Music for a Peaceful Time

The east breeze remains the same as that time,

It loves the weeping willows by the Sui Dyke,
Stroking the green twigs into yellow light.
It is just in the season of Clear and Bright.

Last year in the streets and by capital gate with delight we strolled,
Tonight my concubine's soul wanders as rain and clouds with woe.
Oh, all my life I will be wan and sallow,
How many sad eves shall I spend alone?

# 秦观(1049—1100)

神宗元丰八年(1085)进士。曾任秘书省正字兼国史院编修官等职。受苏轼牵连,他被一贬再贬。最终卒于放还路上。他是"苏门四学士"之一,是一位重要的婉约派词人。他的大多数词作像柳永的词作,与苏轼的词作相离太远,描写男女恋情和放逐后的愁苦。他在《鹊桥仙》中的两行词很有名:"两情若是久长时,又岂在朝朝暮暮。"

**Qin Guan(1049–1100)**

He passed the highest imperial examination in 1085. He once served as a court official mainly compiling and revising the history of the Song Dynasty. Due to the close relation with Su Shi, he was again and again demoted. Finally he died on the way to be pardoned. He was one of the four disciples of Su Shi. He was a very important graceful and unrestrained poet in the Northern Song Dynasty. Most of his *Ci* poems were similar to Liu Yong's and far away from Shu Shi's. They were about love between men and girls and the misery in the demoted areas. The two lines in "Immortals on the Magpie Bridge" are famous:"If the true love grows forever in the hearts of both sides,/They won't care if they can stay together day and night."

## 鹊 桥 仙

纤云弄巧,飞星传恨,银汉迢迢暗渡。金风玉露一相逢,便胜却人间无数。　柔情似水,佳期如梦,忍顾鹊桥归路。两情若是久长时,又岂在朝朝暮暮。

### Tune: Immortals on the Magpie Bridge

The colored graceful clouds woven by the Girl Weaver change into skillful patterns,
Some stars flying quickly in the broad sky convey their deep feelings to each other,
The Cowherd and Girl Weaver cross the Milky Way to have reunion.
When the fragrant jade dewdrops fall into the soft gold breeze here,
The countless trysts in the world have lost their beauty and scent.

Their tender feelings are like gentle water flowing without end,
Their intoxicating reunion, like a spring dream, is so sweet and short,
They cannot bear looking at homeward way, the magpie bridge at all.
If the true love grows forever in the hearts of both sides,
They won't care if they can stay together day and night.

秦 观

## 画 堂 春

东风吹柳日初长,雨余芳草斜阳。杏花零乱燕泥香,睡损红妆。　宝篆烟消龙凤,画屏云锁潇湘。夜寒微透薄罗裳,无限思量。

## Tune: Spring in the Painted Hall

The spring breeze stroking willows, days are becoming longer and longer,
After a shower, the slanting sun shines on the green grasses so fragrant.
Fallen apricot blossoms sweeten the earth for swallows to build nests,
The sleeping beauty still napping, her pink silk skirt gives forth scent.

At night incense burns without stop, but she can't enter a dream,
The white clouds lock the sad Xiang River on the painted screen.
Spring chill penetrates her silk underwear thin,
All the night with deep grief she thinks of him.

## 踏莎行

### 郴州旅舍

雾失楼台,月迷津渡,桃源望断无寻处。可堪孤馆闭春寒,杜鹃声里斜阳暮。　驿寄梅花,鱼传尺素,砌成此恨无重数。郴江幸自绕郴山,为谁流下潇湘去?

### Tune: Treading on Grass

#### In the Inn in Chenzhou

The high building is lost in the thick mist,
In the dim moonlight disappears the ferry,
I look for the fairyland far and near but can't find it anywhere.
The lone inn is shut in spring chill and it's more than I can bear,
At the sun-fading dusk, cuckoos cry sadly: "You'd better go home."

I get some spring plum blossoms from a friend so far away by post,
And from others I receive many letters,
They give me sorrows one after another.
Oh, the Chen River, you should flow around the Chen Mountains in native place,
Why do you flow so far away even to the melancholy Xiang River instead?

秦 观

## 浣 溪 沙

漠漠轻寒上小楼,晓阴无赖似穷秋。淡烟流水画屏幽。　自在飞花轻似梦,无边丝雨细如愁。宝帘闲挂小银钩。

## *Tune: Silk-Washing Stream*

A little spring chill ascends the small storied building,
It is just like in late autumn in the hazy cold morning.
The beauty is sleeping by the screen floating a mist and flowing a stream.

The easy and carefree red flowers are floating as fine as a spring dream,
The endless fragrant drizzle is drifting as light as sorrow leisurely,
With a silver hook she rolls the curtain gazing at the garden dreary.

❋❋❋❋❋❋❋❋❋❋❋❋❋❋❋❋❋

## 如 梦 令

### 春 景

莺嘴啄花红溜,燕尾点波绿皱。指冷玉笙寒,吹彻《小梅》春透。依旧,依旧,人与绿杨俱瘦。

### Tune: Like a Dream

#### Scenery of Springtime

Orioles peck red flowers down flying away one after another,
The tails of swallows break the ripples of the calm green water.
On the cold sparkling jade pipe,
In her fingers slender and white,
The beauty plays the whole "Little Plums" with sorrow.
The same,
The same,
So thin and languid are the beauty and green willows.

※※※※※※※※※※※※※※※※※

## 满 庭 芳

山抹微云,天连衰草,画角声断谯门。暂停征棹,聊共引离尊。多少蓬莱旧事,空回首,烟霭纷纷。斜阳外,寒鸦万点,流水绕孤村。　　销魂,当此际,香囊暗解,罗带轻分。谩赢得青楼,薄幸名存。此去何时见也,襟袖上,空惹啼痕。伤情处,高城望断,灯火已黄昏。

### Tune: Courtyard Full of Fragrance

The high mountains daub the thin clouds at leisure,

The endless withered grass flies to the sky distant,
The painted horn on the city gate blows with sorrow.
Before I start my long melancholy journey in a boat,
We empty the farewell cups of good wine.
How many happy hours come to my mind?
Oh, I see all those intoxicating things
Become mist and clouds in the evening.
Beyond the setting sun, in the blue sky I catch sight of
Cold crows flying homeward like a ten thousand dots,
And a clear brook groaning sadly around the village lonely.

I give my scented purse to my dear beauty as a parting gift,
And we break our love knot of silk lace,
My sweet tender heart is about to break.
Among prostitutes and songstresses a name of fickle lover I get.
When can we meet with delight again? Oh, none of us can tell,
On our red silk sleeves are lots of stains of sad tears.
Turning to have a last look at the green brothel here
Drifting day and night our fragrant beautiful love,
It is lost in thousands of twinkling lights at dusk.

※※※※※※※※※※※※※※※※※※

## 满 庭 芳

晓色云开,春随人意,骤雨才过还晴。古台芳榭,飞燕蹴红英。

舞困榆钱自落,秋千外、绿水桥平。东风里,朱门映柳,低按小秦筝。　　多情。行乐处,珠钿翠盖,玉辔红樱。渐酒空金榼,花困蓬瀛。豆蔻梢头旧恨,十年梦、屈指堪惊。凭阑久,疏烟淡日,寂寞下芜城。

## Tune: Courtyard Full of Fragrance

The grey clouds disappeared at the dawn,
The spring changed her looks as we adored,
It was fine and warm after a heavy shower.
Life filled riverside pavilions and towers,
The flying swallows kicked down the flowers red,
And dancing tired, the coin-like leaves of the elms
At leisure fell one by one on the red-dotted ground.
The swing swayed, the skirt fragrance drifting about,
The bridge touched rising water green.
In the pleasant gentle sleeping breeze,
The willows waved and inside the red gate,
The little beautiful Qin zither was played
Low by the intoxicating beauty with tender sweet affection.

We went for a spring outing to make merry to the satisfaction.
She sat in a pearl-decorated carriage with a greenish covering,
I rode a high horse holding jade reins with red tassels hanging.
Bit by bit our wine kettle was empty,

Like a fairy maiden she was sleepy,

And like a blooming cardamom in early spring, she was thirteen years old.

Oh, now it becomes a fond dream day and night in my mind ten years ago,

Counting the time I'm shocked.

I lean on the railings for long,

The thin mist and pale slanting sun

Fall on the city of Yangzhou at dusk.

❀❀❀❀❀❀❀❀❀❀❀❀❀❀❀

## 八 六 子

倚危亭,恨如芳草,萋萋划尽还生。念柳外青骢别后,水边红袂分时,怆然暗惊。　　无端天与娉婷,夜月一帘幽梦,春风十里柔情。怎奈何、欢娱渐随流水,素弦声断,翠绡香减,那堪片片飞花弄晚,蒙残雨笼晴。正销凝,黄鹂又啼数声。

## Tune: Song of Eight and Six

Leaning alone on the storied pavilion,

Parting hate like fragrant grass appears.

Cut, here and there it still wide grows.

I rode on a piebald beyond the willow,

By water she saw me off with a twig of it in her red sleeves.
All of a sudden I wake up from a short fond dream with grief.

Why did Heaven offer me a girl so beautiful and intoxicating?
Inside the curtains with moonlight, we had dreams of spring.
The ten mile street in the spring breeze was brightened and sweetened by our affection.
Oh, the happy time is gone, day and night with the scented water flowing eastward.
The music of the stringed instrument dies away,
And the aroma of the green silk kerchief fades.
At dusk I can't bear seeing red petals here and there fly,
And a drizzle shed tears groaning endlessly from the sky.
When I stand still feeling melancholy,
Orioles sing some songs quite merry.

## 好 事 近

### 梦 中 作

春路雨添花,花动一山春色。行到小溪深处,有黄鹂千百。飞云当面化龙蛇,夭矫转空碧。醉卧古藤阴下,了不知南北。

秦　观

## June: Happiness Approaching

I wrote in the dreamland.

After a rain the flowers bloom by the paths far and near,
The intoxicating spring scene on the green hills appears.
When I stroll along the path to the privacy of the creek,
I hear the yellow orioles merrily twittering in the trees.

In the blue sky the clouds like
A dragon dance with delight.
Drunk, I sleep in the cane shade,
Not knowing at all where I stay.

❋❋❋❋❋❋❋❋❋❋❋❋❋❋❋❋❋

## 江　城　子

西城杨柳弄春柔,动离忧,泪难收。犹记多情曾为系归舟。碧野朱桥当日事,人不见,水空流。　　韶华不为少年留。恨悠悠,几时休? 飞絮落花时候一登楼。便做春江都是泪,流不尽,许多愁。

## June: A Riverside Town

The willows show tenderness in the west city in spring breeze,

Causing without end in the past hours my deep parting grief,
Like a heavy shower down my faded face fall tears.
The willow tied my returning boat by the pavilion,
We hand in hand gazed at the refreshing light green grass.
Sweetened with our love dew by the red bridge from hearts,
Now my beauty is gone with wind,
The water flows in vain endlessly.

My springtime floating away
Will never come back again.
Boundlessly my hate spreads,
I ask myself when it will end.
I ascend the storied building seeing flowers and catkins flying,
Even my tears with blood fill the east-flowing river of spring,
The water dyed red cannot
Take away all my woe at all.

❀❀❀❀❀❀❀❀❀❀❀❀❀❀❀❀❀❀

## 减字木兰花

天涯旧恨,独自凄凉人不问。欲见回肠,断尽金炉小篆香。　　黛蛾长敛,任是春风吹不展。困倚危楼,过尽飞鸿字字愁。

秦　观

## Tune: Shortened Song of Magnolia Flowers

The beauty's grief is in the remotest corner of the world,
Though she is miserable, no one shows sympathy to her.
If you want to know how painful the charming songstress is,
Just see in the golden burner the incense broken inch by inch.

Her green brows like the distant spring hills knit always,
The light spring breeze cannot blow them smooth again.
For long she leans on the railings in the storied building alone,
Looking at the swan geese flying away becoming dots of sorrow.

※※※※※※※※※※※※※※※※※

## 望　海　潮

梅英疏淡,冰澌溶泄,东风暗换年华。金谷俊游,铜驼巷陌,新晴细履平沙。长忆误随车。正絮翻蝶舞,芳思交加。柳下桃蹊,乱分春色到人家。　　西园夜饮鸣笳。有华灯碍月,飞盖妨花。兰苑未空,行人渐老,重来是事堪嗟! 烟暝酒旗斜。但倚楼极目,时见栖鸦。无奈归心,暗随流水到天涯。

## June: Watching the Tidal Bore

Sparse are the pink plum blossoms,
In the stream melts the iced water,
The east breeze brings spring here unnoticed.
Oh, we once toured the famous Golden Valley,
On the Copper Street hand in hand we roamed,
Fine, on the flat sands arm in arm we strolled.
Sometimes I followed a wrong fragrant cart.
Oh, the catkins flew and butterflies danced,
Joys of spring of life rolled like a sea in our minds.
Under willows lay paths with peaches on both sides,
Here and there they sent the scenery of spring to the huts.

At night in the music of the reed instrument we got drunk,
The colored lanterns outshone the bright moon,
The carriages broke the flowers in full bloom.
The charm of the garden do not fade,
My youthful years flows slowly away.
All sorts of feelings surge in my heart when I again visit here,
In a misty eve, wineshop streamers hang slanting far and near.
I look far, leaning on the railings of the high building,
Now and then I see the perching crows by trees flying.
A slight homesickness in my soft heart seems

秦　观

Flowing to the end of the earth with the stream.

❋❋❋❋❋❋❋❋❋❋❋❋❋❋❋

## 水 龙 吟

小楼连远横空,下窥绣毂雕鞍骤。朱帘半卷,单衣初试,清明时候。破暖轻风,弄晴微雨,欲无还有。卖花声过尽,斜阳院落;红成阵,飞鸳甃。　　玉佩丁东别后。怅佳期、参差难又。名缰利锁,天还知道,和天也瘦。花下重门,柳边深巷,不堪回首。念多情、但有当时皓月,向人依旧。

## Tune: Chanting of Water Dragon

The little storied building near the garden the beauty climbed,
Gazing at him on the finely decorated horse fast away ride.
Half up were rolled the red curtains of the green chamber,
Trying on spring clothes she was so beautiful and fragrant,
It was the season near Pure Brightness.
The east warm breeze blew so gently,
As if playing with a bright day,
The rains stopped and fell again.
The peddling cries of flowers passed.
The slanting sun shone on the yard,
On the well red flowers

Fell shower by shower.

Since he waved farewell to her, jade rings jingling,
He feels painful, all the time groaning and sighing,
The happy time gone, will never again return.
He is joked by fame and wealth in the world.
If Heaven knows his sorrow,
He will also be thin and old.
Far far away, he turned to look at the doors green
And the lane in the shade of weeping willows deep,
With his feelings so painful and sad.
Totally different from the happy past,
The bright moon full of tender love just as before
Will shines on him alone in the firmly shut door.

## 千 秋 岁

水边沙外,城郭春寒退。花影乱,莺声碎。飘零疏酒盏,离别宽衣带。人不见,碧云暮合空相对。 忆昔西池会。鹓鹭同飞盖。携手处,今谁在？日边清梦断,镜里朱颜改。春去也,飞红万点愁如海。

秦　观

## June: A Thousand Autumns

From the waterside and wall of the city,
The light chill of spring retreats secretly.
The shadows of flowers shake in disorder,
The orioles sing sad songs in succession.
In a strange region, from wine I estrange,
Suffering from separation, loose is my belt.
For a long time my charming beauty is out of sight,
Looking at gathering clouds at dusk I moan and sigh.

I recollect at that time in the capital we met by West Pool,
In the carriage we toured the streets under the bright moon,
With cheer we strolled arm in arm everywhere.
Now I alone wander so drearily here and there.
The spring dreams in the capital break,
In the mirror like a heart my face fades.
The intoxicating spring is gone with the gentle breeze,
Ten thousands of flying red petals are the sea of grief.

## 虞 美 人

碧桃天上栽和露,不是凡花数。乱山深处水萦回,可惜一枝如画为谁开? 轻寒细雨情何限,不道春难管。为君沉醉又何妨,只怕酒醒时候断人肠。

### Tune: The Great Beauty Yu

The green peach tree is planted with dew from heaven,
How can she be compared with other flowers common?
She stands in mounts in disorder or by water gurgling,
Oh, the twig of blossoms is like a wonderful painting,
For whom at all does she blossom so pretty and bright?

She displays charm and love in fine rain and cold light,
But the intoxicating spring is too short.
I'm willing to be drunk for her as a lord,
Awake from wine I'm afraid
My heart with pain will break.

秦　观

## 南 乡 子

妙手写徽真,水剪双眸点绛唇。疑是昔年窥宋玉,东邻;只露墙头一半身。　往事已酸辛,谁记当年翠黛颦? 尽道有些堪恨处,无情;任是无情也动人。

### Tune: Song of Southern Countryside

A painter draws a portrait of Cui Hui, a prostitute so famous,
With bright heavily-roughed lips and eyes like autumn water.
A glance at a handsome lad she steels.
As Song's immediate neighbor east,
Above the wall only the upper part of her she shows.

Oh, the past affairs make her frail heart full of sorrow.
Who still remembers her knitted green brows in the days?
After watching the pretty portrait, do you have any regret?
It's a pity for me it has no feeling,
However, even so, it is so moving.

❋❋❋❋❋❋❋❋❋❋❋❋❋❋❋❋❋

## 阮 郎 归

湘天风雨破寒初,深沉庭院虚。丽谯吹罢《小单于》,迢迢清夜徂。　乡梦断,旅魂孤。峥嵘岁又除。衡阳犹有雁传书,郴阳和雁无。

## Tune: Return of the Lover

In the south wind and rain abates severe cold,
The flower garden is deep and floats sorrow.
A popular tune drifts from the tower of the city,
The lively New Year's Eve is long and solitary.

A homesick dream breaks my travelling soul losing its way.
The difficult years one after another are slowly going away.
In Hengyang by wild geese I can get messages of my dear,
But in Chenyang here high and low no wild goose appears.

❖❖❖❖❖❖❖❖❖❖❖❖❖❖❖❖❖

## 调 笑 令

### 莺 莺

春梦,神仙洞。冉冉拂墙花影动。西厢待月知谁共?　更觉

秦　观

玉人情重。红娘深夜行云送,困弹钗横金凤。

## Tune: Song of a Joke

### The Devoted Beauty

In the moonlight I seem
To be in a spring dream,
Entering fairy cavern in the shadows of peach blossoms that slowly moves.
Who can accompany her in the west chamber to appreciate the pretty moon?

She shows me her deep affection
Accompanied by her maidservant
Coming to me like a goddess in the early morning.
On the bed she is tired and sleepy, hairpins slanting.

❉❉❉❉❉❉❉❉❉❉❉❉❉❉❉❉❉

## 南 歌 子

玉漏迢迢尽,银潢淡淡横。梦回宿酒未全醒,已被邻鸡催起怕天明。　　臂上妆犹在,襟间泪尚盈。水边灯火渐人行,天外一钩残月带三星。

### Tune: Southern Song

After a long night the jade water watch stops dropping,
In the high sky the Milky Way is pale lying a bit slanting.
I'm not awake from strong wine completely when my sweet dream breaks,
The cock crows urging the travellers to get up but of daybreak I'm very afraid.

On my arms remain her powder and scent,
With bloody tears my silk sleeves are wet.
By the water some travellers carrying lanterns in a hurry start,
Under the sky hangs a hook of the fading moon with three stars.

❀❀❀❀❀❀❀❀❀❀❀❀❀❀❀❀❀

## 南 歌 子

香墨弯弯画,燕脂淡淡匀。揉蓝衫子杏黄裙,独倚玉阑无语点檀唇。　　人去空流水,花飞半掩门。乱山何处觅行云?又是一钩新月照黄昏。

### Tune: Southern Song

The beauty draws her crescent brows green,

And rubs rouge lightly on her tender cheeks.
With sorrow wearing her favorite pale blue shirt and apricot yellow skirt,
She leans on the jade railings dotting her lips with rouge without a word.

Her sweet lover is gone far and the water in the stream moans,
The flowers fall in showers like tears and the doors half close.
The still mountains cannot find her dear, the rosy cloud floating,
Again the new crescent shows her drear pale face in the evening.

❈❈❈❈❈❈❈❈❈❈❈❈❈❈❈❈

## 临 江 仙

千里潇湘挼蓝浦,兰桡昔日曾经。月高风定露华清。微波澄不动,冷浸一天星。　　独倚危樯情悄悄,遥闻妃瑟泠泠。新声含尽古今情。曲终人不见,江上数峰青。

## June: Immortals by the River

The Xiang River stretches a thousand miles and its green mouth appears,
I recollect drear in a boat the demoted well-known poet had passed here.

The moon high, wind stops and dew sparkles,
The water in the river is clear and waves calm,
In the cold water all the stars in the sky are soaked.

Alone I lean against the tall master with deep sorrow,
Far away floats sad music by the goddesses of the river.
The new tune expresses the feelings present and ancient.
The music ends and the players remain unseen,
On the river lie hills like beauties' brows green.

## 点 绛 唇

醉漾轻舟,信流引到花深处。尘缘相误,无计花间住。 烟水茫茫,千里斜阳暮。山无数,乱红如雨,不记来时路。

## Tune: Roughed Lips

A bit drunk, I take a little painted boat at leisure,
Leaving it float to the depth of peach blossoms.
Because of the fate of this mortal life,
I can't live in the fairyland with delight.

The misty water flows boundless at dusk,

秦 观

And in thousands of miles fades the sun.
In the countless high green mountains,
Red flowers shower down disorderly,
Covering all the paths far and near.
I can't remember how I come here.

## 桃园忆故人

玉楼深锁薄情种,清夜悠悠谁共? 羞见枕衾鸳凤,闷则和衣拥。无端画角严城动,惊破一番新梦。窗外月华霜重,听彻《梅花弄》。

## Tune: Thinking of an Old Friend in Peach Orchard

My frivolous man shuts me in a high jade building deep,
Who spends long cold nights in a lone drear bed with me?
I'm ashamed to see a pair of embroidered lovebirds on the pillow,
When I feel very melancholy I go to bed without taking off clothes.

Suddenly the sad sound of a horn on the city gate
Wakes me up from a sweet dream of spring days.
Outside the window the moon shines bright on the frost thick,
I listen to the famous music of "Plum Blossoms Falling" wholly.

## 如 梦 令

遥夜沉沉如水,风紧驿亭深闭。梦破鼠窥灯,霜送晓寒侵被。无寐,无寐,门外马嘶人起。

## Tune: Like a Dream

The long cold night like a small stream quietly flows,
The wind blows hard and the post station doors close.
I find mice stealing looks at the oil lamp when awake,
The frost sends its chill into my thin quilt at daybreak.
Sleepless,
Sleepless.
All of a sudden out of the door clearly I hear
Horses neigh urging travellers to leave here.

❋❋❋❋❋❋❋❋❋❋❋❋❋❋❋❋❋

## 画 堂 春

落红铺径水平池,弄晴小雨霏霏。杏园憔悴杜鹃啼,无奈春归。　柳外画楼独上,凭栏手捻花枝。放花无语对斜晖,此恨谁知。

秦　观

## Tune: Spring in the Painted Hall

Water rises on a level with the pond banks and paths are covered by flowers fallen,
The light rain now and then falls as if playing with the day intoxicatingly wonderful.
The apricots in the orchard wither and cuckoos cry drear,
The enchanting spring can't help but painfully leave here.

She ascends the high painted building beyond the willows alone,
Leaning on the railings, she twists a twig of blossoms with sorrow.
Without a word she lets it fall in the setting sunshine,
Who knows her sadness in her tender heart and mind?

❋❋❋❋❋❋❋❋❋❋❋❋❋❋❋❋

## 满 庭 芳

碧水惊秋,黄云凝暮,败叶零乱空阶。洞房人静,斜月照徘徊。又是重阳近也,几处处、砧杵声催。西窗下,风摇翠竹,疑是故人来。　　伤怀!增怅望,新欢易失,往事难猜。问篱边黄菊,知为谁开?谩道愁须殢酒,酒未醒、愁已先回。凭阑久,金波渐转,白露点苍苔。

## June: Courtyard Full of Fragrance

Green water chilly, I'm surprised to find autumn come,
The yellow clouds in the wide grey sky gather at dusk,
The leaves of trees fall on the steps in disorder.
Quiet and lonely is the finely-carved chamber,
Outside I wander at leisure in the moonlight.
The Double Ninth Festival will soon arrive,
I hear with sorrow the women everywhere
Pounding clothes for husbands with care.
Under the west decorated red window,
A wind shakes the bamboos to and fro,
Does my intimate visit me here?

I feel so melancholy and drear,
Looking into the distance now and then.
The new love will easily come to an end,
It is so hard to get the joy of affairs in the past.
The yellow chrysanthemums by the fence I ask:
"For whom at all are you now in full bloom?"
Don't say wine can drive away my gloom,
Before I sober up will return again the grief.
For long without a word on the railings I lean,
Gazing at the moon move to the west unnoticed,

秦　观

And clear dewdrops dot moss withering already.

❈❈❈❈❈❈❈❈❈❈❈❈❈❈❈❈❈

## 满 庭 芳

红蓼花繁,黄芦叶乱,夜深玉露初零。霁天空阔,云淡楚江清。独棹孤蓬小艇,悠悠过、烟渚沙汀。金钩细,丝纶慢卷,牵动一潭星。　　时时横短笛,清风皓月,相与忘形。任人笑生涯,泛梗飘萍。饮罢不妨醉卧,尘劳事、有耳谁听？江风静,日高未起,枕上酒微醒。

## Tune: Courtyard Full of Fragrance

The red knotweeds blossom full of vigor,
The yellow reed leaves wither in disorder,
Jade-like dewdrops fall in late night.
Oh, high and vast is the light blue sky,
Over the rivers in the south fly clouds pale.
I row a small painted boat with a single sail,
Quite carefree and leisurely,
Passing misty shoal and islet.
From the clear and calm water I pull
A fishing silk thread with a gold hook,
Shaking the reflections of stars in the stream.

Now and then I play the pipe of a short reed,

Accompanied by the bright moon and the breeze clear,

We melt into one forgetting individual existence here.

People laugh at me as nothing

But a green duckweed drifting.

I go to bed when drunk.

All the worldly troubles

I would not at all take to heart.

The wind over the river is calm,

In the east sky, the sun rises high though,

I'm a bit awake from wine on the pillow.

## 行 香 子

树绕村庄,水满陂塘。倚东风、豪兴徜徉。小园几许,收尽春光。有桃花红,李花白,菜花黄。　　远远围墙,隐隐茅堂。飏青旗、流水桥旁。偶然乘兴,步过东冈。正莺儿啼,燕儿舞,蝶儿忙。

## *Tune: Burning Incense*

The trees surround the village thickly,

The green water fills the pond already.

In the east gentle warm spring breeze,

秦　观

With great interest I wander carefree.
Though little is the garden,
It fills with spring charm.
Pink is the blossom of the peach, a girl's face,
Bright golden yellow is the flower of the rape,
And the blossom of the plum is white like snow.

In the distance stands an enclosing wall very old,
Far away lie dimly some quiet huts thatched.
With cheer flutter the green wine shop flags
By a bridge over water gurgling.
With the interest still remaining,
I climb up slowly the east hill with delight.
In thick leaves pleasantly the orioles cry,
The swallows dance happy high and low in the air,
The butterflies are busy on flowers here and there.

## 米芾(1052—1108)

北宋大书画家。词风豪放、清新、飘逸。他与苏轼多有交往,常唱酬。此词是因苏轼《水调歌头》而作,不失为佳作。

**Mi Fu(1052–1108)**

He was a great painter and calligrapher in the Northern Song Dynasty. The style of his *Ci* poems was uninhibited, fresh and graceful. He and Sushi often rubbed shoulders and wrote and responded to *Ci* poems by each other. He wrote this *Ci* poem in reply to Su's poem. It was an excellent *Ci* poem.

## 水 调 歌 头

### 中　秋

砧声送风急,蟋蟀思高秋。我来对景,不学宋玉解悲愁。收拾凄凉兴况,分付尊中醽醁,倍觉不胜幽。自有多情处,明月挂南楼。　　怅襟怀,横玉笛,韵悠悠。清时良夜,借我此地倒金瓯。可爱一天风物,遍倚栏干十二,宇宙若萍浮。醉困不知醒,欹枕卧江流。

## Tune: Prelude to Water Melody

### At the Mid-Autumn Festival

The autumn wind brings the sounds of pounding cloth,
The crickets at the foot of the wall sing their last songs.
Alone looking at the withering autumn scenery with sorrow,
I'm not so sad as poet Song for his poem of fall well-known.
I drink wine green
To melt my grief.
Still I see scenery lying quiet and desolate.
The bright moon full of feelings so tender
Hangs high over the south storied building.

To dispel the sorrow in my heart flowing,
I play the flute of good jade,
The music is sweet and gay.
In the clear fragrant intoxicating night,
Many times I fill a gold cup with wine.
Seeing the scenery so charming and wonderful,
I lean with cheer through all the twelve banisters.
The world is like duckweeds drifting anywhere.
Now getting drunk as a lord without at all care,
I won't sober up from wine till dawn anyhow,
By the green river, on a pillow on the ground.

# 赵令畤(1051—1134)

宋太祖次子的玄孙。他与苏轼的政治观点一致,交往密切。其词风与秦观的词风相近。他多与苏轼、秦观唱酬。

**Zhao Lingzhi( 1051 – 1134 )**

He was the great-great-grandson of the first emperor's second son in the Song Dynasty. He shared Su Shi's political points of view. He was on friendly terms with Shu Shi. The style of his *Ci* poems was like that of Qin Guan. Still they often wrote and responded to *Ci* poems each other.

## 蝶 恋 花

庭院黄昏春雨霁。一缕深心,百种成牵系。青翼蓦然来报喜,鱼笺微谕相容意。　待月西厢人不寐。帘影摇光,朱户犹慵闭。花动拂墙红萼坠,分明疑是情人至。

## Tune: Butterflies in Love with Flowers

After a spring rain at dusk in the garden it is fine.
My devoted tender heart is again and again twined

赵令畤

With hundreds of threads of love affairs with my charming lover.
Red Girl, the young lady's maidservant comes to me with a letter,
I try my best to figure out in it her devoted sweet meaning.

She stays in the west chamber watching the moon rising.
On the new bamboo curtain the bright moonlight appears,
She is languid leaving the red door half open with cheer.
Suddenly she sees the flowers by the door sway and red petals fall,
She wonders excitedly if her lover always in her mind comes at all.

❁❁❁❁❁❁❁❁❁❁❁❁❁❁❁❁❁❁

## 菩 萨 蛮

春风试手先梅蕊,颊姿冷艳明沙水。不受众芳知,端须月与期。
清香闲自远,先向钗头见。雪后燕瑶池,人间第一枝。

## Tune: Buddhist Dancers

The spring breeze tries blowing open the pistils of plum blossoms,
With cold grace and chilly charm the tree sways by the clear water.
From any other flowers it is so aloof,
But it keeps company with the moon.

Far and near it floats its scent,

On beauties' hair it is first set.
At feasts in heaven it is displayed first
Of all flowers from the human world.

## 蝶 恋 花

卷絮风头寒欲尽。坠粉飘香,日日红成阵。新酒又添残酒困。今春不减前春恨。　　蝶去莺飞无处问。隔水高楼,望断双鱼信。恼乱横波秋一寸。斜阳只与黄昏近。

### Tune: Butterflies in Love with Flowers

Catkins fly in wind and cold comes to an end.
High and low floats blooming flowers' scent,
Day by day, shower by shower the red petals like tears fall.
Drinking old and new wine the beauty gets drunk as a lord,
This spring just as last one she suffers from deep sorrow.

She can ask no one where the butterflies and orioles go.
She leans on the railings of the high building by the water,
And in vain she expects two carp to bring her dear's letter.
Her grief rises again when she sees eve scenery,
Oh, the slanting sunshine is near to dusk only.

赵令畤

## 乌 夜 啼

### 春 思

楼上萦帘弱絮,墙头碍月低花。年年春事关心事,肠断欲栖鸦。　舞镜鸾衾翠减,啼珠凤蜡红斜。重门不锁相思梦,随意绕天涯。

## June: Crow Cawing at Night

### Having Thoughts of Love

Around the curtain of the high building the tender catkins fly,
Away from the flowers below the wall is kept the moonlight.
Spring by spring she misses him bitterly in the end of the world,
She is sad seeing the crows flying round the trees ready to perch.

Fade the green quilts with two lovebirds dancing,
The red candle burns out, its last teardrops falling.
Oh, so many doors can't shut her soul in the yearning dream,
Flying to the remotest part of the earth to seek her sweet free.

# 贺铸(1052—1125)

他是唐朝贺知章后裔。曾任京官和多地长官。晚年退居苏州。退隐之后,忧忧郁郁。他与秦观和黄庭坚齐名。苏轼的四弟子之一张耒说,他是当时首屈一指的词人。词风婉约多样。《青玉案》是其代表作。最后几行词广泛流传:"若问闲情都几许? 一川烟草,满城风絮。梅子黄时雨。"因此,他被称为"贺梅子"。

**He Zhu( 1052 – 1125)**

He was a descendant of He Zhizhang, a well-known poet in the Dang Dynasty. He served as an official in the capital and other cities. In his remaining years, he lived in seclusion filled with sorrow in Suzhou. He enjoyed equal renown with Qin Guan and Huang Tingjian. Zhang Lan, one of the four disciples of Su Shi, praised him as the best poet in the time. The style of his *Ci* poems was subtle and unrestrained. " Green Jade Cup " was his representative *Ci* poem. The last lines were widespread:" If you ask me how much sorrow my heart contains, /See on the plain in the mist the grass growing here and there, /And in the town the weeping willow catkins flying anywhere. /And now and then showers falling/Making green plums yellowing." Therefore, he was called "Plum He".

## 子 夜 歌

三更月,中庭恰照梨花雪。梨花雪,不胜凄断,杜鹃啼血。　王孙何许音尘绝,柔桑陌上吞声别。吞声别,陇头流水,替人呜咽。

### Tune: Song at Midnight

The moon like my brows at midnight shines
On pear blossoms in the yard as snow white.
Oh, pear blossoms are white as snow,
With a tender heart full of deep sorrow,
The cuckoo cries painfully shedding tears with blood.

I have got no information from him, my fickle love,
On the path with mulberry trees we parted gulping down our sobs.
Oh, over there far away we said good-bye gulping down our sobs,
The sparkling water in the field ditch flowing
For our parting lovers whimpers heartbreaking.

## 惜 余 春

急雨收春,斜风约水,浮红涨绿鱼文起。年年游子惜余春,春归不解招游子。　　留恨城隅,关情纸尾,阑干长对西曛倚。鸳鸯俱是白头时,江南渭北三千里。

### June: Cherishing the Remaining Spring

The heavy rain ends the intoxicating spring,
The slanting wind slows the water flowing,
The red flowers float on the rising green water, fishes playing far and near.
I stay far away from hometown treasuring remaining springs year by year,
Oh, spring does not tell me with him to go home.

In the city's outer corner we left our deep sorrow,
Leaning on the railings alone I think of my dear at dusk,
The ends of her letters filled with her concern and love.
Although our hair becomes snow-white,
We are separated by three thousand miles.

贺　铸

## 半 死 桐

重过阊门万事非,同来何事不同归？梧桐半死清霜后,头白鸳鸯失伴飞。　　原上草,露初晞。旧栖新垅两依依。空床卧听南窗雨,谁复挑灯夜补衣!

## June: The Parasol Tree Half Dead

Passing again the west gate of Suzhou I find everything beyond recognition,
We two came here years ago with cheer, but now we cannot return together.
After freezing frost, half of the parasol tree is nearly dead,
Losing its mate, flies alone the lovebird with white head.

On the grass in the wilds,
The dewdrops are just dry.
I stay in the old house, she in a new grave,
But we think of each other night and day.
Lying in the bed we shared so happy alone,
I listen to pattering rain on the south window.
Who would mend my clothes bit by bit,
In the light of a heart-shaped candle dim?

## 陌 上 郎

西津海鹘舟，径度沧江雨。双舻本无情，鸦轧如人语。 挥金陌上郎，化石山头妇。 何物系君心，三岁扶床女！

### Tune: Lover on the Path

In a boat my dear quickly leaves the ferry west,
Straight crossing the Cang River through a rain.
The two small sculls have no feelings,
But their clicking is like their moaning.

Disloyal, he spends all his money, seeking pleasure, and never coming home,
So faithful, she waits for him day and night, nearly becoming a cold stone.
Oh, what can tie his fickle heart to my cold lone bed fast?
Could his three-year-old daughter learning to walk do that?

❈❈❈❈❈❈❈❈❈❈❈❈❈❈❈❈❈

## 减字浣溪沙

楼角初销一缕霞，淡黄杨柳暗栖鸦，玉人和月摘梅花。 笑捻粉香归洞户,更垂帘幕护窗纱,东风寒似夜来些。

## June: Shortened Song of Silk-Washing Stream

Over the corner of a high building just disappears the sunset glow,
In the pale yellow leaves of the weeping willows hide some crows,
In the moonlight the beauty plucks a twig of plum blossoms.

Smiling and twisting it, she goes back to her lonely chamber,
She pulls down the curtain to cover the window screening,
At night the east wind blowing harder, colder it is getting.

## 减字浣溪沙

秋水斜阳演漾金,远山隐隐隔平林。几家村落几声砧。 记得西楼凝醉眼,昔年风物似如今。只无人与共登临。

## June: Shortened Song of Silk-Washing Stream

In the slanting sunlight the breeze ripples the autumn brook,
The distant hills like her brows dimly lie beyond the wood.

From some cottages now and then come the sound of pounding clothes lightly.

In the west building with drunken eyes with my beauty I appreciated the scenery,
Now it is as beautiful and enchanting as that time,
But no one watches it with me on the railings high.

❀❀❀❀❀❀❀❀❀❀❀❀❀❀❀❀❀❀

## 芳 心 苦

杨柳回塘,鸳鸯别浦,绿萍涨断莲舟路。断无蜂蝶慕幽香,红衣脱尽芳心苦。　　返照迎潮,行云带雨,依依似与骚人语。当年不肯嫁春风,无端却被秋风误。

## *Tune: A Bitter Heart*

Around the narrow and winding pool grow weeping willow trees,
Pairs of mandarin ducks play with each other in the water green,
The luxuriant duckweeds stop lotus-gathering boats' way.
Neither butterfly nor bee appreciates the lotuses with scent,
The beautiful pink lotus dress falls leaving her bitter tender heart shown.

At dusk the fading sun shines on waves greeting tidewater flowing home,
The floating clouds now and then sprinkle a rain fine,
The lotus sways in a breeze, to me her grief to confide.
She regrets not having married the spring breeze then,
Now she is left in the cold by autumn wind at present.

## 捣 练 子

砧面莹,杵声齐,捣就征衣泪墨题。寄到玉关应万里,戍人犹在玉关西。

## Tune: Song of Pounding Cloth

The pounding stones are smooth and bright,
And pounding sounds are in unison and high.
After pounding the cloth and sewing it into her husband's clothes,
She makes ink with tears to write his name and address on the post.
It'll travel a thousand miles to the Pass of Jade,
However, his garrison now is a bit farther west.

# 青 玉 案

凌波不过横塘路,但目送、芳尘去。锦瑟华年谁与度?月桥花院,琐窗朱户,只有春知处。　　飞云冉冉蘅皋暮,彩笔新题断肠句。若问闲情都几许?一川烟草,满城风絮。梅子黄时雨。

## Tune: Green Jade Cup

A beauty comes as treading the waves near, then goes away,
I can do nothing but with great admiration and regret gaze
At the fragrant dust rising and departing here.
With whom does she spend her precious years?
By the moonlit bridge or in the flower-filled yard,
In the red door or behind the window finely-carved,
Oh, her scented dwelling place, only spring knows.

At dusk the clouds float away the green plain slow,
I begin to compose a melancholy poem only then.
If you ask me how much sorrow my heart contains,
See on the plain in the mist the grass growing here and there,
And in the town the weeping willow catkins flying anywhere.
And now and then showers falling
Making the green plums yellowing.

贺　铸

## 石州引

薄雨收寒,斜照弄晴,春意空阔。长亭柳色才黄,远客一枝先折。烟横水际,映带几点归鸿,东风销尽龙沙雪。还记出关来,恰而今时节。　　将发。画楼芳酒,红泪清歌,顿成轻别。回首经年,杳杳音尘都绝。欲知方寸,共有几许新愁? 芭蕉不展丁香结。枉望断天涯,两厌厌风月。

### Tune: Song of Shizhou

Light chill is dispelled by a rain fine,
And in the west the setting sun shines,
The beautiful spring scene spreads far and near.
The willow tips begin yellowing by the pavilion,
Who first plucked a willow twig to give his sweet as a parting gift?
In the air drifts the thin mist and on the pond glisten the green ripples,
Reflecting the dots of swan geese on their journey home,
In the east breeze on the green sands disappears the snow.
When years ago I came to the remote region,
As now it was just in the early spring season.

When I was about to start my long cruel travel,
Upstairs the wine shop at a farewell feast so sad,
My beauty sang tears falling down her rouged face,

Just by the groaning water it was an easy farewell.
I have not got any letter from her so far.
In the present time my sweet tender heart
Is piled layer by layer with the unbearable new grief,
As clove overgrowing buds and banana curly leaves.
We look in the directions of our remote parts of the world with yearning,
While the moon sheds its sympathetic light on our faraway storeyed buildings.

❀❀❀❀❀❀❀❀❀❀❀❀❀❀❀❀❀

## 小 重 山

花院深疑无路通。碧纱窗影下,玉芙蓉。当时偏恨五更钟。分携处,斜月小帘栊。　　楚梦冷沉踪。一双金缕枕,半床空。画桥临水凤城东。楼前柳,憔悴几秋风。

### *Tune: Hills by Hills*

It's hard to find her chamber in the garden so deep.
In the swaying shadow of the green window screen,
I saw her intoxicating face like a blooming lotus of jade.
We slept in a bed till the water watch telling us daybreak.
With bloody tears we said good-bye outside,

贺　铸

The curtain bathed in the setting moonlight.

My fond dream is gone and in the room cold,
Remains a pair of gold-embroidered pillows,
And a half empty bed and scented quilts lonely.
She stays by a painted bridge in the east capital.
For years the willows trees before her fragrant boudoir,
In autumn wind wither and shed tears with broken hearts.

❉❉❉❉❉❉❉❉❉❉❉❉❉❉❉❉❉

## 芳 草 渡

留征辔,送离杯。羞泪下,撚青梅。低声问道几时回。秦筝雁促,此夜为谁排？　君去也,远蓬莱。千里地,信音乖。相思成病底情怀？和烦恼,寻个便,送将来。

## Tune: Ferry by Fragrant Grass

Holding the horse rein fine,
She hands him a cup of wine.
From her shy eyes like a rain fall bloody tears,
She twists a twig of green plum fruits so drear,
She asks quite softly when he can return to her arms.
She plays the zither giving forth music high and fast,

"For whom should I play tonight?" she sighs in sorrow.

Then looking at her lover she says in a voice with woe:
"Oh, you'll soon go so far
As to world's remote part
Where no letter can reach.
Try your best to send me
Your lovesickness
And infinite agony."

❋❋❋❋❋❋❋❋❋❋❋❋❋❋❋❋❋

## 人 南 渡

兰芷满汀洲,游丝横路。罗袜尘生步,迎顾。整鬟颦黛,脉脉两情难语。细风吹柳絮,人南渡。　　回首旧游,山无重数。花底深朱户,何处? 半黄梅子,向晚一帘疏雨。断魂分付与,春将去。

### *June: Going to the South across the River*

The riverside shoal was filled with the thoroughworts fragrant,
Over the roads high and low drifted the snow-like gossamer.
With graceful steps she came to me.
Oh, when nearer and nearer got she,
Arranging the hair she displayed her love through her eyes and

brows,
We looked at each other with love but were hard to open our mouths.
Oh, in the gentle breeze the green willow catkins flew far and near,
She went to the river's south shore in a boat like a female celestial.

In vain I recollect the happy hours in those days,
Now the countless mountains surround her place.
In thick flowers she stays in a red door,
I wonder where is my beauty now at all.
The green scented plum fruits are yellowing,
At dusk beyond the curtain a drizzle is falling.
Where will my sad soul go?
The spring will leave alone.

## 国 门 东

车马匆匆,会国门东。信人间自古销魂处,指红尘北道,碧波南浦,黄叶西风。　堠馆娟娟新月,从今夜、与谁同?想深闺独守空床思,但频占镜鹊,悔分钗燕,长望书鸿。

## Tune: The East Gate of the Capital

I ride a horse and she takes a cart in a hurry
To bid farewell at the east gate of the capital.
The saddest for the parting people of all
Is on the dust-covered roads in the north,
And in the south on the surging waves in a river green,
And in the west wind falling the yellow leaves of trees.

In the official station I watch the crescent shed tear-like light,
From now on with whom can I spend the long miserable night?
In the deep boudoir she must miss me painfully on her cold bed,
Divine on the copper mirror for my returning date now and then,
And regret breaking her swallow-shaped jade hairpin and keeping its half.
She is expecting all the time wild geese, messengers with a heavy heart.

❈❈❈❈❈❈❈❈❈❈❈❈❈❈❈❈❈

## 梦 相 亲

清琴再鼓求凰弄,紫陌屡盘骄马鞯。远山眉样认心期,流水车音牵目送。　　归来翠被和衣拥,醉解寒生钟鼓动。此欢只许梦

贺　铸

相亲,每向梦中还说梦。

## June: Making Love in the Dream

I play the zither to please the pretty lady again and again,
I run around her cart to see her powdered and rouged face.
She opens the curtain showing me her love with a smile so enchanting,
With deep sorrow I stare at her scented cart in the crowds disappearing.

Coming back home I go to bed alone with clothes at dusk,
Awake, I feel chilly, hearing a watchman beating the drum.
I dream of making love with her sometimes,
I never forget to tell her about it with delight.

❀❀❀❀❀❀❀❀❀❀❀❀❀❀❀

## 愁 风 月

风清月正圆,信是佳时节。不会长年来,处处愁风月。　心将熏麝焦,吟伴寒虫切。欲遽就床眠,解带翻成结。

## Tune: Sorrow for the Wax and Wane of the Moon

The breeze is cool and moon full now,
Oh, it's really a wonderful night, we should say.
Anyhow it won't stay all the year round,
Anywhere people are sad seeing its wax and wane.

With grief I burn the musk incense,
Reciting poems I accompany insects that now and then sob.
Cold and alone I decide to go to bed,
But when I'm trying to untie my clothes' belt I give a knot.

❀❀❀❀❀❀❀❀❀❀❀❀❀❀❀

## 西 江 月

携手看花深径,扶肩待月斜廊。临分少伫已伥伥,此段不堪回想。 欲寄书如天远,难销夜似年长。小窗风雨碎人肠,更在孤舟枕上。

## Tune: The Moon over the West River

Hand in hand we appreciated the flowers on the deep paths with cheer,

Shoulder to shoulder in the corridor we waited for the moon to appear.

We were filled with grief before we said goodbye.

I cannot bear recollecting the heartbreaking sight.

I want to send her a letter, but she is as far as in heaven,

In the flickering light the bleak night is as a year to spend.

I'm heartbreaking listening to the wind and rain beating the window,

I am just lying on a pillow with a candle beside me in a lonely boat.

## 点 绛 唇

一幅霜绡,麝煤熏腻纹丝缕。掩妆无语,的是销凝处。　　薄暮兰桡,漾下苹花渚。风留住。绿杨归路。燕子西飞去。

### June: Rouged Lips

She sees her dear off and her wet silk kerchief snow-white

Has been dried over the burner with incense so many times.

With it she hides her face tears falling,

Really she is unbearably heartbreaking.

At dusk as if with the beauty in those hours he takes a small boat,
Leaving it drift to the isle full of the white fern flowers with sorrow.
The wind keeping him, he smells the flower with scent from her skirt green.
Turning to gaze at the isle for long and shedding bloody tears he hopes indeed
The swallow on the way back with willows can
Tell her in detail his feeling of separation so sad.

❋❋❋❋❋❋❋❋❋❋❋❋❋❋❋❋❋

## 台 城 游

南国本潇洒,六代浸豪奢。台城游冶。襞笺能赋属宫娃。云观登临清夏,璧月留连长夜,吟醉送年华。回首飞鸳瓦,却羡井中蛙。　　访乌衣,成白社,不容车。旧时王谢,堂前双燕过谁家? 楼外河横斗挂,淮上潮平霜下,樯影落寒沙。商女篷窗罅,犹唱《后庭花》。

### June: Touring the Palace

Jingling, the old capital is so unrestrained and natural,
Here the six dynasties were all steeped in extravagance.
Tai City, the imperial palace situated, is famous for its pretty scenery,

There the emperor composed poems to praise his concubines' beauty.
Thousands of officials climbed the mount to spend summer cool,
In the long nights under the blue sky lingered the jade-like moon,
They recited poems and drank fine wine seeing off the precious time.
The enemy entered the capital burning palace's phoenix-shaped tiles,
The last emperor of the lost dynasty like a frog hid in a well.

With interest I visit again the well-known Black Clothes Lane,
The simple houses replace the splendid ones in the past,
The lane is too narrow to allow any kind of cart to pass.
Will the pair of swallows in the general's mansion fly to other house?
Oh, on the Milky Way hangs the glistening slanting eye-like Plough,
Frost falls on Qinhuai Stream's shoal at its tide low,
Where the dim shadows of the sails move very slow.
The pretty female singer at the window in a little boat with her glistening hair
Still sings the song "Flowers in the Backyard" by the captured king without care.

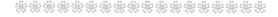

## 望 湘 人

厌莺声到枕,花气动帘,醉魂愁梦相半。被惜余薰,带惊剩眼。几许伤春春晚。泪竹痕鲜,佩兰香老,湘天浓暖。记小江风月佳时,屡约非烟游伴。　　须信鸾弦易断。奈云和再鼓,曲终人远。认罗袜无踪,旧处弄波清浅。青翰棹舣,白蘋洲畔。尽目临皋飞观。不解寄、一字相思,幸有归来双燕。

## Tune: Yearning for the Dear by the Xiang River

The cries of the orioles in disorder come to my pillow,
Open the curtain the fragrance of the red flowers blows,
Drunk, I have a dream quite miserable.
The quilt keeps her remaining aroma,
I'm shocked to find quite loose is my trousers' belt.
How much do I suffer the sorrow for the spring late?
The bloody tears of the king's two concubines on the bamboos remain,
The intoxicating fragrant orchids the well-known poet Qu wore fade.
Now warm and clear are the water of the Xiang River and the sky.
I remember in the time the breeze was gentle and the moon bright,
By the stream I often had trysts with my love.

贺　铸

The strings of the zither are easy to break, just
As happy hours can hardly for long last.
The music ended and she was gone far.
In vain I look for her far and near,
The water is still shallow and clear.
The painted boats come and go on the water flowing,
The green isle is covered with duckweeds blooming.
On high waterside land whole days I stare
In the direction she left with uncombed hair.
I don't know how to send my beauty my grief,
Luckily the pair of swallows returns to our beam.

# 仲殊(生卒年不详)

俗名张挥,法号仲殊。游荡不羁,几为妻毒死,于是弃家为僧。曾先后居于苏州承天寺、杭州宝月寺。与苏轼有交往。最后自缢而死。词浓艳,如《诉衷情》中词句:"三千粉黛,十二阑干,一片云头。"

**Zhong Shu(years of birth and death unknown)**

The poet's name was Zhang Hui. His Buddhist monastic name was Zhong Shu. He loafed about instead of staying at home. He was nearly poisoned by his wife. He left home to be a Buddhist monk in Buddha Temple in Suzhou, and Treasure Moon Temple in Hangzhou. He was on friendly terms with Su Shi. Finally he hanged himself. The style of his *Ci* poems was not plain but gaudy such as the lines in "Baring the Heart":"There are three thousand songstresses and dancers powdered,/Twelve green railings,/And a rosy cloud flying."

## 诉 衷 情

### 寒 食

涌金门外小瀛洲,寒食更风流。红船满湖歌吹,花外有高楼。

仲　殊

晴日暖,淡烟浮,恣嬉游。三千粉黛,十二阑干,一片云头。

## Tune: Baring the Heart

### On Cold Food Day

Out of Gold Emerging Gate, Little Fairy Islet in West Lake
Is extraordinarily beautiful and charming on Cold Food Day.
The lake is full of red boats of prostitutes and songs and music,
Beyond the flowers are the high buildings so delicately painted.

It's fine, warm air floating anywhere,
A thin mist is drifting here and there,
The tourists are drunk as a lord with the beauty and fragrance.
There are three thousand songstresses and dancers powdered,
Twelve green railings,
And a rosy cloud flying.

❈❈❈❈❈❈❈❈❈❈❈❈❈❈❈❈❈

## 诉　衷　情

### 宝　月　山　作

清波门外拥轻衣,杨花相送飞。西湖又还春晚,水树乱莺啼。
闲院宇,小帘帏。晚初归。钟声已过,篆香才点,月到门时。

## Tune: Baring the Heart

### Written in Baoyue Temple

Wearing silk clothes out of Clear Wave Gate, I walk by the West Lake,
Snow-white willow catkins accompany me on the way to my temple.
The West Lake sleeps in the late spring,
In the trees by water orioles madly sing.

The monks sleep quiet and still,
The curtain hangs low and lonely.
The eve comes again.
The chime dies away,
The smoke of incense begins to curl up,
And the moonlight falls on the gate just.

## 南 柯 子

### 忆 旧

十里青山远,潮平路带沙。数声啼鸟怨年华,又是凄凉时候在天涯。　　白露收残月,清风散晓霞。绿杨堤畔问荷花:记得年时沽酒那人家?

仲 殊

## Tune: Southern Song
### Recollecting the Past

The green hills lie ten miles away,
The water rises to the sandy way.
The birds complain about time passing quickly,
Again comes autumn, the season in great misery,
The worst is I'm alone in the earth's remote corner.

The white dew dries under the setting moon, and
The gentle breeze blows away rosy morning glow.
I stand on the bank with the swaying green willows,
I ask the pink lotuses in bloom
With sorrow in the clear pool:
"Do you still remember at that time,
In the shop I drank wine with delight?"

❈❈❈❈❈❈❈❈❈❈❈❈❈❈❈❈❈❈

## 柳 梢 青

### 吴 中

岸草平沙。吴王故苑,柳袅烟斜。雨后寒轻,风前香软,春在梨花。　　行人一棹天涯。酒醒处,残阳乱鸦。门外秋千,墙头红粉,深院谁家?

## Tune: Green Tips of Willow Branches
### In the Old Palace of Wu

On the bank grows grass and beyond it spreads sands far and near.
The old palace of Wu in Spring and Autumn period appears clear,
Mist drifts and willow twigs dance with grace.
After a heavy shower the cold greatly abates,
A breeze brings here faint fragrance,
Spring is in the pears in full blossom.

With an oar's push, the boat seems to pass a mile.
I hear clear when I'm just awake from strong wine
The crows cry in disorder under the sun fading.
Out of the door sways back and forth a swing,
Above the wall shows so heavily a rouged face now and then,
"Whose family does she belong to?" in a low voice I ask myself.

## 夏 云 峰
### 伤 春

天阔云高,溪横水远,晚日寒生轻晕。闲阶静、杨花渐少;朱门

仲　殊

掩、莺声犹嫩。悔匆匆、过却清明,旋占得馀芳,已成幽恨。却几日阴沉,连宵慵困,起来韶华都尽。　　怨入双眉闲斗损。乍品得情怀,看承全近。深深态、无非自许,厌厌意、终羞人问。争知道、梦里蓬莱,待忘了余香,时传音信。纵留得莺花,东风不住,也则眼前愁闷。

## *Tune: Summer Clouds over the Peak*
### Grieving over the Passing of Spring

The clouds fly high and the sky is vast,
And the green stream flows far, and far,
The setting sun shows a rosy halo, shedding cold light.
The courtyard with fading flowers is leisurely and quiet,
Scented catkins fly everywhere, fewer and fewer left,
In the deep closely-shut grand house with a door red,
The voices of the orioles are still childlike and tender.
I'm full of sadness thinking of the spring's departure,
Clear and Bright, day of Tomb-worship is gone drear,
Oh, its fragrance still remains in the yard far and near,
My heart is filled with deep sorrow.
These days dark clouds hang low,
Oh, the whole night I sleep quite soundly,
Getting up I find gone spring scene pretty.

Easy and carefree the leisure misery climbs up my brows,

With love I appreciate the remaining aroma of spring now,
And attend to her in an intimacy careful.
But my deep feelings of faith and truth
Is one-sided love just.
She is cold to my love,
She is shy of others' care, soft and sweet.
I try to seek fairyland in my fond dream,
And to forget her faint scent remaining,
But deep love for me keeps the spring,
Day and night my mind and heart her faint aroma still haunts.
Even I can keep orioles' songs and flowers' scent a time short,
When spring's traces can't be seen anywhere,
Certainly the melancholy sight I can't bear.

# 晁补之(1053—1110)

宋神宗元丰二年(1079)进士。做过京官和地方官。他两次受贬后回家隐居,造筑"归来园",号"归来子"。他是"苏门四学士"之一。他协苏同守扬州。他的代表作为《摸鱼儿》,其中的词句"便似得班超,封侯万里,归计恐迟暮"可与辛弃疾《摸鱼儿》中的词行"更能消几番风雨?"媲美。

**Chao Buzhi(1053–1110)**

He passed the highest imperial examination in 1079. He served as a court official and a local official. He was demoted twice and later he lived in seclusion. He built a garden called "Return Garden" and called himself "Return Scholar". He was one of the four disciples of Su Shi. He once worked under Su Shi in Yangzhou. His representative *Ci* poem was "Groping for Fish" with lines "Even in the Han Dynasty a famous general Ban Chao/ Who was conferred a high title and post in frontier,/Coming back to the capital in his declining years." Some critics said, the lines in the *Ci* poem could compare with the line in Xin Qiji's *Ci* poem "Groping for Fish": "How many times can I bear experiencing wind and rain?"

## 金 凤 钩

### 送 春

春辞我,向何处？怪草草、夜来风雨。一簪华发、少欢饶恨,无计,觅春且住。　春回常恨寻无路,试向我、小园徐步。一阑红药,倚风含露,春自未曾归去。

## Tune: Hook with Gold Phoenix
### Seeing Spring off

Spring bids farewell to me with sorrow,
Where does she with beautiful dress go?
Oh, she is leaving in a hurry, why?
There was wind and rain last night.
My black hair almost becomes frosty,
With much grief and little happiness,
Unnoticed my precious youth is already gone.
In vain I invite spring to stay some time more.

I want to follow spring but don't know her way,
Trying to find her fragrance and traces anyway,
At leisure here and there I walk in my withering garden.
I see a fence of herbaceous peonies blooming with charm,
They dance in breeze with dewdrops glistening,

晁补之

Oh, still here remains so intoxicating the spring.

❀❀❀❀❀❀❀❀❀❀❀❀❀❀❀❀❀

## 临 江 仙

绿暗汀州三月暮,落花风静帆收。垂杨低映木兰舟。半篙春水滑,一段夕阳愁。 灞水桥东回首处,美人新上帘钩。青鸾无计入红楼。行云归楚峡,飞梦到扬州。

### *Tune: Immortals by the River*

The green darkens the shoal by the river in the spring late,
The flowers fall, the wind calms down and lower the sails.
Stroke the boat tenderly the weeping willows.
In the spring water moves half of a punt-hole,
The setting sun brings me a period of sore.

Turning round on Farewell Bridge, I saw
The enchanting beauty rolls up the curtain in my direction looking.
Now Green Bird, love errand can't find the way to her red building.
Those happy days are gone leaving beautiful recollection only,
I hope in a dream to fly to her boudoir in pretty Yangzhou City.

❀❀❀❀❀❀❀❀❀❀❀❀❀❀❀❀❀

## 摸 鱼 儿

### 东 皋 寓 居

买陂塘、旋栽杨柳,依稀淮岸湘浦。东皋嘉雨新痕涨,沙觜鹭来鸥聚。堪爱处,最好是、一川夜月光流渚。无人独舞。任翠幄张天,柔茵藉地,酒尽未能去。　　青绫被,莫忆金闺故步。儒冠曾把身误。弓刀千骑成何事?荒了邵平瓜圃。君试觑,满青镜、星星鬓影今如许!功名浪语。便似得班超,封侯万里,归计恐迟暮。

## Tune: Groping for Fish

### In the Return Garden by the East Mountain

Buying a pool by my home,
I plant the weeping willows,
It is like the Huai River and the Xiang River with hills and trees.
On the east hills falls a new rain and rises the water of the stream,
On the islet gather the gulls and egrets.
In all my life I appreciate tonight best,
The moon and water become one quiet flowing,
Never have I seen the scenery here so charming.
Alone I dance in the great world to my satisfaction.
Above stand the trees to the sky like green curtains,
Below lies at leisure the fragrant carpet-like grass,

晁补之

Drinking up the wine, I'm still unwilling to go back.

Forget those brilliant days
Serving in court far away.
With an official post I was held up.
I was an official of the region once
Leaving my cultivated fields not cared.
In a bronze mirror, I examine my hair,
With care and anxiety,
Oh, it becomes grizzled.
The honor and rank are just nothing but empty talk.
Even in the Han Dynasty a famous general Ban Chao
Who was conferred a high title and post in frontier,
Coming back to the capital in his declining years.

## 洞 仙 歌

### 泗州中秋作

青烟幂处,碧海飞金镜。永夜闲阶卧桂影。露凉时,零乱多少寒螀。神京远,惟有蓝桥路近。　　水晶帘不下,云母屏开,冷浸佳人淡脂粉。待都将许多明,付与金尊,投晓共、流霞倾尽。更携取胡床上南楼,看玉做人间,素秋千顷。

## Tune: Song of Immortals in the Cavern

### Written on the Mid-Autumn Festival in Sizhou

Through green clouds the moon gold-mirror-like
Flies leisurely and carefreely into the vast blue sky.
On the long night in the moonlight lies laurels' shadows.
The dewdrops on the trees and grasses feel a little cold,
In disorder cry cicadas.
Far away is the capital,
But so near is the moon bright.

I draw the crystal curtain aside,
And roll up the mica screen with unmatched pleasure.
The cool moonlight soaks the beauty lightly powdered.
We want to put all the bright moonlight into our wine cups,
And to drink wine till dawn with the flowing rosy glow up.
The enchanting night is very late,
To the south building a chair I take.
As the well-known poet Yu Liang I gaze at the jade-like world,
Appreciating the wonderful endless fall scenery without a word.

# 张耒(1054—1114)

宋神宗熙宁六年(1073)进士。曾任太常少卿等职。"苏门四学士"之一。受苏牵连,一再遭贬。词风不像苏轼那样豪放,而像柳永和秦观那样婉约。在他写给爱妓的《秋蕊香》的词中,就有这样的词行:"别离滋味浓于酒,著人瘦。"

## Zhang Lei(1054–1114)

He passed the highest imperial examination in 1073. He once served as a court official. He was one of the four disciples of Su Shi. Because of the relation, he was demoted again and again. Unlike Su Shi, without power and grandeur, his style was subtle like that of Liu Yong and Qin Guan. Such as "Scent of Autumn Flowers", he wrote for his favorite songstress with the line: "Stronger than wine is the separation taste, /Making thin as a willow branch my waist."

## 秋 蕊 香

帘幕疏疏风透,一线香飘金兽。朱栏倚遍黄昏后,廊上月华如昼。
别离滋味浓于酒,著人瘦。此情不及墙东柳,春色年年依旧。

## Tune: Scent of Autumn Flowers

Through the embroidered green silk curtain of the boudoir thin,
The breeze blows a thread of incense smoke to curl up slowly.
I lean lonely through the high railings in the evening,
In the moonlight bright as day is the corridor winding.

Stronger than wine is the separation taste,
Making thin as a willow branch my waist.
Yet my love is not as deep as the willows by the wall east,
Spring after spring the weeping willows trees become green.

❈❈❈❈❈❈❈❈❈❈❈❈❈❈❈❈❈

## 风 流 子

木叶亭皋下,重阳近,又是捣衣秋。奈愁人庾肠,老侵潘鬓,谩簪黄菊,花也应羞。楚天晚,白蘋烟尽处,红蓼水边头。芳草有情,夕阳无语,雁横南浦,人倚西楼。　　玉容知安否? 香笺共锦字,两处悠悠。空恨碧云离合,青鸟沉浮。向风前懊恼,芳心一点,寸眉两叶,禁甚闲愁。情到不堪言处,分付东流。

张　耒

## June: Song of Gallantry

Tree leaves shower on the riverside land far stretching,
The Double Ninth Festival with misery is approaching.
Again comes the fall and for their remote dears women make clothes.
Day and night I think of my remotest home with heartbreaking sorrow,
My hair at the temples begins to turn grey.
Oh, don't put chrysanthemums on my head,
So ashamed will feel the yellow flowers.
In the eve looking at the sky in the south,
I see the white duckweeds vanishing in vapor curling up slowly,
And the red knotweeds lying by the flowing green water lonely.
The grass gives off scent, a sweet love,
Silent and lonely hangs the setting sun.
The wild geese swim across the mouth of the river,
Alone I lean sad on the railings of the west chamber.

Is she still as pretty as a flower and jade?
We are separated melancholy so far away.
I write many letters and poems, trying to send my deep lovesickness to her.
The blue clouds flying away, Green Bird gets lost in the end of the

world.

Before the cold wind and under the bright moon,

Her love in her tender heart grows still with gloom,

Floating on her brows and any part

Of the face full of intoxicating charm.

Since she cannot pour her grief on the same pillow to me,

Let it with fragrant green water in the river flow away east.

# 周邦彦(1056—1121)

他曾任朝官,主管音乐。他是北宋末年一大词家,善写长调。贵人、学士、市侩、妓女都喜欢他的词。开南宋姜夔、吴文英、张炎一派词风。他写男女恋情、咏物、怀古伤今,其词风与柳永词风相似。但与柳永不同,他的词比较含蓄,无猥亵之语。他嫉妒皇上与歌妓李师师的爱,写了一首词。皇上大怒,将其驱出京城。他临走时写了一首和李师师不忍分别的词。后来皇上听李师师唱此词很感动,又将其召回。

## Zhou Bangyan(1056 - 1121)

He once served as an official in the court, mainly in charge of music. He was a great master of poetry at the end of the Northern Song Dynasty. He was good at writing long tunes. All the people including persons of eminence, scholars, frivolous persons and prostitutes liked his *Ci* poems very much. He started a new school with the followers as Jiang Kui, Wu Wenying and Zhang Yan. He wrote about love between men and women, scenes and meditation on the past. His style was like Liu Yong's. Different from Liu, he was more veiled away from obscenity. He was jealous of the love between the emperor and a famous songstress, writing a *Ci* poem. The emperor was angry and banished him out of the capital. He was so sad, writing another farewell *Ci* poem to her before parting. Later listening to her singing the poem, the emperor was moved and called him back to the capital.

## 满 江 红

昼日移阴,揽衣起,香帷睡足。临宝鉴,绿云撩乱,未忺妆束。蝶粉蜂黄都褪了,枕痕一线红生玉。背画栏、脉脉悄无言,寻棋局。　　重会面,犹未卜。无限事,萦心曲。想秦筝依旧,尚鸣金屋。芳草连天迷远望,宝香薰被成孤宿。最苦是、蝴蝶满园飞,无心扑。

## June: The River All Red

The rising sun slowly moves the shade of the willows gay,
Sleepless the whole night, the beauty still lies on the bed.
When she puts on clothes the sun rises high,
Before the mirror she stays for a little while,
Her hair is like green disorderly clouds,
To do makeup she has no interest now.
The white powder and red rouge on her beautiful face fade,
The line on her face from the pillow looks like red on jade.
She leans on the railings,
Without a word gazing

周邦彦

At the chessboard they played together.

With sadness day and night she wonders
When he will come back to her bed with a scent sweet.
Many merry affairs in the past surge in the heart deep.
She often plays the zither still
Giving forth miserable music.
In the golden boudoir she looks at the distant grass
Wet with the fragrant dew of love from their hearts,
Beside the heart-shaped incense lie the quilts cold.
Her tender heart is filled with unbearable sorrow
Seeing in the garden pairs of butterflies flying at leisure everywhere,
But she is not in the mood to take a fan to swat them here and there.

❋❋❋❋❋❋❋❋❋❋❋❋❋❋❋❋❋❋

## 兰 陵 王

### 柳

柳阴直,烟里丝丝弄碧。隋堤上、曾见几番,拂水飘绵送行色。登临望故国,谁识京华倦客?长亭路,年去岁来,应折柔条过千尺。　　闲寻旧踪迹,又酒趁哀弦,灯照离席。梨花榆火催寒食。愁一箭风快,半篙波暖,回头迢递便数驿,望人在天北。　　凄恻,恨堆积!渐别浦萦回,津堠岑寂,斜阳冉冉春无极。念月榭携手,露桥闻笛。沉思前事,似梦里,泪暗滴。

## Tune: King of Lanling

### The Weeping Willow

The shade of the willows straight forward spreads,
In mist, the twigs like green silk sway with grace.
Sui Dyke of a thousand miles
So far has seen countless times
Painful partings when the catkins fly, and the river the leaves stroke.
Climbing up the height, I look in the direction of my faraway home,
Who still knows me, a thin and tired traveller in the capital?
By the roadside pavilion near the green water of a long river,
In the warm springs or cold autumns year after year,
So many twigs of the willows are plucked away here
To let the hearts of those who leave stay in their dears' hearts anywhere.

Now I try to recollect day and night in my mind those enchanting affairs.
By the dim red candle light in the heartbreaking soft music,
I held a wine cup with my tears to her at the parting banquet.
The pear blossoms urged Cold Food Day to come here again.
I was chilly finding my boat like an arrow quickly going away,

周邦彦

And half of the bamboo punt-hole moving in the warm water tired.
Turning round to have a last look at her, I saw several posts pass by.
The pretty face was already in the north land.

I cannot bear to see a scene miserable and sad,
As I left farther and farther, in my heart, layer by layer, grief heaped.
Circling round was the green water in the river branch flowing east,
Quiet and lonely stood the ferry's lookout,
The setting sun shedding tears went down,
Without end spreads the sceneries of the intoxicating spring.
In the pavilion arm in arm we appreciated the moon hanging,
On Farewell Bridge, face to face we listened to the music once.
Oh, recollecting in my deep heart the happy affairs of true love,
I seem to enter the dream sweet and soft,
Tears fall down my cheeks drop by drop.

❉❉❉❉❉❉❉❉❉❉❉❉❉❉❉❉❉❉❉

## 拜 星 月 慢

夜色催更,清尘收露,小曲幽坊月暗。竹槛灯窗,识秋娘庭院。笑相遇,似觉琼枝玉树相倚,暖日明霞光烂。水盼兰情,总平生稀见。　　画图中、旧识春风面。谁知道、自到瑶台畔。眷恋雨润云温,苦惊风吹散。念荒寒、寄宿无人馆,重门闭、败壁秋虫叹。怎奈向、一缕相思,隔溪山不断。

## Tune: Slow Song of Worship of the Moon and Stars

The dark urged the watchman to beat time,
With dewdrops the dust was unable to fly.
I reached the yard under the dim moon
With the balustrade of scented bamboos.
On a fragrant green winding way,
I saw her in a bright window stay.
With a smile she embraced me.
Oh, I felt she was as a jade tree,
And a rosy cloud of warm and beautiful dawn.
Her wave-like eyes gave enchanting love forth,
Barely I saw such a charming girl.

Oh, the intoxicating portrait of her,
I was once surprised to see somewhere.
Since I met the pretty maiden over there,
I could not leave her warm cloud and sweet shower a moment,
But all of a sudden a terrible cold gale so far away separated us.
Now I live in a lodging alone,
All the doors are firmly closed.

周邦彦

The autumn insects are sadly groaning,
Without a word I stand heartbreaking.
Even the long streams and high mountains
Cannot at all separate my deep lovesickness.

❈❈❈❈❈❈❈❈❈❈❈❈❈❈❈❈

## 芳 草 渡

昨夜里,又再宿桃源,醉邀仙侣。听碧窗风快,珠帘半卷疏雨。多少离恨苦。方留连啼诉。凤帐晓,又是匆匆,独自归去。 愁顾。满怀泪粉,瘦马冲泥寻去路。谩回首、烟迷望眼,依稀见朱户。似痴似醉,暗恼损、凭阑情绪。淡暮色,看尽栖鸦乱舞。

### *Tune: The Ferry by Scented Grass*

I stayed in the Peach Blossom Land
Last night, the second time, so glad.
Drunk, with sadness I again invited the beauty,
We listened to the fine drizzle and hard wind
Knock on the green window, the pearly curtain rolled half.
How painful we were for next morning we had to far part.
Just when she was pouring out like showers her heartbreaking suffering,
The mosquito net decorated with phoenixes showed the first light

of morning.

Again in a hurry and alone,

I began my journey home.

"When can we have our happy reunion?" I sigh drear,

I saw her garment dotted with powder wet with red tears,

My thin muddy horse looked for slow homeward way.

With melancholy I turned to look at the parting place,

In the thin mist my sight was lost,

Faintly I saw the faraway red door.

At home leaning on

The rails with sore,

Oh, as if insane or drunk,

I gaze at the fairyland at dusk.

In my tender heart, layer by layer, piles unbearable grief,

I stare long at perching crows flying up and down trees.

## 夜 飞 鹊

河桥送人处,良夜何其?斜月远堕余辉。铜盘烛泪已流尽,霏霏凉露沾衣。相将散离会,探风前津鼓,树杪参旗。花骢会意,纵扬鞭、亦自行迟。　　迢递路回清野,人语渐无闻,空带愁归。何意重经前地,遗钿不见,斜径都迷。兔葵燕麦,向斜阳、影与人齐。但徘徊班草,欷歔酹酒,极望天西。

## Tune: A Magpie Flying at Night

In the inn near a bridge she said goodbye,
What time at all was the wonderful night?
The fading moon shedding fragrant dew went down drear,
The candle on the bronze plate shed its last drops of tears,
The thick dew wetted travellers' clothes.
The farewell banquet was about to close,
In breeze we listened to a watchman at the ferry beat a drum,
And watched Orion's Belt on a treetop before daybreak just.
My horse knew why I cried in despair,
Even I lifted my whip high with care,
Now and then with sighs and whines the horse stood there still.

She left, my inn seeming far away and country, wide and solitary.
Gradually, died away the people's voice echoing,
I went back to the inn, but sorrow with nothing.
Why do I visit again the place bringing to my deep heart pain?
I look for her lost precious decorations with her scent in vain.
On the path as if in the fairyland I am lost.
The fading sun with a heart sweet and soft
Watches the hollyhocks and oats like her skirt about.
I pace on the grass with our love dew up and down,

Drinking wine, I feel quite depressed,
I look into the west my beauty stays.

## 玉 楼 春

桃溪不作从容住,秋藕断来无续处。当时相候赤栏桥,今日独寻黄叶路。　烟中列岫青无数,雁背夕阳红欲暮。人如风后入江云,情似雨余粘地絮。

### Tune: Spring in the Jade Boudoir

By the Peach Blossom Stream we were in love but finally we parted,
Oh, I know in autumn a lotus root snapped cannot be again connected.
Under the green willows on the red bridge we had a tryst sweet,
Now I stroll alone on the path covered with fallen yellow leaves.

The countless green hills like her brows float into the mist curling up,
The wild geese fly away falling into the stream under the setting sun.
She is with wind the drifting graceful rosy cloud,
My love to her is the catkin sticking to the ground.

周邦彦

## 长 相 思 慢

夜色澄明,天街如水,风力微冷帘旌。幽期再偶,坐久相看,才喜欲叹还惊。醉眼重醒。映雕阑修竹,共数流萤。细语轻轻。尽银台、挂蜡潜听。　自初识伊来,便惜妖娆,艳质美盼柔情。桃溪换世,鸾驭凌空,有愿须成。游丝荡絮,任轻狂、相逐牵萦。但连环不解,流水长东,难负深盟。

### *Tune: Slow Song of Yearning Forever*

The night spreads anywhere clear and bright,
On the streets in the capital flows moonlight,
Before the curtain air drifts a bit cold in a breeze gentle.
As luck would have it, I meet you, my beauty here again,
We look at each other in high glee,
And then we are surprised indeed.
From deep drunkenness of happiness, we are awake.
By the scented green bamboos we sit on the red rails,
Counting the glowworms flying,
And in a sweet voice whispering.
We let the candle listen to us exchanging our love so soft,
For us without a word it cannot help but shed tears warm.

Since the first time I saw you,

In my heart I have left no room

For other things except for your grace, glances and softness.

How we wish tomorrow morn we could be so happily married,

Just like Liu and Ruan marrying the two female celestials so fair,

Or Xiao and Nong riding a pair of phoenixes flying anywhere.

Though you are gossamer or catkins flying far and near,

I believe in the future any time you will turn a deaf ear

To the wooing and pestering of frivolous lads.

Our true love will be double rings chained fast,

And a river flowing without end to the east far,

Our solemn pledges will forever in our hearts.

## 花 犯

### 梅 花

粉墙低，梅花照眼，依然旧风味。露痕轻缀。疑净洗铅华，无限佳丽。去年胜赏曾孤倚。冰盘同宴喜。更可惜、雪中高树，香篝熏素被。　　今年对花最匆匆，相逢似有恨，依依愁悴。吟望久，青苔上、旋看飞坠。相将见、翠丸荐酒，人正在、空江烟浪里。但梦想、一枝潇洒，黄昏斜照水。

周邦彦

## *June: Violation of Flowers*

### The Plum Blossom

Low is the old wall white,
Plum blossoms are bright,
As pretty and intoxicating as before.
The plum with glistening dewdrops
Is like a most beautiful girl with grace
Whose powder has been washed away.
In the vigorous early spring last year on the festival only with her,
I shared the dishes on the jade plate in a remote place of the world.
And what was more attractive
Was all its blossoms are heavy
With snow, like a white quilt, giving off faint scent.

In this early spring, I'll be on a long journey in haste.
Knowing I am about to far go,
She is heartbreaking with woe.
I chant, gazing at her, so beautiful.
All of a sudden, so shocked I am,
The twigs sway and petals shower sobbing.
With unbearable sorrow, I'm away going.
When she bears green fruits fat,
I'll be in a boat travelling so fast

On the misty waves down and up.
Still she will accompany me, but
In drinking fine wine with heavy grief.
I'll be farther and farther away indeed,
In dreams before me under the setting sun will appear
The reflection of her twig of blossoms in the water here.

❋❋❋❋❋❋❋❋❋❋❋❋❋❋❋❋❋

## 水 龙 吟

### 梨 花

素肌应怯余寒,艳阳占立青芜地。樊川照日,灵关遮路,残红敛避。传火楼台,妒花风雨,长门深闭。亚帘栊半湿,一枝在手,偏勾引、黄昏泪。　　别有风前月底。布繁英,满园歌吹。朱铅退尽,潘妃却酒,昭君乍起。雪浪翻空,粉裳缟夜,不成春意。恨玉容不见,琼英谩好,与何人比?

## *Tune: Chanting of Water Dragon*

### The Pear Blossom

The tender pear is still afraid of the remaining cold of spring late,
But she stands in the brilliant sunlight on green grasses with grace.
Her white blossoms brighten the gardens
And shade far and near the roads and paths,

周邦彦

The other remaining red flowers disappear.
Cold Food Day has unnoticed come here,
Envying her enchanting blossoms, the wind and rain do their worst,
Long Gate Palace shuts where the degraded queen shows pity to her.
On the windows press her half wet twigs and leaves,
Oh, in the evening in the sighing and groaning breeze,
With a scented twig in my hand,
I shed tears like showers so sad.

In those fragrant springs
When she was blooming,
The Tang Dynasty emperor loved her, music and songs filling the court.
So matchlessly intoxicating though she was not powdered and rouged at all,
As snow-white concubine Pan refused wine, afraid her face would become scarlet,
And as Princess Wang was playing Pear Leaves bleak to marry a faraway chieftain.
Rarely seen, plum blossoms are like white waves rolling to the sky,
And her fragrant beautiful clothes are so eye-catching at dark night.
How can the plum compare in beauty with the pear?
Jade-like concubine Yang has turned into dust there,

Please don't praise her charming face too much,
Who else at all can with the pear compare but?

❈❈❈❈❈❈❈❈❈❈❈❈❈❈❈

## 苏 幕 遮

燎沉香,消溽暑。鸟雀呼晴,侵晓窥檐语。叶上初阳干宿雨,水面清圆,一一风荷举。 故乡遥,何日去?家住吴门,久作长安旅。五月渔郎相忆否?小楫轻舟,梦入芙蓉浦。

### *Tune: Screened by Southern Curtain*

In early summer, to dispel the wet,
I burn a piece of eaglewood incense.
The birds sing merry on the eaves,
It is fine, with cheer they tell me.
The raindrops on lotus leaves evaporate in early morning,
Like heavily rouged girls the pink lotus flowers blooming
In the gentle breeze dance happy and gay.

My hometown waiting for me is far away,
When can I return my home
In the pretty city of Suzhou?
Oh, too long I have been staying in the capital.

周邦彦

Do my fishing company miss me in May still?
I row a boat into lotus flowers at leisure
In my pleasant sweet dreams very often.

❋❋❋❋❋❋❋❋❋❋❋❋❋❋❋

## 大　酺

### 春　雨

对宿烟收,春禽静,飞雨时鸣高屋。墙头青玉旆,洗铅霜都尽,嫩梢相触。润逼琴丝,寒侵枕障,虫网吹粘帘竹。邮亭无人处,听檐声不断,困眠初熟。奈愁极频惊,梦轻难记,自怜幽独。　　行人归意速。最先念、流潦妨车毂。怎奈向、兰成憔悴,卫玠清羸,等闲时、易伤心目。未怪平阳客,双泪落、笛中哀曲。况萧索、青芜国。红糁铺地,门外荆桃如菽。夜游共谁秉烛?

## Tune: Drinking while Gathering

### The Spring Rain

The heavy fog dispersed last night,
The spring birds still slumber quiet,
And the showers knock on the storied buildings' roofs.
Over the wall the green jade-like flags are the bamboos,
The powder on them has been washed away,
Their tender tips collide in the wind and rain.

Damp, poor is the sound of strings of the instrument,
And the covering of the solitary pillow the cold enters.
With raindrops to the bamboo curtain spiders' nets stick,
The inn in the little village is sleeping silent and lonely.
Listening to the sound of rain on the eaves like sad songs,
Gradually with bitterness I enter a gloomy dream not long.
Oh, I don't know why now and then I wake up,
I cannot recollect anything in the dream at once.
Awake, I feel unbearably gloomy and drear.

I'm eager to go home to embrace my dear,
However, the first trouble is that mud will stop the wheels wet.
Now I know why scholar Yu and Wei staying in the land strange
Were tortured pale and thin with deep sorrow,
Why the musician Ma shed tears with woe.
A fellow traveller plays on the pipe the homesick song with grief,
The music like the north wind drifts into my heart chilly and bleak!
The garden at once changes into the wilds now,
The fallen scented pink flowers dot the ground,
The red cherry blossoms turn into small green fruits out of the door.
Who would carry a lantern accompaning me to have a leisurely walk?

周邦彦

## 满 庭 芳
### 夏日溧水无想山作

风老莺雏,雨肥梅子,午阴嘉树清圆。地卑山近,衣润费炉烟。人静乌鸢自乐,小桥外、新绿溅溅。凭栏久,黄芦苦竹,拟泛九江船。　　年年,如社燕,飘流瀚海,来寄修椽。且莫思身外,长近尊前。憔悴江南倦客,不堪听急管繁弦。歌筵畔、先安簟枕,容我醉时眠。

### *June: Courtyard Full of Fragrance*

I wrote the poem in Lishui county against the
Thoughtless Mountains in summer.

In a breeze, the baby orioles grow up and fly here and there,
In rains, the plum blossoms turn into green fruits fat and fair.
At noon the shade of trees is cool and round.
The land lies low and near stand the mounts,
Damp, the clothes need incense smoke to be dried.
It's peaceful and secluded and crows leisurely fly,
Beyond the old arch stone bridge little,
The rising green water sings pleasantly.
For a long time, lonely and desolate I lean on the red rails,
Watching the yellow reeds and bitter bamboos gently sway.
I seem the banished poet far away drear.

I recollect with deep grief, year by year,

I wander as an official like a petrel migrating,

Across the wide sea and broad rivers, coming

Back all the way to his home, the old nest.

Oh, don't pay attention to fame and wealth,

And just hold a jade wine cup in your hand.

A haggard traveller from the southern land,

I can't bear to listen

To the quick rhythm.

By a banquet with songs of sorrow,

I place a bamboo mat and a pillow

To sleep at once

When I am drunk.

## 西 河

### 京 陵

佳丽地,南朝盛事谁记?山围故国绕清江,髻鬟对起;怒涛寂寞打孤城,风樯遥度天际。　　断崖树,犹倒倚;莫愁艇子曾系。空余旧迹郁苍苍,雾沉半垒。夜深月过女墙来,伤心东望淮水。　　酒旗戏鼓甚处市?想依稀、王谢邻里。燕子不知何世;向寻常巷陌人家,相对如说兴亡,斜阳里。

周邦彦

## Tune: The West River

### In Jingling (Nanjing)

Jingling is a beautiful city in the south of the Yangtze River,
Who in the present time still remember its time so prosperous?
The mountains and water surround the old capital city,
Sleeping on banks the hills look like buns of a beauty.
The raging billows beat the lonely city day and night,
The boats to and fro with full sails float to the horizon.

The trees on the precipices around
Still grow vigorous upside down,
To one of which Sorrowless Girl tied her boat.
There remain the verdant traces of the time old
And the ruins of the barracks half veiled in the thin fog.
At the late night, the moon sheds dew on the city walls,
The Huai Stream where beauties sang flows silent east.

Who can tell me: where is the famous Black Clothes Street
With wineshop streamers fluttering and theatre drums sounding far and near?
I recollect quite clear there once lived the well-known general and premier.
Oh, here it is! Please look at the swallows unaware of the ages

Flying into their nest in the old mansion whose owner changes.
About the rise and fall they are chatting,
With bitterness against the sun slanting.

❋❋❋❋❋❋❋❋❋❋❋❋❋❋❋

## 解 语 花

### 上 元

风销绛蜡,露浥红莲,花市光相射。桂华流瓦。纤云散,耿耿素娥欲下。衣裳淡雅。看楚女、纤腰一把。箫鼓喧,人影参差,满路飘香麝。　　因念都城放夜。望千门如昼,嬉笑游冶。钿车罗帕。相逢处,自有暗尘随马。年光是也。唯只见、旧情衰谢。清漏移,飞盖归来,从舞休歌罢。

## *June: The Flower Knowing Words*

### On the Night of the Lantern Festival

In the breeze, the candles shedding red tears around,
The sparkling dewdrops wet the lotus lanterns about.
The lanterns of different colors reflect each other bright,
The gentle moonlight like water flows on the green tiles,
The thin clouds like light greenish blue silk curtains are up rolled,
In the moon the goddess wants to appreciate the night like snow.
In dresses simple and elegant,

周邦彦

The girls in the land southern
Have slender waists like weeping willows' trunks.
Everywhere are the noises of the flutes and drums,
Countless and disorderly are the shadows of the people,
Over lanes and streets drifts the aroma of ladies' sleeves.

I recollect on the Lantern Festival when curfew was removed
Thousands of the high open red gates were as bright as at noon,
People old and young played and laughed.
My charming dear in a jade-decorated cart
To me smiling waved her handkerchief scented.
I followed the girl on a horse, dust rising after it.
The Lantern Festival comes year after year.
This year without her I'm lonely and drear,
My beauty is far away.
Night is already late,
In a hurry in a simple lone cart I go back,
Letting others until dawn sing and dance.

❋❋❋❋❋❋❋❋❋❋❋❋❋❋❋❋❋❋❋❋

## 过 秦 楼

水浴清蟾,叶喧凉吹,巷陌马声初断。闲依露井,笑扑流萤,惹破画罗轻扇。人静夜久凭栏,愁不归眠,立残更箭。叹年华一瞬,人今千里,梦沉书远。　　空见说、鬓怯琼梳,容消金镜,渐懒趁时匀染。梅风地溽,虹雨苔滋,一架舞红都变。谁信无聊为伊,才减江淹,情伤荀倩。但明河影下,还看稀星数点。

## Tune: Passing the Qin Tower

The bright moon took a bath in the clear creek,
The leaves of trees resounded in a cool breeze,
The noise of carriages and horses died away.
At leisure alone I leaned on the well's rails,
Looking at the pretty girl catching the fireflies,
She broke her painted silk fan to her surprise.
I'm too sad to go to bed
Until about the daybreak.
Oh, precious youth is as short as a moment,
We are a thousand *li* away from each other,
I have neither a dream nor a letter of her.

In vain from her close friends it is heard,
She is afraid to comb her sparse hair with a jade comb,
Before the mirror she is shocked to see her face sallow,
She is even too drear to follow the fashion to make up.
The ground is wet in rainy Season of Yellowing Plums,
In the quiet lonely courtyard grows green moss about,
Red roses like her face fall in succession on the ground.

周邦彦

Who knows my literary talent is gone with my intoxicating beauty half?
Day and night, everywhere yearning for her never leaves my tender heart.
Before dawn what I can do is gazing
In Milky Way at the few stars fading.

❉❉❉❉❉❉❉❉❉❉❉❉❉❉❉❉

## 浪淘沙慢

晓阴重,霜凋岸草,雾隐城堞。南陌脂车待发,东门帐饮乍阕。正扶面垂杨堪揽结。掩红泪、玉手亲折。念汉浦离鸿去何许,经时信音绝。　情切。望中地远天阔。向露冷风清无人处,耿耿寒漏咽。嗟万事难忘,唯是轻别。翠尊未竭,凭断云、留取西楼残月。　罗带光销纹衾叠,连环解,旧香顿歇。怨歌永、琼壶敲尽缺。恨春去、不与人期。弄夜色、空余满地梨花雪。

### *Tune: Slow Song of Waves-Sifting Sand*

The sky was overcast with clouds at dawn,
The frost withered the grasses on the shore.
The fog hid the battlement, and on the path
His finely-decorated chart was ready to start,
The farewell banquet just over and he would say bye to her at any

moment.

Stroking faces the willow twigs with leaves could still be gifts for travellers.

Without a word wiping her tears on the face with blood,

With jade-like hands, as a gift a tender twig she plucked.

Was he in the remotest corner of the world?

She hadn't got his letter from the Green Bird.

She was expecting him the whole night to return to her arms eagerly.

Ascending the height she saw the sky wide and countryside, endless.

In the deserted place the dew was cold and wind clear,

She listened to the water watch dripping water like tears.

Everything between them was still so clear in her mind,

"Why did we easily say goodbye that day?" she sighed.

She kept her cup from being empty, waiting for him to go on drinking.

She asked with deep bitterness in the west sky a white cloud remaining

To hang over the west building to stop the pure fading moon.

The colourful quilts wrinkled, fades the silk ribbon with a loop,

The jade chain of rings is unchained,

The incense he gave her loses scent.

So long shedding tears like rain she sings the songs sad,

She beats tune too hard, in the jade kettle, knocking a gap.

周邦彦

She hates spring leaving with grief,

Without informing her at all indeed.

In the dark silent night it shouldn't have gone anyhow,

Leaving the pear blossoms like snow all over the ground.

✺✺✺✺✺✺✺✺✺✺✺✺✺✺✺

## 解 连 环

怨怀无托,嗟情人断绝,信音辽邈。纵妙手、能解连环,似风散雨收,雾轻云薄。燕子楼空,暗尘锁、一床弦索。想移根换叶,尽是旧时,手种红药。　　汀洲渐生杜若。料舟依岸曲,人在天角。漫记得、当日音书,把闲语闲言,待总烧却。水驿春回,望寄我、江南梅萼。拚今生,对花对酒,为伊泪落。

## *June: Unchaining Double Rings*

I'm unable to get rid of grief anyway,

For my pretty sweetheart is far away,

And I get no message from her.

Oh, with ingenious hands even,

Someone can unchain Double Rings at last,

Our true love can't stop completely just as

When the wind calms and rain ceases remain light fog and clouds thin.

The Swallow Building where stayed the pretty devoted singer is empty,

There lie the music instruments she used once

Covered with thick dust and with fragrant love.

So many times I want to grow with sorrow

New herbaceous peonies to replace the old,

I stop to do so, for the day we planted them I remember clear.

On the shoal the leaves of the wild ginger so luxuriant appear,

Oh, to my love I have no way to have them sent,

Along the river, her boat went to the earth's end.

At first, it seemed the letters she sent to me

Were filled with her love tender and sweet.

Reading them again, I find them silly now,

Oh, I think they should be all burned down.

To the inn by the green stream the enchanting spring returns,

I wish a twig of plum blossoms would be sent to me from her,

In the southeast of the Yangtze River with the previous feelings.

Day by day, year by year, for my love I'll never regret waiting,

To the flowers, I'll alone drink wine

Shedding tears for my dear all my life.

❀❀❀❀❀❀❀❀❀❀❀❀❀❀❀❀❀❀

## 瑞 龙 吟

章台路,还见褪粉梅梢,试花桃树。愔愔坊陌人家,定巢燕子,归

周邦彦

来旧处。　　黯凝伫。因念个人痴小,乍窥门户。侵晨浅约宫黄,障风映袖,盈盈笑语。　　前度刘郎重到,访邻寻里,同时歌舞,惟有旧家秋娘,声价如故。吟笺赋笔,犹记燕台句。知谁伴、名园露饮,东城闲步? 事与孤鸿去。探春尽是,伤离意绪。官柳低金缕。归骑晚、纤纤池塘飞雨。断肠院落,一帘风絮。

## *Tune: Chanting of the Auspicious Dragon*

On either side of the street of brothels gathering,
Again I see sadly the pink plum blossoms fading,
The peach trees begin to blossom.
So deserted is the old green brothel,
The pair of swallows of the days
Return to their home, the old nest.

I stand still thinking of the happy time
When she was in early spring so shy.
In the cold early morn,
She stood at the door,
With a sweet and coy smile and enchaning fragrance she greeted me.
Lightly powdered and rouged, her face was half hidden in the sleeve.

Revisiting the streets and lanes, the old place,
I look for her but I cannot at all find her trace.
Only Autumn Beauty of her companions

Is still as popular as in the former period.

For my beauty I composed many verses,

I can remember some of the lines clearly.

Now who can accompany me like the sweetheart?

We drank unrestrainedly in the well-known garden,

And at leisure in the east city we strolled.

All the hours are gone with a swan alone.

In the early spring, I fail to see her there,

My grief like gossamer drifts everywhere,

Like golden threads, the willow twigs drearily hang.

Towards the evening on a horse in a hurry I go back,

A drizzle sheds tears on the pool.

The courtyard casts me a gloom,

In the wind rolling up and down is the curtain,

Here and there fly the weeping willow catkins.

# 六 丑

### 蔷薇谢后作

正单衣试酒,怅客里光阴虚掷。愿春暂留,春归如过翼,一去无迹。为问花何在?夜来风雨,葬楚宫倾国。钗钿堕处遗香泽。乱点桃蹊,轻翻柳陌,多情为谁追惜?但蜂媒蝶使,时叩窗槅。 东园岑寂,渐蒙笼暗碧。静绕珍丛底,成叹息。长条故惹

周邦彦

行客。似牵衣待话,别情无极。残英小,强簪巾帻;终不似、一朵钗头颤袅,向人欹侧。漂流处,莫趁潮汐。恐断红尚有相思字[※],何由见得。

## Tune: Six Violations

### The Withered Rose

Wearing thin clothes, I taste the newly-made wine,
I regret in a strange region wasting precious time.
I wish the spring for a short while to stay,
But just like a bird it so quickly flies away,
Without leaving its trace anywhere.
Now I can see pink flowers nowhere.
Last night the wind and rain I heard
Burying them like pretty slender girls.
Though silently to another world they are gone,
Their hairpins on earth still give the scent off.
Under the peaches and willows with red petals the paths are covered,
Who takes pity on the flowers, the charming slim maids in Chu palace?
But for the bees and butterflies knocking
At the window lattice miserably weeping.

Sounder and sounder slumbers the garden east,
Thicker and thicker is the shade of green leaves.
Round the fenced red roses in clusters I stroll,

Now and then heaving deep sighs and groans.

A rose stretches a long twig to pull my arm

As if to me to bare her tender fragrant heart,

Showing her parting bitterness endless.

I pluck a fading flower remaining on it,

With great care pinning it on my silk hood.

It can't be compared with a flower in bloom

Quivering on an intoxicating beauty's bun round,

And leaning one side and flirting with men around.

"Oh, lovely rose, don't go away, I cry depressed,

With scented clear green stream's flow and ebb,

On the petal there is a love letter of a palace maid for her dear."※

The cold water of the stream seems flowing into my heart drear.

※ 书生偶然来到御沟边,见一红叶漂在水中,上有题字,急取出,视之,乃诗一首:"流水何太急,深宫尽日闲。殷勤谢红叶,好去到人间。"将其放入箱中。后他娶一宫中遣出的韩姓宫女。结婚当晚,她看到箱中那片红叶。

※ A scholar in the Tang Dynasty saw a red leaf with words floating on the imperial drainage. He picked it out and found there was a poem on it by a court maid: "The green water flows quite fast, /But I live leisurely in the court deep. /Oh, I hope so sincerely the red leaf/Will with water get to the outside world at last." He put it in his suitcase. Later the scholar married the court maid who was allowed to leave the court. On the wedding night she found the red leaf with her poem in his suitcase.

## 关 河 令

> 周邦彦

秋阴时晴渐向暝。变一庭凄冷。伫听寒声,云深无雁影。　更深人去寂静。但照壁孤灯相映。酒已都醒,如何消夜永!

### Tune: Song of the Pass and River

In autumn at dusk it's fine after several days' overcast,
I stand alone in the front courtyard of the inn, very sad.
The withering grasses and trees are soaked in chill.
I hear in the clouds a lonely wild goose cry faintly.

At midnight the room is quiet when a guest is gone,
The flickering candle casts my shadow on the wall.
I just sober up from strong wine,
Oh, how to spend the long night?

## 诉 衷 情

出林杏子落金盘。齿软怕尝酸。可惜半残青紫,犹印小唇丹。南陌上,落花闲。雨斑斑。不言不语,一段伤春,都在眉间。

### Tune: Baring the Heart

On the golden plate are the apricots just picked from a tree.
The girl takes a small mouth of one, for sour her teeth feel,
On the green and purple fruit remain
So clear two lines of blood bright red.

On the winding green path southern,
The flowers shower down at leisure,
Leaving here and there red dots.
Without a word she alone walks,
Oh, the deep spring sorrow
Between her brows shows.

❀❀❀❀❀❀❀❀❀❀❀❀❀❀

## 少 年 游

并刀如水,吴盐胜雪,纤手破新橙。锦幄初温,兽烟不断,相对坐

周邦彦

调笙。　　低声问:"向谁行宿?城上已三更。马滑霜浓,不如休去,直是少人行。"

## Tune: Travelling While Young

The knife of the northern land is as water as bright,
And the salt of the southern land, as snow as white,
The beauty peels a fresh orange with her scented tender fingers.
The chamber is just warmed with the decorated brocade curtains,
The smoke curls up from the incense burner animal-shaped,
With sweet smiles in turn they tune the reed pipe face to face.

She says to him in a voice sweet and low:
"With whom will you sleep tonight cold?
The watchman has beaten three times already.
The frost is so thick and your horse will slip,
You'd better not in a hurry leave,
I can see few people on the streets."

❀❀❀❀❀❀❀❀❀❀❀❀❀❀❀❀

## 少　年　游

朝云漠漠散轻丝,楼阁淡春姿。柳泣花啼,九街泥重,门外燕飞迟。　　而今丽日明金屋,春色在桃枝。不似当时,小楼冲雨,幽恨两人知。

## Tune: Travelling While Young

The grey morning clouds hung quite low and drizzle fell like silk,
Outside the pavilion the spring scene was not so bright and pretty.
A rain falling flowers moaned and willows wept with grief,
A heavy layer of wet mud covered all the lanes and streets,
And with the wet wings in the air flew slow the familiar swallows.

Now on fine days the warm sunlight brightens our chamber of gold,
The spring scenery is on the peach blossoms.
But the hours in the past were more beautiful,
The pavilion was knocked by the wind and rain crying,
Our two hearts shared the chilly feelings of the parting.

❀❀❀❀❀❀❀❀❀❀❀❀❀❀

## 尉 迟 杯

### 离　恨

隋堤路。渐日晚、密霭生深树。阴阴淡月笼沙，还宿河桥深处。无情画舸，都不管、烟波隔前浦。等行人、醉拥重衾，载将离恨归去。　　因思旧客京华，长偎傍疏林，小槛欢聚。冶叶倡条俱相识，仍惯见、珠歌翠舞。如今向、渔村水驿，夜如岁、焚香独自语。

周邦彦

有何人、念我无聊,梦魂凝想鸳侣。

## Tune: Wine in the Cup
### Parting Grief

On Sui Dyke of a thousand miles,
The setting sun sheds its dim light,
The thick mist rises bit by bit on the deep green wood.
The sands by the river bathe in pale light of the moon,
I stay for the night in the thicket of the wood by the bridge.
Ignoring our sad parting the ruthless boat starts its journey,
Soon it passes the mouth of the river.
As a lonely and melancholy traveller,
Drunk I cover myself in a thick quilt trying to enter a dream,
The small boat goes away very slowly with so heavy my grief.

In the flourishing capital city in the days,
We took a walk arm in arm happy and gay,
The little room saw us sleeping in a quilt with cheer.
With all other songstresses and dancers I was familiar,
And with interest I very often long
Appreciated their dances and songs.
Tonight by the fishing village in the station of post,
I spend the drear night as long as a year with woe.
I burn a piece of incense

And murmur to myself:
"I'm lonely and miserable, but really no one
Knows in dreams with my beauty I make love."

## 渔 家 傲

灰暖香融销永昼。蒲萄架上春藤秀。曲角栏干群雀斗。清明后。风梳万缕亭前柳。　　日照钗梁光欲溜。循阶竹粉沾衣袖。拂拂面红如著酒。沉吟久。昨宵正是来时候。

## Tune: Pride of Fishermen

From the incense burner the smoke curling up, long are the days.
On the racks the green grape vines display their graceful waists,
On the winding rails the birds play with one another with cheer.
Pure Brightness, the day of Tomb-worship, is already away here,
Before the pavilion the breeze kisses the twigs of the willows.

The bright sunlight on the beauty's green jade hairpins flowed.
When she passed the steps the white bamboo powder dotted her sleeves,
As if she had drunk a little wine, flush came on her intoxicating cheeks.

周邦彦

Silently I stand here still for a long time,
Oh, all the things just happened last night.

❀❀❀❀❀❀❀❀❀❀❀❀❀❀❀❀

## 忆旧游

记愁横浅黛,泪洗红铅,门掩秋宵。坠叶惊离思,听寒螀夜泣,乱雨潇潇。凤钗半脱云鬓,窗影烛光摇。渐暗竹敲凉,疏萤照晚,两地魂消。　　迢迢。问音信,道径底花阴,时认鸣镳。也拟临朱户,叹因郎憔悴,羞见郎招。旧巢更有新燕,杨柳拂河桥。但满目京尘,东风竟日吹露桃。

### Tune: Recollecting the Tours in Old Days

I recollect sorrow lay on her brows with pale green pigment,
The tears washed away from her face the rouge and powder.
The autumn night entered a sad dream beyond the door.
Awakened by a shower of falling leaves from sad thoughts,
We listened to the sobs of the cold crickets,
And the rain fall thick and fast melancholy.
Half of her hairpins were away from her hair at the temples,
In the candlelight the shadow of the window slowly swayed.
Tonight the chilly bamboos knock at each other outside,
The firefly flickers now and then through the dark night,

We are grieved separated at the ends of the earth.

Oh, so far no letter at all has come here from her.
She often wanders on the paths and in flowers' shade,
With care listening to my horse on the road I left neigh.
Sometimes she tries to go out to the lanes and streets,
But she is afraid to see me for her face fades with grief.
In the old nest on the eaves come the new swallows,
The bridge over the stream is stroked by the willows.
In the capital city over the roads red dust flies here and there,
The east breeze blows open the peach blossoms everywhere.

## 一 落 索

眉共春山争秀。可怜长皱。莫将清泪湿花枝,恐花也、如人瘦。
清润玉箫闲久。知音稀有,欲知日日倚阑愁,但问取、亭前柳。

## Tune: Chain of Jade Rings

With green spring hills my brows vie in beauty,
It's a pity on them all the time stay the wrinkles.
Don't shed tears on the flowers on trees,
Because in this early chilly spring season,

周邦彦

They are as thin and weak as I.

My jade flute lies here long idle,
Oh, fewer and fewer remain my intimates.
Why do I lean on the railings day by day?
Just ask the willow before the pavilion
Seeing us part shedding bloody tears.

❋❋❋❋❋❋❋❋❋❋❋❋❋❋❋❋❋

## 四 园 竹

浮云护月,未放满朱扉。鼠摇暗壁,萤度破窗,偷入书帏。秋意浓,闲贮立,庭柯影里。好风襟袖先知。 夜何其。江南路绕重山,心知谩与前期。奈向灯前堕泪。肠断萧娘,旧日书辞。犹在纸。雁信绝,清宵梦又稀。

### Tune: The Bamboos in the Four Gardens

The clouds accompany the moon bright,
Keeping the red doors from its soft light.
The mice sigh and groan in the holes,
The fireflies steal through the windows
And again study's thick curtains.
In the air very much is the autumn,

I stand still alone with a gloomy heart,
In the shadows of the trees in the yard.
My sleeves first feel the good wind.

Oh, night is very late, what time is it?
In the south of the Yangtze River, roads are surrounded by mounts anywhere,
She cannot at all keep our appointment to have a happy reunion over there.
Before the lamp I can only shed tears without a word.
I'm heartbreaking for her, the prettiest girl in the world,
Her letters in those old days
Lie on the dust-covered table.
At present none of her letters reaches me,
At night I seldom see her in the dreams.

❋❋❋❋❋❋❋❋❋❋❋❋❋❋❋❋❋

## 应 天 长

条风布暖,霏雾弄晴,池塘遍满春色。正是夜堂无月,沉沉暗寒食。梁间燕,前社客。似笑我、闭门愁寂。乱花过,隔院芸香,满地狼藉。　　长记那回时,邂逅相逢,郊外驻油壁。又见汉宫传烛,飞烟五侯宅。青青草,迷路陌。强载酒、细寻前迹。市桥远,柳下人家,犹自相识。

周邦彦

## Tune: Everlasting Woe

The gentle breeze brings warmth here,
Oh, the mist away, the blue sky appears,
Spring water plants fill the pool.
At night there is no bright moon,
Darkness shrouding wholly Cold Food Day night.
In the morn the pair of swallows chats with delight,
In their nest on the beams.
They seem to laugh at me,
Alone and drear the whole day I shut myself behind the door.
Shower by shower flowers like beauties with pink dresses fall
On the ground in disorder,
From the yard comes aroma.

I recollect the day long ago in suburb I saw her by chance,
She first sent me an intoxicating glance in a painted cart.
Again comes Cold Food Day and the palace sends candles
To high-ranking officials in the capital to break their fast.
I take a walk at leisure far and near to seek the old place,
On the path wild with grass like her skirt I lose my way.
With wine I go on looking for our traces.
Far away from the lonely old stone bridge,
There is a familiar hut under the weeping willows,

Before it we bade farewell to each other with woe.

❋❋❋❋❋❋❋❋❋❋❋❋❋❋❋❋❋

## 还 京 乐

禁烟近,触处浮香秀色相料理。正泥花时候,奈何客里,光阴虚费。望箭波无际。迎风漾日黄云委。任去远,中有万点相思清泪。　　到长淮底。过当时楼下,殷勤为说,春来羁旅况味。堪嗟误约乖期,向天涯、自看桃李。想而今、应恨墨盈笺,愁妆照水。怎得青鸾翼,飞归教见憔悴。

### *Tune: Joy of Returning to the Capital*

Cold Food Day and Pure Brightness are coming here,
Scent drifts in the air and flowers glisten far and near.
It is the time to appreciate the charming scene with delight,
But I stay in the place away from my home a thousand miles,
Oh, I spend the spring of precious youth in vain.
In the wind in the river the endless surging waves
Wash the sun, and take in and send out the yellow clouds.
Farther and farther away rolling waves go up and down,
Flowing into the Huai River with my tears of a ten thousand drops.

They pass the downstairs of the storied building we had trysts often.

周邦彦

I sob pouring to you the painful feelings,
On the lonely long journey in the spring.
I sigh for breaking our pledge.
So far away in the world's end,
I appreciate the peaches and pears alone.
Now day and night I think with deep woe,
You write a long love letter drear on rosy paper piece by piece,
Now and then you look at your fading face on water with grief.
Oh, how I wish I could ride on a large phoenix back,
Coming to your arms to show you my faded face sad.

# 阮阅(生卒年不详)

宋神宗元丰八年(1085)进士。做过地方官。宋代地方官妓属于"乐营",也称"乐妓"。长官有宴会,召其歌舞劝酒。客人常与其产生感情。他多写官妓与客人的爱恋之情。词风通俗、坦率,像民歌。

**Ruan Yue(years of birth and death unknown)**

He passed the highest imperial examination in 1085. He served as a local official. In the Song Dynasty when a senior official held a banquet, he asked the licensed prostitutes to sing songs and dance to urge the guests to drink more. They would have love with the guests. He often wrote the love between music girls and their guests. The style of his *Ci* poems was popular and candid like folk songs.

## 洞 仙 歌

### 赠宜春官妓赵佛奴

赵家姊妹,合在昭阳殿。因甚人间有飞燕?见伊底,尽道独步江南,便江北、也何曾惯见。　　惜伊情性好,不解嗔人,长带桃花笑时脸。向尊前酒底,得见些时,似恁地、能得几回细看?待不眨眼儿觑著伊,将眨眼底工夫,剩看几遍。

阮　阅

## Tune: Song of Immortals in the Cavern

I gave the *Ci* poem as a present to a licensed prostitute.

With the same surname, as Zhao's sisters as beautiful,
She should stay with an emperor in Splendid Palace.
But she lives among common people just.
Those people who have seen her even once
Say she is number one beauty in the south of the Yangtze River,
Even in the north of it quite few enchanting girls can match her.

She has a disposition quite soft,
Never losing her temper at all,
She always smiles like a blooming peach.
I have a very precious chance at the feast
To sit just before her intoxicatingly beautiful face.
How many times can I watch close a fairy maiden?
I should keep opening my eyes to have more time
To appreciate her flower-like face and watery eyes.

❈❈❈❈❈❈❈❈❈❈❈❈❈❈❈❈❈❈

## 眼　儿　媚

楼上黄昏杏花寒,斜月小阑干。一双燕子,两行征雁,画角声残。

绮窗人在东风里,洒泪对春闲。也应似旧,盈盈秋水,淡淡春山。

## Tune: Charming Eyes

At dusk climbing the high building I find the cold apricots blossoming,

The slanting crescent like her pretty brows shines on the little railings.

High and low flies a pair of familiar singing swallows,

Two rows of the wild geese are on their journey home,

The horn on the city wall seems to be weeping low with grief.

My dear must be leaning against the window in spring breeze,

With warm tears falling keeping silent.

As before she should still be beautiful,

Her eyes, like clear autumn water so bright,

Her brows, distant spring hills green light.

# 赵企(生卒年不详)

宋神宗时进士。做过地方官。他善于用"移情"的方法,化静为动,化单一为丰富,大大提高画面的审美价值,增加读者的审美情趣。他多写人生的悲欢离合。

**Zhao Qi( years of birth and death unknown)**

He passed the highest imperial examination during the reign of Emperor Shen Zong of the Northern Song Dynasty. He served as a local official. He was good at using the way of "changing one's affection", turning stillness into movement, and singleness into abundance, to lift aesthetic value of a picture, and increase readers' aesthetic taste. He often wrote about joys and sorrows, partings and reunions.

## 感 皇 恩

### 别 情

骑马踏红尘,长安重到。人面依前似花好。旧欢才展,又被新愁分了。未成云雨梦,巫山晓。　　千里断肠,关山古道。回首高城似天杳。满怀离恨,付与落花啼鸟。故人何处也?青春老。

## June: Gratitude to Emperor's Favor

### Parting Grief

I ride a steed treading the dust thick,
Coming back to the thriving capital.
As before the girls' faces are as beautiful as flowers.
We just meet enjoying reunion in the happy hours,
Again we have to part still holding wine cups.
During the short night the showers of our love
Have not moistened at all our long dried heart field.

I'm painful to think of the journey of a thousand *li*,
I have passed the ancient roads, steep passes and mountains high,
Turning round, I find the capital with my beauty as far as the sky.
Seeing flowers falling and hearing birds crying,
I can no longer bear the deep sadness increasing.
Where is my pretty dear?
Youth quickly fades drear.

# 谢逸(1068—1113)

他屡试不第,终身布衣。过着隐逸的生活。词风有花间的浓艳,又有婉约。他有些词可与当时一流词人的词媲美。

**Xie Yi(1068‐1113)**

He failed again and again in the imperial examinations. As a commoner he lived in seclusion in his life. The style of his *Ci* poems was not only rich and gaudy but also subtle and retrained. Some of his *Ci* poems could compare with those of the first-class poets.

## 蝶 恋 花

豆蔻梢头春色浅。新试纱衣,拂袖东风软。红日三竿帘幕卷,画楼影里双飞燕。　　拢鬓步摇青玉碾。缺样花枝,叶叶蜂儿颤。独倚阑干凝望远,一川烟草平如剪。

### Tune: Butterflies in Love with Flowers

Cardamon flowers come out on the tips in early spring.
First time the pretty girl tries on the pink silk clothing,

The gentle breeze strokes her sleeves scented.
The sun rising high, she rolls up the curtains,
In high painted buildings' shadow fly pairs of swallows without care.

With interest she begins to comb her fragrant jet-black sparkling hair,
Putting on it a jade ornament with a queer flower spray,
And bees quivering on the leaves with each small step.
She leans alone on the railings gazing into the distance,
A tract of misty grass lies as even as cut with scissors.

## 江 城 子

杏花村馆酒旗风。水溶溶,飏残红。野渡舟横,杨柳绿阴浓。望断江南山色远,人不见,草连空。 夕阳楼外晚烟笼。粉香融,淡眉峰。记得年时,相见画屏中。只有关山今夜月,千里外,素光同。

### Tune: A Riverside Town

By the water over shops the streamers flutter in a breeze.
The rippling waves murmur in the winding clear stream,

谢 逸

The remaining red flowers fly high and low.
The quiet boat lies empty at the ferry alone,
The luxuriant weeping willows shed thick green shade.
I try to see all the mounts in the southern land in vain,
And I fail to see my intoxicating beauty anywhere,
I can only see green like her skirt here and there.

Last year beyond the pavilion the sun set and dusk spread.
From her snow-like skin came the warm refreshing scent,
Her brows, the distant hills, were drawn lightly.
I recollect in those hours in last spring so clearly
We shared the fragrant pillow behind the screen colorful.
Tonight the moon shines on all the passes and mountains,
Even a thousand miles away it appears
As bright and pure like our love as here.

❉❉❉❉❉❉❉❉❉❉❉❉❉❉❉❉❉

## 千 秋 岁

### 夏 景

楝花飘砌,簌簌清香细。梅雨过,蘋风起。情随湘水远,梦绕吴峰翠。琴书倦,鹧鸪唤起南窗睡。　　密意无人寄,幽恨凭谁洗?修竹畔,疏帘里。歌余尘拂扇,舞罢风掀袂。人散后,一钩淡月天如水。

## Tune: A Thousand Autumns

### Scene of Summer

Chinaberry flowers rustle down on the steps,

Bringing into the lonely chamber faint scent.

The rainy season is gone,

And a breeze blows soft.

My deep affection for him flows away with the sad Xiang River,

In the dream I fly around the green mounts in the land southern.

I am not in the mood at all as usual to play the zither and read books,

Partridges wake me from a nap in the south window in the afternoon.

No one will send my sweet love to him.

To whom can I confide my deep hatred?

Oh, by the bamboos green,

Behind the sparse screens,

With the gentle breeze I dance,

And sing songs with a silk fan.

All the guests wave farewell to me with cheer,

In the water-like sky a pale crescent sheds tears.

# 晁冲之(生卒年不详)

他是"苏门四学士"之一晁补之的从弟。授承务郎。受苏轼牵连而被免责。遂隐居山下。以淡雅的笔触,写尽人世沧桑与复杂心事。他的《汉宫春》是咏梅的名作之一。

**Chao Chongzhi(years of birth and death unknown)**

He was a cousin of Chao Buzhi who was one of the four disciples of Su Shi. Once he was a court official. Because of the relation with Su Shi, he was demoted and he lived in seclusion at the foot of the mountain. In a simple and elegant style, he depicted many vicissitudes of life and his complex feelings. His *Ci* poem "Spring in the Han Palace" was one of the most well-known *Ci* poems describing plum blossoms.

## 临 江 仙

忆昔西池池上饮,年年多少欢娱。别来不寄一行书。寻常相见了,犹道不如初。　安稳锦屏今夜梦,月明好渡江湖。相思休问定何如。情知春去后,管得落花无。

### Tune: Immortals by the River

I recollect on West Pool I often drank with him,
Oh, in those years we were so joyous and happy.
Since parting, he has never sent me a letter,
Even now we meet each other quite often,
We are not as delightful and happy as in those days.

Tonight I have a dream behind the screen of brocade,
Flying in the moonlight across the pool to his bed with delight.
Oh, please don't ask what is lovesickness in the heart and mind.
I know if the intoxicating spring this year is gone drear,
Who can control the fate of fallen flowers far and near?

## 汉宫春

### 梅

潇洒江梅,向竹梢稀处,横两三枝。东君也不爱惜,雪压风欺。无情燕子,怕春寒、轻失佳期。惟是有、南来归雁,年年长见开时。　　清浅小溪如练,问玉堂何似,茅舍疏篱?伤心故人去后,冷落新诗。微云淡月,对孤芳、分付他谁。空自倚、清香未减,风流不在人知。

晁冲之

## June: Spring in the Han Palace
### The Plum Blossom

The plum quite natural and unrestrained,
By the river stretches two or three sprays
To the swaying sparse green bamboo tips.
Oh, the god of flowers shows no sympathy,
Leaving her blown by wind and pressed by snow.
In the warm south with little feelings the swallows
Afraid of the cold of early spring
Miss the period of her blooming.
However, in the vast sky the wild geese,
Year after year from the south are seen
On their homeward way to appreciate her in bloom.

The green lace is the winding shallow clear brook.
The storied house decorated with glistening jade so grand
Is not so good as the low bamboo fence and hut thatched.
She is sad when the poet Lin, her intimate forever left her,
His well-known poem praising her becomes the last words.
Through thin clouds, the pale moon shines anywhere,
And the faint fragrance drifts in the air here and there,
But no one casts her an admirable glance.
Leaning on the bamboos with open arms,

She pays no attention to other

If noticing her grace and aroma.

❉❉❉❉❉❉❉❉❉❉❉❉❉❉❉❉

## 感 皇 恩

寒食不多时,牡丹初卖。小院重帘燕飞碍。昨宵风雨,只有一分春在。今朝犹自得,阴晴快。 熟睡起来,宿醒微带。不惜罗襟揾眉黛。日高梳洗,看著花阴移改。笑摘双杏子,连枝戴。

## *Tune: Gratitude to Emperor's Favor*

It is not long since gone is Cold Food Day,

The peonies in pink buds are just on sale.

Curtain upon curtain in the yard, the swallows can't to and fro fly.

The wind blew very hard and the rain fell thick and fast last night,

There remains one third of the spring scenery.

A young wife, she feels carefree and leisurely

When the rain stops and rises the sun.

From the sound sleep she wakes up,

Seeing her face from wine last night a bit of flush now,

With her silk sleeves she rubs her green moon-like brows.

The sun high she begins to make up before the mirror like a heart,

晁冲之

She watches the shade of the flowers move bit by bit in the yard.
She plucks a twig with red twin apricots smiling,
With care she pins it in her black hair glistening.

# 苏庠(1065—1147)

他隐逸于山林。其词风含蓄、雅致。片言只字,无一点尘埃。其词为宋词中上乘之作。

**Su Xiang(1065 - 1147)**

He lived in seclusion in the mountain forests. The style of his *Ci* poems was reserved and elegant. The words of his *Ci* poems were away from the dust. His *Ci* poems were of the highest order in the Song Dynasty.

## 鹧 鸪 天

枫落河梁野水秋,澹烟衰草接郊丘。醉眠小坞黄茅店,梦倚高城赤叶楼。　　天杳杳,路悠悠。钿筝歌扇等闲休。灞桥杨柳年年恨,鸳浦芙蓉叶叶愁。

## *Tune: Partridge Sky*

In the fall the leaves of the maples shower down and the creek is in ebb tide,

The misty withered grasses connect the open land and hills under

苏　庠

the horizon.
Drunk in the countryside thatched inn, with cheer I dream
In the tower in the red leaves I listen to her singing sweet.

The sky is far, far away,
Long, long is my way.
I'm so melancholy to recollect in the flourishing city
I was dead drunk in the singing girl's songs and music.
Spring after spring by the Farewell Bridge each twig of the willows feels drear,
Autumn after autumn on the parting pool every leaf of the lotuses sheds tears.

# 毛滂(生卒年不详)

初为杭州法曹。苏轼赏其词,推荐与朝。因词《惜分飞》而著名于世。其词风婉雅,近秦观、黄庭坚。

**Mao Pang( years of birth and death unknown)**

He was an official in Hangzhou. Su Shi appreciated his *Ci* poems and recommended him to the court. He was very famous for his *Ci* poem "Sorrow for Separation". The style was subtle and elegant like that of Qin Guan and Huang Tingjian.

## 惜 分 飞

### 富阳僧舍作别语赠妓琼芳

泪湿阑干花著露,愁到眉峰碧聚。此恨平分取,更无言语空相觑。　　断雨残云无意绪,寂寞朝朝暮暮。今夜山深处,断魂分付潮回去。

毛　滂

## Tune: Sorrow for Separation

I saw a singing girl off mile after mile from Hangzhou to Fuyang. With grief I wrote the *Ci* poem.

Her face wet with tears is like a pink flower dewy,
Her knitted sorrowful brows, the green distant hills.
We share the parting torture,
Silently looking at each other.

As the goddess she leaves with clouds and rain fine,
Now we feel so lonely and melancholy day and night.
Tonight in the hills deep I ask the tide in the stream
To take my sad soul to her brothel-gathering street.

❄❄❄❄❄❄❄❄❄❄❄❄❄❄❄❄❄

## 临 江 仙

### 都 城 元 夕

闻道长安灯夜好,雕轮宝马如云。蓬莱清浅对觚棱。玉皇开碧落,银界失黄昏。　　谁见江南憔悴客,端忧懒步芳尘。小屏风畔冷香凝。酒浓春入梦,窗破月寻人。

## Tune: Immortals by the River

### On the Night of the Lantern Festival in the Capital

It is said in the capital the Lantern Festival is so joyful at night,
The carved carriages and high steeds are like clouds in the sky.
The lights in palaces make the roofs of their buildings bright lake.
The colorful lanterns change the city into palaces with open gates,
The Milky Way seems to have fallen on the world of human beings.

Who would visit me from the southeast, a tired traveller heartbreaking?
I have no mood to follow the dust after the carriages with beauties scented.
My dear sits behind the screen, tears wetting her face powdered heavily.
I drink strong wine to get into a dream to forget my deep sorrow,
To keep me company, the moonlight comes in through the window.

※※※※※※※※※※※※※※※※※

## 烛影摇红

### 松窗午梦初觉

一亩清阴,半天潇洒松窗午。床头秋色小屏山,碧帐垂烟缕。枕畔风摇绿户,唤人醒,不教梦去。可怜恰到,瘦石寒泉,冷云幽处。

毛 滂

## June: The Candle Shedding a Red Shadow

### Awake by the Windows in the Shade of Pines

Through the window in the afternoon I see an acre of shade green
And nearly half of the sky of the exuberant leisure high pine trees.
By the bed stands a little screen with autumn scenery,
The green gauze net seems drifting wisps of thin mist.

Outside a breeze moves the shade,
From a spring dream I am awake,
How I wish it hadn't ended soon.
I just arrived at a pretty place cool,
On the gravels flowed a spring cold and clear,
And chilly clouds at leisure flew far and near.

# 郑少微(生卒年不详)

他因《鹧鸪天》这首咏梅词而声名卓著。他用朦胧手法,句句在写梅,又似乎处处在咏梅花一样冷艳的美人,处处在咏梅花一样高洁的词人。是在写梅花呀?写美人呀?写词人呀?都是,都是。朦胧美是最美的。

**Zheng Shaowei( years of birth and death unknown)**

He was well-known for his *Ci* poem "Partridge Sky" about a plum tree. In misty way, he wrote every line praising the plum tree, but he seemed to be praising a beauty, or the poet. Was it the plum, the icy beauty or the noble poet? It was the plum, the beauty and the poet. Misty beauty is the most beautiful.

## 鹧 鸪 天

谁折南枝傍小丛,佳人丰色与梅同。有花无叶真潇洒,不向胭脂借淡红。　　应未许,嫁春风。天教雪月伴玲珑。池塘疏影伤幽独,何似横斜酒盏中。

## June: Partridge Sky

Who plucks the twigs of the plum from the land southern
Putting them in my small garden beside my flower clusters?
With snow-white color the plum is a beauty like jade.
With blossoms without leaves, it sways with easy grace,
She never borrows light red from rouge anyhow.

I think she may not have promised up till now
To get married to the warm gentle spring breeze blowing.
To keep her company, heaven leaves the moon shining.
The clear pool reflects her thin shadow lonely and quiet,
She is so willing to shed her shadow on the cups of wine.

# 司马槱(生卒年不详)

他曾为高官。以艳词闻名。据传他在上任地方官途中,一日昼寐驿站。梦见一穿古衣的美女,执板唱此词上阕,歌罢而去。他续成此曲。他住房下面,乃南齐名妓苏小小之墓。其词有二首存世。

**Sima You ( years of birth and death unknown )**

He once served as a senior official. He was well-known for his love *Ci* poems in flowery style. One day on the journey to taking office, he had a nap in the post station dreaming of a beauty singing upper half of the *Ci* poem with a clapper. Then she went away. Later he composed other half. It was said under the house he stayed there was the tomb of the famous prostitute Su Xiaoxiao in the Southern Qi Dynasty. He has only two *Ci* poems extant.

## 黄 金 缕

家在钱塘江上住。花落花开,不管流年度。燕子又将春色去,纱窗一阵黄昏雨。　　斜插犀梳云半吐,檀板清歌,唱彻《黄金缕》。望断行云无去处,梦回明月生春浦。

司马樆

## Tune: Gold Thread Garment

As a female singer I live by the Qiantang River,
By turns any kind of flowers fall and open, and
Spring comes with delight and leaves with grief.
Swallows take away the enchanting spring scene,
Beyond the screen a shower falls in the twilight.

On her hair like dark clouds quivers a comb fine,
In her white hand with company of clappers of hardwood,
She sings the love song "Gold Thread Garment" with gloom.
Awake from a dream I find her as a goddess with clouds disappearing,
I only see over the Farewell Ferry the moon like her brows slow rising.

# 秦湛(生卒年不详)

秦观之子。有人称他的词句"藕叶清香胜花气"。他的词虽属婉约派,但已注入刚健因素。

**Qin Zhan( years of birth and death unknown)**

He was the son of Qin Guan. Some critics said that his *Ci* poems were like the scent of lotus leaves, stronger than that of lotus flowers. His *Ci* poems though belonged to the subtle school, but were added the vigorous elements.

## 卜 算 子

### 春 情

春透水波明,寒峭花枝瘦。极目烟中百尺楼,人在楼中否?
四和袅金凫,双陆思纤手。拟倩东风浣此情,情更浓于酒。

## Tune: Song of Divination

### Stirring of Love

The spring comes here and the water is limpid,
In cold air the flower twigs with buds are thin.

秦　湛

I strain my eyes looking into her storied building at the end of the world,
Does she lean on the railings also gazing into my room without a word?

The incense burning, my beauty moved a pair of dice
Very lightly with her hands tender and snow-white.
I ask the spring breeze to blow my yearning far away,
But stronger than wine it sticks to my heart and brain.

# 徐俯(1075—1141)

黄庭坚外甥。作词不因袭他人,包括他舅舅。他独辟蹊径。

**Xu Fu(1075–1141)**

He was Huang Tingjian's nephew. But he didn't follow any one's *Ci* poems including his uncle's. He created a new style of his own.

## 卜 算 子

天生百种愁,挂在斜阳树。绿叶阴阴自得春,草满莺啼处。
不见凌波步,空忆如簧语。柳外重重叠叠山,遮不断、愁来路。

## Tune: Song of Divination

I have in my heart sorrow of a hundred kinds,
Hanging on the trees in the setting sunshine.
The spring smiles proud in the leaves green,
The orioles sing with cheer in the grass deep.

I can neither see my beauty's steps like that of goddess graceful,

徐　俯

Nor at all can I be intoxicated in her songs matchlessly beautiful.
Mounts one after another stand beyond the willows,
But in no way they can stop the coming of sorrow.

# 叶梦得(1077—1148)

宋哲宗绍圣四年(1097)进士。曾任翰林学士、龙图阁直学士等职。晚年隐居于山林之中。词风近苏轼。《贺新郎》中的词句"谁为我,唱金缕"受人赞崇。

**Ye Mengde(1077–1148)**

He passed the highest imperial examination in 1097. He served as a senior official. In his later years he lived in seclusion in the mountain forest. The style of his *Ci* poems was like that of Su Shi. The lines in "Congratulations to the Bridegroom" were eulogized:"Oh, who at all for me sings in a voice so sweet and pleasant/"Gold Thread Garment", a popular song by singers maiden?"

## 贺 新 郎

睡起流莺语,掩苍苔、房栊向晚,乱红无数。吹尽残花无人见,惟有垂杨自舞。渐暖霭、初回轻暑。宝扇重寻明月影,暗尘侵、上有乘鸾女。惊旧恨,遽如许。　　江南梦断横江渚。浪粘天、葡萄涨绿,半空烟雨。无限楼前沧波意,谁采苹花寄与。但怅望、兰舟容与。万里云帆何时到,送孤鸿、目断千山阻。谁为我,唱金缕。

叶梦得

## June: Congratulations to the Bridegroom

Awake from a sound dream of spring,
I hear a pair of orioles gaily chatting.
In the courtyard the red petals toward eve
Cover the ground dotted with moss green.
The remaining flowers are blown away by the wind wholly,
There the weeping willow trees sway with the breeze only.
It's getting warmer and warmer,
Gradually comes early summer.
I take out an old fan never leaving her once
Covered with scented dust full of her love,
On it dimly I recognize the female immortal flying to the moon with grace.
I get shocked I am still heartbreaking to recollect those enchanting days.

Our dream was broken, we're so sad
On an green islet in the southern land.
Cold water rises becoming mist and rain fine,
Darkening nearly half of the sky on the horizon.
She may be leaning in the storied building, gazing far,
Will she pick a duckweed and send it to me from afar?
Really I hope in vain with deep sorrow

She is in a boat returning to my home.

When will her sail from a thousand *li* away reach here?

I only see a swan goose in countless mounts disappear.

Oh, who at all for me sings in a voice so sweet and pleasant

"Gold Thread Garment", a popular song by singers maiden?

❀❀❀❀❀❀❀❀❀❀❀❀❀❀❀❀❀

# 虞 美 人

### 雨后同干誉、才卿置酒来禽花下作

落花已作风前舞,又送黄昏雨。晓来庭院半残红,惟有游丝,千丈胃晴空。 殷勤花下同携手,更尽怀中酒。美人不用敛蛾眉,我亦多情,无奈酒阑时。

## *Tune: Great Beauty Yu*

After a rain, I invited two of my friends to drink under
the pear-leaved crab apples. I wrote the *Ci* poem.

Before a wind the flowers dance happy and gay,

In the eve with cheer they see off the rain again.

In the morn the fallen red flowers cover the yard here and there,

Only the gossamer flies ten thousands of meters high in the air.

I invite my friends to sit under the flowers of pear-leaved crab apples

叶梦得

To enjoy cups of good wine one by one with pleasure, hand in hand.
Oh, beauties, please don't knit your intoxicating brows drear,
I'm also sad when the kettle is empty and we'll say bye here.

# 刘一止(1078—1160)

宋徽宗宣和三年(1121)进士。累官中书舍人、给事中。当时,他的《喜迁莺》一词盛传京城,他一时有"刘晓行"之号。

**Liu Yizhi(1078–1160)**

He passed the highest imperial examination in 1121. He served as a court official. His *Ci* poem "Joyous Migrant Orioles" spread far and wide in the capital. He was called "Liu goes on a journey early in the morning".

## 喜 迁 莺

### 晓 行

晓光催角。听宿鸟未惊,邻鸡先觉。迤逦烟村,马嘶人起,残月尚穿林薄。泪痕带霜微凝,酒力冲寒犹弱。叹倦客、悄不禁重染,风尘京洛。　　追念人别后,心事万重,难觅孤鸿托。翠幌娇深,曲屏香暖,争念岁华飘泊。怨月恨花烦恼,不是不曾经著。这情味,望一成消减,新来还恶。

刘一止

## Tune: Joyous Migrant Orioles

### On a Journey Early in the Morning

The horn hastens daybreak,

Sleeping birds are not awake,

A cock crows loud firstly.

Still in a pretty dream is

The misty meandering hamlet by the solitary creek.

The horses neighing, travellers are up ready to leave,

The setting moonlight gets out through the green treetops.

The wine can't keep out the cold, my tears frozen by frost.

Though I'm a tired and languid guest anywhere,

I'm reluctant to get dirty in the capital life there.

Since I left my beauty heartbreaking at that time,

I have been tortured by deep grief day and night,

It's hard to find a lone swan goose to send my dear a letter.

Now my intoxicating beauty leans on the fragrant curtains,

Or lies behind the deep warm green screens lonely and drear,

How can she know I'm on a hard travel at the end of the year?

When I see flowers like her face and her brows the moon,

Unbearable grief rises from my deep heart and mind soon.

Since I have experienced such things,

In those years, the troubled feelings,
I hope sincerely, will quickly calm down.
But new grief more intense comes round.

# 汪藻(1079—1154)

宋徽宗崇宁二年(1103)进士。累官中书舍人,兼直学士院,迁兵部侍郎,拜翰林学士。后受弹劾免职。他喜欢让歌妓在宴会上唱他的词。主要受苏轼的影响,他语言优美、幽默。

**Wang Zao ( 1079 – 1154 )**

He passed the highest imperial examination in 1103. He served as a senior official. Finally he was impeached and removed from office. He liked to ask songstresses to sing his *Ci* poems at banquets. Mainly influenced by Su Shi, his *Ci* poems were of fineness and humour.

## 醉 落 魄

小舟帘隙,佳人半露梅妆额。绿云低映花如刻。恰似秋宵,一半银蟾白。　　结儿梢朵香红扐。钿蝉隐隐摇金碧。春山秋水浑无迹,不露墙头,些子真消息。

## Tune: Drunk in Dire Straits

In the small painted boat through the crack of the curtain,

I see on a beauty's face half of a plum blossom ornament.
Her green hair sets off the yellow artificial flower carved-like,
Her forehead is just like half of the moon so gentle and bright
Of the Mid-autumn Festival in the finest hour.

At her left temple sways a cicada-like flower,
Sending out a kind of intoxicating green sheen of gold.
Spring hills are her brows, fall water her eyes, not shown.
How can I at all see
If she has love for me?

# 曹组（生卒年不详）

宋徽宗宣和三年(1121)进士。曾任阁门宣赞舍人、睿思殿应制。其词多俗语、噱语、艳词。词风近秦观。他《卜算子》中的几句词得到人们的称赞，特别是词人的称赞："著意闻时不肯香，香在无心处。"

**Cao Zu( years of birth and death unknown)**

He passed the highest imperial examination in 1121. He served as a court official. The style of his *Ci* poems was similar to Qin Guan's with popular, amusing and gaudy words. The lines in "Song of Divination" were appreciated by people, especially by poets: "With intention, one can't smell her fragrance anyhow, / Unconsciously he can find her delicate scent all around."

## 忆 少 年

年时酒伴，年时去处，年时春色。清明又近也，却天涯为客。 念过眼光阴难再得。想前欢，尽成陈迹。登临恨无语，把阑干暗拍。

## Tune: Recollecting Early Youth

In the year I had a good time

With my company of wine

Enjoying lively beautiful scenery of spring.

Now again Clear and Bright is approaching,

Oh, but she is in the remotest corner of the earth.

Time with water flowing away will never return.

The joy and merriment we shared

Become the trails here and there.

Grief fills my heart when I ascend the height again,

I can do nothing but look far patting gently the rails.

❈❈❈❈❈❈❈❈❈❈❈❈❈❈❈❈❈

## 卜 算 子

松竹翠萝寒,迟日江山暮。幽径无人独自芳,此恨凭谁诉?
似共梅花语,尚有寻芳侣。著意闻时不肯香,香在无心处。

## Tune: Song of Divination

At dusk in a deep valley, with only bamboos and pines,

The orchid stands graceful in the pale setting sunlight.

The secluded path empty, no one appreciates her scent,

To whom can she pour out in her heart grief and hate?

曹　组

She wants to confide to the plum her lofty moral opinions,
She hopes on the path someone to seek aroma will appear.
With intention, one can't smell her fragrance anyhow,
Unconsciously he can find her delicate scent all around.

❈❈❈❈❈❈❈❈❈❈❈❈❈❈❈❈

## 青　玉　案

碧山锦树明秋霁。路转陡,疑无地。忽有人家临曲水。竹篱茅舍,酒旗沙岸,一簇成村市。　　凄凉只恐乡心起。凤楼远、回头谩凝睇。何处今宵孤馆里,一声征雁,半窗残月,总是离人泪。

## Tune: Green Jade Cup

After a shower the green hills set off the frosted red leaves.
The path covered with withering grass is winding and steep,
And here all of a sudden it seems to stop.
Then I see, overlooking the winding pond
Stand the yellow bamboo fences and huts thatched,
The streamers of wine shops flutter by the sandbank,
In the distance lies at random misty hamlets.

The desolation all round makes me homesick,
My dear in her lonely boudoir is far, far away,

Turning round I gaze into her direction in vain.
Where is my inn so lonely tonight?
Overhead a wild goose lonely cries,
Half of the pink windows are in the setting moon,
I can't help shedding tears like a rain with gloom.

# 万俟咏(生卒年不详)

曾任大晟府制撰。当时人称其词平而工,和而雅,甚至称其为词之圣者。他《长相思》中几行词特别受人推崇:"一声声,一更更。窗外芭蕉窗内灯。此时无限情。"

**Moqi Yong(years of birth and death unknown)**

He served as an official in the court in charge of music. The style of his *Ci* poems was delicate with simple words but deep meaning. He was even praised as the sage of *Ci* poems. Four lines in his *Ci* poem "Yearning Forever" were held in esteem by people:"Drop by Drop, /Watch by Watch. /Beyond the window shiver the banana leaves, inside flickers dim light, /I think of your enchanting face and deep devoted love the whole night."

## 木 兰 花 慢

恨莺花渐老,但芳草、绿汀洲。纵岫壁千寻,榆钱万叠,难买春留。梅花向来始别,又匆匆结子满枝头。门外垂杨岸侧,画桥谁系兰舟。　　悠悠。岁月如流。叹水覆、杳难收。凭画阑,往往抬头举眼,都是春愁。东风晚来更恶,怕飞红拍絮入书楼。双燕归来问我,怎生不上帘钩?

## Tune: Slow Song of Magnolia Flowers

I hate flowers fading and orioles growing up,
Fragrant and refreshing grasses, you see but
Green all over the low riverside land.
No matter how high stand the crags,
And how many the coin-shaped leaves lie bleak on the ground,
The flourishing scented spring will not slow its steps anyhow.
The plum just said good-bye to the spring lately,
She has borne green round fruits on all her twigs.
On the greenish bank by the red bridge no beauty ties her boat
To the trunk of the weeping willow as the Girl Without Sorrow.

How long are our love affairs gone by?
Like a river they flow east day and night.
The aromatic clear water in a small kettle
Poured on the ground can't be got again.
Leaning alone on the red painted railings,
I see everything full of sorrow of spring.
Towards evening the east cold wind is blowing harder and harder,
Afraid of petals and catkins entering my study, I draw the curtains.
However, the pair of returning swallows in a low voice ask me,
Why not hook up the curtain and let them come to the red beam?

万俟咏

## 长 相 思

### 雨

一声声,一更更。窗外芭蕉窗里灯,此时无限情。 梦难成,恨难平。不道愁人不喜听,空阶滴到明。

### Tune: Yearning Forever

#### Rain

Drop by drop,
Watch by watch.
Beyond the window shiver the banana leaves, inside flickers dim light,
I think of your enchanting face and deep devoted love the whole night.

I cannot enter a sweet dream,
My grief can't at all be eased.
Without caring my gloomy mood, falls the rain
Continuously on the empty steps until daybreak.

❈❈❈❈❈❈❈❈❈❈❈❈❈❈❈❈❈

## 诉 衷 情

一鞭清晓喜还家,宿醉困流霞。夜来小雨新霁,双燕舞风斜。

山不尽,水无涯,望中赊。送春滋味,念远情怀,分付杨花。

## Tune: Baring the Heart

I am so happy and ready to go home when my whip breaks the dawn,
On a horse I'm not wholly awake, for last night I got drunk as a lord.
Through all the night, a drizzle has been falling and it stops now,
In the gentle warm breeze a pair of swallows dances up and down.

There stand countless green mountains,
And flow clear streams one after another,
I have so long a way to my hometown in the mood drear.
I have been so sorrowful seeing spring off year after year,
And yearning for my enchanting beauty night and day,
I ask the flying willow catkins to take my feeling away.

❈❈❈❈❈❈❈❈❈❈❈❈❈❈❈❈

## 长 相 思

### 山 驿

短长亭,古今情。楼外凉蟾一晕生,雨余秋更清。　　暮云平,暮山横。几叶秋声和雁声,行人不要听。

万俟咏

## Tune: Yearning Forever

### A Post Station by a Mountain

Either in the past or present pavilions by roads
Are all filled with heartbreaking parting sorrow.
The crescent like brows with a halo rises outside the post station,
After a rain so melancholy and lonely is the scenery of the autumn.

In the eve the clouds hang thin,
And the distant mounts lie dim.
Green leaves sob, wild geese moan south flying,
To them the travellers cannot bear at all listening.

❀❀❀❀❀❀❀❀❀❀❀❀❀❀❀❀

## 忆秦娥

### 别　情

千里草。萋萋尽处遥山小。遥山小。行人远似,此山多少。　　天若有情天亦老。此情说便说不了。说不了,一声唤起,又惊春晓。

## Tune: Recollecting the Beauty in Qin

### Parting Grief

The grass stretches a thousand *li*,

Small the dim distant hill seems.
Oh, small seems there the hill distant,
But the leaving traveller looks smaller,
They look similar, oh, at all how much?

Heaven will be old if he has true love.
I can hardly explain it clearly,
Oh, I can not clearly explain it.
All of a sudden I hear a cock crowing,
To my surprise spring day is breaking.

# 田为(生卒年不详)

曾充大晟府典乐。善琵琶。视歌伎舞女为知音。

**Tian Wei ( years of birth and death unknown )**

He served as an official in the court in charge of music. He was good at playing pipa. He regarded songstresses and dancers as his intimates with true love.

## 南 柯 子

### 春 思

团玉梅梢重,香罗芰扇低。帘风不动蝶交飞。一样绿阴庭院锁斜晖。 对月怀歌扇,因风念舞衣。何须惆怅惜芳菲,拚却一年憔悴待春归!

## Tune: Southern Song

### Thoughts of Love

The plum twigs are heavy with plump fruits green,
On the clear water float the new round lotus leaves.
Without wind the curtain still, outside a pair of butterflies flies,

The green-shaded courtyard shuts in the pale setting sunlight.

Under the bright moon, I yearn for the maiden singer's fan,
In the gentle warm breeze, I think of her green skirt of dance.
It's unnecessary to remember the fragrant past spring in a mood drear,
I'm ready to be wan and sallow the whole year to wait for spring here.

❋❋❋❋❋❋❋❋❋❋❋❋❋❋❋

## 南 柯 子

### 春 景

梦怕愁时断,春从醉里回。凄凉怀抱向谁开?些子清明时候被莺催。　　柳外都成絮,栏边半是苔。多情帘燕独徘徊,依旧满身花雨又归来。

## Tune: Southern Song

### Scene of Springtime

I'm afraid when I'm awake the sorrow will also be awake,
When I'm drunk as a lord, quietly spring comes back again.
Oh, to whom can I tell my unbearable sadness?
The orioles urge Pure Brightness to go quickly.

田 为

Outside the window catkins here and there fly,
By the red railings the green moss grows wild.
The pair of swallows returns with raindrops and red petals,
They feel lonely and sorrowful on the beam in their nest.

# 徐伸(生卒年不详)

曾为朝官,管音乐。后出知常州。此词为想念被妻所驱的宠妾而写,因此出名。

**Xu Shen( years of birth and death unknown)**

He served as an official in the capital in charge of music, later a prefect of Changzhou. He was well-known for this *Ci* poem, in which he poured out his devoted love for his concubine driven away by his wife.

## 转调二郎神

闷来弹鹊,又搅碎、一帘花影。漫试著春衫,还思纤手,熏彻金猊烬冷。动是愁端如何向,但怪得、新来多病。嗟旧日沈腰,如今潘鬓,怎堪临镜? 重省。别时泪湿,罗衣犹凝。料为我厌厌,日高慵起,长托春酲未醒。雁足不来,马蹄难驻,门掩一庭芳景。空伫立,尽日阑干倚遍,昼长人静。

## Tune: Changed Tune of a God

Bored, he shoots a pebble with a catapult at a magpie singing,

徐　伸

Beyond his expectation, for a very short time greatly shaking
On the curtain, the flowers' shadows.
When he tries on old spring clothes,
He thinks of her hand so white and tender,
The ash is a bit cold in the incense burner.
Wherever he goes he can't get rid of grief,
Oh, pity, to make the matter worse even,
He has been ill.
His waist is thin,
And his hair like dark clouds in the past is grey,
He can't bear seeing in the mirror his faded face.

He remembers when he said goodbye to her,
He found her tears wetting her pink silk shirt.
Her shirt must still be wet,
Her heart is about to break.
Still she is on the bed when the sun rises high,
She pretends to be sick of wine in spring time.
No wild goose comes here with his letter so far,
And no horse stays neighing outside her boudoir,
The scented scenery in the yard she shuts.
She gazes at the grass like his globe just,
And leans through all the railings whole day with gloom,
The day is as long as a year, quiet and lonely is her room.

# 陈克(1081—1137)

曾为京官。词风闲雅,近唐温庭筠和韦庄。他的《菩萨蛮》中的词句"绿窗春睡轻"为人们称颂至今。

**Chen Ke(1081－1137)**

He was a court official. His *Ci* poems were elegant and leisurely like those of Wen Tingyun and Wei Zhuang in the Tang Dynasty. His *Ci* poem, "Buddhist Dancers" with the line "Behind the green windows the beauty cannot enjoy a spring dream sound." has been praised through the ages.

## 菩 萨 蛮

赤阑桥尽香街直,笼街细柳娇无力。金碧上青空,花晴帘影红。黄衫飞白马,日日青楼下。醉眼不逢人,午香吹暗尘。

## Tune: Buddhist Dancers

The bridge with red railings leads to the beautiful straight street,
The weeping willows shade it with their twigs slender and sweet.
The high golden splendid mansions are lost in the vast blue sky,
Flowers' shadows redden and sweeten the curtains in the sunlight.

陈　克

The dandy in yellow garment speeds by on a white horse,
Day after day, he makes merry with beauties in brothels.
Drunk, he doesn't cast his dim eyes to anyone
Leaving behind the fragrant red clouds of dust.

❈❈❈❈❈❈❈❈❈❈❈❈❈❈❈❈❈❈❈

## 菩 萨 蛮

绿芜墙绕青苔院,中庭日淡芭蕉卷。蝴蝶上阶飞,烘帘自在垂。
玉钩双语燕,宝甓杨花转。几处簸钱声,绿窗春睡轻。

## *Tune: Buddhist Dancers*

The grass-covered wall surrounds the yard wild with moss green,
At noon under the pale sunlight curl up the Bajiao banana leaves.
The butterflies dance high and low over the still steps,
The green curtain hanging at ease, with breeze sways.

On the jade hooks, a pair of swallows with deep love chatters,
The weeping willow catkins drift around an old well at leisure.
Some young girls play the game with cheer, throwing coins on the ground,
Behind the green windows the beauty cannot enjoy a spring dream sound.

# 朱敦儒(1081—1159)

曾任鸿胪少卿。大部分时间隐居于江湖之畔。他《相见欢》中的几行词颇受时人赏识:"试倩悲风吹泪过扬州。"

**Zhu Dunru(1081‑1159)**

He once served as a court official and in most of his life time he lived in seclusion by rivers and lakes. The lines in "Joy at Meeting" were appreciated by people:"Oh, please, the painful weeping autumn wind, /Blow my miserable bloody tears/To Yangzhou, the front not near."

## 水调歌头

### 淮阴作

当年五陵下,结客占春游。红缨翠带,谈笑跋马水西头。落日经过桃叶,不管插花归去,小袖挽人留。换酒春壶碧,脱帽醉青楼。　楚云惊,陇水散,两漂流。如今憔悴,天涯何处可销忧。长揖飞鸿旧月,不知今夕烟水,都照几人愁。有泪看芳草,无路认西州。

朱敦儒

## Tune: Prelude to Water Melody

### In Huaiyin

In the days in Wuling, near the old capital,

Oh, we went for a spring outing in company.

With red hats and green bands talking and laughing in glee,

On horses we quick crossed the west end of the clear stream.

Unconsciously we bathed in the setting sun,

When we passed the Peach Leaves Ferry just,

A beauty warmly invited us for the night to stay,

With her little pink silk sleeves around my waist.

The beauty with a kettle urged us to empty cups one after another,

Drunk, we took off our hats and unbuttoned our brown silk garments.

Shocked was my pretty dear,

Our deep love disappeared,

We were separated in the earth's corners remote.

Day and night missing her, I'm wan and sallow,

I can dispel my sorrow and lovesickness nowhere in the world.

I beg the swan goose and the moon to send my yearning to her,

I wonder how many people are full of grief

Seeing the lone water and sad mist this eve.

With tears I gaze at the grass with our love dewdrops,

Oh, when can we again enjoy sweet hours as before?

## 相 见 欢

金陵城上西楼,倚清秋。万里夕阳垂地大江流。　中原乱,簪缨散,几时收？试倩悲风吹泪过扬州。

### Tune: Joy at Meeting

I lean in the tower on the west city gate
Of Jinling on a chilly clear autumn day.
The setting sun sheds tear-like light on a thousand *li* land with sorrow,
With sighs and groans without end to the east the Yangtze River flows.

The enemy coming, the central plain is in disorder,
High and low officials escape to the land southern.
When can we recover lost rivers and mountains?
Oh, please, the painful weeping autumn wind,
Blow my miserable bloody tears
To Yangzhou, the front not near.

朱敦儒

## 鹧 鸪 天

唱得梨园绝代声。前朝惟数李夫人。自从惊破霓裳后,楚奏吴歌扇里新。　　秦嶂雁,越溪砧。西风北客两飘零。尊前忽听当时曲,侧帽停杯泪满巾。

### Tune: Partridge Sky

In the singing circle through the ages in our country,
Lady Li sings most beautiful in the former dynasty.
When the enemy caught the capital she escaped to the south lonely and sadly,
She sings in wine shops, with the names of the popular songs on her fan.

The wild geese fly here from the north for the winter so cold,
The women pound cloth to make clothes for husbands remote.
As her friend I happen to meet her and listen to her old songs with grief,
With a cap on the head slanting I stop drinking, tears wetting my kerchief.

# 周紫芝(1082—?)

宋高宗绍兴十二年(1142)进士。历官枢密院编修,出知兴国军。他自幼酷爱晏几道的词,词风清新、婉约、曲折,内容多为男女的恋情和思念。《鹧鸪天》因有以下几行词而十分著名:"如今风雨西楼夜,不听清歌也泪垂。"

## Zhou Zizhi(1082 –?)

He passed the highest imperial examination in 1142. He served as an official in the capital. He was fond of Yan Jidao's *Ci* poems in his childhood and the style of his *Ci* poems was fresh, subtle and tortuous. Mostly he wrote the love and yearning between men and women. "Partridge Sky" was very famous with the lines: "Tonight the wind and rain beat the west storied building full of sorrow, /I'm unable to hear your drear song, but my tears still wet my clothes."

## 醉落魄

江天云薄,江头雪似杨花落。寒灯不管人离索。照得人来,真个睡不著。　　归期已负梅花约,又还春动空飘泊。晓寒谁看伊梳掠。雪满西楼,人在阑干角。

周紫芝

## Tune: Drunk in Dire Straits

Over the river the white clouds hang low under the sky,
On the head of it, like catkins, snow here and there flies.
No sympathy at all the cold lamp shows
To the traveller trying to get asleep alone.
Oh, the light makes me unable to have a dream happy.

I fail to keep the solemn promise before parting sadly
That I will come to her arms when the plums are in blossom.
The spring rolls up her veil showing her charming appearance,
I still wander in the remote regions but.
In the morn who will see her dress up?
The snow covers thick the west storied building,
And she leans so sad on a corner of the railings.

❈❈❈❈❈❈❈❈❈❈❈❈❈❈❈❈

## 鹧 鸪 天

一点残红欲尽时,乍凉秋气满屏帏。梧桐叶上三更雨,叶叶声声是别离。　　调宝瑟,拨金猊。那时同唱鹧鸪词。如今风雨西楼夜,不听清歌也泪垂。

## Tune: Partridge Sky

The red candle sheds the last drops of tears drearily,
The early autumn cool fills the screens and curtains.
A heavy rain falls on the parasol leaves in the third watch,
My parting grief is poured out by each leaf and each drop.

With your snow-white fingers, the jade zither you played,
And I poked the ash in the lion-shaped burner of incense.
We sang happy together at the time
"Partridge Sky", in a voice so high.
Tonight the wind and rain beat the west storied building full of sorrow,
I am unable to hear your drear song, but my tears still wet my clothes.

❈❈❈❈❈❈❈❈❈❈❈❈❈❈❈❈❈

## 踏 莎 行

情似游丝,人如飞絮。泪珠阁定空相觑。一溪烟柳万丝垂,无因系得兰舟住。　　雁过斜阳,草迷烟渚。如今已是愁无数。明朝且做莫思量,如何过得今宵去!

周紫芝

## June: Treading on Grass

Our love is like gossamer long and thick,
I'm a catkin everywhere flying with wind,
Two pairs of eyes with tears look at each other so drear and sad.
A thousand green twigs of the willows hang on the brook banks,
But my beauty's painted boat, they are unable to tie.

Beyond the lonely setting sun the wild geese pass by,
On the misty islet, the grass like her skirt is dimly seen,
Oh, my tender sweet heart is filled with unbearable grief.
Oh, please, at present don't think of tomorrow,
I have to consider how to spend tonight alone.

# 赵佶(1082—1135)

即宋徽宗。他做了二十五年的皇帝。1127年被掳北去,过了九年耻辱的俘虏生活,后死于黑龙江境内。他政治上昏庸无能,生活上穷奢极侈。善诗词。他在囚禁期间写的词《燕山亭》是他所有诗词中成就最高的,可与李后主有"春花秋月何时了"词行的《虞美人》相媲美。

**Zhao Ji( 1082 – 1135)**

Zhao Ji was the Emperor Huizong in the North Song Dynasty. He ruled the country for twenty five years. He was captured and sent to the north as a captive in the year 1127. He lived a shameful life in captivity for nine years. He died in Heilongjiang Province. He was fatuous and incompetent in politics and extremely extravagant and luxurious in life. He was good at poetry. The *Ci* poem he wrote in captivity "Pavilion by Hills" marked the highest achievement of all his poems. It was said this *Ci* poem could compare with "Great Beauty Yu" by Li Yu, the last emperor of the Southern Tang Dynasty with the line "When will the spring wind and autumn moon end?"

赵　佶

## 眼　儿　媚

玉京曾忆昔繁华。万里帝王家。琼林玉殿,朝喧弦管,暮列笙琶。
花城人去今萧索,春梦绕胡沙。家山何处,忍听羌笛,吹彻梅花。

### *Tune: Charming Eyes*

Sometimes I recollect drear the past flourishing capital,
The home of an emperor of a ten thousand *li*'s country.
There are magnificent palaces, pretty artificial hills and beautiful gardens,
In the morning in the palaces melodious music of all kinds refreshed the heart,
In the evening there were so many lines of musicians ready to play.

Now people scatter and the city of flowers becomes a desolate place,
I still dream of it in the desert here with deep sorrow.
I again and again asks myself:"Where is my home?"
As a captive how can I bear listening to the Qiang flute
Play the sad tune, "Plum Blossoms Fall" with gloom?

## 燕山亭

### 北行见杏花

裁剪冰绡,轻叠数重,淡著胭脂匀注。新样靓妆,艳溢香融,羞杀蕊珠宫女。易得凋零,更多少无情风雨。愁苦。问院落凄凉,几番春暮。　　凭寄离恨重重,这双燕,何曾会人言语。天遥地远,万水千山,知他故宫何处。怎不思量,除梦里有时曾去。无据。和梦也新来不做。

### Tune: the Pavilion by Hills

#### Seeing the Apricot Blossom While Going North

The apricot blossom seems the layers of silk cold and delicate,
Cut very carefully by the tender snow-white hands quite skilful.
With rouge light,
In the latest style,
She is charming and far and near drifts her refreshing scent,
Before her the beautiful maidens in the palace are ashamed.
Intoxicating sweet spring leaving, she is easy to fade,
How can she endure the ruthless wind and rain again?
Grief fills my mind and heart,
And I inquire the lonely yard:
"How many times have you seen the late spring off here?"

赵　佶

And I also want to ask with endlessly falling bloody tears
My old friends on the nest, the pair of swallows
To send to the relatives my unbearable sorrow,
But they look at me still, not knowing at all my words.
I have passed countless rivers and mounts in the world,
Now I am staying in its remotest corner.
Where in those years was my old palace?
Not a moment it ever leaves my heart even,
Sometimes I can reach there in my dreams.
Oh, I know dreams mean at all nothing,
But recently I have no dream of spring.

# 廖世美(生卒年不详)

词家称他的词如一再吟咏会沁人心扉,终身不忘。他的词堪称绝妙,殊不多见。其词有二首存世。

**Liao Shimei( years of birth and death unknown)**

It is said if his *Ci* poems were read again and again they would enter the readers' hearts and stay there forever. His *Ci* poems were so excellent that few other *Ci* poems could compare with. Only two of his *Ci* poems are extant.

## 好 事 近

### 夕 景

落日水熔金,天淡暮烟凝碧。楼上谁家红袖?靠阑干无力。
鸳鸯相对浴红衣,短棹弄长笛。惊起一双飞去,听波声拍拍。

## Tune: Happiness Approaching

### Scenery at Dusk

The fading sun reflected in water is like gold melting,
The mist seems especially thick when dim it is getting.

廖世美

I wonder to whose family the pretty girl in red belongs,
Leaning on the railings weary and lethargic very long.

In the water a pair of mandarin ducks washes their red clothes.
The long flute is played giving forth music in the small boat,
Starting the intoxicated pair,
Flapping their way in the air.

# 李清照(1084—约1151)

她是首屈一指的女词人。她是宋代可与第一流的男词人抗衡的女词人。她嫁与丞相之子,夫妻相亲相爱。金兵南犯,她随夫逃至江南。丈夫死后,她流寓金华、绍兴、杭州。其词风早期明快,后期凄凉深婉。早年,其词多描写少妇的情感,如在《如梦令》中的句子:"知否?知否?应是绿肥红瘦!"晚年,其词描写她的孤独和痛苦,如《声声慢》中的句子:"寻寻觅觅,冷冷清清,凄凄惨惨戚戚。乍暖还寒时候,最难将息。"以上名句到处吟唱。

## Li Qingzhao(1084 – about 1151)

She was the best poetess and she could rival first-class poets in the Song Dynasty. She married the son of a prime minister. They loved each other. When the soldiers of Jin invaded southward, with her husband, she escaped to the southern land. When her husband died, she wandered, staying in Jinhua, Shaoxing, and Hangzhou. In her early years, she wrote *Ci* poems in a fresh, chaste style. In her later years, she wrote *Ci* poems in a reserved and subtle style. In early years, her *Ci* poems depicted the feeling of young ladies, as the lines in "Like a Dream": "But, you don't know at all, how do you know? /The red is thin, the green fat." In her later years, her *Ci* poems displayed her sorrow and desolation as the lines in

"Slow, Slow Song": "I search and search for something to console myself here and there, /But I find there is nothing but cold and desolation everywhere, /I feel so dreary, sad and lonely. /Now warm and now cold it is, /It's difficult to take care of me." Above lines have been recited and sung everywhere.

## 点 绛 唇

蹴罢秋千,起来慵整纤纤手。露浓花瘦,薄汗轻衣透。 见客入来,袜刬金钗溜。和羞走。倚门回首,却把青梅嗅。

## Tune: Rouged Lips

Playing on the swing for some time,
She has never felt so weary and tired,
She relaxes her hands tender and delicate.
The dew is heavy and the flowers, so thin,
The light sweat wets her silk dress.

Seeing come in a young male guest,
With quick steps only in green socks,
Shyly she leaves and her hair pins fall.
Leaning on the door she turns round slow with a charming grace,
Smelling a green plum fruit and stealing a glance at the man gentle.

## 减字木兰花

卖花担上,买得一枝春欲放。泪染轻匀,犹带彤霞晓露痕。
怕郎猜道,奴面不如花面好。云鬓斜簪,徒要教郎比并看。

### Tune: Shortened Song of Magnolia Flowers

Cheerful from a flower load I buy
A flower in bud in the spring time.
Its petals are like rosy clouds in the morn,
And its dew, fragrant sparkling teardrops.

Seeing the bud just like a pretty young girl I am afraid
My husband will think it is more beautiful than my face.
I pin it slanting in my dark-cloud hair,
"Who is prettier?" I ask him to compare.

❀❀❀❀❀❀❀❀❀❀❀❀❀❀❀

## 醉 花 阴

薄雾浓云愁永昼,瑞脑消金兽。佳节又重阳,玉枕纱厨,半夜凉初透。　东篱把酒黄昏后,有暗香盈袖。莫道不销魂,帘卷西风,人比黄花瘦。

李清照

## Tune: Drunk in the Shade of Flowers

With the thin mist and thick clouds, how to spend the dreary long day?
The incense burns solitary and drear in the gold burner animal-shaped.
Again comes the Double Ninth Festival in autumn,
On the jade-like pillow behind the gauze curtains,
In the dead of night I feel the bleak cold entering my tender heart.

At dusk I drink before the blooming chrysanthemums in the garden,
The cold faint scent flows into my pink silk sleeves.
Oh, the hours will make a lonely wife full of grief,
The west wind rolls up the curtain seeing with sorrow
My pretty face thinner than charming flowers yellow.

❈❈❈❈❈❈❈❈❈❈❈❈❈❈❈

## 如 梦 令

昨夜雨疏风骤,浓睡不消残酒。试问卷帘人——却道"海棠依旧"。知否?知否?应是绿肥红瘦!

### Tune: Like a Dream

Last night the rain was light and the wind very hard,
Sound sleep has not dispelled my wine effect so far.
"What about the crab-apple tree?" with misery I ask.
"As yesterday", a maid rolls curtains saying so.
"But, you don't know at all, how do you know?
The red is thin, the green fat." I say with sorrow.

❋❋❋❋❋❋❋❋❋❋❋❋❋❋❋❋

## 武 陵 春

风住尘香花已尽,日晚倦梳头。物是人非事事休,欲语泪先流。 闻说双溪春尚好,也拟泛轻舟。只恐双溪舴艋舟,载不动许多愁。

### Tune: Spring in the Land of Peach Blossoms

The wind stops and all the flowers fall on the ground with scent,
I have no mood to comb my fluffy hair though in the morn late.
All the things are the same just as before,
But to another world my husband is gone,
Before I can pour out my woe, my tears stream down my cheeks.

李清照

I'm told still intoxicating is the spring scenery of the Twin Creeks.
I want to have a tour in a boat,
But I think with much sorrow,
Small and light it is
It will probably sink.

## 一 剪 梅

红藕香残玉簟秋。轻解罗裳,独上兰舟。云中谁寄锦书来？雁字回时,月满西楼。　花自飘零水自流。一种相思,两处闲愁。此情无计可消除,才下眉头,却上心头。

## Tune: A Twig of Plum Blossoms

Fall coming, red lotuses wither, scent fades and bamboo mat feels cold.
With loneliness and desolation very slowly taking off my green silk coat,
I take an orchid boat alone in a dull mood.
When quietly rises the bright round moon,
My boudoir is bathed in its cold light.
Wild geese pass by the sky in a line
Bringing me no message from my dear.

The flowers here and there drift drear,
The water weeps miserable.
The deep love between us
Makes us full of sorrow in two places.
Oh, it's a pity I can't dispel it even a bit,
To get it away from my brows, I try very hard,
But almost at once it comes into my sweet heart.

❋❋❋❋❋❋❋❋❋❋❋❋❋❋❋❋❋❋

## 凤凰台上忆吹箫

香冷金猊,被翻红浪,起来慵自梳头。任宝奁尘满,日上帘钩。生怕离怀别苦,多少事、欲说还休。新来瘦,非干病酒,不是悲秋。　　休休!这回去也,千万遍阳关,也则难留。念武陵人远,烟锁秦楼。惟有楼前流水,应念我、终日凝眸。凝眸处,从今又添,一段新愁。

## Tune: Playing the Flute on Phoenix Terrace

Cold is the burner lion-shaped, burns out the incense,
The red quilts on the bed are left like waves in a mess,
Getting up for long, I'm too tired to make up.
The heart-shaped mirror is covered with dust,
The sun already rises to the hook of the green curtain.

李清照

The tragic parting never leaves my mind for a moment,
How many melancholy things in my tender heart sweet,
I tried to tell him, I stopped when he was leaving even.
I am thin recently, to my surprise,
But it has nothing to do with wine
Nor with woe about the fall.

Really I had no way at all.
He was determined to start his travel, leaving me alone sad,
Having sung a thousand times a parting song "The Yang Pass",
I was unable to move him with me to stay.
Now he is in the southern land so far away,
I'm in the quiet boudoir shrouded completely in a heavy mist in the late spring.
No one knows my grief but the creek shedding tears before my storied building.
I lean on the red railings, gazing at the distance for his returning boat,
The bleak water on the horizon flows into my heart with new sorrow.

❋❋❋❋❋❋❋❋❋❋❋❋❋❋❋❋❋❋

## 菩 萨 蛮

风柔日薄春犹早,夹衫乍著心情好。睡起觉微寒,梅花鬓上残。
故乡何处是,忘了除非醉。沉水卧时烧,香消酒未消。

## Tune: Buddhist Dancers

It is in early spring, with the breeze gentle, the sunlight weak,
Wearing double layered vernal dress, I'm at ease and carefree.
Getting up after a nap, I feel the chill invading my tender skin,
On my hair the fragrant and pretty plum blossoms fade already.

Oh, where is my beautiful dear native town?
Except drunkenness, I can't forget it anyhow.
At night the incense begins to burn when I go to bed,
At dawn it burnt out all, I still haven't sobered up yet.

❀❀❀❀❀❀❀❀❀❀❀❀❀❀❀❀❀

## 南 歌 子

天上星河转,人间帘幕垂。凉生枕簟泪痕滋。起解罗衣聊问夜何其。　　翠贴莲蓬小,金销藕叶稀。旧时天气旧时衣,只有情怀不似旧家时!

## Tune: Southern Song

In the sky the Milky Way with sweet love turns slow,
In the world the curtains of my red boudoir hang low.

李清照

The bamboo pillow and mat cold and drear
Is wet here and there with my bloody tears.
Taking off my garment and going to bed,
I find the lonely night is already very late.

On the underwear are the lotus seedpods of feather green,
And glistening golden thread-embroidered sparse leaves.
Oh, in those old days are the clothes and weather,
My feelings differ from the time with my husband.

❈❈❈❈❈❈❈❈❈❈❈❈❈❈❈❈❈

## 永 遇 乐

落日熔金,暮云合璧,人在何处?染柳烟浓,吹梅笛怨,春意知几许?元宵佳节,融和天气,次第岂无风雨?来相召,香车宝马,谢他酒朋诗侣。　中州盛日,闺门多暇,记得偏重三五。铺翠冠儿,撚金雪柳,簇带争济楚。如今憔悴,风鬟霜鬓,怕见夜间出去。不如向、帘儿底下,听人笑语。

### *Tune: Joy of Eternal Union*

The melting gold seems the enchanting rosy setting sun,
In the eve out of colored clouds the jade-like moon comes,
Oh, where at all is my dear?

In mist, willows feel drear,

Who plays on the flute "Plum Blossoms Fall" sad somewhere?

How much intoxicating spring floats here and there in the air?

On the Lantern Festival tonight,

It is pleasantly warm and fine,

But at any moment will come heavy rain and wind hard.

With so beautifully decorated horses, and fragrant carts,

My friends, some of intimates far and near in wine and verse

Invite me to appreciate lanterns, but I reject with polite words.


Years ago when the capital was prosperous,

Girls in spring of youth got much pleasure,

And had a great interest in the festival in the days.

Wearing small bonnets with green feather inlaid,

And dark-cloud hair with willow twigs of golden threads,

To vie in beauty and fashion delightedly we were dressed.

Now I'm wan and sallow,

My hair looks like snow,

At night to go out I'm not in the mood.

I'd better stay alone in the quiet room,

Behind the curtains hanging listening

To young people talking and laughing.

❈❈❈❈❈❈❈❈❈❈❈❈❈❈❈

李清照

## 渔 家 傲

天接云涛连晓雾,星河欲转千帆舞。彷佛梦魂归帝所。闻天语,殷勤问我归何处? 我报路长嗟日暮,学诗谩有惊人句。九万里风鹏正举。风休住,蓬舟吹取三山去!

## Tune: Pride of Fishermen

In the morning the big waves roll to the sky and drifts a thin mist pale,
On the Milky Way thousands of sails high and low dance with waves.
In the dream I come back to the heavenly palace high.
Expressing his own concern, Supreme Being inquires,
"Please tell me as a traveller in the world where you are going."

I reply, "I have a long way to go, and it is already in the evening,
I have composed wonderful poems, but no use they seem."
The roc flies up to the sky as high as ninety thousand *li*.
"Oh, hard wind, please don't stop," I loudly shout,
"And take my boat to the three fairy isles anyhow."

## 小 重 山

春到长门春草青。红梅些子破,未开匀。碧云笼碾玉成尘。留晓梦,惊破一瓯春。　　花影压重门。疏帘铺淡月,好黄昏。二年三度负东君。归来也,著意过今春。

### Tune: Hills by Hills

Spring reaches the Long Gate Palace and green dots the garden,
The wild plums by the green river begin to blossom with charm,
But most of them are too shy to show their faces to the appreciators.
The fresh scented emerald green tea has been crushed into powder,
Awake in the morn, a fond dream remains in my brain,
I take a cup of the new refreshing tea to drive it away.

At dusk the shadows of the aromatic flowers sway on the doors,
On the green curtains hanging low the leisurely moonlight falls,
With the scenery and scent the eve is enchanting.
In two years, I fail to live up to the god of spring,
Now I'm so happy for my husband comes here,
Oh, I'll enjoy the beautiful spring with my dear.

李清照

## 怨 王 孙

湖上风来波浩渺,秋已暮、红稀香少。水光山色与人亲,说不尽、无穷好。　莲子已成荷叶老,清露洗、蘋花汀草。眠沙鸥鹭不回头,似也恨、人归早。

## Tune: Complaint of Princess

The breeze blows, and the waves appear on the lake,
The withering fall like a fading lady is already late,
The red flowers are sparse and the fragrance floats rare.
Dear to us are the green hills and water here and there,
Their beauty on earth
Is really beyond words.

The lotus seeds come out and the flowers grow old,
The sparkling jade-like dewdrops now and then roll
On the fading white clover ferns and green duckweeds.
The egrets do not look at us, lying on the sands at ease,
It seems that they hate greatly
The tourists leaving them early.

## 诉 衷 情

夜来沉醉卸妆迟,梅萼插残枝。酒醒熏破春睡,梦远不成归。人悄悄,月依依,翠帘垂。更挼残蕊,更撚余香,更得些时。

### Tune: Baring the Heart

At night, drunk, I go to bed without taking off my adornments,
The plum twigs on my hair on the pillow with lovebirds wither.
I dream I am on a long journey back home in the north lost,
The scent sobers me up and here the beautiful dream stops.

My husband away, I'm lonely and solitary,
The moon shines on the window lovingly,
The melancholy green curtains hang down.
Taking away faded twigs on my hair about,
I twist them fragrance remaining
Without end until next morning.

❋❋❋❋❋❋❋❋❋❋❋❋❋❋❋

## 渔 家 傲

雪里已知春信至,寒梅点缀琼枝腻。香脸半开娇旖旎,当庭际,

李清照

玉人浴出新妆洗。　造化可能偏有意,故教明月玲珑地,共赏金尊沉绿蚁,莫辞醉,此花不与群花比。

## Tune: Pride of Fishermen

In the thick snow there is the beautiful spring message,
The red plum blossoms embellish the jade-like twigs.
The tree is delicate with her half open face full of charm,
Standing with grace in the scented green-dotted courtyard,
She looks like a beauty just having bathed.

Nature has partiality for her charming face,
To set off the red, she makes the moon especially bright.
Let's with pleasure lift our gold cups of the green wine,
Don't stop, please until daybreak go on and on drinking,
Other flowers cannot compare with her so intoxicating.

❈❈❈❈❈❈❈❈❈❈❈❈❈❈

## 添字采桑子

窗前谁种芭蕉树?阴满中庭,阴满中庭,叶叶心心,舒卷有余情。　伤心枕上三更雨,点滴霖霪,点滴霖霪,愁损北人,不惯起来听。

## Tune: Expanded Song of Gathering Mulberry Leaves

The plantain before the window, who plants?
Its thick shade fills the pretty little courtyard.
Heart and leaves,
Heart and leaves,
With deep love it rolls up and unfolds.

On the lonely and melancholy pillow,
Hearing the rain in the dead of night
Dropping on leaves, I groan and sigh.
Drop by drop,
Drop by drop,
In the north of the Yangtze River born and bred,
I'm not used to listening to the whole night rain.

## 行 香 子

草际鸣蛩,惊落梧桐。正人间天上愁浓。云阶月地,关锁千重。纵浮槎来,浮槎去,不相逢。　　星桥鹊驾,经年才见,想离情别恨难穷。牵牛织女,莫是离中。甚霎儿晴,霎儿雨,霎儿风。

李清照

## June: Burning Incense

In the grasses the crickets weep with grief,
Frightening into falling the parasol leaves.
Deep loneliness and sorrow fill the world and heaven,
In heaven the moon is the ground and clouds, the steps,
How many barriers lie between the Cowherd and the Girl Weaver?
Even in a craft going from the sea to the boundless heaven river,
And coming down to the ground,
You can't meet with them anyhow.

Magpies gathering there, a bridge across Milky Way appears,
It is a pity, they have unforgettable reunions only once a year,
Day and night in their hearts the pain of separation flows.
Probably many times they have said good-bye with woe,
They stand quiet.
Oh, now sunshine,
Now rain,
Now gale.

## 玉 楼 春

### 红 梅

红酥肯放琼苞碎,探著南枝开遍未。不知酝藉几多香,但见包藏无限意。　道人憔悴春窗底,闷损阑干愁不倚。要来小酌便来休,未必明朝风不起。

## Tune: Spring in the Jade Boudoir

### The Red Plum Blossom

To burst the pink jade-like plum buds are ready,
Are all plum blossoms opening on sunny twigs?
How much fragrance do they get?
How much love do they contain?

With a fading face staying behind the window,
I cannot bear leaning on the railings with woe.
Come here, and appreciate plum blossoms while drinking wine,
Oh, the chilly wind in the early spring will blow hard at any time.

李清照

## 满 庭 芳

小阁藏春,闲窗锁昼,画堂无限深幽。篆香烧尽,日影下帘钩。手种江梅更好,又何必、临水登楼。无人到,寂寥恰似,何逊在扬州。　从来知韵胜,难堪雨藉,不耐风揉。更谁家横笛,吹动浓愁。莫恨香消玉减,须信道、扫迹难留。难言处,良萧淡月,疏影尚风流。

## Tune: Courtyard Full of Fragrance

In the little chamber the early fragrant spring hides,
The leisure windows lock the scenery in the daytime,
Deep and quiet sleeps the painted hall.
And thin incense coils have burnt all,
The shadow of the sun goes down the hooks of the curtain,
By the water the plum tree planted by me is in full blossom.
But I have no interest to ascend the building storied,
Facing the green scented water to appreciate scenery.
No one comes here,
I'm lonely and drear,
As poet He staying solitary in Yangzhou wrote sad poems about the plum.

The charm of the aromatic plum tree has all the time been praised too much,

She can neither bear being beaten by a rain,

Nor can she endure being blown by a gale.

Who plays "Plum Blossoms Fall" on the flute

Increasing in my tender mind and heart gloom?

Don't be sad about the fragrance fading,

And like snow the plum blossoms falling.

Its traces may disappear, you must believe,

Eternally the true affection there will be.

Oh, I realize now it is really too hard

To describe my feelings in my heart.

I see so charming and elegant the shadows of the flowers,

Under the pale moon beyond the window in fine hours.

❉❉❉❉❉❉❉❉❉❉❉❉❉❉❉❉❉❉

## 孤 雁 儿

藤床纸帐朝眠起,说不尽、无佳思。沉香断续玉炉寒,伴我情怀如水。笛声三弄,梅心惊破,多少游春意。 小风疏雨萧萧地,又催下、千行泪。吹箫人去玉楼空,肠断与谁同倚?一枝折得,人间天上,没个人堪寄。

## Tune: A Lonely Wild Goose

In the morn on the cane bed,

李清照

With a cloth net heart-shaped,
I'm awake from a dream,
My heart fills with grief.
The eaglewood incense burns away and cold is the burner,
Accompanying me with feelings like the groaning water.
Someone plays "Plum Blossoms Fall" somewhere,
Making the plum trees blossoming here and there,
The spring comes and the fields are full of life.

Then the breeze groans and the drizzle sighs,
Causing me to shed like showers a thousand lines of bloody tears.
My husband playing the tune is dead, the chamber cold and drear,
Who would lean on the railings with me to dispel my woe?
I pluck a twig of scented pink plum blossoms with sorrow,
But on earth and in heaven,
To whom can I get it sent?

❀❀❀❀❀❀❀❀❀❀❀❀❀❀❀❀❀

## 蝶 恋 花

泪湿罗衣脂粉满,四叠阳关,唱到千千遍。人道山长水又断,潇潇微雨闻孤馆。　　惜别伤离方寸乱,忘了临行,酒盏深和浅。好把音书凭过雁,东莱不似蓬莱远。

## Tune: Butterflies in Love with Flowers

The tears wet wholly our garments and powder dots our faces,
Four times we sisters have sung the parting song so miserably,
And will sing it with unbearable grief a thousand times.
The green hills and blue water are lost on the horizon,
In the lone inn, we listen to the rain pattering.

We are heartbreaking before the sad parting,
And we forget at all with too deep sorrow
To notice how much wine our cups hold.
In the future we can ask wild geese to send letters to each other,
And Donglai, a quite remote place, is not so far away as heaven.

❄❄❄❄❄❄❄❄❄❄❄❄❄❄❄❄❄

## 声 声 慢

寻寻觅觅,冷冷清清,凄凄惨惨戚戚。乍暖还寒时候,最难将息。三杯两盏淡酒,怎敌他晓来风急?雁过也,正伤心,却是旧时相识。　　满地黄花堆积,憔悴损,如今有谁堪摘?守着窗儿独自,怎生得黑!梧桐更兼细雨,到黄昏、点点滴滴。这次第,怎一个愁字了得!

李清照

## Tune: Slow, Slow Song

I search and search for something to console myself here and there,
But I can find there is nothing but cold and desolation everywhere,
I feel so dreary, sad and lonely.
Now warm and now cold it is,
It's difficult to take care of me.
Two or three cups of wine weak
Cannot keep out at all
Chilly wind in the morn.
The grief floats into my heart
When I see under the sky vast
The wild geese fly away.
They are my old friends.

The courtyard is filled with the chrysanthemums yellow,
I'm thin and haggard with deep grief in the autumn cold,
And I'm too sorrowful to pluck the blooming flowers.
I just sit at the window to spend the miserable hours,
How hard to stay till dusk.
But when it finally comes,
A rain begins to thick and fast fall
On the parasol trees drop by drop.
Oh, the word "sorrow" is not enough to describe

The state of my mind tortured cruelly all the time.

❋❋❋❋❋❋❋❋❋❋❋❋❋❋❋

## 念 奴 娇

萧条庭院,又斜风细雨,重门须闭。宠柳娇花寒食近,种种恼人天气。险韵诗成,扶头酒醒,别是闲滋味。征鸿过尽,万千心事难寄。　　楼上几日春寒,帘垂四面,玉阑干慵倚。被冷香销新梦觉,不许愁人不起。清露晨流,新桐初引,多少游春意。日高烟敛,更看今日晴未?

## Tune: Charm of a Maiden Singer

The courtyard feels lonely and desolate,
The wind sighs and sheds tears a drizzle,
I shut all the doors and gate quite drear.
The coquettish willows and flowers fear
Cold Fold Day approaching,
The weather is so annoying.
I spend lonely time composing the poems with rare rhyme,
Layer by layer grief piling, on and on I drink strong wine.
The swan geese disappear on their homeward way,
Who else would send my love to my dear far away?

For days my boudoir is pervaded by spring cold,
In a miserable sleep many red curtains hang low,
I'm not in the mood to lean on the solitary railings of the chamber.
The quilts cold and incense burnt I'm awake from a dream beautiful,
With deep sorrow I can no longer lie in the solitary bed.
In the early morning dew falls drop by drop without end,
From the twigs of paulownias crawl out buds tender and green,
Oh, now, I have interest to go out to appreciate the spring scene.
With the rising sun disperses the fog,
I wonder if it'll be a fine day or not?

※※※※※※※※※※※※※※※

## 鹧 鸪 天

暗淡轻黄体性柔,情疏迹远只香留。何须浅碧深红色,自是花中第一流。　　梅定妒,菊应羞。画栏开处冠中秋。骚人可煞无情思,何事当年不见收。

## June: Partridge Sky

The fragrant laurel wears dull or light yellow dress like a maiden,
With little affection, she often hides alone in the deep mountains,
She spreads aroma far and near refreshing the heart.
Though without the color of light green and red dark,

Of all flowers she belongs to the first rate.

The plum is jealous of her charming face,
And the chrysanthemum feels ashamed smelling her scent.
When standing with grace in full bloom by the painted rails,
In the cool and desolate mid-autumn she ranks the first.
Without enough love, poet Qu hadn't written about her.

❀❀❀❀❀❀❀❀❀❀❀❀❀❀❀

## 浣 溪 沙

绣面芙蓉一笑开,斜飞宝鸭衬香腮,眼波才动被人猜。　一面风情深有韵,半笺娇恨寄幽怀,月移花影约重来。

## *Tune: Silk-Washing Stream*

Her smiling face is like a blooming pink lotus with green leaves,
The slanting hair pins on her hair set off her fragrant red cheeks,
Her amorous glance shows her secret in the heart.

Her face with a flush displays her coquettish charm,
She writes her anger at him on half piece of rosy paper for a long time,
Still she invites him for a tryst in the flower shadows in the

moonlight.

## 好 事 近

风定落花深,帘外拥红堆雪。长记海棠开后,正伤春时节。　酒阑歌罢玉尊空,青缸暗明灭。魂梦不堪幽怨,更一声啼鴂。

### Tune: Happiness Approaching

The wind calming down, the ground outside the curtain
Is covered with piles of the red and white flowers fallen.
I often recollect in those days with gloom,
When the crab-apples were in full bloom,
It was in spring and people felt depressed.

I drink good wine alone until the night late,
Songs stop, I'm drunk, and empty the cup,
The incense in the green burner burns up.
My soul can't bear the deep sorrow in the dream,
Somewhere comes a cry of a cuckoo with grief.

## 点 绛 唇

寂寞深闺,柔肠一寸愁千缕。惜春春去,几点催花雨。　　倚遍阑干,只是无情绪。人何处,连天芳草,望断归来路。

## Tune: Rouged Lips

In the lonely quiet deep love-fading boudoir,
A thousand threads of sorrow twine my heart.
Though I value the spring scene,
Oh, still it so quickly leaves me,
The raindrops speed the falling of the flowers.

Day by day in the unbearable lonesome hours,
One by one I lean through the railings drear.
In the remotest region is my husband dear,
The fragrant grass like his green robe stretches to the sky,
My miserable eyes are fixed on his way back all the time.

❀❀❀❀❀❀❀❀❀❀❀❀❀❀❀❀❀

## 庆 清 朝 慢

禁幄低张,雕栏巧护,就中独占残春。容华淡伫,绰约俱见天真。

李清照

待得群花过后,一番风露晓妆新。妖娆艳态,妒风笑月,长殢东君。　　东城边,南陌上,正日烘池馆,竞走香轮。绮筵散日,谁人可继芳尘?更好明光宫殿,几枝先近日边匀。金尊倒,拚了尽烛,不管黄昏。

## Tune: Slow Song of Celebrating the Good Dynasty

Over the peonies is the tent painted,
And around them the red rails thick,
They are in full bloom like with beautiful dresses in the late spring.
Some stand with grace wearing white faces so delicate and charming,
Like in heaven fairy maidens.
When all other flowers fade,
They are beauties, washed and dressed in dew and breeze in the morn.
The other peonies wear pink looks quite gorgeous, enchanting and soft,
Playing with the warm breeze and bright moon
And god of spring as a spoiled girl of childhood.

Through the city gate east,
And on the paths in fields,
The people appreciate them in their fragrant carts with cheer,
The warm sun shines on the gardens and riverside pavilions.

The flower fair is over and banquets end,
When can we thoroughly enjoy ourselves?
Bright Palace with peonies in bloom is open tonight,
The dark dusk everywhere except the palace arrives.
One after another we empty wine cups
Until at night when the candle burns up.

## 瑞 鹧 鸪

### 双 银 杏

风韵雍容未甚都,尊前甘橘可为奴。谁怜流落江湖上,玉骨冰肌未肯枯。 谁教并蒂连枝摘,醉后明皇倚太真。居士擘开真有意,要吟风味两家新。

## Tune: Auspicious Partridge

### Twin Ginkgoes

Though the ginkgo is neither charming nor elegant,
At banquets the orange serves only as her servant.
Nobody taking pity on her, by water she lives a vagabond life,
With jade bones and ice skin, the ginkgo neither fades nor dies.

I pluck the green twin ginkgo nuts leaning on each other on a heavy

twig,
As the drunken emperor, leaning on his concubine to appreciate peonies.
I open them carefully with tender fragrant love,
Their hearts and mine are sweet—becoming one.

## 浣 溪 沙

### 春 景

小院闲窗春色深,重帘未卷影沉沉,倚楼无语理瑶琴。 远岫出山催薄暮,细风吹雨弄轻阴,梨花欲谢恐难禁。

## *Tune: Silk-Washing Stream*

### Scene of Springtime

Beyond the leisure window in the little yard,
The enchanting spring is almost wholly past.
The curtains still hang low,
And thick are their shadows.
Leaning on the railings silent,
I begin to play the Yao zither.

Over distant green hills float grey clouds,

Urging the twilight to come earlier round.
The gentle breeze brings the drizzle,
And the weather changes gradually.
The white blossoms of the pears
Fade and they are falling there.

❋❋❋❋❋❋❋❋❋❋❋❋❋❋❋❋❋

## 殢 人 娇

玉瘦香浓,檀深雪散,今年恨探梅又晚。江楼楚馆,云闲水远。清昼永,凭栏翠帘低卷。　　坐上客来,尊前酒满,歌声共、水流云断。南枝可插,更须频剪,莫直待、西楼数声羌管。

### *June: A Charming and Lingering Beauty*

Jade-like plum blossoms are thin and their fragrance thick,
The snow melts showing reddish brown branches and twigs,
This year to appreciate the plum blossoms is again too late.
The green curtains hang low as sleeping sound all the day,
I lean on the railings gazing at the clouds flowing into water at ease,
In a waterside tower he must be enjoying wine with a beauty in glee.

Here in chamber west

Come my female guests.

The cups are filled with wine,

The sweet songs and music rise

With refreshing scent far and near flying.

The plums facing the south are blossoming,

To pin them in your hair, please pluck the plum blossoms more,

Don't wait till the chamber sends out music "Plum Blossoms Fall".

❀❀❀❀❀❀❀❀❀❀❀❀❀❀❀❀

## 如 梦 令

长记溪亭日暮,沉醉不知归路。兴尽晚回舟。误入藕花深处。争渡,争渡。惊起一滩鸥鹭。

## Tune: Like a Dream

I often recollect at dusk by the pavilions I enjoyed in a boat outings,

As a pretty young girl I was intoxicated with the scene so charming.

Greatly satisfied with the excursion I lost my way,

Entering the depth of the lotus flowers by mistake.

I shouted in surprise, get through, quickly get through,

Starting out the gulls and egrets on the bank of the pool.

# 吕本中(1084—1145)

做过朝廷高官。他的词俚俗、清新,有民歌风味,广受欢迎。

**Lü Benzhong(1084 - 1145)**

He served as a senior official in the court. He wrote *Ci* poems in a vulgar and fresh style, like folk songs enjoying high popularity.

## 采 桑 子

恨君不似江楼月,南北东西。南北东西,只有相随无别离。  恨君却似江楼月,暂满还亏。暂满还亏,待得团圆是几时?

## *Tune: Song of Gathering Mulberry Leaves*

I hate you couldn't be the moon over the storied building by the river,
No matter in the south, north, west or east,
No matter in the south, north, west or east,
It always accompanies me and never leaves.

I hate you are just like the moon over the storied building by the river,

吕本中

When it is just full, it begins to wane.
When it is just full, it begins to wane,
Oh, when can we have reunion again?

# 李持正（生卒年不详）

政和五年（1115）进士。他的词受到词家特别是苏轼的赞扬，广为流传。

**Li Chizheng ( years of birth and death unknown )**

He passed the highest imperial examination in 1115. His *Ci* poems were praised highly by the poets, especially by Su Shi, and spread far and near.

## 人 月 圆

小桃枝上春风早，初试薄罗衣。年年乐事，华灯竞处，人月圆时。禁街箫鼓，寒轻夜永，纤手重携。更阑人散，千门笑语，声在帘帏。

### *Tune: Reunion under the Full Moon*

In the early spring breeze, the peaches are blossoming,
Feeling a bit warm all the people try on silk clothing.
The Lantern Festival arriving here our great joy year after year lies
In the lights of all shapes and colours brightening the earth and sky,

李持正

And in people's reunions under the sweet and soft full moon.

Over the streets are the deafening sounds of drums and flutes,
Long is the night and a little, the cold,
The lads take the girls' hands like snow.
People scatter when the night is late,
Talking and laughing loud, they get
Into curtains hanging lowly
Of ten thousands of houses.

# 李邴(1085—1146)

他是崇宁五年(1106)进士。曾任朝廷高官。此词写一位美丽的少女写作时的情态,新颖别致。

**Li Bing(1085–1146)**

He passed the highest imperial examination in 1106. He once served as a senior official in the court. The *Ci* poem described the expression of a pretty young girl when she was writing something. It was new and exquisite.

## 木 兰 花

### 美 人 书 字

沉吟不语晴窗畔,小字银钩题欲遍。云情散乱未成篇,花骨欹斜终带软。　　重重说尽情和怨,珍重提携常在眼。暂时得近玉纤纤,翻羡缕金红象管。

## *Tune: Magnolia Flowers*

### A Beauty Writing Characters

On a fine day at the windows a beauty is deep in thought muttering,

李　邴

She fills the paper with little words but far from revealing her feeling.
Her thoughts as floating clouds, her letter can't be completed,
Her hands are beautiful and strong still with female softness.

The letter tells him in detail in her heart love and grief,
Again and again words "treasure" and "help" are seen.
Reading the letter I seem to be close to the beauty white and tender,
And begin to admire in her fragrant hand the gold-inlaid brush even.

# 向子諲(1085—1152)

做过京官。后隐居江湖。他是一位爱国词人。他把自己所写的词编为《酒边词》,分为两卷——《江南新词》和《江北旧词》。前者作于衰落时代,后者作于繁华时代。

**Xiang Ziyin(1085–1152)**

He once served as an official in the capital. Later he lived in seclusion. He was a patriotic poet. He wrote "*Ci* Poems by the Cups". He divided it into two parts, "New *Ci* poems in the south of the Yangtze River", written in declining period, and "Old *Ci* poems in the north of the Yangtze River", in flourishing period.

## 秦 楼 月

芳菲歇,故园目断伤心切。伤心切,无边烟水,无穷山色。　可堪更近乾龙节,眼中泪尽空啼血。空啼血,子规声外,晓风残月。

## Tune: The Moon over the Qin Tower

In the southern land in late spring flowers fade,
The lost land is out of sight and my heart breaks.

向子諲

My heart breaks.
Boundless are the mist and water,
And endless, the green mountains.

I can't bear to think approaching is emperor's birthday,
My tears are exhausted and blood falls down my face,
Blood falls down my face.
Beyond now and then the heartbreaking cries of the cuckoo,
Sighs the morning breeze and sheds tears the setting moon.

# 蒋兴祖女(生卒年不详)

其父蒋兴祖为县令。金兵南侵,将城包围。其父拼命抵抗,至死不屈。其母及兄皆被杀害。她被金兵掳去,送往北方。途中题词于驿站墙上。时年仅十五岁,很漂亮,善写诗词。

**Daughter of Jiang Xingzu(years of birth and death unknown)**

Her father was a county magistrate. When Jin invaders surrounded the county, he fought against them desperately until he was killed by them. Her mother and brother were also killed. She was caught. On the way she was sent to the north, she wrote this *Ci* poem on the wall of the post station. She was just fifteen years old and very beautiful. She was good at composing poems.

## 减字木兰花

### 题雄州驿壁

朝云横度,辘辘车声如水去。白草黄沙,月照孤村三两家。　飞鸿过也,万结愁肠无昼夜。渐近燕山,回首乡关归路难。

蒋兴祖女

## June: Shortened Song of Magnolia Flowers

I wrote the *Ci* poem on the wall of the post in Xiongzhou County in the North.

The dark clouds fly across the sky in the early morning,

The carts rumble northward as the water sadly groaning.

In the desolate region the grass is white and the sands, yellow,

The moon sheds tears on two or three huts in a village alone.

The swan geese fly southward silently,

Day and night my tears fall endlessly.

When I approach in the north enemy's capital,

Turning round I find returning home impossible.

# 李重元(生卒年不详)

他作《忆王孙》词四首,包括春词、夏词、秋词和冬词。此处收录"春词"。

**Li Zhongyuan( years of birth and death unknown)**

He composed four *Ci* poems of "Recollecting Prince", including spring, summer, autumn, and winter. The following is a *Ci* poem of spring.

## 忆 王 孙

### 春 词

萋萋芳草忆王孙,柳外楼高空断魂。杜宇声声不忍闻。欲黄昏,雨打梨花深闭门。

## Tune: Recollecting Prince

### Spring

The grass with the dew of our love grows wild
With its scent stretching to the distant grey sky.
Beyond the willow trees,

李重元

In the high brothel green,

Leaning on the rails,

Looking far in vain,

The beauty misses her dear beyond the grass with deep sorrow.

She cannot bear hearing the cuckoo sadly crying "Return home!"

The evening draws near, she shuts the door drear,

The rain beats the white pear blossoms, our dear.

# 李玉(生卒年不详)

有人说"风流蕴藉,尽在此篇"。他的词只收录这一首。

**Li Yu( years of birth and death unknown)**

It is said that the urbane charm in this *Ci* poem is matchless. Only one of his *Ci* poems is extant.

## 贺 新 郎

### 春 情

篆缕消金鼎。醉沉沉、庭阴转午,画堂人静。芳草王孙知何处?惟有杨花糁径。渐玉枕、腾腾春醒。帘外残红春已透,镇无聊、殢酒厌厌病。云鬓乱,未忺整。　　江南旧事休重省。遍天涯寻消问息,断鸿难倩。月满西楼凭阑久,依旧归期未定。又只恐、瓶沉金井。嘶骑不来银烛暗,枉教人、立尽梧桐影。谁伴我,对鸾镜。

## Tune: Congratulations to the Bridegroom

### Stirring of Love

From the gold burner the incense smoke curls up,

李 玉

Drinking one cup after another she is dead drunk.
The shadows of trees in the yard turn to the west a bit,
The magnificent painted hall sleeps quiet and solitary.
Seeing grass like his robe spreading to the sky,
She heaves from her tender heart a deep sigh:
"Where are you, I can see you in the dreams drear?"
The willow catkins shower on paths far and near.
For a short time she lies on the lone pillow fragrant,
Now having sobered up she is languid and indolent.
The spring is late outside the curtain green,
Only a few red flowers remaining on trees.
She feels bored and desolate all day,
Drinking fine wine again and again.
Her hair like dark clouds is in a mess,
She is too weary and sleepy to dress.

She can't bear recollecting in southeast the hours in his warm arms.
Anywhere in the world any information of her handsome sweetheart,
So far in her solitary chamber she has not heard,
Nor swan goose has brought his love letter to her.
Leaning on the rails of the moonlit west building,
All the time she is thinking of his date returning,
And she is so afraid day and night their sweet love is gone at all.
The candle burning away, she hears no horse neighing at the door,
The sweet moon seeing us sleeping on the same pillow falls down,

The shadows of the parasol trees disappear on the steps and ground.
She groans and moans
With deep love sorrow:
"Who would accompany me to look with true love and care
At my fading face in the mirror shaped like lovebirds in pair?"

# 吴淑姬(生卒年不详)

  吴淑姬之父是秀才。她是女词人中之佼佼者,写了五卷词,妙处不减李清照。

**Wu Shuji( years of birth and death unknown)**

  Her father passed the imperial examination at the county level. She was a great poetess. She wrote five collections of *Ci* poems. A critic said she could compare with Li Qingzhao.

## 小 重 山

谢了荼蘼春事休。无多花片子,缀枝头。庭槐影碎被风揉。莺虽老,声尚带娇羞。  独自倚妆楼。一川烟草浪,衬云浮。不如归去下帘钩。心儿小,难着许多愁。

## *Tune: Hills by Hills*

The rose leaf raspberries fade and gone is spring,
But a few white petals like pretty girls glistening,
With fragrant dewdrops still smile with cheer on the tips of the trees.
The shadows of the locust trees in the yard are broken by the breeze,

Young orioles have grown up already,
They sing still with coquettish shyness.

I lean with sorrow on the railings of the lone boudoir,
Gazing at the vast expanse of the wave-like sad grass,
Against the background of the floating white clouds.
I think I'd better go back to pull the curtains down.
My heart is too small
To hold the grief all.

※※※※※※※※※※※※※※※※

# 长相思令

烟霏霏。雪霏霏。雪向梅花枝上堆。春从何处回。　　醉眼开。睡眼开。疏影横斜安在哉。从教塞管催。

## Tune: Song of Yearning Forever

The mist drifts here and there,
The snow flies here and there.
The snow covers all the branches of the plum trees,
When will the spring reach here with pretty scene?

I open my drunken eyes,

吴淑姬

I open my sleepy eyes.

Where is the reflection on the water of the plum blossoms on a twig slanting?

Oh, leave the bamboo flute blow the sad music "Plum Blossoms Falling".

# 乐婉(生卒年不详)

乐婉是杭州乐妓。她与施酒监相爱。离别时,施赠词于乐:"相逢情便深,恨不相逢早。识尽千千万万人。终不似,伊家好……"乐回以此词。

**Le Wan(years of birth and death unknown)**

She was a music prostitute in Hangzhou. She was in love with a supervisor of wine. Before leaving, the man gave her a farewell *Ci* poem. She wrote the following *Ci* poem in reply.

## 卜 算 子

### 答 施

相思似海深,旧事如天远。泪滴千千万万行,更使人、愁肠断。要见无因见,拚了终难拚。若是前生未有缘,待重结、来生愿。

### Tune: Song of Divination

At parting, the lover presented a *Ci* poem to the prostitute and she gave him the *Ci* poem in reply.

My love for him is as deep as the sea,

乐　婉

As far as the sky are our hours sweet.
Though I shed thousands of lines of bloody tears,
I can't stop his journey so far away from me drear,
My heart almost breaks.

If we can't meet again,
I'd better give up my love for him forever,
But I can hardly put it away even a moment.
If we had no predestined relationship,
Oh, let's in the next life get married.

# 聂胜琼(生卒年不详)

聂胜琼乃京城名妓。李之问至京,与聂胜琼一见倾心。相聚几月。别后不到十日,她作此词寄李。李途中得之,藏于箱中。后为妻所得。见其情真意切,让夫娶其回家。妻妾终身和悦。

**Nie Shengqiong(years of birth and death unknown)**

She was a famous prostitute in the capital. Li Zhiwen came to the capital. Li and she fell in love with each other at the first sight. They stayed together for several months. In less than ten days after Li Zhiwen left, she posted the *Ci* poem to him. He got it on the way and put it in the suitcase. Li's wife found it. Finding her love to him so deep and devoted, she asked Li to bring her home as a concubine. All life Li's wife and Nie lived together friendly and harmoniously.

## 鹧 鸪 天

### 寄李之问

玉惨花愁出凤城。莲花楼下柳青青。尊前一唱《阳关》后,别个人人第五程。　　寻好梦,梦难成。况谁知我此时情。枕前泪共帘前雨,隔个窗儿滴到明。

### Tune: Partridge Sky

A prostitute posted the *Ci* poem to her lover,
an official going home.

As a faded flower I'm so sorrowful,

I accompany you out of the capital,

Under the high Lotus Tower green willows are weeping.

Before a cup of wine I sing a farewell song heartbreaking,

Crying loud I watch you going slow away.

To have a sweet dream I try night and day,

But I fail to have it in broken sleeps at last.

Who knows my bitterness in my deep heart?

My bloody tears on the lonely pillow

And a rain outside the green window

Falls drop by drop

Till the dim dawn.

# 陈与义(1090—1139)

宋徽宗政和三年(1113)进士。他做过副丞相。评论家说他有的词超过黄庭坚甚至苏轼。

**Chen Yuyi( 1090 - 1139 )**

He passed the highest imperial examination in 1113. He once served as a vice prime minister. Some critics said some of his *Ci* poems were better than those of Huang Tingjian, even Su Shi.

## 虞 美 人

大光祖席,醉中赋长短句

张帆欲去仍搔首,更醉君家酒。吟诗日日待春风,及至桃花开后却匆匆。　歌声频为行人咽,记著樽前雪。明朝酒醒大江流,满载一船离恨向衡州。

## *Tune: Great Beauty Yu*

At farewell banquet, getting drunk, I wrote the *Ci* poem.

All the sails lifted, I linger here just,
One by one emptying the wine cups.

陈与义

I remember reciting poems we were expecting spring breeze day by day,
Now the fragrant peaches begin to blossom, in a hurry I will go far away.

The maiden singer sings songs with sobs and sighs,
I will remember her at the farewell feast all the time.
Tomorrow sobering up, I will be on the sad Xiang River in a boat,
And it will sail to the city of Hengzhou with a full load of sorrow.

# 张元干(1091—约1170)

官至将作少监,是一位杰出的爱国词人。早年词的风格婉媚。南渡后,词的风格变为豪放。他写过两本词集。为辛派词人的先驱。

**Zhang Yuangan(1091 – about 1170)**

He once served as a senior official. He was an outstanding patriotic poet. In his early years the style of his works was graceful. When he lived in the southern land for the invasion of Jin, it became uninhibited. He wrote two collections of Ci poems, pioneering the school of Xin Qiji.

## 兰 陵 王

### 春 恨

卷珠箔。朝雨轻阴乍阁。阑干外、烟柳弄晴,芳草侵阶映红药。东风妒花恶。吹落梢头嫩萼。屏山掩、沉水倦熏,中酒心情怯杯勺。 寻思旧京洛。正年少疏狂,歌笑迷著。障泥油壁催梳掠。曾驰道同载,上林携手,灯夜初过早共约。又争信飘泊? 寂寞。念行乐。甚粉淡衣襟,音断弦索。琼枝璧月春如昨。怅别后华表,那回双鹤。相思除是,向醉里、暂忘却。

张元干

## Tune: King of Lanling

### Grief of Springtime

I roll the pearly curtains up,
The morning rain stops just.
In the sunshine beyond the bamboo rails,
The misty willow twigs dance with grace,
The scented grass invades the steps setting off the herbaceous peonies.
The evil spring wind is jealous of the flowers like enchanting beauties,
Blows down all the young flowers on tips green.
Behind the heavy beautifully-decorated screens,
I have no mood to light eaglewood incense,
Oh, of getting drunk I'm very much afraid.

Just in the old capital at that time,
When I was young and unbridled,
I invited the beauty out attracted by her songs so intoxicating.
In the scented oil-painted cart, she was made up so charming,
We drove to and fro on the imperial streets fast,
And toured the gardens and parks hand in hand.
When the Lantern Festival ended, she lay in my arms in the dark,
I had never thought I now roam here and there with a heavy heart.

As a wanderer so solitary and lone,

I think of the merry affairs with woe.

The sweet scent of her clothes is weaker,

The strings of the instrument are broken.

Her face is as beautiful as before.

When can she in my heart at all

As a crane from a remote place return?

Day and night deep yearning for her

Except in drunkenness, the world of gloom,

Fills my heart and mind without any room.

## 菩 萨 蛮

### 三月晦,送春有集,座中偶书

春来春去催人老,老夫争肯输年少。醉后少年狂,白髭殊未妨。插花还起舞,管领风光处。把酒共留春,莫教花笑人。

## *Tune: Buddhist Dancers*

### At a Party in Late Spring

People grow old when spring comes and goes round and round,

Though old already, to young people I do not want to lose out.

Being drunk, I'm unrestrained like a youngster,

My moustaches are white, but it does not matter.

张元干

I pin pink flowers in my white hair and dance with cheer,
Enjoying enchanting spring sight and sound far and near.
Let's lift cups of good wine and invite it to stay some time more,
And don't let the flowers laugh at us for not valuing time at all.

# 吕渭老(生卒年不详)

他的词在南宋很有名。词风婉媚深窈。著有《圣求词》。

**Lü Weilao(years of birth and death unknown)**

His *Ci* poems were well-known in the Southern Song Dynasty. The style was graceful and profound. He wrote "*Ci* Poems Admired by Sages".

## 薄 幸

青楼春晚。昼寂寂、梳匀又懒。乍听得、鸦啼莺弄,惹起新愁无限。记年时、偷掷春心,花间隔雾遥相见。便角枕题诗,宝钗贳酒,共醉青苔深院。　　怎忘得、回廊下,携手处、花明月满。如今但暮雨,蜂愁蝶恨,小窗闲对芭蕉展。却谁拘管。尽无言、闲品秦筝,泪满参差雁。腰支渐小,心与杨花共远。

## *Tune: A Fickle Lover*

Spring late and I stay in the green boudoir alone.
Quiet and still, the days seem filled with sorrow,
Languidly I dress myself up.

吕渭老

Somewhere all of a sudden,

I hear the crows cawing and orioles crying,

My heart full of grief seems to be breaking.

I remember years ago in those sweet days,

I showed him stealthily my love like jade,

In the clusters of flowers through the mist, we looked at each other.

We inscribed poems on the horns decorated on the pillow fragrant,

I changed my hairpins of gold with wine so dear and fine,

In the yard wild with green moss, we drank too much wine.

How can I forget when the full moon

Shone over pretty flowers in bloom,

We walked with cheer,

Slowly far and near,

Now and then we sat on seats arm in arm,

In the long winding corridor in the dark.

Dusk comes and rain falls,

Bees and butterflies sob,

Before the leisure window, the Bajiao trees spread their leaves.

In the world and heaven, who cares me, a charming girl bleak?

Without a word, so sad,

I play the zither like mad.

My tears like a rain drop by drop fall on the pegs

Like a line of wild geese flying on homeward way.

In the present thinner and thinner my waist is,

Catkins, please, fly far with my heart to him.

❈❈❈❈❈❈❈❈❈❈❈❈❈❈❈❈❈

## 选 冠 子

雨湿花房,风斜燕子,池阁昼长春晚。檀盘战象,室局铺棋,筹画未分还懒。谁念少年,齿怯梅酸,病疏霞盏?正青钱遮路,绿丝明水,倦寻歌扇。　　空记得、小阁题名,红笺青制,灯火夜深裁剪。明眸似水,妙语如弦,不觉晓霜鸡唤。闻道近来,筝谱慵看,金铺长掩。瘦一枝梅影,回首江南路远。

## *Tune: Choosing a Hat*

The rain now and then wets the flowers in bloom around,
In the scented breeze swallows fly slanting up and down,
The waterside attic is quiet and long the days.
With my friend I play a Chinese chess game,
Watching the jade pieces on the board languid,
To move any of them, I have no at all interest.
I ask myself day and night: "Who thinks of me?"
Seeing green plum fruits I feel sour at the teeth,
I have been away for long from wine with a heavy heart.
The elm leaves like copper coins shade roads and paths,
The green weeping willow twigs like silk stroke the clear brook

吕渭老

water,

I'm tired of sweet songs of songstresses and charming grace of dancers.

I now and then think of that happy night,
In the attic under the bright candle light,
On a piece of rosy writing paper very fine and rare,
We wrote the poems and our names in the warm air.
Her eyes were like clear water of spring,
Her voice, moving sound of the strings,
In the frosty early morn, we heard cocks cry drear.
In the present time from one of her sisters I hear,
She is too weary and sad to turn a page of the music score,
Always she shuts herself deep in the finely-decorated door.
She is so thin like a twig of plum blossoms here with sorrow,
But she is far away in the south of the Yangtze River, I know.

# 朱翌(1097—1167)

朱翌这首词的另一题为《雪中看西湖梅花作》。其词风自然大雅,留有空白,让人想象,像一幅水彩画。

**Zhu Yi( 1097 – 1167)**

He gave another title of the *Ci* poem, "Appreciating the Plums by the West Lake". The style is simple and elegant, leaving blanks for people to imagine, like a water colour painting.

## 点 绛 唇

流水泠泠,断桥横路梅枝亚。雪花飞下,浑似江南画。　　白璧青钱,欲买春无价。归来也,风吹平野,一点香随马。

### *Tune: Roughed Lips*

The green water gurgles melodious,
The plum twigs from the path near
The broken bridge stretches out.
The snow falls on the ground,
What a beautiful painting of the southern land scenery!

朱　翌

You are unable at all to buy the enchanting spring early,
No matter how precious jade and how much money you have.
Now from the waterside scene of the West Lake I come back,
Over the open fields a spring breeze blows soft,
The faint plum fragrance follows my fast horse.

# 岳飞(1103—1142)

他是最著名的抗金将军。他屡次打败金兵,收复大批沦陷的国土,后被召回处死。其词《满江红》为千古咏唱。

**Yue Fei(1103 - 1142)**

He was the most well-known general fighting against the Jin invaders. He had defeated the invaders many times and recovered many of the lost areas. He was called back and put to death later. The *Ci* poem "The River All Red" has been sung through the ages.

## 小 重 山

昨夜寒蛩不住鸣。惊回千里梦,已三更。起来独自绕阶行。人悄悄,帘外月胧明。　白首为功名。旧山松竹老,阻归程。欲将心事付瑶琴。知音少,弦断有谁听?

## Tune: Hills by Hills

Last night the cold crickets chirped without end,
Waking me up from a dream a thousand *li* away.

岳　飞

At chilly midnight alone,
Round the steps I strolled.
In the courtyard it was still and quiet,
The bright moon hung lone in the sky.

Fighting fearlessly for the recovery of the land lost,
I see in a mirror I have my black hair turned to frost.
I want to return to my old bamboos and pines there to live in seclusion,
But all returning roads and paths have been stopped without exception.
I try to reveal my feelings through the zither in vain,
Now in our vast country invaded I have few intimates.
I know even if I pluck hard all the strings,
Who would listen to my music so exciting?

## 满 江 红

怒发冲冠,凭栏处、潇潇雨歇。抬望眼,仰天长啸,壮怀激烈。三十功名尘与土,八千里路云和月。莫等闲、白了少年头,空悲切！　　靖康耻,犹未雪。臣子恨,何时灭！驾长车,踏破贺兰山缺。壮志饥餐胡虏肉,笑谈渴饮匈奴血。待从头、收拾旧山河,朝天阙。

## Tune: The River All Red

My angry long hair pushes up my hat,

I lean on the railings agitated and sad,

Gradually stops the rain.

Lifting up high my head,

To the sky with clouds I sigh so loud,

My chest with ambition rolling about.

Day and night in eight thousand miles I fight enemies anywhere,

But I regard the fame in the thirty years as flying dust in the air.

Don't waste the precious time,

And let black hair turn white,

Or you'll be painful in vain.

The two emperors' disgrace

Has not been wiped out at all in my heart.

My hatred increasing day and night so far

Certainly has not at all disappeared.

I'm determined to drive a war chariot

To break the high Helan Mountains through.

Hungry, I'd take the invaders' flesh so brutal,

Thirsty, I'd drink the blood of the enemy so ferocious.

I cherish ambition to drive out of our country invaders.

When I recover all the mountains and rivers in our country lost,

I'll welcome with great respect two emperors in the capital before.

# 康与之(生卒年不详)

他的词自然朴素,像民歌。他擅长写少妇悲痛之离情以及妓女的情态。

**Kang Yuzhi(years of birth and death unknown)**

His *Ci* poems were natural and simple like folk songs. He was good at describing the misery of separation of young married women, and the soft feeling of prostitutes.

## 长 相 思

### 游 西 湖

南高峰,北高峰,一片湖光烟霭中。春来愁杀侬。 郎意浓,妾意浓。油壁车轻郎马骢,相逢九里松※。

## Tune: Yearning Forever

### Go Sightseeing around the West Lake

There stands the South Peak,
And nearby the North Peak,
A mist drifts over the pretty lake scenery.

The spring brings me unbearable sadness.

Deep was his affection,
Deep was my affection.
He rode a piebald steed and I was in an oil-painted cart light,
We had our sweet engagement in the lakeside Nine Mile Pines.※

※ 苏小小是南齐钱塘名妓,但红颜薄命,英年早逝。她常乘油壁车观赏西湖。一日,她遇骑青白马的英俊少年,一见钟情。她吟了一首诗,约他到西陵松柏下,相订终身:"妾乘油壁车,郎跨青骢马,何处结同心,西陵松柏下"。

※ Su Xiaoxiao was a famous prostitute in Hangzhou in the Southern Qi Dynasty. She died very young. One day, when she was appreciating the beautiful scenery of the West Lake in an oil-painted cart, she met a young man on a piebald. They fell in love at first sight. She led him to the pine wood to have an engagement, while singing a song of her own: "I take a cart oil-painted, /you ride a horse white and green. /Where shall we have our engagement delighted? /By the Xiling Bridge under the pine trees."

❈❈❈❈❈❈❈❈❈❈❈❈❈❈❈❈❈

康与之

## 满庭芳
### 寒 夜

霜幕风帘,闲斋小户,素蟾初上雕笼。玉杯醽醁,还与可人同。古鼎沉烟篆细,玉笋破、橙橘香浓。梳妆懒,脂轻粉薄,约略淡眉峰。　清新歌几许,低随慢唱,语笑相供。道文书针线,今夜休攻。莫厌兰膏更继,明朝又、纷冗匆匆。酩酊也,冠儿未卸,先把被儿烘。

## Tune: Courtyard Full of Fragrance
### Cold Night

Outside the curtain blows the wind and congeals frost,

But inside the scented little room is leisurely and warm,

Over the window lattice just rises the moon bright.

The white jade cups are filled with the good wine,

With cheer my sweetheart and I empty them again and again.

In the ancient burner burns eaglewood incense heart-shaped,

With her snow-white fingers,

She peals an orange fragrant.

She is too languid and lazy to make up beautifully,

Her charming face is powdered and rouged lightly,

And her brows are drawn pale green roughly with a brush.

How many new popular songs has she already lowly sung?

Slowly singing,

She says smiling:

"We should not sew and write tonight at least,

And don't forget to add oil to the lamp please,

You'll be very busy tomorrow,

Doing something of your own."

When she finds I get drunk, with a few sweet words

Without taking off my hat, she warms our quilt first.

# 韩元吉(1118—1187)

曾任吏部侍郎。他与范成大、陆游、辛弃疾等以词唱和。

**Han Yuanji(1118–1187)**

He served as a court official. He was a friend of Fan Chengda, Lu You and Xin Qiji. When one wrote a *Ci* poem, the others came up with another in reply.

## 六州歌头

### 桃　花

东风著意,先上小桃枝。红粉腻,娇如醉,倚朱扉※。记年时。隐映新妆面,临水岸,春将半,云日暖,斜桥转,夹城西。草软莎平,跋马垂杨渡,玉勒争嘶。认娥眉凝笑,脸薄拂燕脂。绣户曾窥,恨依依。　　共携手处,香如雾,红随步,怨春迟。消瘦损,凭谁问？只花知,泪空垂。旧日堂前燕,和烟雨,又双飞。人自老,春长好,梦佳期。前度刘郎,几许风流地,花也应悲。但茫茫暮霭,目断武陵溪,往事难追。

## June: Song of Six States

### The Peach Blossom

When the affectionate east breeze comes to

The little charming peach tree first in bloom.

So heavily powdered and rouged just,

It's like a beauty coquettish as drunk,

It leans on the door red.※

Still clearly I recollect

Last year setting off green willows with cheer

A fascinating newly made-up face appeared.

Near the bank, almost half

Of the spring has passed.

Under the warm sun and clouds,

Just in the west of the little town,

Across the slanting bridge,

On the grass soft and thick,

Riding a horse I saw her at the ferry shaded with willows weeping.

So many colorfully decorated horses with pleasure vied in neighing.

She made eyes at me with a smile winsome,

Her pink face was like a peach in blossom.

Several times I peeped at her in the fragrant boudoir,

My grief has never for a moment left my tender heart.

韩元吉

Now along the paths we strolled I walk alone,

My leisure steps only the falling flowers follow,

The scent from the peaches drifts in the air,

With regret at the late spring scenery I stare.

Why am I so thin and weak?

No one but the flowers see,

My tears with blood fall down drop by drop in vain.

The pair of swallows in the grand house in the days,

In the rain and mist up and down flies.

I grow old so quickly to my surprise,

Spring is pretty forever with enchanting flowers,

Day and night I dream of the intoxicating hours.

I come to the fairyland to look for the beauty from the earth,

But I lose my way there and I have to come back to the world.

※ 崔护进士落第,清明日,独游京城南郊。口渴叩门求饮。一少女开门,设坐,递以杯水。她独依小桃,注目良久,脉脉含情。次年清明,崔护再来寻少女。老者启门说,闺女已昏睡一年。他入门呼其名,女乃醒。两人结为夫妇。

※ Cui Hu failed in the highest imperial examination. On Clear and Bright, he walked in the southern suburb of the capital. Feeling thirsty, he knocked at a door and asked for water. A beautiful girl opened the door. She invited him to sit on a chair and gave him a cup of water. Leaning on a peach tree in blossom, she looked at him with a shy smile while he was drinking water. On the same day next year, he again knocked at the door, but an old man opened it and said his daughter has been sleeping lethargically for a year. He hurried in and loudly called her by name. She was awakened. Later they got married.

# 朱淑贞(生卒年不详)

朱淑贞在宋朝女词人中排名第二。她自小聪明,善写诗词。成人后,十分漂亮。她嫁与商人,常郁郁不乐。她的词充满幽怨悲愤。留世之作有《断肠词》。

**Zhu Shuzhen(years of birth and death unknown)**

She was the second best poetess in the Song Dynasty. She was very clever and good at writing poems in her childhood. When she grew up, she was beautiful. She married a businessman and often felt depressed. Her *Ci* poems were filled with pent-up feeling of grief and indignation. She left us a collection of *Ci* poems, "Heartbroken Poems".

## 谒 金 门

### 春 半

春已半,触目此情无限。十二阑干闲倚遍,愁来天不管。　好是风和日暖,输与莺莺燕燕。满院落花帘不卷,断肠芳草远。

## Tune: Pay Homage to the Golden Gate
### Half of Spring Gone

Half of the intoxicating spring is already away,
The pretty scenery causes sorrow without end.
I lean through the twelve balustrades one by one alone,
God does not at all care for me overladen with woe.

The breeze is enchanting and sunshine warm,
But I have no mood to appreciate them at all,
I give them to the orioles and swallows dancing in pairs in the air.
I cannot bear seeing the yard covered with fallen flowers anywhere,
Behind the quiet and solitary curtain on the lonely bed I lie,
I'm so sad missing him in scented grass beyond the horizon.

❄❄❄❄❄❄❄❄❄❄❄❄❄❄❄❄❄

## 眼 儿 媚

迟迟春日弄轻柔,花径暗香流。清明过了,不堪回首,云锁朱楼。午窗睡起莺声巧,何处唤春愁?绿杨影里,海棠亭畔,红杏梢头。

朱淑贞

## Tune: Charming Eyes

Spring day long, warm sunlight strokes willow twigs tender,
Over the path far and near drifts the pleasant faint fragrance.
Pure Brightness, the day of Tomb-worship away,
I cannot endure recollecting the miserable days,
The heavy clouds under the sky shroud my lonely red chamber.

Awake from a nap I hear the oriole outside the window twitter,
Where is the bird causing spring sorrow?
Is it in the shadows of the green willows,
By the pavilion of flowering crab-apples or,
On the twig tips of the blossoming apricots?

❉❉❉❉❉❉❉❉❉❉❉❉❉❉❉❉❉❉

## 菩 萨 蛮

山亭水榭秋方半,凤帷寂寞无人伴。愁闷一番新,双蛾只旧颦。
起来临绣户,时有疏萤度。多谢月相怜,今宵不忍圆。

## Tune: Buddhist Dancers

In late fall, the pavilions on hills by the water are attractive,

Behind the quiet curtain I feel lonely without any company.

My grief increases day and night,

My brows are knitted all the time.

Getting up, I lean on the window with sorrow,

The fireflies now and then at midnight glow.

The crescent in the sky feels sympathy for me,

She cannot bear to turn round tonight at least.

## 菩 萨 蛮

### 咏 梅

湿云不渡溪桥冷。娥寒初破东风影。溪下水声长。一枝和月香。人怜花似旧,花不知人瘦。独自倚阑干,夜深花正寒。

## Tune: Buddhist Dancers

### Ode to the Plum Blossom

The dark rainy clouds hang low,

The bridge by the bank lies cold.

Through the clouds floats out the crescent,

The plum tree sways its shadow with grace.

The stream flows to the distance giving forth very long sound,

In the moonlight a twig of the blossoms gives off scent around.

I'm glad to see again the plum in blossom, as before as beautiful,
But she does not know at all I am becoming thinner and thinner.
Alone I lean on the banisters with grief,
In the dead of night chilly the plum feels.

❈❈❈❈❈❈❈❈❈❈❈❈❈❈❈❈

## 清 平 乐

恼烟撩露,留我须臾住。携手藕花湖上路,一霎黄梅细雨。　　娇痴不怕人猜,和衣睡倒人怀。最是分携时候,归来懒傍妆台。

### Tune: Music for a Peaceful Time

We stroll on the dykes of West Lake with the lotuses blooming,
All of a sudden falls a drizzle of the season of the Plums Yellowing.
Oh, annoying mist drifts and irritating dew drops,
For a short time in a waterside pavilion we stop.

Unable to control my excitement,
I lie in his arms in pink garment.
I'm so painful and reluctant to him to say farewell,
Returning home, I lean lazily on the dressing table.

## 清 平 乐

风光紧急,三月俄三十。拟欲留连计无及,绿野烟愁露泣。　倩谁寄语春宵？城头画鼓轻敲。缱绻临歧嘱付,来年早到梅梢。

### Tune: Music for a Peaceful Time

It is the thirtieth of the third month, a pressing day,
Immediately the pretty spring scene will go away.
The charming spring from leaving I have no way to keep,
Over the green fields the mist sheds tears and dew weeps.

Who can be asked to give the spring at night a message?
The drum moans and groans low on the wall of the city,
With feeling it urges the spring next year
To come to the twigs of the plums earlier.

## 念 奴 娇

冬晴无雪,是天心未肯,化工非拙。不放玉花飞堕地,留在广寒宫阙。云欲同时,霰将集处,红日三竿揭。六花翦就,不知何处施设。　应念陇首寒梅,花开无伴,对景真愁绝。待出和羹金鼎手,为把玉盐飘撒。沟壑皆平,乾坤如画,更吐冰轮洁。梁园燕客,夜明不怕灯灭。

## Tune: Charm of a Maiden Singer

There is no snow in the whole winter,
It is because heaven has no intention,
Not for Mother Nature lacks the skills.
No snow falls on the ground even a bit,
It is kept in Cold Palace in the moon.
The clouds are gathering with gloom,
And ice crystals are about to mass,
The red sun rises three rods at last.
Snowflakes of six angles have been made,
But where in the world will they be spread?

The plum in bloom, heaven knows
Without company of white snow,
Her purity can't be shown to people.
I am expecting the god will at ease
Sprinkle jade-like snowflakes from the high sky to earth,
Filling gullies, making as pretty as a painting the world.
So pure and bright the jade-like moon will appear,
Shining on guests at hotels and feasts with cheer.
The night will be as a sunny day as bright,

And we will have no fear when lamps die.

✺✺✺✺✺✺✺✺✺✺✺✺✺✺✺✺✺

## 阿 那 曲

梦回酒醒春愁怯,宝鸭烟销香未歇。薄衾无奈五更寒,杜鹃叫落西楼月。

### Tune: A Pleasant Song

When I sober up from drunkenness, the spring fills me with anxiety and fear,
The smoke from the incense burner dissipates but the aroma doesn't disappear.
In a solitary thin quilt,
I feel at midnight chilly.
The cuckoo cries bleak till the moon bright
Over the west storied building out of sight.

# 李吕(1122—1198)

其词明艳妩媚,有晏几道的风采。

**Li Lü(1122–1198)**

His *Ci* poems were lovely and charming like Yan Jidao's.

## 鹧 鸪 天

### 寄 情

脸上残霞酒半消,晚妆匀罢却无聊。金泥帐小教谁共?银字笙寒懒更调。　人悄悄,漏迢迢。琐窗虚度可怜宵。一从恨满丁香结,几度春深豆蔻梢。

## *Tune: Partridge Sky*

### Sending Her Love to Him Far Away

She is awake from wine, on her face fading the flush,
At night she is so idle and bored still after making up.
Who shares with her gold powder-decorated bed curtain?
She is too languid to tune the reed pipe wind instrument.

She listens to the water watch dripping in the boudoir quiet,
Behind the little window she wastes another precious night.
Hatred fills the buds of the clove just like a girl of fourteen years old,
In some late springs the buds on cardamom tips are steeped in sorrow.

## 姚宽(1105—1162)

他擅长用不同形式的比喻表达意义与情感。

### Yao Kuan (1105 - 1162)

He was good at describing things and feelings with different forms of metaphors in his *Ci* poems.

## 生 查 子

### 情 景

郎如陌上尘,妾似堤边絮。相见两悠扬,踪迹无寻处。 酒面扑春风,泪眼零秋雨。过了别离时,还解相思否?

## Tune: Mountain Hawthorn

### Feelings and Settings

You seem to be the dust on the road,
I, the dikeside catkin of the willow.
We meet by chance in the air,
Oh, now we fly here and there.

A breeze blows the flush from wine on my snow-white face,
My eyes shed bloody tears without end like an autumn rain.
Today when we waves good-bye here,
Will you in future think of me drear?

## 洪迈(1123—1202)

其词有弦外之音。

**Hong Mai(1123–1202)**

His *Ci* poems had overtones.

### 踏 莎 行

院落深沉,池塘寂静。帘钩卷上梨花影。宝筝拈得雁难寻,篆香消尽山空冷。　钗凤斜攲,鬓蝉不整。残红立褪慵看镜。杜鹃啼月一声声,等闲又是三春尽。

### Tune: Treading on Grass

The yard is deep and lonely,
The pond is quiet and still.
Rolling up the curtains, she only sees the pear blossoms' shadows with pain,
With zither in her arms, she forgets to tune on the wild-geese-carved pegs,
The incense burns out and cold the hills on the screens.

Slanting lies the sparkling hairpin like a phoenix green,
At the temples the ornaments like black cicadas are not in good position,
The rouge on her face fading she doesn't want at all to see it in the mirror.
The cuckoo cries "Go home" again and again in the moonlight,
So easily the pretty and fragrant spring without a trace goes by.

# 陆游(1125—1210)

陆游多地当文官,也在边疆当过武官。他是著名的爱国诗人,也是当时第一词人。他有两首词天下有名。一首是《钗头凤》,描写他对前妻唐琬的苦苦思念。他娶唐琬后,夫妻恩爱。但母亲不喜欢她,将其赶走。两人另嫁再娶。一日两人邂逅沈园。唐琬派人送来酒菜,自己不陪。他十分伤感,在沈园墙上写下这首传世之作。另一首是咏梅的《卜算子》,有这两行:"零落成泥碾作尘,只有香如故。"

**Lu You(1125 - 1210)**

He served as a civil official in many places and a military official in the frontier. He was a famous patriotic poet and the best poet in his times. Two of his *Ci* poems were well-known to all. One was "Phoenix Hairpins", which described his painful missing of his former wife Tang Wan. They loved each other. His mother hated her driving her out. He got remarried and she married again. Later they met by chance in the Shen Garden. Tang Wan had someone sent food and wine without accompanying him. He was very sad, and wrote this masterpiece on the wall of Shen Garden. Another one was "Song of Divination", with the lines: "Fading, the beauty falls on the earth, ground to dust, /However, her intoxicating scent remains the same just."

## 卜 算 子

### 咏 梅

驿外断桥边,寂寞开无主。已是黄昏独自愁,更著风和雨。　　无意苦争春,一任群芳妒。零落成泥碾作尘,只有香如故。

### Tune: Song of Divination

#### Ode to the Plum Blossom

By the little post station near the broken bridge,
With no appreciator, a plum is blossoming lonely.
At the growing dusk she is filled with deep sorrow,
The rain and wind beat her in snow-white clothes.

Not wanting to vie with others in beauty in spring scene,
She stay with grace alone avoiding their jealous cheeks.
Fading, the beauty falls on the earth, ground to dust,
However, her intoxicating scent remains the same just.

陆　游

## 钗 头 凤

红酥手,黄滕酒。满城春色宫墙柳。东风恶,欢情薄。一怀愁绪,几年离索。错,错,错。　春如旧,人空瘦。泪痕红浥鲛绡透。桃花落,闲池阁。山盟虽在,锦书难托。莫,莫,莫!

## Tune: Phoenix Hairpins

With her rosy hands and forever love so deep,
She handed me a cup of wine with yellow silk sealed.
Spring filled the city and willows kissed the wall of an old palace.
However, the east wind brought the human world chill and evil,
Too short were our days pleasant.
Grief fills our hearts and breasts,
We are separated for several years long.
Wrong, wrong, wrong!

Spring remains unchanged,
But she is thinner in vain,
Her tears wet her handkerchief embroidered with flowers.
The peach blossoms like her face fall shower by shower,
By the pool so desolate the pavilions and kiosks are.
Never for a moment does our pledge leave our hearts,
But we can't exchange letters full of woe.

No, no, no!

## 秋波媚

### 七月十六晚登高兴亭望长安南山

秋到边城角声哀,烽火照高台。悲歌击筑,凭高酹酒,此兴悠哉!
多情谁似南山月,特地暮云开。灞桥烟柳,曲江池馆,应待人来。

### Tune: Enchanting Autumn Waves

#### At Night in the Happy Pavilion, I looked at South Mountain in Chang'an, the old capital.

When autumn comes to the frontier city the sound of the horn is drear,
The beacon-fire from the capital shines bright on the Happy Pavilion.
I can't help playing the zither,
On the height I pour a libation,
In my heart surges the determination of recovering the country.

With love so sweet the bright moon over the South Mountain
Pushes the curtains of grey clouds open.
By the Farewell Bridge the misty willows
And near the Qu River the kiosks and towers high
Must be waiting so eagerly for our army to arrive.

陆　游

## 鹊　桥　仙

一竿风月,一蓑烟雨,家在钓台西住。卖鱼生怕近城门,况肯到红尘深处？　　潮生理棹,潮平系缆,潮落浩歌归去。时人错把比严光,我自是无名渔父。

### Tune: Immortals on the Magpie Bridge

A fishing rod in the wind and moonlight,
A straw cap in a thick mist and rain fine,
I live in the west of fishing site of Yan Guang, a hermit.
To sell fish I am quite afraid to go to the gate of the city,
How would I go even
To city's busy streets?

When the tide flows I go out quick in a small boat fishing,
When the tide rises highest I tie it to a willow tree swaying,
When the tide ebbs, singing the fishing songs leisurely I go home.
I am regarded as a hermit by the water and mountains well-known,
But out-and-out I am
An unknown fisherman.

## 诉衷情

当年万里觅封侯,匹马戍梁州。关河梦断何处,尘暗旧貂裘。胡未灭,鬓先秋,泪空流。此生谁料,心在天山,身老沧洲。

### Tune: Baring the Heart

To seek fame and rank alone I rode a steed

Travelling in the frontier a ten thousand *li*.

Where does my dream of the rivers and mountains end?

The past dust covers my military coat of the fur of sable.

The invaders have not been driven out of our country,

Already my black hair at the temples becomes frosty,

In vain like a rain tears fall.

Oh, who would have thought,

I live at leisure by the Mirror Lake,

But in the frontier, my heart stays?

## 恋绣衾

不惜貂裘换钓篷,嗟时人、谁识放翁。归棹借、樵风稳,数声闻、

陆　游

林外暮钟。　　幽栖莫笑蜗庐小,有云山、烟水万重。半世向、丹青看,喜如今、身在画中。

## *Tune: Liking the Embroidered Quilt*

I get a fishing boat in exchange of a sable fur coat,
Of all people at the present time, I sigh and groan,
Oh, no one understands me.
In a returning boat at ease,
I hear with the wind through the trees so clear
The evening bell sounding several times drear
From the temple beyond the wood quiet.

Oh, don't laugh at my poor hut shell-like,
I own the mounts and clouds,
The mist and water all around.
In about half of my life I remember clearly,
I see in the paintings the beautiful scenery.
Now I am greatly glad
In real pretty scene I am.

# 唐琬(生卒年不详)

她嫁与表哥陆游后,夫妻唱和,如鱼得水。陆游母亲不喜欢这位有才华的媳妇,逼迫陆游休了她。两人各自又成婚。一天他们在沈园相逢。唐琬让人给陆游送来美酒佳肴,自己没来相陪。陆游题《钗头凤》于墙上,她回以此词。不久,她郁郁而死。

**Tang Wan ( years of birth and death unknown )**

She was married to Lu You, her cousin. The couple loved each other with great happiness, they enjoying writing poems togethcr. But his mother didn't like the talented daughter-in-law, forcing him to devoice her. They each remarried. One day they met in the Shen Garden. She had fine wine and delicious dishes sent to him at once without joining him. He wrote a *Ci* poem "Phoenix Hairpins" and put it on the wall. She wrote the *Ci* poem in reply. Not long after she died of sadness.

## 钗 头 凤

世情薄,人情恶,雨送黄昏花易落。晓风干,泪痕残。欲笺心事,独语斜阑。难,难,难! 人成各,今非昨,病魂常似秋千索。角声寒,夜阑珊。怕人寻问,咽泪装欢。瞒,瞒,瞒!

唐　琬

## June: Phoenix Hairpins

Worldly things are evil,
Human feelings are thin.
The rain sees off the withering flowers and the eve.
The wet fallen flowers and grass dry in morn breeze,
But my tear stains are clearly seen in the sad mirror.
Shall I pour out my woe on the rosy writing paper?
I lean alone on the rails murmuring something in my heart.
Hard, hard, hard!

Separated for several years, we are full of pain,
We cannot at all return to the past happy days,
My sick soul in the dreams is like a swing rope.
The sound of the horn from the city wall is cold,
When the lonely night ends,
Afraid of my grief being read,
I swallow my bloody tears pretending to be in spirits high.
Hide, hide, hide!

# 传陆游妾(生卒年不详)

陆游娶她后,二人恩爱。半年后被陆游母亲赶走。

**The *Ci* poem is said to be composed by Lu You's concubine (years of birth and death unknown).**

When he married her as a concubine, they loved each other. After half a year, she was driven out by his mother.

❀❀❀❀❀❀❀❀❀❀❀❀❀❀❀

## 生 查 子

只知眉上愁,不识愁来路。窗外有芭蕉,阵阵黄昏雨。 晓起理残妆,整顿教愁去。不合画春山,依旧留愁住。

### Tune: Mountain Hawthorn

On my brows I see sorrow,
Where I got it, I don't know.
Outside the window weeps a Bajiao banana tree,
Showers shed tears one after another in the eve.

I'm absorbed in dressing up in the morn,

Trying hard to get away the sorrow all.

I shouldn't have drawn my brows like spring hills,

Because sorrow almost at once goes back there still.

# 范成大(1126—1193)

南宋高宗绍兴二十四年(1154)进士。曾任参知政事等职。他是南宋最著名的词人之一,风格婉约,多写自己的闲适生活。他的《鹊桥仙》是吟咏牛郎织女的宋词中的三大名篇之一。其中有三行词很有名:"新欢不抵旧愁多,倒添了、新愁归去。"其它两首词是欧阳修和秦观所写。

**Fan Chengda(1126–1193)**

He passed the highest imperial examination in 1154. He once served as a senior official. He was one of the most well-known poets in the Southern Song Dynasty, belonging to the subtle and unrestrained school. He often described his leisure and comfortable life. His "Immortals on Magpie Bridge" was one of the three most well-known *Ci* poems in the Song Dynasty describing the stories about the Cowherd and the Girl Weaver. In the *Ci* poem the three lines are famous:"The new joy is much less than the old woe,/Finally with grief old and new,/Oh, there they make their adieu." The other two were written by Ouyang Xiu and Qin Guan.

范成大

## 蝶 恋 花

春涨一篙添水面。芳草鹅儿,绿满微风岸。画舫夷犹湾百转,横塘塔近依前远。　江国多寒农事晚。村北村南,谷雨才耕遍。秀麦连冈桑叶贱,看看尝面收新茧。

### June: Butterflies in Love with Flowers

In a breeze a rod high rises the spring water.
On the banks sway gently the grass fragrant,
With the green water the young yellow geese play.
Along the stream the painted boat winds its way,
The well-known high Tiger Hill Tower seems to be so near.

The region of rivers and lakes is cold and farming, late here.
In the south and north big waterside village,
Just before Grain Rain plowing is finished.
The heading wheat spreads to the distant hills and cheaper are mulberry leaves,
The peasants are ready to gather in the new silk worm cocoons and wheat.

## 鹊桥仙

### 七夕

双星良夜,耕慵织懒,应被群仙相妒。娟娟月姊满眉颦,更无奈、风姨吹雨。　　相逢草草,争如休见,重搅别离心绪。新欢不抵旧愁多,倒添了、新愁归去。

## Tune: Immortals on the Magpie Bridge

### The Seventh Evening of the Seventh Moon

The two stars in the fine night are eagerly expecting to have merry reunion

The Cowherd and the Girl Weaver stop plowing and weaving with cheer,

The fairy maidens are so jealous of their reunion so happy.

The goddess of the moon knits her brows like distant hills,

The goddess of wind quick goes away,

Leaving behind her the wind and rain.

For a very short time they will meet,

It is better not to meet and soon leave,

The meeting will also cause parting sorrow.

The new joy is much less than the old woe,

Finally with grief old and new,

Oh, there they make their adieu.

❈❈❈❈❈❈❈❈❈❈❈❈❈❈❈❈

## 霜天晓角

范成大

晚晴风歇,一夜春威折。脉脉花疏天淡,云来去、数枝雪。　　胜绝,愁亦绝。此情谁共说。惟有两行低雁,知人倚、画楼月。

### Tune: Morn Horn under the Frosty Sky

It is fine and a wind calms down in the eve,
The chill of all the night abates a great deal.
Under the pale sky the clouds at leisure fly,
And a few of the plums show the faces shy,
The twigs seem to be dotted with snow fragrant.

The scenery of early spring is the most beautiful,
Oh, so unbearable is my bitterness.
To whom can I confide my sadness?
Where is my pretty dear?
Over there only appear
Two lines of wild geese flying low,
They see clear my sweetheart alone
Under the moon leaning on the railings

Of the solitary painted storied building.

❀❀❀❀❀❀❀❀❀❀❀❀❀❀❀

## 鹧 鸪 天

嫩绿重重看得成,曲阑幽槛小红英。酴醾架上蜂儿闹,杨柳行间燕子轻。　　春婉娩,客飘零,残花残酒片时清。一杯且买明朝事,送了斜阳月又生。

### Tune: Partridge Sky

Here and there sway the green leaves tender and fresh,
In the winding quiet fence smile the little flowers red.
On the trellis of the rose leaf raspberries the bees run wild,
Through the willow twigs to and fro the swallows fly lithe.

The scenery of spring is so beautiful,
But as a guest here and there I wander.
Before the fading flowers I drink to forget for a moment woe of spring,
I go on drinking to see off the setting sun and moon until next morning.

# 杨万里(1127—1206)

南宋高宗绍兴二十四年(1154)进士。曾任秘书监。他是南宋有名的词人。词风清新、活泼、自然。本词中有两行词很有名:"未见秋光奇艳,看十五十六。"

**Yang Wanli( 1127 – 1206)**

He passed the highest imperial examination in 1154. He served as a senior official in the court. He was a very famous poet in the Southern Song Dynasty. The style of his *Ci* poems was fresh, lively and natural. In the following *Ci* poem the two lines are famous:"Oh, to appreciate the most beautiful autumn night scene,/We have to wait patiently till the fifteenth and sixteenth."

## 好 事 近

月未到诚斋,先到万花川谷。不是诚斋无月,隔一庭修竹。　如今才是十三夜,月色已如玉。未是秋光奇艳,看十五十六。

## June: Happiness Approaching

The moonlight has not reached my study,

It has come first to my garden so pretty.
Tonight my study has got no light of the moon,
For a bamboo wood before it leaves it in gloom.

It is the thirteenth night,
And the moon, jade-like.
Oh, to appreciate the most beautiful autumn night scene,
We have to wait patiently till the fifteenth and sixteenth.

# 严蕊(生卒年不详)

严蕊为军营妓女。善歌舞,色艺冠一时。间作诗词。朱熹以有伤风化为其罪名,将其入狱,加以鞭打,不予水饭,要她坦白。她宁死不屈。朱熹调离,岳霖继任。岳霖同情她,让其写词辩白,遂成《卜算子》。

**Yan Rui(years of birth and death unknown)**

She was a prostitute in a military camp. She was the prettiest girl in the time and good at singing and dancing. Sometimes she composed poems. An official going on a circuit accused her the crime of sleeping with an official and put her into prison and whipped her, giving her neither food nor water, and asking her to confess her crime. She didn't yield. A new official came and showed sympathy to her, asking her to prove her innocence by a *Ci* poem. The following is her *Ci* poem.

## 卜 算 子

不是爱风尘,似被前缘误。花落花开自有时,总赖东君主。　去也终须去,住也如何住!若得山花插满头,莫问奴归处。

### Tune: Song of Divination

I don't like being a licensed prostitute anyway,
It is my poor lot driving me on this hard way.
At a fixed time flowers opening and falling
Are certainly decided by the god of spring.

After all, this place I have to leave,
And this life I can no longer keep.
If I wear wild flowers at the temples,
Please don't ask me where I'll stay.

❈❈❈❈❈❈❈❈❈❈❈❈❈❈❈❈❈

## 如 梦 令

道是梨花不是。道是杏花不是。白白与红红,别是东风情味。曾记。曾记。人在武陵微醉。

### Tune: Like a Dream

Pear blossoms, they look like,
But they are not.
Apricot blossoms, they look like,

But they are not.

The trees boast of two colored blossoms, the white and red ones,

From their sweet hearts east breeze blows out special pure love.

Oh, I remember,

Oh, I remember,

Once in fairyland I loved the trees

Along the Peach Blossom Stream.

# 张孝祥(1132—1170)

南宋高宗绍兴二十四年(1154)进士。做过高官。他是南宋著名的爱国词人,支持北伐计划。他词风豪放,是辛弃疾的先行者。他的《念奴娇》是有历史意义的名篇。

**Zhang Xiaoxiang(1132–1170)**

He passed the highest imperial examination in 1154. He served as a senior official. He was a patriotic poet supporting the plans to recover the lost land. The style of his *Ci* poems was bold and unrestrained and he was the pioneer of the school of Xin Qiji. His "Charm of a Maiden Singer" was a famous historic *Ci* poem.

## 念 奴 娇

### 过 洞 庭

洞庭青草,近中秋、更无一点风色。玉鉴琼田三万顷,著我扁舟一叶。素月分辉,银河共影,表里俱澄澈。怡然心会,妙处难与君说。　　应念岭表经年,孤光自照,肝胆皆冰雪。短发萧骚襟袖冷,稳泛沧溟空阔。尽挹西江,细斟北斗,万象为宾客。扣舷独啸,不知今夕何夕。

张孝祥

## *Tune: Charm of a Maiden Singer*
### Crossing the Dongting Lake

The Dongting Lake joins the Grass Lake here,
The Mid-autumn Festival is drawing very near,
Over the pretty and charming lake blows a gentle breeze.
The vast water is as a mirror and jade as bright and even,
My little boat like a leaf drifts on the sparkling water slow.
Into the waves the light of the moon and the Galaxy flows.
The world is clear and transparent.
I feel myself melting into the water,
At the wonderful scene, who looks?

In the moonlight so sweet and cool,
Oh, I think of being a high official in the past,
Like ice and snow, pure and cold was my heart.
My sleeves are simple and clean though sparse my hair
Leaving my boat go at ease, I'm at leisure without care.
I want to take the Big Dipper as a cup, drinking
All the water in the Yangtze endlessly flowing.
With everything on earth and in heaven as a guest happy,
Knocking on the board now and then with great interest,
Looking at the bright sky I whistle high,
Forgetting fame and rank and even time.

# 辛弃疾(1140—1207)

他是南宋著名的爱国词人。二十一岁参加抗金义军。他日后在《永遇乐》中回忆道:"四十三年,望中犹记,烽火扬州路。"历任湖北、江西、湖南、福建、浙东安抚使等职。被免职后,闲居几达二十年。到了晚年,又得以任用,但不久又被免职。终于抑郁而终。其词风慷慨悲壮、沉郁悲凉。在宋代诗词界,他与苏轼齐名,被认为是豪放派的代表。

**Xin Qiji(1140－1207)**

He was a very famous patriotic poet in the Southern Song Dynasty. He took part in the fights against the Jin invaders when he was only twenty-one years old, as he wrote in "Joy of Eternal Union": "Forty-three years slips. /With heartbreaking sadness I again and again look back, /I fought the enemy in Yangtzou day and night like mad." Then he served as a local official. He was dismissed from office and lived idle for nearly twenty years. Later he was reinstated, but before long, he was dismissed. Finally he died of dejection. The style of his *Ci* poems was fervent and solemn, depressed and bleak. He enjoyed equal renown with Su Shi in the *Ci* poems in the Song Dynasty. He was also regarded as the representative of bold and unconstrained.

辛弃疾

## 清 平 乐

### 博山道中即事

柳边飞鞚,露湿征衣重。宿鹭窥沙孤影动,应有鱼虾入梦。一川明月疏星,浣纱人影娉婷。笑背行人归去,门前稚子啼声。

### Tune: Music for a Peaceful Time

#### The Night View on the Way to the Bo Mountain

I rode a horse quickly passing the green willows,
Wet with the glistening dewdrops are my clothes.
An egret squints at the sands, its shadow shaking,
It must be in a dream seeing a fish near swimming.

The bright moon and the sparse stars are reflected in the water,
A beauty washes the yarn by the water, her reflection graceful.
At the door a baby cries all of a sudden,
Hearing the cries, she gets up at once.
Seeing a stranger on the way, with a smile so shy,
The beauty turns back home with little steps lithe.

## 青 玉 案

### 元 夕

东风夜放花千树。更吹落,星如雨。宝马雕车香满路。凤箫声动,玉壶光转,一夜鱼龙舞。　蛾儿雪柳黄金缕,笑语盈盈暗香去。众里寻他千百度,蓦然回首,那人却在,灯火阑珊处。

### *Tune: Green Jade Cup*

#### On the Night of the Lantern Festival

The east wind blows open the colored lanterns like flowers,

And put down the meteor-like fireworks shower by shower.

The young lads ride the decorated horses fast,

And the charming girls sit in the carved carts,

They send forth the fragrance over the streets and roads.

The music from the bamboo flutes floats high and low,

The full moon gazes at the bustling earth with delight,

The fish and dragon lanterns dance like crazy all night.

The girls wear moths and willow twigs with gold threads on the hair,

They talk and laugh loudly, their delicate scent dispersing in the air.

A thousand times I seek my love,

Turning my head all of a sudden,

Oh, there, I see my pretty lover

Under the dim light of the lanterns.

辛弃疾

## 丑奴儿

### 书博山道中壁

少年不识愁滋味,爱上层楼。爱上层楼,为赋新词强说愁。而今识尽愁滋味,欲说还休。欲说还休,却道天凉好个秋。

### Tune: An Ugly Girl

I wrote the *Ci* poem on the wall on the way to the Bo Mountain.

When I was young I didn't know what was sorrow,

I liked ascending storied buildings.

I liked ascending storied buildings,

For I wanted to compose the poems about sorrow.

Now I know what is real sorrow thoroughly,

When I'm about to pour out my sorrow I stop.

When I'm about to pour out my sorrow I stop,

I just say what a cool and pleasant fall it is.

## 定 风 波

### 暮 春 漫 兴

少日春怀似酒浓,插花走马醉千钟。老去逢春如病酒,唯有,茶瓯香篆小帘栊。　　卷尽残花风未定,休恨,花开元自要春风。试问春归谁得见? 飞燕,来时相遇夕阳中。

### *Tune: Calming Disturbance*

I wrote the *Ci* poem at will in late spring.

When I was young, my feelings of spring were as strong as good wine,
Flowers on my hair, I rode a steed drinking a hundred cups of wine fine.
Old I seem drunk when spring comes,
I find with chill I have nothing but
The tea kettle, the round incense, and so small the curtains.

The vernal wind kicks down all flowers without exception,
Oh, don't hate it though it is cruel,
Without it flowers will not bloom.
Who sees where spring go?
Only the flying swallows.
Dear swallows, when you are on your homeward way,

Under the fading pink sunlight, you will meet it again.

❋❋❋❋❋❋❋❋❋❋❋❋❋❋❋❋❋

## 鹧 鸪 天

### 代 人 赋

陌上柔桑破嫩芽,东邻蚕种已生些。平冈细草鸣黄犊,斜日寒林点暮鸦。　　山远近,路横斜,青旗沽酒有人家。城中桃李愁风雨,春在溪头荠菜花。

### *June: Partridge Sky*

I wrote the *Ci* poem for other.

By the paths the breeze breaks mulberry buds,
I see with interest in my east neighbors' huts,
From their tender cocoons some young worms crawl out.
On the ridges of hills wild with grass the calves moo loud,
In setting sunlight in the cold wood dots of crows are seen clear.

The green mountains stand at leisure high and low, far and near,
The paths wind their ways to the roads and streams,
The green streamer of a wine shop waves in a breeze.
In the city the peaches and plum blossoms worry about the wind and rain,

Spring is on the shepherd's purse flowers by the creek and pathways.

❀❀❀❀❀❀❀❀❀❀❀❀❀❀❀

# 祝英台近

## 晚　春

宝钗分,桃叶渡,烟柳暗南浦。怕上层楼,十日九风雨。断肠片片飞红,都无人管,更谁劝啼莺声住?　　鬓边觑,试把花卜归期,才簪又重数。罗帐灯昏,哽咽梦中语:是他春带愁来,春归何处?却不解带将愁去。

## Tune: Slow Song of Zhu Yingtai

### Late Spring

Oh, either with half of the golden hairpin,
We said good-bye at Peach Leaves Ferry,
The mist with my grief enveloped the willows weeping.
In the present I'm afraid of ascending storied buildings,
I meet cold rain and hard wind nine out of ten times in the air.
The heartbreaking pink petals like beauties fly here and there,
I can't bear the sight sad.
Who can with misery ask
The orioles to stop singing the melancholy songs?

Looking slantingly at the flowers on my hair long,

Oh, I take them down counting the petals to divine his returning date,

Wearing them on the hair, I take them down and count the petals again.

Behind the dimly lit silk curtain,

In the dream I sob to my lover:

"Spring brings here sorrow,

But now where does it go?

I don't know why spring leaves

In a hurry, giving sorrow to me."

## 汉宫春

### 立春日

春已归来,看美人头上,袅袅春幡。无端风雨,未肯收尽余寒。年时燕子,料今宵、梦到西园。浑未办、黄柑荐酒,更传青韭堆盘？　　却笑东风从此,便薰梅染柳,更没些闲。闲时又来镜里,转变朱颜。清愁不断,问何人、会解连环？生怕见、花开花落,朝来塞雁先还。

## Tune: Spring in the Han Palace

### The Beginning of Spring

With slow steps the pretty spring again comes,

On beauties' heads are the swallows silk cut.
The cruel wind and rain are unwilling
To take away the chilly air remaining.
Swallows leaving sad last year
Are dreaming of coming here
Back to west flower-covered garden.
I haven't prepared with a heavy heart
The mandarin orange wine at meals,
Spring cakes with vegetables green.

I laugh at the east wind,
From now on being busy
Yellowing plums and greening willows by paths and water.
At its leisure it comes to the scented heart-shaped mirrors,
Making the pink faces fade.
My grief seems not to end,
I ask with extremely sorrow:
"Who can disperse my woe?"
I'm so greatly afraid to look
At the flowers fall and bloom.
In the morn the wild geese fly back north,
And closely follow them, my sad thoughts.

辛弃疾

# 水 龙 吟

## 登建康赏心亭

楚天千里清秋,水随天去秋无际。遥岑远目,献愁供恨,玉簪螺髻。落日楼头,断鸿声里,江南游子。把吴钩看了,栏杆拍遍,无人会、登临意。　休说鲈鱼堪脍,尽西风、季鹰归未？求田问舍,怕应羞见,刘郎才气。可惜流年,忧愁风雨,树犹如此！倩何人唤取,红巾翠袖,揾英雄泪！

## *Tune: Chanting of Water Dragon*

### Climbing up Eye-Pleasing Pavilion in Jiankang (Nanjing)

The clear fall is displayed in the southern land of a thousand miles,
The green Yangtze River flows east day and night with the blue sky.
Straining my eyes I look far at the miserable mountains
Like a beauty's screw hair buns and emerald hair pins.
With the increasing indignation and hatred,
Under the fading sun in the building storied,
In the melancholy cries of a lonely swan goose losing its way,
A traveller in the south of the Yangtze I miss my native place,
For a long time I gaze at the sharp sword,
And with it I beat through the railings all.
Why do I ascend the building high?

I am sure no one at all can realize.

Now colder and colder the north west wind blows,
In my hometown cooked perches are well-known,
I won't return home in mounts and fields without care,
Nor will I buy any house and piece of land over there,
For I'd be ashamed if I can't become a hero to recover the lost land.
Just like water precious time flows away and will never come back.
The land of our country beautiful and vast
Is in the wind and rain so cruel and hard.
Whom can I ask with unbearable grief
To call a beauty in a singing hall green,
With pink kerchiefs and green sleeves here,
To sweep away tenderly a hero's warm tears?

## 念 奴 娇

### 书东流村壁

野棠花落,又匆匆过了,清明时节。划地东风欺客梦,一枕云屏寒怯。曲岸持觞,垂杨系马,此地曾经别。楼空人去,旧游飞燕能说。　　闻道绮陌东头,行人长见,帘底纤纤月。旧恨春江流不断,新恨云山千叠。料得明朝,尊前重见,镜里花难折。也应惊问:近来多少华发?

辛弃疾

## Tune: Charm of a Maiden Singer

I wrote the *Ci* poem on a wall at a village.

Wild birch pear blossoms fall,
Day of Tomb-worship is gone
With people's sorrowful mourning tears in haste.
The breeze blows me from a spring dream awake,
The chill invades me on a lonely pillow bloody tears falling,
By the winding stream the horse was tied to a willow weeping,
And we drank with heartbreaking sadness farewell wine.
Ever since I can't bear looking back on the parting sight.
Now the scented chamber is quiet and solitary,
Only the swallows remember our love romantic.

In the east brothel street, I hear
Behind the curtain she appears
With intoxicating brows like in the sky graceful jade-like crescent.
The spring stream flows eastward with my old grief without end,
And into clouds and mounts floats new sorrow.
Even if at a feast we meet each other tomorrow,
How can I pick with pleasure
The pretty flower in a mirror?
She'd be so shocked to say, looking at me:
"How much has your white hair increased?"

## 贺 新 郎

### 赋 琵 琶

凤尾龙香拨,自开元霓裳曲罢,几番风月?最苦浔阳江头客,画舸亭亭待发。记出塞、黄云堆雪。马上离愁三万里,望昭阳宫殿孤鸿没※,弦解语,恨难说。　　辽阳驿使音尘绝,琐窗寒,轻拢慢撚,泪珠盈睫。推手含情还却手,一抹《梁州》哀彻。千古事,云飞烟灭。贺老定场无消息,想沉香亭北繁华歇。弹到此,为呜咽。

## Tune: Congratulations to the Bridegroom

### Pipa

On the sandalwood lute with a couple of phoenixes on its tail,
The tune "Rainbow Clothes", an imperial concubine Yang played,
How many times has the full moon hung in the sky since the Tang Dynasty?
The banished poet felt heartbreakingly sorrowful listening to a lady lutenist
Playing the lute with bloody tears who shared the same experiences in life.
Again a beautiful princess Wang on her long way of thirty thousand miles
To marry a chieftain.

辛弃疾

With unbearable grief,
Getting through the high Yang Pass,
Under snow-gathering clouds dark,
She turned and saw a swan goose disappearing over the palace alone.※
The strings with love in her heart were able to convey deep sorrow
Which in words could hardly be clearly expressed.

A young beauty behind the cold window at present,
Misses her dear in the frontier and from him she has long lost information.
She begins to pluck the pipa lightly and slowly with her pink slender fingers,
Tears falling drop by drop from the lashes glistening.
The fragrant pipa is filled with deep tender feelings.
When she plays a sad frontier tune, she cannot bear.
Historic events in our country any time anywhere
In the drifting grey clouds and thick mists disappear.
The lutenist in the Tang palace never again appears,
The scene of the emperor and concubine Yang appreciating peonies is gone.
When she plays to this romantic sweet affair she with woe breaks into sobs.

※ 王昭君是四大美人之一。她是汉元帝时一宫女。汉元帝宫中"美人三千",无暇亲自挑选侍寝美人,因而从画师呈上的肖像中

挑选宫中美女。宫中女子都纷纷行贿画师,但昭君就是不送钱财。结果,送礼物的皆被美化,她被丑化。她与皇上咫尺千里。后被指派以公主身份远嫁匈奴酋长。在漫漫旅途中,她用琵琶弹奏悲伤的曲子《桃叶》。到了北方,因不习惯那儿的生活,她日日夜夜思念家乡。忧忧郁郁,英年早逝,38岁即魂归故土。

※ Wang Zhaojun, was one of the four most beautiful ladies in ancient China. She was a maid in the imperial palace in the Han Dynasty. The emperor chose a beauty for a night from the portraits by a painter. All the beauties, except Zhaojun bribed him. The painter beautified those who gave him bribes and he drew her portrait much uglier than she was. She had no chance to see the emperor. She was ordered to be married to a chief of a tribe as a princess. On the long journey, she played the sad tune on pipa, "Peach Leaves". In the north, she was not accustomed to the life there, thinking of her parents day and night. She felt melancholy and died in the prime of life. At thirty eight, her soul returned to her hometown.

※※※※※※※※※※※※※※※※※

## 贺 新 郎

### 别茂嘉十二弟

绿树听鹈鴂,更那堪、鹧鸪声住,杜鹃声切。啼到春归无寻处,苦

辛弃疾

恨芳菲都歇。算未抵、人间离别。马上琵琶关塞黑,更长门翠辇辞金阙。看燕燕,送归妾。　将军百战身名裂。向河梁、回头万里,故人长绝。易水萧萧西风冷,满座衣冠似雪。正壮士、悲歌未彻。啼鸟还知如许恨,料不啼清泪长啼血。谁共我,醉明月?

## Tune: Congratulations to the Bridegroom
### Saying Farewell to My Twelfth Cousin

Hearing in the green trees the pelicans cry,
How can I bear the sad songs' fall and rise,
In a melancholy and lonely mood,
From the partridges and cuckoos?
They ruthlessly cry until spring is gone and nowhere to be found,
They deeply regret that the enchanting flowers fall on the ground.
But much less they are suffering
Than the humans who are parting.
On a horse playing pipa, the princess entered the frontier to marry a chieftain sadly.
In a carriage the disfavored queen left the court for the Long Gate Palace lonely.
The new king was killed in the court,
His mother went to hometown sore.

General Li fought a hundred battles but finally to the enemy he surrendered.

On the small stone bridge he saw his friend off going back to the capital.

He looked into his hometown a ten thousand *li* away,

He bade farewell to his friend and there he had to stay.

Beside the Black River the cold west wind sobbed and groaned,

The prince and friends in white seeing the knight off with woe

Who was going to kill Qin's king and the man

So loudly and excitedly the heroic songs sang.

If the birds knew the painful partings above,

What they shed would not be tears but blood.

Oh, from now on who would accompany me here

Under the bright pretty moon to get drunk drear?

❈❈❈❈❈❈❈❈❈❈❈❈❈❈❈❈❈

## 木兰花慢

### 滁州送范倅

老来情味减,对别酒,怯流年。况屈指中秋,十分好月,不照人圆。无情水都不管,共西风、只管送归船。秋晚莼鲈江上,夜深儿女灯前。　　征衫,便好去朝天,玉殿正思贤。想夜半承明,留教视草,却遣筹边。长安故人问我,道愁肠殢酒只依然。目断秋霄落雁,醉来时响空弦。

辛弃疾

## Tune: Slow Song of Magnolia Flowers
### Seeing My Assistant off in Chuzhou

Old, my interests greatly decline.

Facing the farewell cup of wine,

I'm afraid of precious time away flowing.

The Mid-autumn Festival is approaching,

But in the vast sky the bright sweet full moon

Won't shine on us gathering in a happy mood.

The flowing water so ruthless

Doesn't care about our agony,

Together with the wind west

Sending your little boat away.

I think you'll enjoy the perches and water shields in the fall rivers,

And before lamps into late night you'll talk with family members.

Then still wearing the clothes on the long and hard journey unchanged,

You'll present yourself before the emperor wanting men wise and able.

You will be asked

To examine drafts

And help him to plan

To recover lost land.

If my friends in the capital ask about me,

Oh, tell them I drown with wine my grief.

Drunk, I draw the bowstring shooting at a wide goose without arrow,
And see the frightened bird from the high sky falling down very slow.

❀❀❀❀❀❀❀❀❀❀❀❀❀❀

## 永 遇 乐

### 京口北固亭怀古

千古江山,英雄无觅,孙仲谋处。舞榭歌台,风流总被,雨打风吹去。斜阳草树,寻常巷陌,人道寄奴曾住。想当年,金戈铁马,气吞万里如虎。　　元嘉草草,封狼居胥,赢得仓皇北顾。四十三年,望中犹记,烽火扬州路。可堪回首,佛狸祠下,一片神鸦社鼓。凭谁问:廉颇老矣,尚能饭否?

## Tune: Joy of Eternal Union

### Thinking of the Past in the Northern Pavilion in Jingkou (Zhenjiang)

The mountains and rivers remain the same,
But it is very hard to find the heroes great
Like Sun, Wu's king, in the land southern.
His well-known outstanding achievements
Together with the halls for song and dance
Vanish in winds and rains leaving no mark.
A native pointing at the trees under fading sunray

辛弃疾

Tells me in the narrow winding grass-dotted lane,
Once had lived in childhood so famous a king Liu.
With a spirit of recovering lost land he was imbued,
He won so many battles in those years,
With armored horses and flashing spears.

Without preparation, his son tried to recover the land lost,
And cut his great deeds in the high mountains in the north,
He fled away in a hurry.
Forty-three years slips.
With heartbreaking sadness I again and again look back,
I fought the enemy in Yangzhou day and night like mad.
Now in the lost land resounds with drums in glee.
Oh, who would ask me filled with unbearable grief:
"Oh, so old and weak you are at the present,
To recover the lost land, do you have strength?"

❋❋❋❋❋❋❋❋❋❋❋❋❋❋❋❋❋

## 贺 新 郎

### 同父见和再用韵答之

老大那堪说。似而今、元龙臭味,孟公瓜葛。我病君来高歌饮,惊散楼头飞雪。笑富贵千钧如发。硬语盘空谁来听? 记当时、只有西窗月。重进酒,换鸣瑟。　　事无两样人心别。问渠侬:

神州毕竟,几番离合？汗血盐车无人顾,千里空收骏骨。正目断关河路绝。我最怜君中宵舞,道"男儿到死心如铁"。看试手,补天裂。

### Tune: Congratulations to the Bridegroom

I stayed idle at home. A friend came to see me. We discussed the strategies to fight the invaders and recover the lost land. We wrote *Ci* poems in reply to each other. The *Ci* poem is one of mine.

Old, without achievement outstanding,

Really I have nothing worth mentioning.

We have aspiration nowadays

Just as in the past those days.

When I was sick, you came to me and sang loudly,

Frightening away the snow on the building storied.

We regard high position and great wealth as feather,

But now who would listen to our words so sonorous?

At that time no one comforted us full of sorrow,

But for the moonlight through the west window.

Oh, let's empty some more wine cups,

Changing low-key music into high one.

On the national affairs people have different opinions,

I want to ask those without courage at all with tears:

"Do you know since the Qin Dynasty how many times
Has heaven seen our big sacred country unite and divide?"
Now steeds are used to pull too heavy salt-loaded carts,
It's no use at all to buy their bones from the places far.
On the roads my sight is lost
With snow to invaded north.
I appreciated you when you danced at midnight best,
Singing excitedly:"Men's will is like iron until death."
We'll do all we can with our hands
To repair the holes in the sky vast.

❀❀❀❀❀❀❀❀❀❀❀❀❀❀❀❀

## 满 江 红

敲碎离愁,纱窗外、风摇翠竹。人去后、吹箫声断,倚楼人独。满眼不堪三月暮,举头已觉千山绿。但试把一纸寄来书,从头读。　　相思字,空盈幅;相思意,何时足?滴罗襟点点,泪珠盈掬。芳草不迷行客路,垂杨只碍离人目。最苦是、立尽月黄昏,阑干曲。

### June: The River All Red

Outside the window screens,
Wind shakes bamboos green,

Breaking my deep grief of separation.
Since we said farewells to each other,
I have no interest at all to play the vertical bamboo flute,
The whole day I lean on the railings in a miserable mood.
I can't bear in the late spring seeing flowers flying here and there,
I find drear the mountains are dyed green like his robe everywhere.
I read the letter of him far away,
Word by word, again and again.

Several pink pages are filled
With words of lovesickness.
But his feelings of love
Seem not to be enough.
Tears wet my clothes
And my hands also.
He will not lose the way back covered with the skirt-like grass,
But the willow twigs will stop me from seeing him returning far.
Oh, for me it is really the most suffering time
Leaning on the railings watching the moon rise.

## 满 江 红

### 暮 春

家住江南,又过了、清明寒食。花径里、一番风雨,一番狼藉。红粉暗随流水去,园林渐觉清阴密。算年年、落尽刺桐花,寒无力。　　庭院静,空相忆。无说处,闲愁极。怕流莺乳燕,得知消息。尺素始今何处也,彩云依旧无踪迹。漫教人、羞去上层楼,平芜碧。

## June: The River All Red

### Late Spring

Now I live in the south of the Yangtze River.
Gone Cold Food Day and Qingming Festival,
The intoxicating spring is already away.
Destroyed by the ruthless wind and rain,
The fallen flowers like beauties on the paths
With charming scented skirts lie near and far.
Some pink petals leave with water unnoticed,
The shade of the green trees thickens bit by bit.
Spring after spring, year after year,
When flowers fall from paulownias,
The cold declines.

The yard quiet,
In vain day and night bitterly I yearn for her.
To whom can I confide my heartfelt words?
I am tortured hard with heartbreaking sorrow.
I hate singing orioles and dancing swallows
To know in the heart and mind my deep grief.

When will my beauty send a love letter to me?

Where is she with dark hair?

How can I with sadness bear

To climb up step by step the storied building

to see the grass with our love dew stretching.

❋❋❋❋❋❋❋❋❋❋❋❋❋❋❋❋

## 满 江 红

### 饯郑衡州厚卿席上再赋

莫折荼蘼,且留取一分春色。还记得,青梅如豆,共伊同摘。少日对花浑醉梦,而今醒眼看风月。恨牡丹笑我倚东风,头如雪。　榆荚阵,菖蒲叶。时节换,繁华歇。算怎禁风雨,怎禁鹈鴂!老冉冉兮花共柳,是栖栖者蜂和蝶。也不因春去有闲愁,因离别。

### Tune: The River All Red

I gave a farewell banquet to my friend who was going to take the post of prefect. I presented him a *Ci* poem. I had something more to say, so I wrote the second one, the following one.

Don't pluck rose leaf raspberries

Just in order to keep a little bit

辛弃疾

Of spring beauty here.

I still remember clear

We picked green fruits of plums

Cheerfully like soya beans just.

When young as if drunk or in a dream I looked at flowers,

Now I watch the spring scene carefully in wakeful hours.

I hate peonies to laugh at me

Standing in a warm wind east,

With sparse hair snow-white.

Elm pods fall dancing tired,

Oh, calami grow leaves again.

The charming season is away,

The luxuriant scene vanishes leaving no mark.

The cruel wind and rain nearly break my heart,

I can hardly bear hearing cuckoos cry:"Go home."

With me flowers and weeping willows grow old,

But bees and butterflies are busy as before.

However, I know my leisure sorrow is not

Caused by leaving of spring

But our heartbreaking parting.

# 破 阵 子

## 为陈同甫赋壮词以寄

醉里挑灯看剑,梦回吹角连营。八百里分麾下炙,五十弦翻塞外声,沙场秋点兵。 马作的卢飞快,弓如霹雳弦惊。了却君王天下事,赢得生前身后名。可怜白发生!

## Tune: Dance of the Cavalry

I posted the *Ci* poem with great aspiration to my friend.

Drunk, poking the oil light bright, I watch the sword in my hand,
Sobering up, I listen to the horns sounding in all military camps.
The roast beef is distributed among the soldiers,
The music instruments play martial compositions,
In fall the soldiers form into lines going to battle fields.

So fast as flying in the air with dust rising run our steeds,
The bows shoot arrows at enemies with thundering sounds.
I am determined to drive all invaders of our country out,
And win the reputation before and after my death.
It's a pity white hairs begin to grow on my head.

❋❋❋❋❋❋❋❋❋❋❋❋❋❋❋

辛弃疾

# 南 乡 子

### 登京口北固亭有怀

何处望神州？满眼风光北固楼。千古兴亡多少事？悠悠,不尽长江滚滚流！　年少万兜鍪,坐断东南战未休。天下英雄谁敌手？曹刘。生子当如孙仲谋！

## Tune: Song of Southern Countryside

### Ascending the Northern Tower in Jingkou（Zhenjiang）

Oh, where is the invaded vast central plain I long to see all the time?
Ascending Northern Tower in Jingkou anywhere I see pretty sights
So many dynasties have been away,
One after another through the ages,
Only the Yangtze before our eyes still flows day and night eastward.

Sun Quan, still young in those years, with ten thousands of soldiers
Occupied the south of the Yangtze River fighting endlessly.
Of all the great heroes in our country, who can match him?
Oh, only Cao Cao and Liu Bei, and no other one.
Cao said:"If you want a son, he should be Sun."

## 木兰花慢

中秋饮酒将旦,客谓前人诗词有赋待月,无送月者。因用《天问》体赋。

可怜今夕月,向何处、去悠悠?是别有人间,那边才见,光影东头?是天外空汗漫,但长风浩浩送中秋?飞镜无根谁系?姮娥不嫁谁留? 谓经海底问无由,恍惚使人愁。怕万里长鲸,纵横触破,玉殿琼楼。虾蟆故堪浴水,问云何玉兔解沉浮?若道都齐无恙,云何渐渐如钩?

### Tune: Slow Song of Magnolia Flowers

At a banquet, we drank nearly until dawn on the night of Mid-autumn Festival. One of the guests said some of forefathers wrote poems waiting for the moon, but no one wrote a poem seeing the moon off. So I wrote the *Ci* poem by using the pattern of "Asking the Moon Questions".

How lonely is the moon tonight,
Oh, westward you leisurely fly!
Where will you step by step go?
Is there a similar big world also?
I just see you rise in the east slowly,
As if in the universe vast and empty,

辛弃疾

The long long wind blows you far and far around,

Then who ties you, the rootless flying mirror round?

Who keeps the intoxicating goddess from being married out of the moon?

You are said to swim through bottom of seas but without at all being proved.

I am very afraid

The huge whales

That dash around like mad far and near

Will break the jade towers and pavilions.

The toad can swim everywhere,

But what about the jade hare?

If you are safe and sound all the long way,

How can you become hook-like crescent?

❈❈❈❈❈❈❈❈❈❈❈❈❈❈❈❈

## 贺 新 郎

邑中园亭,仆皆为赋此词。一日,独坐停云,水声山色竞来相娱。意溪山欲援例者,遂作数语,庶几仿佛渊明思亲友之意云。

甚矣吾衰矣。怅平生、交游零落,只今余几! 白发空垂三千丈,一笑人间万事。问何物、能令公喜? 我见青山多妩媚,料青山见我应如是。情与貌,略相似。　　一尊搔首东窗里。想渊明《停云》诗就,此时风味。江左沉酣求名者,岂识浊醪妙理? 回首叫、云飞风起。不恨古人吾不见,恨古人不见吾狂耳。知我者,二三子。

## *Tune: Congratulations to the Bridegroom*

Out of post I stayed idle in the countryside. I built a new residence, a garden and pavilions. I sat in one of the pavilions called Stopping Clouds Pavilion designed according to the ideal of famous hermit Tao, thinking of my relatives and friends.

Now I am weak and old.

My heart fills with sorrow

When I think my old friends

Scatter with only a few left.

My white hair has grown so long, almost three miles,

I dismiss everything in the world with a casual smile.

I wonder if there is anything that can please me.

How intoxicating I find the mountains jade green,

I think they also find me very handsome.

Our appearances and feelings are similar

Oh, we seem to be melting into one nearly.

When in the west window drinking leisurely,

I seem to enter poet Tao's fairyland, a true recluse.

I am so lucky we must share exactly the same mood.

In the south of the Yangtze, the drunkard scholars seek fame,

Oh, the life essence in the sweet wine they cannot at all taste.

Lifting my head I sigh to the vast sky loud,

The wind begins to blow and fly the clouds.

I don't regret I can't see the real scholars in the past,

However I hate they can't see me behave like mad.

I have one or two

Only intimates true.

※※※※※※※※※※※※※※※

## 水 调 歌 头

壬子三山被召,陈端仁给事饮饯席上作。

长恨复长恨,裁作短歌行。何人为我楚舞,听我楚狂声?余既滋兰九畹,又树蕙之百亩,秋菊更餐英。门外沧浪水,可以濯吾缨。　一杯酒,问何似,身后名?人间万事,毫发常重泰山轻。悲莫悲生离别,乐莫乐新相识,儿女古今情。富贵非吾事,归与白鸥盟。

## Tune: Prelude to Water Melody

Called back to the temporary capital (February, 1193), a friend gave me a farewell banquet when I wrote the *Ci* poem.

My hate long, long

Is cut into short songs.

Who'd excitedly for me dance,

And listen to me sing like mad?

I've planted thoroughworts and orchids of more than one hundred *mu*,

The autumn chrysanthemums by the path and brook are my main food.

A creek before my gate gurgling I hear,

I can wash my hat with the water clear.

To my mind,

A cup of wine

Is much better than the reputation after death.

In the country low and high officials at present

Think totally upside down the importance of anything.

The saddest thing is the members of a family parting,

The happiest is the meeting of the new intimates,

They are the feelings of all people through ages.

I regard wealth and honour as floating clouds as insignificant,

I'm eager to return to be white gulls' neighbor by clear water.

# 姜夔(约1155—1209)

姜夔布衣终身。当时的大词人杨万里、范成大和辛弃疾都赞赏他的词。他精通音律,自创十七种调式。其词写爱情之处很多,但与柳永、黄庭坚和秦观的作品不同,毫无猥亵成分。他也有一些对国家命运担忧的词。他的《暗香》和《疏影》是咏梅的绝唱。他的《扬州慢》也是名篇。

## Jiang Kui( about 1155–1209)

He didn't take any official post all his life. His *Ci* poems were praised highly by the first-class poets such as Yang Wanli, Fan Chengda and Xin Qiji in his times. He was good at temperament. He created seventeen tune patterns, very harmonious and gentle. Most of his *Ci* poems were about love, different from those of Liu Yong, Huang Tingjian and Qin Guan, away from flashiness and lewdness. Some of his *Ci* poems showed his care to the motherland. His *Ci* poems "Faint Fragrance" and "Sparse Shadows" were best for all times describing plums. "Slow Song of Yangzhou City" was also very famous.

## 点 绛 唇

### 丁未冬过吴松作

燕雁无心,太湖西畔随云去。数峰清苦。商略黄昏雨。 第四桥边,拟共天随住。今何许。凭阑怀古。残柳参差舞。

### Tune: Rouged Lips

#### Passing by Wujiang County in the Winter of the Year Ding-wei(1187)

From the north, line after line wild geese,

In the west of Tai Lake fly south at ease

With the clouds in fall clear.

The hills so quiet and drear

Are now brewing a rain of evening.

Near the Fourth Bridge I'm willing

To be a leisure and carefree recluse as poet Lu in the Tang Dynasty.

Where are the scholars who live in mounts and by rivers like him?

I lean on the railings of the storied building recollecting the past,

In the cold wind the withered weeping willows in disorder dance.

姜　夔

## 鹧鸪天

己酉之秋,苕溪记所见

京洛风流绝代人,因何风絮落溪津？笼鞋浅出鸦头袜,知是凌波缥缈身。　　红乍笑,绿长颦。与谁同度可怜春？鸳鸯独宿何曾惯,化作西楼一缕云。

### Tune: Partridge Sky

By Tiao Stream, moved by unlucky lady,
I wrote the *Ci* poem in the autumn of
the year Ji-you(1189).

She is a matchless beauty in the flourishing capital,
Why does she come here like a catkin on the rivulet?
She wears big shoes and silk stocks, showing her feet snow-white,
With charming scent she walks with little steps graceful and lithe,
Like the fairy maiden in heaven, treading on flowing green waves.

For a short while her smiling face like a blooming lotus she displays,
More often than not she knits her green brows enchanting.
With whom does she spend the beautiful and lonely spring?
A pair of mandarin ducks never sleeps without their partners,
She wishes to be a rosy cloud as a goddess flying to her lover.

## 鹧 鸪 天

### 元夕有所梦

肥水东流无尽期,当初不合种相思。梦中未比丹青见,暗里忽惊山鸟啼。 春未绿,鬓先丝。人间别久不成悲。谁教岁岁红莲夜,两处沉吟各自知。

## Tune: Partridge Sky

### A Dream on the Night of the Lantern Festival

The Fei River flows day and night with our lovesickness eastward,
We shouldn't have planted true love in our tender hearts each other.
Your beautiful image in the dreams
Is not as clear as the picture I keep.
I'm often waked up by birds in mounts at midnight.

So far the fragrant spring hasn't greened the wilds,
My hair has become white at the temples.
Long separation makes our misery fade.
The Lantern Festival year after year, I know
Night after night increases really our sorrow.

姜　夔

## 杏花天影

丙午之冬,发沔口。丁未正月,道金陵。北望淮楚,风日清淑,小舟挂席,容与波上。

绿丝低拂鸳鸯浦。想桃叶、当时唤渡。又将愁眼与春风,待去;倚栏桡,更少驻。　　金陵路、莺吟燕舞。算潮水、知人最苦。满汀芳草不成归,日暮;更移舟,向甚处?

## *Tune: Shadows under Apricot Blossom Sky*

In winter of the year Bing-wu(1186), in a boat I went to Huzhou from Miankou through Jinling where I anchored it. In early spring I saw green buds on willows by Peach Leaves Ferry, Peach Leaves, the two beauties, I thought of the willows on the streets and lanes in Hefei city where my lover and I strolled hand in hand. Knowing I am farther and farther away from my dear, I cannot bear to leave.

The green silk-like willow twigs stroke the ferry.
At that time, my dear like Peach Leaves, so pretty
Left here slow in a small painted boat
Across the Qinhuai stream with sorrow.
I watch the weeping willow buds like her sad eyes.
I'm ready to the melancholy scene to say good-bye,

But still I lean on the oars

And for some time I stop.

In Jinling over the roads and paths,

The orioles sing and swallows dance.

In the world flows and ebbs

Know my deep sorrow best.

The desolate riverside land

Is wild with skirt-like grass.

Towards evening I wonder so drear

Where will I take my boat with tears?

## 暗 香

辛亥之冬,予载雪诣石湖。止既月,授简索句,且征新声,作此两曲。石湖把玩不已,使工妓肄习之,音节谐婉,乃名之曰《暗香》《疏影》。

旧时月色,算几番照我,梅边吹笛?唤起玉人,不管清寒与攀摘。何逊而今渐老,都忘却、春风词笔。但怪得、竹外疏花,香冷入瑶席。　　江国,正寂寂。叹寄与路遥,夜雪初积。翠尊易泣,红萼无言耿相忆。长记曾携手处,千树压、西湖寒碧。又片片吹尽也,几时见得?

姜　夔

## Tune: Faint Fragrance

In a boat through heavy snow I went to Fan Chengda's home as a guest in winter of the year Xin-hai (1191). Asked by him I wrote two *Ci* poems, "Faint Fragrance" and "Sparse Shadows", appreciated by him greatly.

In those hours, the moonlight
Shone upon me several times.
I played the bamboo flute by the plums sweet,
And also awakened my beauty in a love dream
To pluck blossoms regardless of the cold.
Springs flowing away I'm growing old,
I feel so sorrowful and possibly I am unable
To compose good poems as in the old days.
From the blossoms beyond the bamboos now and then
Come bit by bit to the feast table the pleasant cold scent,
I can't help writing rhymes worthy of the blossoms.

In the region of the southeast of the Yangtze Rivers,
Unable to have a gay dream I feel quite lonely.
How can I send a twig to my faraway beauty?
Furthermore, snow covers the roads and paths far and near.
Green wine and red petals miss her without end with tears,

I watch the flowers, thinking of the pink face in the past.
We once appreciated them with deep love hand in hand,
Thousands of pretty plum trees blossoming
Were reflected on cold West Lake rippling.
Again one by one, the blossoms fall to the ground,
When will they again with pretty faces come around?

❊❊❊❊❊❊❊❊❊❊❊❊❊❊❊❊❊

## 疏　影

苔枝缀玉,有翠禽小小,枝上同宿。客里相逢,篱角黄昏,无言自倚修竹。昭君不惯胡沙远,但暗忆、江南江北;想佩环、月夜归来,化作此花幽独。　　犹记深宫旧事,那人正睡里,飞近蛾绿※。莫似春风,不管盈盈,早与安排金屋。还教一片随波去,又却怨、玉龙哀曲。等恁时、重觅幽香,已入小窗横幅。

### Tune: Sparse shadows

The intoxicating jade-like blossoms
Decorate a plum twig moss-covered,
Oh, a beauty indeed.
A pair of birds green
Closely to each other on the twig perch.
In the alien place I happen to meet her

姜　夔

Against the slender bamboos leaning
Without a word in the quiet evening.
A charming concubine of the imperial court
Married a chief of a tribe in desert of north,
Not accustomed there, she misses her home day and night.
Her soul from the remote region returns in the moonlight,
With tingling jade pendent hanging low,
Changing into the lone plum with sorrow.

I still remember the princess so young and beautiful
Sleeping sound, a sleeping beauty, by day in a palace.
When a plum blossom fell on her forehead, an adornment, a popular one.※
But the cold spring wind blows hard day and night showing at all no love
To the flowers in full bloom like the charming beauties so delicate and graceful,
Not as the emperor making a gold room for the girl a childhood playmate.
Now blossoms fall on the stream, flowing far and near.
Seeing the sight I can't help drop by drop shedding tears.
When I listen to the tune, Plum Blossoms Falling from the flute of jade.
Soon all the enchanting blossoms will be gone in the wind with scent.

If at that time I want to appreciate her beauty and charm,
I can recollect on the curtain her painting with a sad heart.

※ 宋寿阳公主,白日睡含章殿檐下,梅花落额上,成五出花,拂之不去,经三日,洗之方落,宫女奇之,竞相效之,称梅花妆。

※ In the Song Dynasty, in the daytime princess Shou Yang slept under the eaves of a palace. A plum blossom fell on her forehead becoming one with five colors. It couldn't be whisked away. Three days later it was washed away. The court maids liked it very much. They drew a plum blossom on their foreheads called plum blossom adornment.

## 扬 州 慢

淳熙丙申至日,予过维扬。夜雪初霁,荠麦弥望。入其城,则四顾萧条,寒水自碧。暮色渐起。戍角悲吟。予怀怆然,感慨今昔,因自度此曲,千岩老人以为有黍离之悲也。

淮左名都,竹西佳处,解鞍少驻初程。过春风十里,尽荠麦青青。自胡马窥江去后;废池乔木,犹厌言兵。渐黄昏,清角吹寒,都在空城。 杜郎俊赏,算而今、重到须惊。纵豆蔻词工,青楼梦好,难赋深情。二十四桥仍在,波心荡、冷月无声。念桥边红药,

姜　夔

年年知为谁生！

## Tune: Slow Song of Yangzhou City

On Winter Solstice of the year Bing-shen(1176), I passed by Yangzhou invaded Again and Again. Seeing the desolate scene in and out of the city, I felt so distressed.

In Yangzhou whose fame spreading the world round,
In the long and broad well-known Huai River's south,
And on a road quite near
West Bamboo Pavilion,
I dismount from a horse for a short time.
I pass the flourishing street of ten miles,
Oh, now it is covered with thick wild green wheat.
Since the city was tramped by enemy horse heels,
Desolate broad ponds and trees tall
Fear to talk of battle fires and swords.
The eve is gradually approaching with sorrow,
The horn from the city gate moans and groans
Through the whole empty city.

Poet Du appreciated it greatly,
If he came back here one day,
He would be greatly amazed.

Even he was good at writing girls' beauty, so charming,

And sweet spring dreams in the green singing buildings,

He could not describe his feelings so chilly and miserable.

The Twenty-fourth Bridge misses the merry hours silent,

And under it clear waves with grief gurgle,

The moon shivers on them without a word.

The herbaceous peonies red

By the old bridge depressed

Year after year bloom

After all, for whom?

❋❋❋❋❋❋❋❋❋❋❋❋❋❋❋❋❋

## 长 亭 怨 慢

予颇喜自制曲,初率意为长短句,然后协以律,故前后阕多不同。桓大司云:"昔年种柳,依依汉南;今看摇落,凄怆江潭;树犹如此,人何以堪!"此语予深爱之。

渐吹尽、枝头香絮,是处人家,绿深门户。远浦萦回,暮帆零乱向何许?阅人多矣,谁得似长亭树。树若有情时,不会得青青如此! 日暮,望高城不见,只见乱山无数。韦郎去也,怎忘得玉环分付。第一是早早归来,怕红萼无人为主。算空有并刀,难剪离愁千缕。

姜　夔

## Tune: Slow Song of Farewell Pavilion

Seeing willows swaying by rivers, I think of miserable parting lovers, and then of our lovers parting heartbreaking.

Little by little a warm spring wind
Blows away all the willow catkins.
Deep willows' shade
Covers all the gates.
The stream winds its way to the distance,
At dusk where are sails going in disorder?
No one has seen so many parting people to their lovers with tears
Saying good-bye as the weeping willow by the Farewell Pavilion,
Day and night by the water standing.
Oh, if she had tender sweet feelings,
She wouldn't wear in her glee
The pretty clothes gaily green.

In the evening out of sight
Is Hefei we had happy time.
There lie only hills in a mess
Like her fragrant green dress.
I remember when we were parting with sorrow,
"Your words I'll never forget," I said with woe.

She burst into sobs streaming down tears sad:
"You should as early as possible come back,"
"I'm a red petal so lonely
Falling anywhere helpless."
Even now in my hand I had a sparkling sword,
Thousands of threads of grief, I couldn't cut off.

❈❈❈❈❈❈❈❈❈❈❈❈❈❈❈

## 庆 宫 春

双桨莼波,一蓑松雨,暮愁渐满空阔。呼我盟鸥,翩翩欲下,背人还过木末。那回归去,荡云雪,孤舟夜发。伤心重见,依约眉山,黛痕低压。　　采香径里春寒,老子婆娑,自歌谁答。垂虹西望,飘然引去,此兴平生难遇。酒醒波远,正凝想、明珰素袜。如今安在,惟有阑干,伴人一霎。

## *Tune: Celebrating Spring in Palace*

Through water shields with two oars we rowed our boat,
The raindrops from the pine trees wet my straw clothes,
Grief clouds shroud water and land at dusk.
Like an old friend, I greet the familiar gulls.
They fly at leisure seeming to fall before me,
Then they shave my back and tips of the trees.

姜　夔

I remember clear when last time I left here,
Snow fell thick on the ground far and near,
My leaf-like boat began a long lonely journey.
I'm sad, thinking of leaving Rainbow Bridge.
Now hills far and near along the river lie
Like her green brows near the dewy eyes.

Passing Spice-gathering Creek I drink to keep out cold air,
To the hills and water I dance without any anxiety and care,
And I sing in a high voice but no beauty answers.
I see the arch bridge leaving farther and farther,
The boat goes as riding a wind as fast,
Oh, now my pleasure reaches a climax.
Awake, looking at the waves with our tears flowing away,
I miss my charming beauty day and night in the old days
Wearing sparkling ear rings and silk socks with jade.
Where is the pretty face always in my mind at present?
Only the railings of the green high building
Accompany me in the short dream of spring.

❋❋❋❋❋❋❋❋❋❋❋❋❋❋❋❋❋

## 齐 天 乐

庾郎先自吟愁赋,凄凄更闻私语。露湿铜铺,苔侵石井,都是曾听伊处。哀音似诉。正思妇无眠,起寻机杼。曲曲屏山,夜凉独自甚情绪？　　西窗又吹暗雨。为谁频断续,相和砧杵？候馆迎秋,离宫吊月,别有伤心无数。幽诗漫与,笑篱落呼灯,世间儿女。写入琴丝,一声声更苦。

## *June: A Sky of Joy*

When in the room I recite a melancholy poem of love very famous,

I hear in the wall the crickets chirp sadly as parting lovers whisper.

Outside the door with dewdrops,

By a stone well with green moss,

Oh, people hear them

Moan and complain.

Hearing them, the young wife can't enter a dream,

Going to the quiet and empty chamber to weave.

Looking at the mounts along the winding stream on the screens with tears,

How she wishes to send clothes to her dear husband in the remote frontier.

A rain begins to fall outside the west windows.

Why do the crickets on and on sign and groan?

Do they want to join in pounding

Cloth for making winter clothing?

The exiled officials in autumn wind drear and cool,

And the king kept in captivity under the full moon,
Will be certainly heartbroken when hearing the sad sound.
Moved by the cries, on the paper I pour my feelings out.
I laugh at the children with lamps catching crickets,
Here and there in the fences of green bamboo twigs.
Oh, if people in the world compose a tune of their chirps,
The strings will give forth the saddest music on the earth.

❈❈❈❈❈❈❈❈❈❈❈❈❈❈❈❈❈

## 念 奴 娇

余客武陵,湖北宪治在焉。古城野水,乔木参天。余与二三友日荡舟其间,薄荷花而饮,意象幽闲,不类人境。秋水且涸,荷叶出地寻丈,因列坐其下,上不见日,清风徐来,绿云自动。间于疏处窥见游人画船,亦一乐也。揭来吴兴,数得相羊荷花中。又夜泛西湖,光景奇绝。故以此句写之。

闹红一舸,记来时尝与鸳鸯为侣。三十六陂人未到,水佩风裳无数。翠叶吹凉,玉容消酒,更洒菰蒲雨。嫣然摇动,冷香飞上诗句。　　日暮青盖亭亭,情人不见,争忍凌波去? 只恐舞衣寒易落,愁人西风南浦。高柳垂阴,老鱼吹浪,留我花间住。田田多少,几回沙际归路。

## Tune: Charm of a Maiden Singer

Many times with some friends I took a boat floating in the lakes leisurely in the southern land. I found the scenes wonderful, totally different from the world. I wrote the fairyland in the *Ci* poem.

My boat goes through the lotus flowers vying in beauty,
On the way leisurely and carefree to the deep recesses.
I'm greeted by pairs of mandarin ducks here and there.
On the thirty six ponds floats no other boats anywhere,
The pleasant cool breeze
Strokes the lotus leaves.
The flowers are her cheeks blushing with wine,
A shower drifts on her pink face from wild rice.
She gives me a sweet smile filled with charm,
Cold scent congeals into a poem in my heart.

At dusk she waits for him with green leaves like canopy of a chariot,
Oh, she waits and waits, still her handsome sweetheart does not appear,
She is reluctant to tread on the waves back home anyhow.
But I fear in the coming cold her pink skirt will fall down,
And a west wind over the south pond will cause my sorrow.
With gentle grace sways the shade of the tall weeping willows,
In the green pond the old fishes push the waves,

The pretty scene invites me in flowers to stay.
Oh, charming lotus, how many times have I strolled along the sands?
I linger here a long time gazing with grace at the scented lotus dance.

❀❀❀❀❀❀❀❀❀❀❀❀❀❀❀❀

## 侧　犯

### 咏　芍　药

恨春易去,甚春却向扬州住。微雨,正茧栗梢头弄诗句。红桥二十四[※],总是行云处。无语,渐半脱宫衣笑相顾。　金壶细叶,千朵围歌舞。谁念我、鬓成丝,来此共尊俎。后日西园,绿阴无数。寂寞刘郎,自修花谱。

## *Tune: Side Invasion*

### Ode to the Herbaceous Peony

Anyhow the intoxicating spring will soon go,
But it's still luxuriant anywhere in Yangzhou.
Under the grey sky a drizzle drifts everywhere like a mist,
On herbaceous peonies' tips hang buds with flavor poetic.
Twenty four beautiful girls like graceful female celestials
On the Twenty-fourth Bridge play the flutes with cheer,[※]
Giving forth the charming music as if from the high sky.
The blooming herbaceous peonies like girls with smiles

Take off half of their pink dresses silent,
Making goo-goo eyes at the appreciators.

The golden red flowers set off the thin green leaves,
And the pretty girls sing and dance with rosy cheeks.
Who takes great care
Of me with grey hair
And comes here with me to empty wine cups?
When to the west garden the summer comes,
Here and there the green will be fat and thin, the red.
I'll write a book depicting a herbaceous peony face.

※ 二十四桥,即吴家砖桥,因二十四位美人吹箫于桥上而得名。这二十四位美人一说是天上仙女,另一说为扬州美女。

※ The Twenty-fourth Bridge used to be called Wu Jiazhuan Bridge. On a moon-lit night, twenty four beauties played the vertical bamboo flutes on it. From then on it has been called the Twenty-forth Bridge. The beauties were said to be fairy maidens or the beautiful girls in the city of Yangzhou.

❋❋❋❋❋❋❋❋❋❋❋❋❋❋❋❋

姜　夔

## 角　招

为春瘦,何堪更、绕西湖尽是垂柳。自看烟外岫,记得与君,湖上携手。君归未久,早乱落香红千亩。一叶凌波缥缈,过三十六离宫,遣游人回首。　　犹有,画船障袖,青楼倚扇,相映人争秀。翠翘光欲溜,爱著宫黄,而今时候。伤春似旧,荡一点、春心如酒。写入吴丝自奏。问谁识、曲中心,花前友。

### Tune: Horn Invitation

I am thinner and thinner for spring sorrow,

How can I bear seeing the lakeside willows?

Alone looking at the hills beyond a mist,

Oh, I remember last time still quite clearly,

We toured arm in arm the West Lake so pleasant.

Not long after you left the pink plum petals fell

On a thousand Mu of the land by the beautiful lake.

Now my little boat goes through the mist and waves.

When it passes the thirty-six temporary palaces one after another,

I can't help turning to look at them again and again with affection.

In the painted boats the songstresses hide half their faces with their sleeves,

And the beauties wave fans in their snow-white hands in the brothels

green,
On and by the lake they vying in beauty and brilliance.
The glistening green bird feather on their hair appears,
And their faces with yellow powder are charming.
But just as before I am filled with grief of spring
That is really as strong as wine
Rippling in my heart and mind.
I write it in the tune of Wu, in many sorrowful hours,
And play it on the strings with tears before the flowers.
But in the world, no matter in the capital or in mounts, who
Knows my feelings of missing intimates in spring in the tune?

❋❋❋❋❋❋❋❋❋❋❋❋❋❋❋❋❋❋

## 解 连 环

玉鞍重倚,却沉吟未上,又萦离思。为大乔能拨春风,小乔妙移筝,雁啼秋水。柳怯云松,更何必、十分梳洗。道郎携羽扇,那日隔帘,半面曾记。　　西窗夜凉雨霁,叹幽欢未足,何事轻弃。问后约、空指蔷薇,算如此溪山,甚时重至。水驿灯昏,又见在、曲屏近底。念唯有夜来皓月,照伊自睡。

### *Tune: Unchaining Double Rings*

Leaning on a jade saddle of a steed,

姜　夔

I couldn't at all bear to take leave,

In my heart rising the unbearable parting sorrow.

Sister Qiao plucked pipa as spring breeze blows,

And her younger sister gently moved the strings of the zither,

With carved wild geese on its pegs crying over the fall water.

The intoxicating girls wore hair fluffy,

But for them it was quite unnecessary

To comb the hair

With great care.

"Through the curtain", the elder sister said,

"I saw you clear first time with a gay face

Taking a silk fan

In your pink hand."


At midnight, the west window felt cold and rain stopped just,

Our merry making on the warm bed being far from enough.

I left her in a hurry alone in that empty room, why?

She sobbed: "When will you come back to my side?"

Pointing at roses, I promised to return to her when they fall,

But at that time I really didn't know the returning time at all.

I sighed, "When can I come back to the water and mountains?"

Now the candle is very dim in the lone waterside post station.

Half asleep I seem to have gone far

As if entering her fragrant boudoir.

Awake I know there is only the moon shining

On her fading face with bloody tears dripping.

❀❀❀❀❀❀❀❀❀❀❀❀❀❀❀

## 鬲溪梅令

丙辰冬,自无锡归,作此寓意。

好花不与殢香人。浪粼粼。又恐春风归去绿成阴。玉钿何处寻。　木兰双桨梦中云。小横陈。漫向孤山山下觅盈盈。翠禽啼一春。

### June: The Plum across the Stream

Returning from Wuxi, I applied the implication in winter of the year Bing-chen in the *Ci* poem.

The pretty plum blossom can stay with her dear a short time only,
In the scented winding stream glisten here and there clear ripples.
When spring breeze leaves and green trees form deep shade,
Far and near on the grass I cannot at all find her scented trail.

In a dream, as on clouds, I rowed a boat on the rippling waves with my dear lover,
In the south or north of the Yangtze River I had never seen a girl so beautiful.

Now in vain I go to the Lonely Hills looking for the blossom so charming.

Finding her nowhere I can only hear the green birds sing in the whole spring.

## 琵 琶 仙

《吴都赋》云:"户藏烟浦,家具画船。"唯吴兴为然。春游之盛,西湖未能过也。己酉岁,予与萧时父载酒南郭,感遇成歌。

双桨来时,有人似、旧曲桃根桃叶。歌扇轻约飞花,蛾眉正奇绝。春渐远,汀洲自绿,更添了、几声啼鴂。十里扬州,三生杜牧,前事休说。　　又还是、宫烛分烟,奈愁里、匆匆换时节。都把一襟芳思,与空阶榆荚。千万缕、藏鸦细柳,为玉尊、起舞回雪。想见西出阳关,故人初别。

## Tune: Immortal of Pipa

While going sightseeing in a boat in Wuxing in the year Ji-you(1189), I thought of the old friends.

Oh, a girl rows a small painted boat with two oars coming near,

I'm surprised to see her like the two sisters in Hefei, my dears.

She moves her silk fan away her face to get petals falling,

Her brows like the moon are so beautiful and enchanting.

The pretty and fragrant spring is late,

The shoal is wild with the green fresh,

From the distant luxuriant wood

Come a pelican's cries with gloom.

In the ten mile street

Of Yangzhou in glee,

I had merry affairs with female singers in boudoirs.

They are still at the bottom of my brain and heart,

I can't bear to talk about them again.

Now again comes Cold Food Day.

With heartbreaking bitterness,

I notice seasons change quick.

I give my whole fragrant thoughts

To on the steps the fallen elm pods.

With thousands of twigs hiding a young crow,

The tender graceful brow-like weeping willows

Swayed before the farewell feast with catkins like snow flying in the air.

On that day we said farewell shedding tears together like a rain over there.

姜　夔

## 凄 凉 犯

绿杨巷陌秋风起,边城一片离索。马嘶渐远,人归甚处,戍楼吹角。情怀正恶。更衰草寒烟淡薄。似当时、将军部曲,迤逦度沙漠。　　追念西湖上,小舫携歌,晚花行乐。旧游在否?想如今、翠凋红落。漫写羊裙,等新雁来时系著。怕匆匆、不肯寄与误后约。

### *Tune: Violation of a Tune*

The fall wind blows over the lanes and streets with willows green,
The city of Hefei in danger of being invaded is desolate and bleak.
The horses go farther and farther away,
The frightened people scatter in haste,
From the city gate comes horn sound worried.
I feel in the remote frontier lonely and dreary,
I see from withered grass a thin mist slow rise.
And I remember quite clear just as at that time,
The soldiers led by the well-known general
Wound their way across the lonesome desert.

I recollect on the West Lake in the city of Hangzhou,
I often invited female singers in a small painted boat,
Drinking with cheer to appreciate the lotus flowers.

Are there far and near any trails of our happy hours?
Looking in the direction of the West Lake I think there,
The green fades and the red flies in the air everywhere.
In a letter I tell her I'll see her when lotuses bloom next year,
I'll tie it to a leg of a wild goose flying south, a letter courier,
But I'm rather afraid in a hurry it will soon come back,
Without sending out the letter and we'll miss our chance.

❀❀❀❀❀❀❀❀❀❀❀❀❀❀❀❀❀❀

## 霓裳中序第一

亭皋正望极。乱落江莲归未得。多病却无气力。况纨扇渐疏，罗衣初索。流光过隙。叹杏梁、双燕如客。人何在，一帘淡月，仿佛照颜色。　　幽寂。乱蛩吟壁。动庾信、清愁似织。沉思年少浪迹。笛里关山，柳下坊陌。坠红无信息。漫暗水、涓涓溜碧。飘零久，而今何意，醉卧酒垆侧。

### Tune: The First One of Rainbow Clothes Tunes

Standing on the land by the water I look far with sorrow,
Faded lotus flowers fall in a mess and I cannot go home.
I am so weak and often sick,
Seldom I use the fan of silk,
Silk clothes hang on the clothe-rack idle.

姜　夔

The precious time so quickly passes by.
In my lonely room on the beam in the nest,
The pair of swallows will soon go as guests.
Where day and night in my heart is she?
Through the curtain the pale moonbeam
Shines on my intoxicating dear.

It is quiet and bleak far and near,
Beneath the wall crickets sob in disorder.
Oh, the situation, so lonely and miserable,
In declining years I can hardly bear.
When young I wandered anywhere.
In Hefei City I listened to her sing songs and play the flute in her boudoir,
I strolled with her cheerful under the weeping willows in lanes arm in arm.
Oh, her face fades
Already in vain.
I see the green water with flowers away gurgling,
And as a leaf here and there I have been floating.
Now I don't want to get drunk
And sleep by the wine vat just.

❈❈❈❈❈❈❈❈❈❈❈❈❈❈❈❈❈

## 惜红衣

吴兴号水晶宫,荷花盛丽。陈简斋云:"今年何以报君恩,一路荷花相送到青墩。"亦可见矣。丁未之夏,予游千岩,数往来红香中,自度此曲,以无射宫歌之。

簟枕邀凉,琴书换日,睡余无力。细洒冰泉,并刀破甘碧。墙头唤酒,谁问讯、城南诗客。岑寂。高柳晚蝉,说西风消息。虹梁水陌。鱼浪吹香,红衣半狼藉。维舟试望,故国。眇天北。可惜渚边沙外,不共美人游历。问甚时同赋,三十六陂秋色。

## Tune: Cherishing the Red Dress

In Wuxing the water is clear, called crystal palace. In summer of the year Ding-wei (1187), lotus flowers in full bloom were seen everywhere. Deeply touched with the scene, I wrote the Ci poem.

Autumn coming, the mat and pillow invite the cool,
To spend a long day I play the zither and read books.
After a long nap I still feel a bit weak.
With cold water I wash the fruits clean,
And then with a knife cut them open.
I cannot borrow wine from a neighbor,
No one at all has visited my poor house,

姜　夔

A stranger here I stay in the south town.
It is a place lonesome and desolate,
In high willows cicadas chirp sadly,
Telling the west wind will soon arrive.

Along the glistening lake winds a dyke
Like a path and over the water shallow
Lies an old arch bridge just as a rainbow.
The fishes play with duckweeds sending forth the scent refreshing,
The red flowers of the lotuses fade like beauties far and near flying.
I tie the boat to the trunk of a willow and stand on the bank,
With deep grief I look in the direction of the lost north land.
Oh, on the islet covered with fragrant green grass,
I can't walk arm in arm with my pretty sweetheart.
When can I appreciate the autumn scenery with her
Who like a lotus flower wears her favorite pink skirt?

❈❈❈❈❈❈❈❈❈❈❈❈❈❈❈❈❈❈

## 水 龙 吟

黄庆长夜泛鉴湖,有怀归之曲,课予和之。

夜深客子移舟处,两两沙禽惊起。红衣入桨,青灯摇浪,微凉意思。把酒临风,不思归去,有如此水。况茂陵游倦,长干望久,芳心事、箫声里。　　屈指归期尚未。鹊南飞、有人应喜。画阑桂子,留香小待,提携影底。我已情多,十年幽梦,略曾如此。甚谢郎、也恨飘零,解道月明千里。

## Tune: Chanting of Water Dragon

I visited Shaoxing. A friend and I took a boat floating in the Jian Lake. He wrote a *Ci* poem yearning for going back and asked me to write a *Ci* poem in reply.

In late night our boat goes into the depth of the lake,
It starts up the pairs of water fowls flattering away.
To the oars come the lotus flowers like girls' red clothes,
The calm waves are rocked by the green lamp in the boat,
In the dead of night I feel cold a bit.
I hold a cup of wine against the wind,
Pointing at the pure water I take an oath now,
I'll return to my beautiful love's arms anyhow.
Far and near I'm so tired of in a boat wandering.
Day and night she waits far for my boat returning.
In her solitary and lonely room,
She plays sad the bamboo flute.

I don't know when I can go back.
My pretty dear will feel very glad

Seeing the magpie returning to the tree before her door with my love.

Before the railings the laurels will keep scent a little time for me just,

In their shadows we'll stroll arm in arm pleasant.

In the present time I'm actually too sentimental

Having dreams for ten years

Of separations and reunions.

Oh, my friend, you also hate wandering everywhere most of your life,

You'll also write "the moon shines on us separated by a thousand miles."

# 吴文英(约 1212—约 1272)

南宋最重要的词人之一。他一生没做过官,但也不是隐士。他与辛弃疾和姜夔交往甚密。他继承周邦彦词风。他有三首《莺啼序》,每首有二百四十字,为词中最长的调子。此处选其中两首。

**Wu Wenying( about 1212 – about 1272)**

He was one of the most important poets in the Southern Song Dynasty. He neither held any official post nor did he live as a hermit. He rubbed elbows with Xin Qiji and Jiang Kui. He followed the style of Zhou Bangyan. He boasted of three of his *Ci* poems,"Prelude to Orioles Twitter". Each has two hundred and forty words, the longest tune. Here are two of his " Prelude to Orioles Twitter".

## 莺 啼 序

残寒正欺病酒,掩沉香绣户。燕来晚、飞入西城,似说春事迟暮。画船载、清明过却,晴烟冉冉吴宫树。念羁情、游荡随风,化为轻絮。　　十载西湖,傍柳系马,趁娇尘软雾。溯红渐、招入仙溪,锦儿偷寄幽素。倚银屏、春宽梦窄,断红湿、歌纨金缕。暝堤空,

吴文英

轻把斜阳,总还鸥鹭。　　幽兰旋老,杜若还生,水乡尚寄旅。别后访、六桥无信,事往花委,瘗玉埋香,几番风雨。长波妒盼,遥山羞黛,渔灯分影春江宿,记当时、短楫桃根渡。青楼仿佛,临分败壁题诗,泪墨惨淡尘土。　　危亭望极,草色天涯,叹鬓侵半苎。暗点检:离痕欢唾,尚染鲛绡,䲪凤迷归,破鸾慵舞。殷勤待写,书中长恨,蓝霞辽海沉过雁,漫相思、弹入哀筝柱。伤心千里江南,怨曲重招,断魂在否?

## Tune: Prelude to Orioles' Twitter

In remaining chill,
With wine I'm sick.
Behind the fine door I shut myself with gloom,
Burning day and night the incense of eaglewood.
The swallows come back quite late,
Flying to and fro near the West Lake
To tell all the travellers nearly gone is beautiful spring time.
The painted boats with music carry away Clear and Bright,
Over green trees float white clouds at leisure.
My deep sorrow of homesickness unbearable
Changes into willow catkins flying far and near.

I stayed beside the pretty West Lake for ten years.
I tied my horse to a lakeside weeping willow,
Appreciating the scenery and songs in a boat.

Then I strolled along the bank and got lost in spring scene,

Coming into the Peach Blossom Stream, fairyland in glee,

A maiden brought me the beauty's invitation of true love.

Oh, lying in her arms, with happiness, as a lord I got drunk.

The spring was long and my dream short.

Her red tears drop by drop began to fall,

Wetting her fan and skirt woven in the threads of gold pure.

Tourists went home, the dykes with scent remaining a lure,

All the intoxicating scenery of the setting sun was left

To gulls and egrets to appreciate to their heart's content.

The graceful orchids grow old on the land,

The wild gingers become green on the bank,

In a region of lakes and rivers, life without her I couldn't enjoy.

Now finally I come back here with dreams of pleasure and joy.

Oh, in Hangzhou I look for her everywhere,

To my disappointment, I find her nowhere.

Our sweet love faded like in late spring falling flowers,

She was buried like a pink petal by wind and showers.

In those days the lake's water was jealous of her glances with charm,

The green hills envied her brows sleeping on her beautiful face calm.

We lay in a boat on fishing-light-reflected water in a happy mood,

Just as poet Wang greeted in a boat his dears, Peach Leave and Root.

吴文英

Before parting I wrote a poem about what is in the deep hearts all,
With woe on the splendid wall of the green building, the brothel.
Now the thick dust covers the red tears and black ink.

From the farewell pavilion for a while we stayed in,
I look at the green grass like her skirt extending to the horizon,
It occurs to me half of my hair already becomes snow-white.
In my pocket is kept her handkerchief sending scent out,
With the stains of her bitter tears and happy saliva about.
A phoenix losing its way
Won't sing sweet and gay,
Nor will dance happy before a mirror broken.
Night and day I think of writing her a letter,
Pouring out my yearning of many years for her so strong,
But no wild goose flies between a vast sky and water long.
Also it's in vain to compose my sadness into the music heartbreaking.
Over the south of the Yangtze River of a thousand *li* float sad feelings.
If I play the music to call back her soul from another world,
Oh, I wonder whether her soul exists at all and where is hers.

❋❋❋❋❋❋❋❋❋❋❋❋❋❋❋❋

## 莺 啼 序

横塘棹穿艳锦,引鸳鸯弄水。断霞晚、笑折花归,绀纱低护灯蕊。

润玉瘦,冰轻倦浴,斜拖凤股盘云坠。听银床、声细梧桐,渐搅凉思。　　窗隙流光,冉冉迅羽,诉空梁燕子。误惊起、风竹敲门,故人还又不至。记琅玕、新诗细掐,早陈迹、香痕纤指。怕因循,罗扇恩疏,又生秋意。　　西湖旧日,画舸频移,叹几萦梦寐。霞佩冷,叠澜不定,麝霭飞雨,乍湿鲛绡,暗盛红泪。练单夜共,波心宿处,琼箫吹月霓裳舞,向明朝、未觉花容悴。嫣香易落,回头澹碧销烟,镜空画罗屏里。　　残蝉度曲,唱彻西园,也感红怨翠。念省惯、吴宫幽憩,暗柳追凉,晓岸参斜,露零沤起。丝萦寸藕,留连欢事,桃笙平展湘浪影,有昭华秾李冰相倚。如今鬓点凄霜,半箧秋词,恨盈蠹纸。

## *Tune: Prelude to Orioles' Twitter*

In Hengtang of Suzhou in a boat we went through lotuses leisurely,

Pair by pair mandarin ducks on the lake played with the water gaily.

We toured the lake till appeared the sunset glow,

Plucking charming lotus flowers we went home.

The red black gauze bed-curtain kept light away.

My beauty was slender and snow-white like jade,

After a shower she seemed to be especially cold and pure,

On the bed her hairpins were slanting and bun loose, a lure.

I am listening to the parasol leaves

Falling on the well fence in a breeze,

Chilly fall will soon reach the place of the world.

吴文英

Oh, thinking of the past I feel time flies like a bird,
Our beautiful and fragrant love affairs have been away for years,
Coming back, the pair of swallows find their old nest disappeared.
I start at the sound at the gate locked,
Oh, it is the swaying bamboos' knock
Instead of my dear coming to me singing a sweet song.
On the bamboo she cut a poem with her nails for long,
Oh, here it sways still with clear marks,
But they become the things of the past.
She complained with grief to me once,
Her colored silk fan, I wouldn't love
When cold autumn with the wind arrived there.


On West Lake we left our boat drift anywhere,
Oh, those happy sweet hours are flowing without end in my heart and mind,
The ripples sparkled on the cool lake and scented mist floated low and high.
Her tears happy and warm
Wetted handkerchiefs all.
We made love at the night in a thin quilt
In the little boat on the murmuring ripples.
Then to her heart's content, she played the bamboo flute,
And danced with gay smile under the bright tender moon,
Until the moon was setting.

She was a lotus blooming.
The red flowers so easily fall on the ground,
Over the green water vanish the rosy clouds,
In the painted silk screens alone the mirror like two hearts hangs.

On the sad withered red and green in a dreary voice cicadas sang
In Suzhou in the West Garden very beautiful.
I recollect clearly with deep sorrow so often,
With a maiden singer, I stayed there to have a rest
For the night in the thick willow shade by the lake.
Just as a lotus root snaps but its fibers stay forever firmly joined,
Later we shared a bamboo mat with wave—like patterns with joy.
Now frost dots my hair and desolation fills my brain and heart,
In half of a box are sheets of paper full of my love poetry drafts.

# 蒋捷(约1245—1305后)

南宋度宗咸淳十年(1274)进士。宋亡不仕,隐居太湖竹山。著《竹山词》。内容以忆昔伤今为主。词风近辛派。《一剪梅》中,"红了樱桃,绿了芭蕉"是脍炙人口的名句。

**Jiang Jie(about 1245 – after 1305)**

He passed the highest imperial examination in 1274. When the state was subjugated, he didn't held any official post and lived in seclusion in the Bamboo Mountain by the Taihu Lake. He wrote "*Ci* Poems in the Bamboo Mountain". In his *Ci* poems he recalled his past and grieved over the changed society. The style was akin to Xin's. In the *Ci* poem "At Twig of Plum Blossoms", the two lines won universal praise:"At that time, red the cherries will be, / And the bananas will become green."

## 虞 美 人

### 听 雨

少年听雨歌楼上,红烛昏罗帐。壮年听雨客舟中,江阔云低,断雁叫西风。　而今听雨僧庐下,鬓已星星也。悲欢离合总无情,一任阶前点滴到天明。

## Tune: Great Beauty Yu

### Listening to the Rain

When young I listened to a rain in a dance hall high,
Behind the silk curtains the red candles shone bright.
In prime of years I listened to a rain in a travelling boat,
The river broad, the wind hard, a wild goose cried alone.

I listen to the rain in an old temple at present,
Frost has dotted my sparse hair at the temples.
I'm apathetic to the joy and sorrow, reunions and partings,
I listen to the rain drop on the empty steps till next morning.

❀❀❀❀❀❀❀❀❀❀❀❀❀❀❀❀❀❀

## 一 剪 梅

### 舟 过 吴 江

一片春愁待酒浇。江上舟摇,楼上帘招。秋娘渡与泰娘娇,风又飘飘,雨又萧萧。　何日归家洗客袍?银字笙调。心字香烧。流光容易把人抛,红了樱桃,绿了芭蕉。

## June: A Twig of Plum Blossoms
### My Boat Passing by Wujiang

My deep sorrow needs to be drowned with fine wine.
On the river my boat goes through waves low and high,
Out of the curtains of the storied wine shops beck me in the smiling beauties.
The boat passes slow the Pretty Songstress Ferry and Lucky Songstress Bridge.
The wind blows chilly and hard,
And the rain falls thick and fast.

When can I get home and have my dust covered clothes washed,
And listen to my dear play the silver pipe in the chamber warm,
With incense burning heart-shaped?
How rapidly the time flows away!
At that time, red the cherries will be,
And the bananas will become green.

# 后　记

我译唐诗宋词已四十余年。其量均达九百余首,取"九九重阳吉祥"之意。在这个过程中有新一辈译者顾怡燕的加入。我的译诗生涯始于"插队"岁月。我带着一本破旧的英汉辞典和一些唐诗宋词的手抄本,离开喧闹的上海,来到平静的江南农村。那儿,远远近近,只见小桥流水。春天桃红柳绿,秋天荷艳菊香。那儿不是桃花源,不是仙境吗?那儿比桃花源,比仙境更好,因为它一直存在。有一个传说:刘晨、阮肇去天平山采草药。他们又渴又饿。忽见山上有泉水,水边有一桃树和两个美女。二美女给他们喝水、吃桃。又领他们上山,当晚双双成亲。过数月,两人想回家告诉父母喜讯。二女不许。又过数月,两人坚持要回,二女痛哭不已。两人答应当天即回。到山下,父母早已不在,世上已过六代。两人知遇仙女,却总找不到归去之路。古诗词中去过仙境的人,再也回不去,而我随时可以回去。

晚上我望着皎皎的月亮,听着潺潺的流水,背诵英汉辞典,翻译唐诗宋词。写江南水乡的诗人或为告老还乡者,如范成大,他写了《四时田园杂兴》:"昼出耘田夜织麻,村庄儿女各当家。童孙未解供耕织,也傍桑阴学种瓜。"或为经水路去他处者,如张继,他写了《枫桥夜泊》:"月落乌啼霜满天,江枫渔火对愁眠。姑苏城外寒山寺,夜半钟声到客船。"或为漂泊江南者,如白居易,他写了《忆江南》:"江南好,风景旧曾谙。日出江花红胜火,

# 后　记

春来江水绿如蓝。能不忆江南?"我在不少作品中能做到忘我,跨越时空,把自己变成作者,到实境中(半数作品)或模拟实境中体会,进入"第二种"境界,译出最美、最好、最符合原文意义的译文。我得到最大的审美享受。我融合在江南水乡里。歌曲《江南情》唱出了我的心声:"江南美,烟雨迷离,你在江南的小桥流水里。江南美,最美的是你……江南美,柔情似水,你在江南的唐诗宋词里。江南美,最美的是你……"

高考恢复后,我考入上海师范大学外国语学院,后到上海大学外国语学院任教。我全力以赴翻译唐诗宋词。暑寒假到有文化的地方,去体会实境。如去扬州,因为杜牧写了《寄扬州韩绰判官》:"……二十四桥明月夜,玉人何处教吹箫?"远在西安的杜牧问朋友,你每晚在二十四桥上教歌女吹箫?二十四桥因桥上有二十四位美人吹箫而得名,美人一说为仙女,另一说为扬州美人,是仙女呀?还是扬州美女呀?这便产生了朦胧美,朦胧美是世上最美之物。二十四桥还在。因为杜牧写了《赠别》:"……春风十里扬州路,卷上珠帘总不如。"因为欧阳修写了《朝中措》:"平山阑槛倚晴空,山色有无中。手种堂前垂柳,别来几度春风?"欧阳修守扬州,修平山堂,并在堂前植杨柳,传为千古佳话。平山堂和杨柳均在。如去杭州,因为康与之写了《长相思》:"南高峰,北高峰,一片湖光烟霭中。春来愁杀侬。郎意浓,妾意浓。油壁车轻郎马骢。相逢九里松。"

现在,我体会到了所有作品中的实境。作品达到了意美、音美(押韵十分严密)和形美。出于意美、音美和形美的考虑,本部译作对个别专有名词或同一个词采用不同的译法。这部译作所收录宋词的数量在中外宋词译作中独占鳌头,在翻译质量上

— 719 —